RULES OF
ENGAGEMENT

✳ ✳ ✳

GORDON KENT

BERKLEY BOOKS, NEW YORK

RULES OF ENGAGEMENT

A Berkley Book / published by arrangement with
the author

PRINTING HISTORY
Previously published in Great Britain
G. P. Putnam's Sons hardcover edition / October 1999
Berkley mass-market edition / April 2001

The Penguin Putnam Inc. World Wide Web site address is
http://www.penguinputnam.com

Visit the author's Web site at
www.navnov.com

ISBN: 0-425-17858-7

BERKLEY®
Berkley Books are published by The Berkley Publishing Group,
a division of Penguin Putnam Inc.,
375 Hudson Street, New York, New York 10014.
BERKLEY and the "B" design
are trademarks belonging to Penguin Putnam Inc.

PRINTED IN THE UNITED STATES OF AMERICA

10 9 8 7 6 5 4 3 2 1

To our shipmates and squadron-mates,
who will know the facts from the fictions

1

He was only a small man in a dark raincoat. He wore glasses, speckled now with raindrops. A minor bureaucrat, you would have said. Nobody. Completely forgettable.

He turned into a wet little pocket park and followed the lighted path for twenty meters and then turned away into the darkness on a set of log steps that climbed steeply behind rhododendrons. At the top was room enough for two or three people who could, if they wanted, look at the Amsterdam skyline, or, if they looked down, watch the heads of people on the path below—if there had been any people.

He watched the path. After three minutes, a woman appeared. She had entered from the other direction and was coming slowly along through the pools of light, moving with the rolling caution of pregnancy. He watched her, watched behind her, then slipped down through the wet bushes and was beside her.

The woman, startled, swayed back, then seemed to recognize him and to pull herself in, as if protecting herself or her child. He spoke rapidly, very low; he might have been selling her something useful but not interesting—insurance, perhaps. She chewed her upper lip, messing the too-red lipstick.

Traffic hummed beyond the park, but here in the rain there were only the two of them, and they might as well have been in the privacy of a locked room for all the attention they drew.

The man asks her something. He seems urgent.

She shakes her head.

He says two or three words. His body is stiffer. What has he said: Are you sure? You won't? We can't?

She shakes her head more quickly, and tries to pull away.

He took his right hand from his raincoat pocket and slashed her throat from side to side, and she fell back on the black asphalt, her red blood pumping out and spreading into a puddle of water like ink.

The man walked away.

Seven minutes later, he was in a taxi. He took a white card from his gray pocket, found a black pen and with it made a mark beside the first of four names on a list. A small minus sign.

2247 ZULU. MID-ATLANTIC.

"Spy?"

"Huh? Yes, Rafe?"

"Remember we're in EMCON, and stay shut down for Christ's sake until I give the word, got it?"

"Yeah, yeah, I know."

Alan Craik glanced aside at the SENSO, a senior chief so good at his craft that Alan felt like a kid with him. Alan always wanted to ask him a kid's questions—How do you know that? How do you do that? How, why, why, but—? He *was* a kid, he thought miserably, a beginner among men made mature by their skills.

"Goin' for a ride," Rafe said. The elaborate casualness,

the cowboy intonation, was what Alan didn't have, at once both real coolness and overdone, flyboy bravado.

Alan's innards dropped to his socks as the plane roared from the catapult. He should be getting used to it, he thought; why couldn't he be casual and cool? Was anybody else afraid he was going to be sick? Did anybody else think they were going into the black ocean instead of the night sky?

And would he ever be able to make a carrier takeoff and not think of his warrior father and what a burden it was to be the warrior's son?

MARCH 15. 0121 ZULU. NEAR HEATHROW.

Where the road makes a bend toward Iver, there is a stone bridge over a little river. At the Iver end of the bridge, if you look to the right, a sign is visible among the branches announcing the private grounds of a fishing club; there is a metal gate.

The unremarkable man in the raincoat and eyeglasses turned down toward this gate, hardly slowing although the path was dark and wet. He produced a key, unlocked the gate, and went through. As he had in Amsterdam, he went up the bank instead of along the path, this time examining the fence with a tiny flashlight and satisfying himself that the old breaks and holes were still there. The lock and the gate, it appeared, were mostly symbolic.

Again, he waited and watched. The sky was dull copper from London's light on the low clouds; out on the bridge, glowing spheres of mist formed around streetlamps. After six minutes, a silhouette moved slowly to the center of the stone bridge—an overweight man, black among the bare black branches; he leaned over, seemed to study the water but actually looked up and down the fishing length. Then he, too, let himself in at the gate; unlike the small man, he moved uncertainly, and he swore once and then put on a light that he carried covered in his fingers so that only bits of it seemed to fall at his feet. He came along the fisherman's path, breathing heavily.

The man in the raincoat spoke a name. Fred. Not quite a whisper, hoarse, betraying an accent: *Fr-r-red.* The other man turned. He was a little frightened. In the soft light from the bridge, he could be seen to have heavy lips and the kind of thick eyelids that look as if they have been weeping.

The man in the raincoat went down to him. He spoke with what seemed to be urgency, one hand extended, the other in his coat pocket. Again, there was a sense of selling something, of persuasion; his head cocked as Fred lowered his eyes; he might almost have been trying to get below Fred's face, to look up into it. A word was audible, as if it was so important it had been spoken louder, extended: *money.*

Fred rubbed his fat chin. Both men looked around. Fred looked up at the glowing sky, said something, laughed. Nervous laughter.

The smaller man leaned in again. He repeated the question. Well? Yes or no?

Whatever Fred said, it was barely muttered, certainly not emphatic; but it was enough, and the smaller man smiled, nodded, took Fred's upper arm and squeezed the muscle, then patted it. *Good dog.* Fred grinned.

They spoke for another two minutes. Mostly, the small man explained. Fred nodded or muttered understanding. Then, abruptly, the smaller man hit Fred on the arm again and walked off.

Eight minutes later, he was standing beside a telephone in the shadow of a closed pub. He lit his tiny flashlight. He took out the white card. He passed over the first name with its minus sign. His pen touched Fred's name. He made a small plus.

The pen passed down to the third name: *Clanwaert.*

He checked his watch. Then he dialed a number in Moscow and waited while the long, clumsy connection was made, all that antiquated technology, and a man's voice answered, and he said, "Tell them, 'Get ready.'""

0136 ZULU. MID-ATLANTIC.

Six thousand feet above the water, buffeting at four hundred and thirty knots, alpha golf seven zero seven was flying search patterns. An aged S-3B hardly younger than her crew, she was getting tired. The men inside were getting bored.

Below, the black Atlantic roiled in a March squall, unseen, silent to the four men in the darkened old aircraft.

The S-3B was searching the mid-Atlantic for a homebound U.S. battle group. Running opposing-force exercises on the carrier you relieve is an old tradition in the fleet, and no outbound battle group CO wants to be found by the smart-assed flyers of the carrier he is replacing. So AG 707 was the forward scout, trying to find a battle group hidden somewhere between Gibraltar and Cape Hatteras.

"I think you got us way too far south, Spy," the pilot said now. "Where you think these fuckers are hiding, the South Pole?"

The squadron intelligence officer is often called "Spy"—if he isn't called worse. Alan Craik was a new Spy—a very junior grade lieutenant, his ensign's wetness hardly dried behind his ears. The pilot, Rafehausen, didn't much like him. But he called him "Spy" and not something worse because Craik was the only IO he'd ever known who was willing to crawl into a tired old beast like AG 707 and put in his hours with the grown-ups.

As the old line went, How is an intel officer like Mister Ed? *He can talk but he can't fly.*

But this kid did.

Seven hours in an ejection seat was still torment to him. But there were rewards for Alan Craik, not least the discovery that he was good at the "back end" craft—reading the screens, coaxing discoveries from radar and computer.

And there was the reward, to be earned slowly, of being accepted by the flyers.

And by his father.

"Come on, Spy, give us a break."

Before he could answer, Senior Chief Craw broke in, "He's doin' just fine, sir; give him some slack. He's tryin' to find the ass on the gnat that lives on a gnat's ass."

Rafe groaned. The old aircraft shook itself like a dog and plowed on through the night.

0141 ZULU. MOSCOW.

Nikkie Geblev the go-getter punched his Touch-Tone phone and cursed Gorbachev the president and Yeltsin the mayor and anybody else responsible for his not living in New York, or maybe LA, and tried for the third time to beat the phone into submission: *Get through, you fucker!* he wanted to shout at it. Make connections! Be a winner!

Nikkie Geblev was surrounded with electronic gadgets that had begun their existences in Japan and Taiwan and Italy and then had had the luck to be on a truck that had been hijacked in Finland. Nikkie was an entrepreneur. A New Soviet Man. A Eurocapitalist. A crook.

"At last," he said aloud. He was making money, relaying this call.

He heard it ring at the other end, then he picked up.

"What?" a man's voice said.

"I'm looking for Peter from Pravda."

Pause. Resignedly: "Peter went to Intertel."

Nikkie didn't want to know anything about who the man was or what was going to happen next, but he couldn't help the images that rose in his mind—a tough man, unshaven, cruel—ex-military, hungry, impatient—Nikkie had dodged the draft because of Afghanistan and he didn't like to think of the way ex-military would treat him if they knew. They had grenades—guns—

Nikkie cut off the images by saying, "Peter says 'Get ready.'"

He broke the connection. He was sweating and his knees felt weak.

0439 ZULU. MID-ATLANTIC.

Everybody in the squadron called the plane Christine, after Stephen King's killer car. And Christine *was* a killer. Her nose had taken the head off a sailor during a cat shot; squadron myth said bits of him were still embedded in her radome. Long ago, in her first life as an S-3A, she had fired the rear ejection seats without human help, sending the back-end aircrew into ESCAPAC and smashing their legs on their keypads. Now, rekitted as an S-3B, she was like an aging queen with a face-lift—older than she looked, and *nasty.*

She expressed herself tonight in vibrations and the unpredictable. Odd vacillations in a gauge. False readings from a fuel tank. A nut that could be seen slowly unscrewing itself just beyond the copilot's window. Nothing serious, because Christine was not in one of her killer moods; only minor, constant, nerve-picking trivia. A mean old aircraft for a long, dull mission.

Boredom and discomfort. Old aircraft smells, engine noise, the abrasion of personality on personality. *Four hours down; three to go,* Alan thought. He yawned. Where was the battle group? Why did he care?

Christine shivered and gave him a temporary blip and made his heart lurch, and then he saw it was nothing.

What was in his lunch box? Should he drink some coffee?

How come Craw had stood up for him like that?

Would any of these guys ever begin to like him?

How many hours to go?

"Hey, Spy, what's the word? I'm not going all the way to fucking Ascension Island! What's the program, man?"

Bicker, bicker. Rafehausen would never like him, he supposed. What you might call a difference in culture.

Still. "I want to get where I can catch it in a wide sweep, Rafe."

"They won't go that far out of their way! These bastards have been one hundred and ninety days at sea. Which you haven't!" Rafe wanted to stay closer to the carrier. He wanted to show that he thought that this was Mickey-Mouse fun and games. He wanted to scream that this was bullshit.

The copilot, a nervous j.g. everybody called Narc, sucked up to Rafe. "Yeah, wait till *you've* been out for your one-ninety, Spy. Nobody wants to make it one ninety-one." Then, purely for Rafehausen's benefit, "Only the fuckin' Spy—" They laughed, the sounds tinny in his intercom.

Alan felt himself blush. He tried to see if Senior Chief Craw was grinning, but he could make out only helmet and mask in the green light of the screens. But it wouldn't have mattered if the man's head had been bobbing with laughter. He knew people thought he was funny. Because he was serious, he was funny. There was something peculiar in that. Well, it was true: nothing was Mickey Mouse to Alan. He took even games very seriously.

Alan tried to think of something to say, something that would be funny and cool and would make them like him, but by then Rafe and Narc had forgotten him and his grids and his plots; they were bickering about fuel and the readings Christine was giving them.

How many hours to go?

Nothing ever happens, he thought. Somewhere, things must be happening. Somewhere.

He thought of Kim. He resisted thinking of Kim, her inescapable eroticism a painful pleasure in these surroundings. Beautiful. Rich. Fun. Sex, my God. A woman who would—

Think of the radar screen instead. The pale green blank, with its hypnotic moving radius.

Kim in the bed in Orlando. Kim laughing, nude. Kim—

Think of the radar screen.

How many hours to go?

0459 ZULU. BRUSSELS.

He had circles under his eyes now as he came into the air terminal, but he was little different from the others. Businessmen getting a jump on the day—businesswomen, too. They carried sleek attachés and laptops and were dressed for success, but nobody looked very bright yet.

The rain had ended but the tarmac was still wet. He came out of the terminal, took a taxi to a hotel within the airport, and, when he had dismissed the car, walked away toward the terminal he had just come from. A half-mile brought him to an area of sheds, more like a factory than an airport. Without pausing, he went between two of the buildings to a loading dock where trucks would be backing in another hour. He checked his watch, then the sky. No sign of the sun yet.

He waited in the shadows. He did not lean against the wall, despite his fatigue. He was a man of will, not easily recognized as such because of his fussiness and his pedantic attention to detail—the flashlight, the list.

Clanwaert plodded toward him through a shallow puddle. Clanwaert was a plodder, the thing he prized about the man. Unsurprising, steady. Capable of change? Perhaps not. In the pocket of the raincoat, his hand tightened on a piece of steel wire.

He called to Clanwaert from the shadows. Clanwaert tried to see him, failed, perhaps caught the glint of his eyeglasses because he began to search for a way up on the loading dock. To his right was a Dumpster, which might have offered handholds to a younger or more agile man. Instead, he walked fifty feet the other way and struggled up a steel ladder like an exhausted swimmer coming out of a pool. He plodded back toward the shadows.

The man in the raincoat spoke for a full minute. His tired voice had the same tone of urgency, a kind of metallic hopefulness. Would Clanwaert? This great opportunity. More money.

But Clanwaert resisted. His voice rose; even invisible

in the darkness, he was a man taking a stand. Surprising, to anybody who had seen his heavy plodding, he was a man of passion—and, it seemed, of hatred for the man in the raincoat. The word *traitor* hissed out.

"That is all dead now," the man in the raincoat said.

Clanwaert raged at him. Perhaps the man had meant that a god was dead, for Clanwaert resisted, the way people resist a threat to their religion. At last, he ran down, gave a rumble or two, fell silent.

"I am sorry," the other man's voice came clearly from the shadow. "Look out there." One hand appeared in the light. Clanwaert turned to follow where it pointed.

The steel garrote fell over his face silently and tightened; heavy as he was, the smaller man was able to deal with him. Exercise of the will, passion of a different kind.

Grunting, he dragged Clanwaert to the edge of the loading dock and rolled him into the Dumpster.

Twenty minutes later, he was in a terminal different from the one at which he had landed. He found a telephone in a bank of telephones, half of them occupied now by businesspeople making their arrangements for the day. He put his note card in front of him as he cradled the telephone and began to punch the buttons: another call to Moscow. As the connection was being made, he put a minus sign next to Clanwaert's name.

"Yes?" the tight voice said in Moscow.

"Tell them, 'Go.' "

He put the instrument back and looked at the last name on the list. *Bonner.* He touched it with his pen. He sighed. Bonner. He made a small question mark next to the name. For a few seconds, he hesitated there, apparently unsure of himself for the first time—made so by fatigue or by the thought of Bonner, and whatever difficulties that name represented.

0615 ZULU. MID-ATLANTIC.

"Spy? You shut down back there?"

The night was almost over. Alan's hand hovered over

the switch that would shut the back end down. Once he threw it, the old computer ("the best technology of the 1970s") would die and the radar sweeps would end. Their search for the homebound battle group would be over.

But he didn't want to give up. "What if the BG went north of the Azores?" he said into the intercom. "Radar might have missed them if they hid between those islands."

"Come on—shut down! This mission is over!"

He hated to let go. One more sweep, one more experiment—he didn't believe there were problems that couldn't be solved.

His hand wavered over the switch but didn't touch it.

"*We* went way north of the Azores coming back in '86," Craw said in his Maine twang. Craw always sounded like a comedy act but was a deeply serious man who couldn't understand why people smiled when he spoke. "Admiral Cutter, there wa'nt anything he wouldn't do to keep from bein' found, no sir."

"Oh, great," Rafe moaned. "Jeez, Senior Chief, whose fucking side are you on? I want a slider and the rack! Spy, next time have your great idea before I'm almost in the stack, for Christ's sake."

Narc nosed in with, "Anyway, we're in EMCON." EMCON—Emission Control Condition.

But the senior chief's voice was as stubborn as a lobsterman's defending his right to put traps where his father and his grandfather had. "We're not inside fifty miles just yet. Look heah—" This to Alan. "Set up the sweep as we turn nawth. The stack's offset this way anyhow."

"Oh, Christ—!" he heard Rafe say.

Alan peered forward, just able to read the compass. He set up the sweep as the senior chief had instructed; let Rafe contradict them with a direct order if he cared so much. As the compass touched north he punched the keyboard, and the radar expanded to cover hundreds of miles of ocean. Craw watched from his own board as the circular picture of their world appeared, at the center their aircraft. To the east were the fourteen ships of their own battle group. Two blips showed visibly larger than the rest; their carrier, USS *Thomas Jefferson*, and, unusual for peacetime, a second carrier, the *Franklin D Roosevelt*. To the north and west were the Azores, more than two hundred miles away and showing only as grainy blobs. Alan sorted out those shapes, the real islands' outlines stored somewhere in his brain along with a knowledge of the effects of this radar; his fingers coaxed more detail from the computer, put the name PICO in bright green capitals on the island to which it belonged.

Just south of the main island, two faint blips glowed. He tabbed each on the computer and updated it until he had a standard course and speed. *Bingo!* He was excited by the chase now, oblivious of Rafe.

"Two UNID surface contacts! Range two-ninety. Christ, Senior, we must have some duct."

"She's a beauty."

"Speed thirty to forty knots. One big banana and one little banana. I think—I think, guys—" His fingers worked the keyboard as he prepared to place the contacts in the datalink.

Rafe's voice sliced into his excitement. "This is the Mission Commander—just to remind you two. I just put us fifty miles out from the carrier and we're in EMCON. *Do not rotate or radiate!*" He was silent for a second or two to let it sink in. "Now shut down the back end!"

Alan debated the notion of rebellion. He was angry, but he knew part of the anger was fatigue. What the hell— Rafe was in command; let him take the flak if there was any. But still—Fuck it. He pushed the switch, and the radar image collapsed on its center and was gone. He began to clean up his side of the aircraft.

0619 ZULU. MOSCOW.

Number 1743 was a nondescript office building put up sometime after the Great Patriotic War, vaguely influenced by Western designs of the fifties, so probably from the seventies. It had a central entrance and a guard who was nothing more than a presence—an aging man in two sweaters who sometimes had this or that to sell. He would be no trouble.

There were four men. Despite differences, they looked alike because they were all of the same age and they had all led the same life—former *Spetsnaz.* Three of the four needed a shave; none of them wore a tie or a hat.

The guard waved them to stop.

The first man put a hand on the old man's chest and pushed him gently back while the others went past. Then the man told him to lie facedown, showing him a pistol. The old man lay down. The young man shot him in the back of the head.

They trotted up the two flights of stairs and turned right and trotted to a door that said VENUX in English characters. Inside were fluorescent lights and head-height partitions in cheap beige fabric, a sense of modernity and busyness rare in that building, in that city.

The four men went through the door, took out silenced Type 51 Kalashnikovs, and began firing through the partitions. They sprayed the room methodically, and when one ejected a clip he would drop it into a bag and slam home another and resume shooting. Men and women were screaming and trying to run away, and a man looked over a partition by jumping up and down until he was hit. Others were heroic and tried to shield the fallen, until they were hit, too.

Two of the men went from cubicle to cubicle, shooting each body in the head, alive or dead. The third man guarded the door, while the fourth took a device from his backpack, carried it to the center of the room, and, checking his watch, tripped a timer.

They trotted out one after another, covering each other, the first one firing at the horrified people in the corridor, and each one after him, firing as he ran, to the stairs, down the stairs, and they were gone.

The bomb blew and fire belched from the smashed windows.

0624 ZULU. MID-ATLANTIC.

Christine was seconds from the wire. She had two thousand pounds of fuel—plenty for one landing, dicey if she had to go around again and nobody up to give her more. To Rafehausen, Christine felt like a reluctant partner at the prom—she did what he wanted, just not exactly in time to his moves. *Mushy,* he thought.

Rafe wanted to see the boat. He didn't dare glance at the altimeter; instead, he was staring into the darkness, trying to find the lens—the cluster of lights at the port bow that would guide him down. Where was the fucking lens?

Then Christine broke out of the squall and there was too much light, too much brightness, as if the whole reflective surface of the deck had struck his dark-accustomed eyes at once. He winced. At the same time, he found the lens, and the voice inside his head that was really eight years of flying experience said *Wrong!* Wrong set of lights, it meant.

Wrong.

Wrong for landing.

Wrong for me. And this inner voice, which the good pilot hears like an angel's whisper, said much more: it said Power; it said Go; it said airspeed lift altitude move MOVE! All in an instant because the lights were not set for an S-3B, meaning that the tension on the wires was wrong and the instructions were wrong, and the boat was expecting somebody else.

Rafe wanted to look over his shoulder for the F-14 that might be landing right on top of him.

And the voice said *Wrong:* you're trying to land on the wrong fucking boat.

Blinding light all around him. The deck was there there there THERE! The tail slammed down; the plane lurched; Rafe went to high power—

—and they didn't stop. No blow to the ribs. No neglected junk flying past them in the false wind of deceleration. Only hurtling down the deck on the edge of airspeed, night vision shot to shit by the landing lights, sparks rooster-tailing from their hook, and a second later falling over the front end into the dark without a hope, yet hoping, praying.

All of them astonished and scared and seeing nothing but light as they flashed down the deck of the wrong carrier—not seeing the startled air officer in Pri-Fly, not seeing the deck crew flinch back from them, not seeing the man who was down on the catwalk, safe but still flattening himself against the far bulkhead as if he thought they would take his head off, their lights flashing on the name patch on his left breast: *Bonner, S.*

2

Alan clenched his teeth. Even in the back end, the light
as they came out of the squall had dazzled him, yet he
had stayed braced. Then, the failure to stop had tricked
his senses; he had even leaned into his harness as if the
hook had caught. Now, as they came off the bow, he felt
the plane falling. Light vanished; everything was blackness and electronic green. And then, climbing agonizingly
away from the black water as if crawling out of a hole,
he felt Christine decide not to kill them.

"Bolter, bolter," Craw muttered.

"Shut up!" Rafe bellowed.

"Hookslap?" Narc said.

"It wasn't my lens." Rafe was incapable of dishonesty,
at least about flying—and at least to another pilot. He cut
the back end off the intercom and said to Narc, "It wasn't
my boat! Fuck, fuck fuck fuck FUCK. Twelve hundred
pounds of fucking fuel left! We gotta land on the wrong
fucking boat!"

• • •

On the flight deck, the Landing Signal Officer was already jabbering to PriFly, where a paunchy commander in a yellow jersey with "Miniboss" across the chest was staring into the rain.

"What the hell?" the Miniboss (the Assistant Air Officer) moaned.

"It was an S-3. We haven't got an S-3 up."

"You *sure?* You better be *sure!*"

"I'm sure."

Miniboss turned away from his bubble window and muttered, "Well, I'm not," and he hollered at a lieutenant he didn't know to check the sheets for an outstanding S-3. Had they got the goddam count wrong or what? And while you're at it get somebody up here who knows S-3s even if you have to wake the squadron's skipper because that sonofabitch is going to come around again; and he said into his mike to the LSO, "What's he going to do?"

"We're under EMCON; I'm not in contact."

"The way I read it, he's from the *Jefferson.* Get his fuel load."

"We're under EMCON."

"Well, get out from under! Set the lens for an S-3 and find if he can get back to his own boat! If he can't, prepare to receive." He turned away to order somebody to keep the Combat Air Patrol airborne until it was over; get their fuel and estimated time aloft; while you're at it—

The LSO had already had the lens reset. He was already prepared to receive. He had expected to recover two F-18-As; the lens had been set for them. He imagined the S-3 catching a wire set for the much lighter F-18-A and winced.

All in a night's work.

Rafe caught the flare of lights that signaled him to try again. Narc had talked on the ball to the LSO and told him that their fuel was down. So, the worst was going to happen: he, LT George Rafehausen, veteran carrier pilot, sometime wingman of the squadron skipper, was going to land on the wrong boat. Rafe blew out his breath in disgust.

This time he kept it simple. By the numbers. He gentled Christine into the approach. His angle of attack was perfect. At least he'd make a good landing.

Then he watched as the carrier began to turn.

He had to chase the turn. His numbers went out the window. They were turning away from the squall to help him, but that made no odds to him. Why weren't things ever easy?

"Smoke in the tunnel," Spy's voice said over the intercom.

There was a break, then Senior's voice: "Tape's still turning. Friction fire. Gawdamned Christine." Then, "I'll get it."

The brightness of the deck was close.

"No time," Rafe said. "Senior, stay strapped; I'm putting this sucker down."

Rafe coughed as the smoke hit him. Why wasn't he wearing his mask? His eyes watered. This time he kept the carrier in sight. He had his landing well in hand again; he could feel it. Again the light hit him, and then the deck reached up and slammed the plane.

His angle was too steep. Not by much, just some instant's inattention in the fumes. Too steep and too soon, and the tail smashed the deck just forward of the one wire. Bitched. Rafe felt it and was into high power, and the plane shot off into the looming dark.

Another bolter. He couldn't believe it.

The LSO was already on to Pri-Fly. "Hook snapped," he said.

"Oh, shit."

"Readying the net."

"Understood."

Hooks take a beating. Crews check them after every

landing. But they can miss a hairline fracture, especially if a man is thinking about his wife or his debts or his future. Or maybe in this case it was Christine, trying something new.

Anyway, they had lost their hook.

On the flight deck, men in blue jerseys were clearing away the broken hook. Others in red jerseys stood by— the crash crew.

The LSO announced the hooksnap to a stunned audience of four and said that the barrier was being rigged. Asked for their gas status: eight hundred pounds.

Alan, for once, was unworried. Sometimes, ignorance *is* bliss. His father had told him tales of landing crippled aircraft into the "barrier," which Alan, as a kid, had seen as a giant volleyball net raised across the deck to catch wounded planes. His father used to say he had done it so often they called him "Net" at the club. He said it was the easiest landing in the world.

And, after all, you have no choice. There is no other way to put a hookless aircraft down on a flight deck—not one that keeps the pieces together.

Senior Chief Craw seemed more worried about the smoking computer tape. He unclipped his harness and lunged for the tunnel behind their seats, wrestled with the box, and swung it open. The smell got worse. Alan, now concerned for Craw because he was unstrapped and the break might come at any time, grabbed his thermos and, without thinking, poured cold coffee over the fire.

The smell changed from burned electrics to burned coffee.

The plane banked. Craw slammed against his seat and then slipped into it. The plane banked again.

"Make ready!" Rafe growled.

Senior Chief Craw was clumsy getting his straps clipped. The aircraft turned hard, and Craw winced. Alan realized that the man's hands were burned.

Alan reached up under his own safety toggles and pulled the clips. Free from the waist up, he leaned across the aisle and pushed the Senior Chief back in his seat, then moved the man's hands away from the straps. Surprisingly, getting the prongs into the clips turned out to be easier on somebody else.

"Here we go!" Rafe said.

Alan slammed back into his seat and reached over his shoulder for his harness straps. They weren't there. Of course not; he was leaning back on them.

"Ejection positions!" Narc snapped.

He forced himself to move slowly: lean forward, reach up and over your shoulder. Get one. Flip it out into position and pat around for the other. Find it. Lean back. Don't think about ejecting. Clip one restraint. No problem. Clip the other. Regain your landing posture and brace. Only now do you have time to think, *If we'd had to eject while the straps were off, I'd be dead.*

And then, he realized that he didn't feel airsick. He felt fine. His mind was strangely, eerily clear. He felt ready for—was that Death, just down there ahead of them? No, it couldn't be. He felt ready, then, for whatever came next. It was liberating, not having to think.

He wanted to tell Rafe not to worry; that Rafe would catch the barrier just fine. He wanted to tell his father that he, his son, would be okay in the Navy; give him some slack. Yes, he had needed to experience this. He felt good.

"Good lineup."

"Four hundred pounds fuel."

"You're left."

"Good lineup."

"Power."

"Nose up—nose up—POWER!"

Thirty thousand pounds of airframe hurtled into the net stretched above the wire and the wire strained and the tail rose and the whole mass skidded down the deck to the limit of the wire's extension and the tail slapped down with a final crack, and alpha golf 707 came to a dead stop.

Christine was home.

She snarled. She still had enough fuel to bitch with.

Rafehausen had put her down with as little damage as could be hoped for. Christine would fly again, even though most barrier survivors are scrap from the moment the net is pulled off.

The LSO had sweated through the calls and brought this bird home. Now, he drawled to the waiting ship:

"Beautiful landing, American flyboy. Welcome aboard USS *Franklin D. Roosevelt*—your home away from home."

It was the first hint Alan had that they were on the wrong boat.

He understood perfectly when Rafe's shaking voice whispered over the intercom, "Nobody say a fucking word to me. Not a fucking word!"

Alan was not feeling too well himself. The coolness of moments before had vanished, leaving, not airsickness, but real nausea. He had been wrong: Death *had* been waiting on the boat, grinning at Christine as she roared by, throwing sparks like a welder's torch. *Catch you next time,* Death had signaled. Or the time after. Or sometime.

Reality check.

Alan breathed in the stinking air and tried to focus on something else. The wrong boat. That meant—his father's boat. He had just landed on his father's carrier. That brought him to. He felt the old reaction—welcomed it as relief from the aftershock of the close call—the old shortness of breath and slight dread. Perhaps it was simply expecting too much of every meeting, or perhaps it was fearing that too much was expected of him. Always, always when he was preparing to meet his father in all those years they had lived apart, there had been this reaction.

So he sat in the net-wrapped plane, numbly watching figures in red and orange as they hustled to clear the flight deck for incoming CAP craft, scuttling around Christine like ants servicing the queen.

He loved his father. He feared his father. Where was the balance between those things?

And Alan Craik, thinking only of himself and his father, did not guess, could not guess, that a man who would change his life was out there among the hurrying jerseys.

3

In a stall of a men's room in the Brussels airport, the small man stood over the toilet, a cigarette lighter in one hand and the white card in the other. Most days of his adult life, he had gone through this little ceremony, burning the day's notes to himself, a secret act of defiance and a terrible act of hubris—"wanting to be caught," the psychologists (whom he despised) would have said. They would have been quite wrong. No part of him, physical or mental, wanted to be caught. The very idea made him smile.

He looked down the list. Two minus signs. He was sorry to have lost them; he would have much preferred those signs to be pluses. The minus signs were like defeats. But they would not discourage him. Depression came more easily with fatigue; he knew himself that well. Still— He flicked the lighter and touched the flame to the corner of the card. As the flame spread toward his fingers he watched Bonner's name and his question mark disappear, then dropped the burning paper to the water and flushed.

He wished that the question surrounding Bonner could

be so easily disposed of. Bonner, to his profound regret, was out of his reach just then.

He pulled himself up and marched to a ticket counter and bought a seat on a flight to Naples.

0723 ZULU. MID-ATLANTIC.

Alan stepped down to the flight deck and wavered, rubber-legged. He made himself cross toward the catwalk as if he felt cool and strong, not wanting anybody to see his weakness. Craw came behind him. Alan had already lost track of Rafe and Narc; when had they got out of the plane? He took his helmet off—the plain helmet of a beginner, without nickname or logo. You had to earn the boastful, joking graphics that aircrew lavished on their helmets. He had no idea what he would use, if he was ever allowed. He could imagine what Rafe would choose for him—a winged asshole?

He was cold, but the fine, stinging spray of rain was a relief, the clean sea air a tonic after the aircraft. Moving at twenty knots, the carrier made a wind that seemed to blow him clean.

He turned, looked past the senior chief at Christine. She was already being moved to an elevator, one wing folded, her tires blown. Irrationally, he felt at that moment an uncomplicated affection for her.

Craw's hand touched his shoulder. Alan jumped. "I appreciate what you did there, sir. Helping me."

"I-uh—hey. How're your hands?"

Craw held up palms shiny with burn ointment. "I got more grease on me than a slider."

And they both laughed. They laughed because it was funny just then, laughed because they had survived and were alive to see another fireball rise over the Atlantic.

And Craw said, "You goin' to do all right, sir."

They grinned at each other across the divide that separates officer from enlisted, despite age, experience, knowledge of life and death.

"We gawt to clear outta here," the senior chief said. "Aircraft incoming."

They walked together down the nonskid catwalk toward the ready room, the debrief, the awful meatballs that sailors call "sliders," supposedly so greasy that one will slide the length of a table with a minimal shove; toward this floating world of maleness, this tangle of stresses, traditions, affections, hidden feelings; walked toward it in a momentary but perfect companionship. At the door to the light lock, they hesitated, and Alan opened the door because he thought Craw's burned hands wouldn't let him do it. They exchanged a look, and Craw was gone.

Alan, the shock of the landing fading, realized that he had never felt so content.

And ready to meet his father. Somewhere on board, probably tomorrow.

He stepped through into the darkness of the light lock. The far door was just closing on Craw's heels, the wedge of light folding to nothing. Alan, blind from the glare of the deck, was aware only of a bulk nearby before he was wrapped in an embrace.

"Welcome aboard, kiddo."

"*Dad.*" He returned the embrace, glad of it, glad of the darkness that hid their embarrassment.

"You okay?"

"I'm fine."

"My SDO woke me up. How'd you like the net? Fun, huh?"

They moved into the passage, Alan squinting at the brightness, chattering too fast. "I've got to do the debrief. You know, the new guy gets the dumb job? You look great, Dad. Yeah, what a ride—"

"I'll walk along."

His father was a commander, CO of an attack squadron of A-6s. He would be hard-pressed for sleep, but he had sacrificed it for these minutes in the dark hours of a morning to be with his son. He could not say so. He could only do it, make his being there stand in for any expression of emotion.

They had last seen each other three weeks before at the O club. That had been different. This, Alan realized, was the first time in an operational environment. It was a little like the moments with Craw—looking across a divide with new eyes, getting something new back. Yet they chatted of trivia. Everything was hidden.

Until, at the debrief door, his father grasped his shoulders. "Proud of you," he said—and abruptly turned away.

On the flight deck, silence marked the end of the twelve-cycle flight day. The glare was turned off, and only disembodied blue flashlights pierced the dark, darting about as if searching for something—as if, perhaps, they sensed the traitor whose existence was not yet known, like hounds looking for a scent. They moved in silence, only the wind generated by the *Roosevelt*'s twenty-plus knots sounding where earlier jet engines had shattered the night.

Thirty-six inches below the flight deck, bunkrooms of snoring ensigns finally achieved real sleep, free from jet-blast deflectors and engines screaming for launch, free from the "THWACK-thud" of jets making the trap right over their heads.

Alan tumbled into an empty sack and was instantly asleep. He dreamed old dreams of examinations for which he was unprepared and woke at last still locked in their fear of failure.

In another part of the ship, Petty Officer First Class Sheldon Bonner stripped to his skivvies and lay back on his rack, an envelope in his left hand. It had already been opened, the letter inside already read. Yet, he took the paper out and read it again. He yawned. *Dear Dad*, it began. Unconsciously, Bonner smiled. He held the letter above him. *Dear Dad, How are you doing? Everything here is A-OK, but I get tired of Navy schools. I bet you have an exciting time in the Med.*

Bonner read it all through. He got paper and a ballpoint from his locker and lay down again, this time on his side, and began to write. *Dear Donnie. Great to get your letter. I am thinking of that time we fished for trout in Idaho, remember, I bet you forgot. We had some great times, you bet. You do what your old man tells you and make the most of that school, your future is secure if you do good there. Now I am serious about this. I want you to make chief, super chief, unlike your old man, you got potential to do anything. Aim for the stars.* He wondered if that was too much. No, he meant it. His kid could be anything. Anything!

0953 ZULU. MOSCOW.

In Moscow, a cold rain was falling. In the old KGB building, now the SVRR building (and called "the old KGB building" by everybody), Darya Ouspenskaya stared at her window, tracking the drops that streamed down it like tears. She muttered aloud, *"Il pleut sur la ville comme il pleure dans mon coeur,"* and smiled at herself. Down in the street, a few people hurried, shoulders hunched against the downpour. *My poor Moscow,* she thought. The city looked even dirtier in the rain.

Darya Ouspenskaya was overweight but still pretty, a jolly woman who radiated good humor. Men liked her, found her sexually attractive because her face seemed to promise that everything would be taken lightly; any mistakes or failures would be laughed away. She humored them all, slept with none. She was long since divorced from a man she hardly ever thought of anymore. Her few sexual adventures were short-lived now, never allowed to be serious.

Her telephone rang. She picked it up with habitual distaste, an ancient dial phone that felt greasy no matter how much she bribed the babushka to sterilize it. Darya wanted a new telephone, green or gold, Touch-Tone, something reeking of high tech and smartness.

"The Director will see you now," a female voice said. "At once."

She avoided the lift, which might again be stopping only at every other floor, and walked up the two flights of broad stone stairs. Big muscles in her calves and thighs raised her; she enjoyed feeling them work. She wore clothes picked up in London, "the Raisa Look," everybody now mad to imitate Gorbachev's wife.

"Go right in," the secretary said. She was younger, inexplicably severe-looking; Darya, by keeping her supplied with perfume and little favors, had overcome that severity and now got special bits of gossip from her, preferred access to her boss.

Director Yakoblov was sitting at his desk with his face down in a file, his bald spot pointed at her. He had a cold. He breathed heavily and blew his nose into a tissue and swore. A plastic bag at his feet was half filled with soiled tissues.

"What have you got?" he said.

"You should be in bed," she said; between them, such words had no sexual connotation.

"Rotten, simply rotten," he said. "But if I stayed home, they'd think I wasn't indispensable, and then you'd have my job. What have you got?"

"Efremov."

He groaned.

"You directed me to look into his disappearance."

"I know what I did! My God, Ouspenskaya—!" He clutched his forehead. "Aaah! I need antibiotics, they give me decongestants! Well?"

"He seems to be gone. His apartment has not been visited in three days. I ordered an entry; I have the report, but the essence is his clothes and so on are there, as is money, keys, even a passport." She paused.

"Go on, go on." He blew his nose.

"He has a second flat near the Gorki statue, under the name Platonov. Internal Security had it wired; I suspect he knew all that. Not a beginner, after all. He had a woman there sometimes, always the same. A little delicate."

The Director looked at her over another white tissue.

"The daughter of Malenkov the gangster. We assume the other listening devices were his."

He blew his nose. "Continue."

"I interviewed her myself. She is terrified of her father. She is married to one of his boys; one or the other will kill her if they find out about Efremov, she says. As if Papa didn't already know. She hasn't seen him in"—she checked her notes—"ten days. She was to meet him at the flat three days ago, but he didn't appear. That checks out with Internal's records—she was there for an hour alone, then left. Anyway, she doesn't know where he is, she says, has no plans to meet him in some other place, and so on and so on.

"You believe her?"

"Oh, yes. She's a scared little thing. I threatened her a bit, she almost fainted. She needs to be questioned by somebody with more time than I have, really go over everything, her memory might turn up a clue. But we'd have to promise her something good—protection from her husband, maybe. Maybe her father, as well."

He waved a tissue.

She looked up at him. He stopped sniffling and stared back. "I've had a look at his computer files. Surprisingly—mm—bland. I make no judgments, as you know, but—if I were the famous Sherlock Holmes, I would say they are significant for the fact that they are so insignificant."

"Well, after all, his agents are run by underlings. He has how many agents?"

"He claims eighty."

The Director looked up. " 'Claims'?"

Ouspenskaya, with a tiny shrug, said, "We pay for eighty; I am not entirely convinced that I see the files for eighty."

The Director nodded, gloomy, as if his worst fears about her cynicism were confirmed.

"No evidence in his shredder or the burn box. By that,

I mean only that there is no indication that this was a man preparing to leave. Everything points rather to a man who, mm, is not with us against his will."

She looked, waited. The Director opened a drawer and took out a nasal spray, stuck it up one nostril, and shut the other with a finger. "Continue," he said. He sprayed.

"His computer may have been purged of some files. It's hard to say, impossible for me, in fact; I'm not an expert. That computer, as I've told you a thousand times, is an antique and not to be trusted. American secretaries have better computers on their desks than you and I have in our—" He was waving his free hand at her, meaning *Shut up, shut up, I've heard it over and over.* "Well. The sum and substance is that Efremov has disappeared and I've found no evidence of anything. He's gone. Kaput. Disappeared. What is it the British say? 'Done a bunk'?"

" 'Taken a powder,' the Americans say. A colloquialism I don't understand at all."

"Face powder? Or, sleeping drafts used to be called powders. Quite nonsensical."

The Director threw himself back so hard that his chair springs made a catlike noise; he sniffed, then worked his nose up and down. "Efremov," he said. "I like him. I *trust* him. Don't you trust him?"

"He is devoted to his work." She knew that she would gain no advantage with this man by claiming to have suspicions. In fact, she was afraid of Efremov and stayed away from him.

"All right. What are your suspicions?"

"Director! You hurt my feelings. Why must I have suspicions?"

He cleared his throat, like a man preparing to spit. "Between ourselves," he said, "I admire your suspicious nature. Tell me what you think. I won't necessarily believe you."

She stared at the distant window. "I surprise myself by having no suspicions. Odd. I think I don't know enough yet. But that makes me suspicious, because I have been

looking into the man's life for two days and it is all—
bland. Like the creation of a perfect bureaucrat. And why
not? Colonel Efremov has a splendid record, some might
say brilliant; he has no 'past,' no quirks, no secret life except the girlfriend. Still—" Her voice trailed off. "He has
decentralized his work over the past four years. One might
say it is an example of *perestroika*. Or one might say it is
the opposite—obfuscation. He has divided his agents into
somewhat irregular groups for purposes of administration
and created his own subsections to handle them. Nothing
wrong, exactly, but—he has followed the CIA model of
creating false entities, companies on the new free-market
model, and using them to mask his organizations. Nothing
wrong, but they are a little difficult to track."

"Accountability?" the Director said hoarsely.

"Financing, to be sure."

"False agents?" The Director sounded heartbroken.

"I have no evidence of such a thing. But—!" She stood
up. "Suppose the girl's gangster father learned something,
maybe from her, maybe with his taps, maybe somewhere
else—let's say that he learned that his daughter's KGB
colonel—sorry, SVRR colonel—was making money from
his elaborate administrative structure. Let us just say he
learned that we are paying for agents who don't exist. He
confronts Efremov. He says, 'Do such-and-such for me, or
I tell your bosses.'"

" 'Such-and-such?' "

"Oh—information about KGB—SVRR—penetration of
foreign businesses, or a lever on contracts, or—my God,
you know how illegal money is made as well as I!"

The Director blew his nose. "Proceed."

"And Efremov says no, or he tries to exercise some
power of his own, and Papa has him killed. Or, another
scenario, Efremov kills himself!"

"Rather Lermontov, that."

"I agree. Or he leaves the country."

The Director rubbed his already red eyes. "Or he could
be lying in a stalled car in the snow beside a back road he

took by mistake on the way to his dacha." He looked at her between his fingers. "We mustn't overlook the accidental." He studied her face. "There's something more. Come on."

She shook her head vigorously; her brown hair bounced back and forth. "Only an anomaly. Nine months ago, he set up another of his entities to support four agents. For him, perfectly normal procedure—except that all his other entities support twelve to fifteen agents."

"That doesn't seem much to me."

"His *best* four agents. You know how he liked to brag—keeping a secret and bragging at the same time. Like those note cards he always had in his pocket, writing down the most important things he was doing that day: something a rank beginner would know better than to do. He would brag of something that one of his agents had brought him, then cover his tracks by hiding the nationality or some such. In fact he was deliberately transparent about some things—their jobs, for example. I knew that he had an agent who was on the maintenance staff at NATO in Brussels, for example. Also somebody in the American military. Those and two others had been set up in this new entity."

"The others?"

She shook her head. "One I think was a woman. That's all I can tell at this point in time. If you'd allow me some expert support to go into his computer—"

He shook his head. "Keep it in the house." He spat into his tissue and looked at the result. "Maybe he'll turn up. Maybe he's just sulking someplace. Maybe he's dead." The contents of the tissue made him even gloomier. "Maybe it's we who are dead, hmm? Moscow, the city of the dead? I would have been reprimanded for treason for saying that once. Now, I wish there was somebody to reprimand me."

1038 ZULU. MID-ATLANTIC.

He reported to a lieutenant commander in the inboard intel center. Peretz was a slouching, slightly bald man his father's age who had sick-looking circles under his eyes and a constant air of gloom.

"You Mick Craik's son?"

"Yes, sir."

"Siddown, siddown. Your father and I go way back. In fact, the first squadron I served with." Peretz wore glasses and used them like an academic, looking over the tops or pointing them for emphasis. Now, he pulled them down his nose and stared at Alan. "I understand you *fly*."

"Yes, sir."

"Gonna stay with it?"

"I want to."

Peretz made a face, half-grotesque; his gloom was a mask for a sardonic sense of humor, Alan realized. He pushed his glasses up. "What do the flyboys call you?"

"Spy."

"Could be worse. 'Dickhead' is a favorite. You get along?"

"I think so."

Peretz nodded, a rapid head movement that made his shoulders bob. Looking at his hands, he said, "You know the other battle group found us last night."

"Oh, shit."

Peretz looked up at him. His eyes were shrewd and perhaps amused. "Did you do a wide radar sweep just before you made the stack last night?"

Alan flushed. "We weren't in EMCON."

"*JFK* thought somebody found them last night. They were sure we'd be on them." He looked up from his fingers. "No report was made."

"No, sir."

"You didn't know you'd flashed them?"

Alan hesitated. Should he protect Rafe? He thought that Peretz was trying to teach him something, that this was between two intel officers, the flyers not part of it. He took a chance. "I caught two bananas south of Pico and ID'd one as the *Kennedy*. Was I right?"

Peretz nodded. He seemed fascinated by his own fingertips, even sniffed them from time to time. "How come you didn't give us a blast?"

"Are we in trouble over this?"

"We? You mean, you and your pilot? Naw. This is between *Kennedy*'s IO and me and the gatepost."

"I thought the admiral would be pissed."

"He is. But you're too young to feed to an admiral. He wouldn't get any satisfaction from reaming you out; admirals want commanders or higher." Peretz grinned at his hands. "A Brit wrote after World War II that flag officers are best thought of as old ladies who need very careful handling." He raised his eyebrows and glanced at Alan. "Keep it in mind."

"I didn't report it because my mission commander— let's say he ruled the mission was over."

Peretz swung forward, hands on knees. "Okay. Learning time. You had important information and you didn't do with it what you're supposed to. It's no good saying to yourself it's his call and he'll take the heat. You going to do this in a combat situation? You're an *intelligence* officer—you have a responsibility. I don't care how much you like to fly! Information, information! You let us down. You let yourself down." He leaned back. "And I'd have done the same thing." He smiled. "You must be pretty good with that TACCO rig, to pick them up like that."

"It was iffy."

Peretz nodded. "As a TACCO, next time let the intelligence officer in you decide whether the iffy stuff is worth following up. Okay? End of lecture." He waved a hand. "Nobody gets in trouble over this one." He did the same rapid head-nod. "You want to belong. Am I right? You want to be one of the boys. Aviators are a funny lot." He chuckled. "I coach my daughter's soccer team. All girls. They taught me a lot about aviators. I began to see aviators completely differently once I learned to look at them as a girls' soccer team."

Alan thought he was supposed to laugh, did, felt like a traitor to his mates, and said, "Girls?"

"Yeah. Think about it. Lots of nervous laughter. Very cliquey. Full of insecurity. Always clustering around the most popular girl—that is, the guy with the most clout with the skipper, or the best landing grades. Love gossip. Get in corners and giggle together. Share secrets a lot—snicker, snicker. Try it. It might make you worry less about being an IO."

He was, Alan thought, a disappointed man who had found a little fantasy to cover his own failure. Granted, being a Jewish IO would be even harder than being Alan Craik; and he guessed that Peretz came across to flyers as a weird nerd, to boot. Still, the idea of his squadron as a cabal of prepubescent girls had its appeal. He changed the subject by saying, "How do I get back to my ship?"

"You don't. Not till we hit the first liberty port. They're cutting orders for you to stay here with me until then." He saw Alan's stricken face. "This is important! You're going to do a lieutenant's job—learn the joint-ops template and brief it on your boat. You brief the squadron commanders, air wing, ship's captain, the works. I would have had to pull somebody over here from your boat, otherwise."

Alan thought of the flying hours missed. That, he realized, was precisely what Peretz had so gently read him out for—thinking more of the flying than his real job.

"Sounds good." Did he mean that?

He found his father in his squadron's ready room. His father grabbed him, held on to his arm to keep him from escaping while he explained something to two other officers. They moved into the passage, and then his father continued to carry on brief exchanges with passing men while he talked to Alan. His father seemed to know everybody, so that every few words he was interrupting himself with, "Hey, Jack," "George, how're they hanging this morning?" "Smoker, good to see you—" His eyes flicked constantly away from Alan, up and down the passage, as if he were a politician looking for constituents. Perhaps he was; being a squadron commander has its political side.

"So," he said, "you get some sleep? *Hiya, Gomer.*"

"I was wiped."

"*Bill.* I hear you're going to be here a few days. *Kincaid, I want a report on Florio's mother—if it's cancer, give him compassionate. Yeah, today.* You meet Bernie Peretz?"

"Yeah, I—"

"*Hey, Deek, stand by, man, I need to talk to you.* What'ja think?"

"I liked him."

"You did. *Hey, Mac.* Yeah, Bernie's an okay guy. Uh—he's getting out, you know." His father said that in a faint tone of warning, meaning—what? That he shouldn't take Peretz too seriously? Shouldn't use him as a model?

"Why's he getting out?"

"Passed over for commander. *Phil, you guys stank yesterday. This isn't the Mongolian Navy we're running here. We care, get me?* He didn't make the cut. Bernie's okay, but—he likes to stay home with the kids and the dog. He's good at what he does, though—learn what you can from him. Word to the wise: do good on this one, it's all money in the bank. You do these briefings, your name gets around—it's all part of the profession."

"You always used to tell me that doing my best was all that mattered."

Why had he said that? Already, he had put that prickly hedge between them. *Let him say whatever he wants,* an inner voice cautioned. But too late.

"Doing your best *and* having other people know it. You gotta be practical, kiddo. Something you're not very good at—they don't teach it in the ivory tower, right?"

Don't rise to it, the inner voice said. *This is as hard for him as for you.* It was the old opposition. Style. Culture.

His father said, "Anyway, we'll have a look at Naples together, okay?"

"Palma."

"*Your* boat's going to Palma; *we're* making liberty at Naples. You're on *this* boat, kid."

"Oh, God! Dad, *Kim*'s meeting me at Palma!"

"Kim? The redhead with the big gazumbahs I met at Shakey's with you?"

And he lost it. "Goddammit, Dad—!"

"Oh, sorry—I meant to say, 'the young lady with the enormous intellect.' *Snake—Jackson, hey—*"

He yanked his arm away. "Dad, Kim and I are practically engaged!"

His father gave him a strange look. His eyes stopped flicking up and down the passage. He took plenty of time, perhaps thinking of something and then deciding to say something else. "Like father, like son, huh?"

"You said it; I didn't." His father's record with women was abysmal: he had been married twice, both failures, the first to Alan's mother, the second to a fleshy woman named Thelma who had had huge breasts and the brain of an ant, although she had been smart enough to get out after eight months. Alan almost said, *When I get married, I mean to stay that way,* but he bit the words off. Instead, forcing himself to be calmer, he said, "You're talking about somebody you don't know anything about," and his cheeks flamed.

His father made a face. "Sorry, she looked like Son of Thelma to me. Give me her address, I'll get a message to her you'll be in Naples." Again, he looked at Alan strangely. "I think there's a lot I don't know about you all of a sudden."

1311 ZULU. LANGLEY, VIRGINIA.

George Shreed heaved himself off his metal canes and into his chair, propping the canes against the desk, supported on a decorative turning that was faintly worn from years of such use. His shock of gray hair stood up on his head, rather startling, almost as if he had had it styled that way, looking not unlike the Nobel winner Samuel Beckett. He lit a cigarette and turned to the morning book—pages of already digested and analyzed intelligence, winnowed, prioritized, emphasized, and most of it crap, he thought. He flipped pages. One item caught his eye; unthinkingly, he put a little tick next to it. *Moscow. Massacre in office building. At least thirty dead in military-style attack. Probable organized crime but target not clear. Spetsnaz-style execution of aged security guard. Unconfirmed dummy company.* He looked back a page, then ahead, jumped to the Russian and area forecast section and again did not find what he wanted. "Sally!" he said harshly, pressing down a button. "We had a Not Seen on Yuri Efremov a couple days ago, Moscow. Get some details." He returned to his briefing book.

1323 ZULU. MOSCOW.

The stink of fire and chemicals lay in the damp air even after the fire was out. A police detective, hands plunged into the pockets of his cheap ski jacket, stared gloomily at the building's doorway as another body bag came down.

"Thirty-one," the cop next to him said.

"How do you know it's thirty-one? You've put the pieces together, have you?"

"Thirty-one bags."

"Imbecile." He crossed the wet street and pushed through the firemen. As an investigation, this was going to be a joke. What the firemen hadn't bitched up, the bomb squad had. They'd be a week just working out how many dead they had.

"Hey, sir, that's where they found the old man." A plain-clothes cop he knew pointed toward the floor near the far wall. "Back of the head, close range—typical stuff."

Typical, my ass, he thought, *it didn't get to be typical until fucking Gorbachev showed up with his freedom and his shit.* Aloud, he said, "Ex-mil."

"Yes, sir."

The detective trusted the man, knew him to be more or less honest, perceptive when he wasn't too lazy to think. "So?" he said, bobbing his head toward the upstairs. Water, he saw, had spilled down the stairs and was leaking through the ceiling. Broken pipes.

"I seen it ten times in the last few years. You know. Exmil for hire, they're fucking good at it, fucking Rambos. It's mafia." He had been talking to people in the building and could give a quick summary of what was up there—the big room with thin partitions, computers, lots of telephones, some kind of high-tech business. "So they wouldn't pay off the gangsters, they got hit," he said with a shrug.

"Computers? Western money?"

"I dunno. This is just what the people in the building say."

It didn't click for him. He was slower to reach conclusions but reached sounder ones when he did; maybe that's why he was a detective. "Let's have a look," he said.

"Fucking mess up there."

"No kidding." He started up the stairs, keeping near the wall where there was less water.

1441 ZULU. MID-ATLANTIC.

Peretz had nothing for him yet, and he wandered down to the JO wardroom for lack of anything to do. Carriers are carriers, your own or somebody else's: a lot of hours to kill. He wished he had work, or— He thought of Kim.

Narc was sitting alone at a table. Heading for him, Alan remembered Peretz's fantasy about the girls' team; he tried it here. Five pilots were laughing too loud a few feet away; another pair were muttering together with their heads close. Raise the pitch of the laughter, blur your eyes and give them longer hair—my god, it might work! He thought of Peretz's edged description: *insecurity, cliquishness, rivalry . . .*

"Hey, Narc."

"You know we're gonna be on this boat for five fucking days?"

"I'm fine, thanks; how nice of you to ask. And how are you this morning?"

"I'm pissed off. I don't have a dad to entertain me while I'm aboard, okay?"

"Okay, okay—sorry. Hey, I haven't seen Rafe."

Narc snorted. "Our pilot and senior chief have already left. Nice, huh? Skipper pulled them back the first chopper they could get. Isn't that swell! They go, I stay."

Alan, despite himself, tuned out the content, listened only to the tone; was this Peretz's jealousy, preadolescent gossip? He was wondering if Narc could make it as an eleven-year-old girl when Narc leaned forward and said, "I think I'm a better pilot than Rafe—don't you?"

"Rafe's pretty good," Alan muttered. He was trying to keep from chuckling, and Peretz's imagery came to him. He let Narc jabber on; inside his own head he was crushing the image of the young girls. Such a petty revenge might be fine for a man who was leaving the Navy; it could only get Alan into trouble. He put the notion aside, thought instead of his father's comments about his girl.

"Absolutely," he said. That was all Narc demanded of him—sympathetic sounds.

"Right."

His father had no right to speak to him like that, he thought, then saw that of course he had; what was galling was that it was such a cheap shot, especially from him. Alan had once heard his father referred to as "Mattress Mick," knew he was a womanizer.

"You bet," he said to Narc's vaguely heard complaints.

He felt Narc actually liking him, warming to his support. "I mean," Narc was saying, "I don't take anything away from the guy; he put Christine into the net and didn't total her. Good job. I give the fucker his due. But goddammit, it all started with him trying to land on the wrong boat. Jesus H. Christ! Is that first-class flying? Is it?"

"Well—"

"Right! And what's his punishment? Do you know what his punishment is? Huh?"

"What?"

"He's gotta buy a beer for everybody who repaints Christine. Huh? Get it?"

Alan didn't get it. He supposed somebody would paint out the damage to Christine's face-lift—so what?

"Look, Spy, this is how it goes. When you put a plane on the wrong carrier and it needs work, they repaint it, see, with their logo and their markings. In effect, it's a plane from this carrier's S-3 squadron now. Get it? So then it gets sent home to our carrier and it has to be repainted again with our logo and our marks. See? Well, every officer and EM in the squadron will want a hand on a spray gun to say he helped, see, so Rafe has to buy beer for the squadron. Well, what the hell is that? A guy puts a plane down on the wrong boat and we wind up with a fucking beer party. Is that right?"

Narc was outraged. He was not the brightest guy ever to join the Navy, but he was not far from wrong in believing he had been born to fly. He wanted to be an astronaut. He took it all very seriously.

"Maybe we could reintroduce flogging," Alan made the mistake of saying.

Narc stared at him, finally got it, said, "Your human interaction is piss-poor, did anybody ever tell you that? I'm saying this for your own good. You don't get along."

"Jeez, I thought I was lovable."

"See? Always destructive digs. Now, my guess is you were never on a sports team. Am I right?"

"Actually, I was."

Narc's eyes narrowed. "What team?"

"Wrestling."

"*Wrestling!* You wrestled?" Narc looked shocked. "Were you any good?" Had he been any good? Mostly, he'd been a skinny kid too small for his age who'd spent his adolescence doing the things he most feared because he thought he was a coward—going in the winter without a coat, swimming across a lake at night, wrestling. He'd hated it, and so it had become even more important to do it. Had he been any good? "Nah," he said.

For three years, he had learned all the holds, the take-downs and the escapes; he got so good at them that the coach had him teaching other wrestlers. But he was physically weak, and he hardly ever won a match. Then, in the summer after his junior year, he put on a spurt of growth and grew right into the weight class of the team's best wrestler, the state runner-up. He never got into a match again, was a training partner for the good one. At the season's end, the coach gave him a letter anyway, something he had desperately wanted, and that night he took it down to the Iowa River and dropped it in, because it was part of his code then that real rewards didn't come for trying hard; they came for succeeding.

"I don't see you wrestling," Narc said.

Alan smiled at him. "Ever try it?"

"Jesus, no. The dumbest guys I ever knew were wrestlers." Clearly, Alan had confused him. "Do it in college?"

Alan shook his head, laughing now. "I made sure I picked a college that didn't have a wrestling team." In fact, he'd picked a college that had no teams at all, only intramural sports. He had conducted his life like that in those days, with a rigid adolescent morality, rules, abrupt changes of direction. Ironically, he had put on bulk and muscle his first year in college and would then have been the wrestler he had wanted to be. He hadn't realized that until, his second week in the squadron, he had been packed off to be the guinea pig for a new self-defense course put on by the Marines at Quantico. He had loved it, learned a lot about street fighting, and had told the skipper it was great. Later, other officers, coming back limping and bruised, had accused him of being a practical joker.

"I played soccer and baseball," Narc said, his tone indicating that these were real sports and that they gave him an authority Alan lacked. Narc went on to explain his theory of human interaction based on team experience. He ended by saying, "No offense, Craik, but the way I read it, you're a loner, do you get my meaning?"

"You mean I'm a loner."

"That's right."

"Wrestlers get like that. Four years in somebody else's armpit, you want a little space."

"You need to learn to interact. I bet you weren't in a fraternity."

"You're right."

"See? That's where you really learn in college. Human skills. I paid a lot of attention to that side of it. You ever notice how I handle Rafe, for example?"

Alan hadn't, but he said, "Mmmm," in an appreciative way.

"That's my point. You understand what I'm saying? You're in his face all the time—like that shit with the BG and the radar. You made it sound like he had to do it because it was some big moral thing. I'd have made it a game, a team thing. See, it's really a kind of management thing. Management skills. That's what sports are all about. I expect to be an astronaut, right? That's a team effort all the way. I'll be way ahead in that department."

"Afraid I'm a little late for a sports team."

"Never too late to improve yourself. That's one of my beliefs. I have a book I'd like you to read. Will you read it?"

Alan was surprised that Narc read any books at all. He said that of course he'd read it.

"It'll change your life."

Alan wondered if he wanted his life changed. That brought him somehow back to his father, then to a question as to whether all the changes he had made had simply been tacking back and forth across the unchangeable fact of being Mick Craik's kid.

0420 ZULU. LANGLEY, VIRGINIA.

A bored clerk watched the low-level traffic feed in, now and then routing a message to file or analysis. Most of it, she knew, ended up somewhere in the attic of a mainframe computer, bytes on a chip that would be dust-covered from neglect if dust were allowed there. She yawned. Her eyes stung with fatigue. She sipped cold coffee.

Somebody had got herself murdered in Amsterdam. *Big deal,* she thought, *you should live in DC.* Hey, the somebody was a possible agent. She looked at the clock. *Oh, Christ,* she thought, *four hours to go yet!* A woman in Amsterdam. *Yuck. Oh, gross.* It made her slightly sick—a pregnant woman killed with a knife. *Who does these things?* "Lover of assistant naval attaché, Turkish mission." That was it? One murder, one pair of hotpants. Big deal. She routed it toward the back burner.

MARCH 16 – 19, 1990. MID-ATLANTIC.

Peretz was a born teacher. Alan learned more from him in four days, he thought, than he had in months of Navy schools. Peretz was crippled by a cynical wit, a submerged though very real arrogance. Yet he loved intelligence.

Once, in those four days, Alan said to him, "HUMINT's a dying craft." He had learned that in intelligence school: HUMINT—human intelligence, "spies," was history; the future belonged to technology.

"Should I write that down?" Peretz had said. He had made this joke several times, pretending that Alan had said something so important it should be kept for posterity. "Jeez, I wish I had pen and paper. Maybe I can just commit it to memory. Now, how did it go? 'HUMINT's a dying craft.' Boy, that's really beautifully put."

"Okay, you don't agree."

"Not me, sonny. It's folks like the KGB—sorry, the SVRR. You think they have seven hundred thousand employees because they believe HUMINT's a dead issue?"

"And look where they are. They lost. It's over."

"Communism lost, so HUMINT's a dead issue. I think I missed a logical connection there someplace. Does your mind always work that way?"

Alan repeated to him some of the wisdom that he had

learned in intelligence school, and Peretz laughed out loud at him. "Oh, to be young again!" he said. "Look, Al—" He had taken to calling him "Al," a name he had hardly heard since high school. "—satellites are wonderful, spy planes are superb, NSA is the greatest organization of its kind in the world. But without the guy on the spot, they're just fodder for the bean-counters. You need both, SIGINT and HUMINT. Americans love technology; for one thing, it's expensive, and we trust things that cost a lot. Anything as cheap as a spy is immediately suspect to us. But you can really get hurt by old-fashioned human intelligence. How do you think the Soviets got the atomic bomb?"

"Forgive me, but I think your example says it all. That was more than forty years ago." Alan chuckled; he knew Peretz well enough by then to be able to say, "Come on—*spies?*"

"Al, right now you're in love with your computer and your radar. That's fine. But I keep trying to tell you, you're an intelligence officer. *Be intelligent.*" Peretz saw his skepticism. He sighed. "My greatest fear is, somebody's going to plant an agent on me and I'll be the unwitting means for some two-bit country to learn something that will hurt us—South Africa. France. Israel. One of the Arab states. You think I'm living in the past. Wrong end of the stick, chum: I'm living in the future. You wait until low-tech countries start going after our shit. You'll see how important HUMINT is, in spades." He shrugged. "Okay, so you need to grow up some. Come on, I'll buy you a slider while you're aging."

They worked late together one day, running the new template through its paces. Alan knew he was good at it, had even proposed an improvement that Peretz fastened on to. Now, pleased with themselves, at ease with each other, they sipped cold coffee in the intelligence spaces, feet up.

"You know this is my last tour," Peretz said.

Alan tried to think of a politic thing to say.

"Your dad told you I'm out, didn't he?"

"Yes, sir."

Peretz began to play with his fingers. "I could give you a lot of reasons why. They're on my fitreps, right? But, between you and me—let me tell you this, because I see in you another . . . guy who might have to make the same choices. *I wouldn't make the sacrifice.* You understand what I mean?" He made a face, sighed. "I wouldn't make the sacrifice. Of my doubts, of my jokes, of my family. Of myself. What I mean is, if you stay in—there's a cost." He shrugged. "I didn't want to pay it." He looked at Alan. "You sure you want to pay it?"

He wasn't sure at all. He didn't yet know Peretz well enough to say what he really feared: I'm only here until I prove something to my dad.

The last morning, Alan went to say goodbye. They were anchored in the Bay of Naples. Alan was excited, mostly about the imminent meeting with his girl, an imminence of sex that was so powerful he was sure he smelled of it. Sailors and women, oh boy—it was all true!

"I'm on my way, sir."

"Hey, it's been good. Your dad's a lucky guy. Listen—" He held Alan's arm. "Stay, in touch. I mean that."

"I will."

And he would. His father wouldn't approve, but he would stay in touch with Peretz.

Alan ran his father down in the squadron ready room. They shook hands, neither moving to an embrace because other men were nearby. The distance that had opened between them had not been closed, and Alan found himself dodging the suggestion that they get together in Naples.

He would think later of the time thrown away, time they might have had together, valuable only when it was too late.

4

It was a day of the kind they make tourist brochures about, the bay deep blue and sparkling with the sun; toward Capri, the water looked greener, and the boats heading for the island trailed crisp, white wakes. In the other direction, Vesuvius seemed unthreatening behind a thick rim of beachfront development.

Petty Officer First Class Sheldon Bonner was not impressed. He liked Vesuvius well enough—enjoyed checking it out each time a sea tour brought him here—but "See Naples and Die" sounded stupid to him. The volcano looked a little dimmer today he thought—more smog, more people down along the bay, more cruddy towns. But what he liked about Vesuvius was its lurking menace, and one day, he was sure, it would crack open again and pour ash and lava down on all the crud, and the bay would be cleansed and the air would be clear again. That would be worth seeing.

"Hey, Boner."

A body joined him in the line. He didn't even look back to see who it was. He grunted.

"Hey, Boner, gonna get some?"

"What else do you think we visit this shithole for?"

"Great pussy here, huh, Boner?"

"So-so."

"You're a fucking cynic, you know that, Boner? Your old lady know you got such high standards in pussy?"

Bonner carried on these conversations without thinking. Most talk, he had found, was done on autopilot. Men lived their real lives someplace else, hustling each other about what great sex they had, or what bad sex they had, how drunk they were last night, how they were mistreated, misunderstood, ripped off by the system; inside, they were thinking about other things entirely. He, for example, was thinking about money.

The line lurched forward and a speaker boomed out, "Boat away." He gave his name, started down the ladder. Below, a boat was just moving away from the ship, the water opening between them a deeper, blackening blue. He descended into shade and felt cold.

Another boat nudged up and men began to file aboard. Bonner followed, clutching his toilet kit.

"You been this place before?" the E2 next to him said. Bonner remembered him from the hangar deck, a kid just out of high school.

"Lots."

"It true they got a guy with a humongous prick at Pompeii?"

"Depends what your standard of comparison is."

The kid laughed and turned red. He started to tell Bonner how he and his buddies were going to rent a car and drive to Pompeii and see the porn. Bonner tuned out. It was no good telling them that the train was a lot cheaper and easier. It was no good telling them the porn was stupid. It was no good telling them anything. They were young. Let them get ripped off by the Italian car rental agency, screwed by every gas station and trattoria; let them pay some ancient Guinea a hundred times what he was worth to be told a lot of bullshit about Pompeii. They were young and stupid—and in three to five years, they'd be out of the Navy or they'd be on their way to passing him by. They'd be headed for chief, and he'd still be a PO1.

Sheldon Bonner, PO1-For-Life. He thought of it as a title. He'd been busted twice, come back both times to PO1, knew now he would never rise beyond it. The hot-shots got their promotions on the backs of people like him, who made them look good. Were they grateful? Not a chance. They got the promotion, changed the uniform, hung out with their own kind and laughed at him behind his back. He knew. He'd had buddies who'd done that.

"Hey, you see that guy?" The kid nudged him. He was jerking his head toward a young man just coming aboard. Officer, Bonner thought, even in the civilian clothes. Behind him was a huge black man Bonner recognized as a super chief.

"What about him?"

"That's my skipper's son. Isn't that amazing?"

He looked to be a perfectly normal, snot-nosed j.g., from all that Bonner could see. "What's fucking amazing?"

"He's the skipper's son."

"I'm not amazed."

"He came in on that S-3 that took the net four nights ago. Maybe you didn't hear." He sounded suddenly apologetic, as if he had just realized that what was wonderful to his novice eyes bored the shit out of an old man like Bonner.

Bonner grunted. He didn't much care about officers. They had almost nothing to do with him. He resented them, but this was simply a fact of life; everybody who wasn't an officer resented them. But it was a given, part of their world, like the law of gravity. He watched as the super chief seemed to surround the young officer, protecting him. Old Dad had seen to that.

"Nice to have somebody to wipe your ass for you," he said. The boy snickered. It wasn't officers Bonner really resented, it was hotshot enlisted like this super chief, clearly younger than Bonner, already making better money. This one, he supposed, got there by being black.

"We're the biggest minority in the fucking world," Bonner said.

"Who?"

The boat separated itself from the carrier. The breeze freshened as soon as they swung away. Bonner shivered, then put his face up as they swung into sunlight. "White guys," he muttered.

Did he really believe that? Bonner was never quite sure what he believed. Other people seemed to have fierce, clear beliefs, but he was aware only of large areas of dislike or grievance or distrust. The White Power guys, for example; they really believed all that, but when he talked to them, they sounded bananas. He knew guys in the Klan; they were out of it, too, he thought. No, what he hated about the Navy, about the world, was something so huge, so unexplainable, that you couldn't make a cause of it. It was, finally, himself alone, and then this huge Other. That was the enemy. All *that*.

Not that he didn't think that black guys got ahead these days because they were black. They did. Also women. But those were just parts of it, just little bits you could see of something huge and hidden.

What he was sure of, what he really knew, was that nobody ever got anything without being crooked somewhere. Find a rich guy, he'd show you a crook. The difference between people with money and people without money was that the ones with hadn't got caught.

"Hey, man, is this Naples really as bad as they say?" the kid said. He looked nervous. He was like a young chicken, waiting to be plucked. He touched something in Bonner, maybe his attachment to his son.

Bonner began to talk to the kid about Naples. He gave him good advice, even though he knew it was wasted.

"Use a fucking condom. The whores here have AIDS for breakfast."

• • •

Alan Craik let Senior Chief Petty Officer Gibbs shepherd him to the door of the Hilton. Gibbs apparently considered it his duty to keep watch over the skipper's kid; this could have annoyed the hell out of Alan, but he decided not to let it.

"I think I can get through the front door by myself, Chief."

Gibbs grinned. He was an enormous man, almost too big for the Navy's specs. "Naples's a dangerous place, Mr. Craik."

"Yeah, but the Hilton isn't. Thanks for baby-sitting me."

Gibbs grinned. Alan found the grin patronizing.

"Chief, I used to live in this town. Granted I was only nine. Kids learn a lot. *Capisce?*" Gibbs looked skeptical. "My dad was assigned to NATO here. I used to live—right up there." He pointed up toward the Vomero, hardly visible now between the high-rises. He tried out the Italian he had been practicing in secret, the dimly remembered language of childhood. *"Ero un piccolo scugnizz' americano; ho visto tutto, tutto, d'accordo?"* He made it a joke, laughed, although what he really remembered was that this was where his parents' marriage had fallen apart. Not because of Naples, but because of the Navy.

"Okay, okay, Lieutenant. Take care, you hear?"

The big man ambled to the curb, then darted into the traffic and was across the street and gone.

Alan went through the doors and into the lobby that seemed familiar because it was international, therefore almost American, in the style of the American century. The woman at the concierge's desk was stunning, bringing back all of Naples to him in an instant: not a girl, a woman, ample, a Sophia Loren face. Like the maid when he was nine, his friend, who had taught him Italian because she spoke no English. Teresa. Married to a little shrimp of a man who abused her.

"Per favore, signora."

"Yes, sir?" She wasn't going to let him speak Italian, he saw.

"A guest named Hoyt? Initial K?" Had Kim been able to get here?

"Twelve-thirty-one, sir. The telephone is right through there."

His knees felt weak. He hadn't seen her for six weeks. She had been a new experience for him before he sailed, a poor little rich girl with an appetite. Now, heading for the phones, he was thinking that maybe those nine days were a fiction; maybe he remembered them wrong. And then there was what his father had said about Kim—implying that she was stupid, a bimbo, an easy lay.

But she was here. He had sent a message, and she had jumped on a plane and come.

"Kim? Alan."

"Oh, God! Come on *up!*" She giggled. "I've been shopping."

When she opened her door, he saw what she'd been shopping for. They hardly managed to get the door closed before they were at each other.

PO1 Bonner picked his way around the pimps, dodged the plainclothes cops, and gestured away the child pickpockets who were waiting for the carrier's crew. He changed twenty dollars at the booth by the dock, causing a black-market money changer (probably a cop) to assume a look of deep grievance; then he walked quickly up away from the water and headed into the first tobacco store.

"Camels. And a carty di telyphono."

"Bene." Bonner dropped fifteen thousand lire and the man counted the correct change. Bonner believed that every Italian would cheat him if given the chance, but he never gave them that chance, and he believed they knew it. It was part of his idea of himself that he had to project an image of toughness and knowingness, or the world would cheat him.

"Gratzy," he said. The man only nodded.

Every minor crook and sex merchant in southern Italy would be there to greet a major American ship, he believed. The streets of Naples teemed with criminals, anyway, he was sure; today, their numbers would be multiplied— dwarves pretending to be children, mothers who had made cripples of their children to start them on a life of begging, men got up as nuns, transvestites there to lure naive kids into alleys. Bonner was walking through a city of tricksters. It was like this wherever he went; as a result, he never enjoyed himself.

He walked through a narrow street of shops and came out into the great piazza in front of the old Bourbon palace, then along the front of the palace. A few other sailors were already sightseeing there; these were the nerds, the serious ones, what Mattingly called the jerkoffs; one of them even had a guidebook and was reading to his buddy. Bonner walked along behind them. He passed the statues of the Bourbon kings, elevated above him in niches, below each one a stone rectangle and a kind of curb at the bottom. He passed the third of the four kings, and no one watching him could have said for sure whether he looked down and saw the chalked circle on the small curbstone, but when he had walked the length of the palace he turned, without changing his pace, and angled across the piazza, along in front of the curving porticoes that are a little like those of St. Peter's in Rome, and headed into the Via Chiaia. And nobody watching him could have known that seeing the chalked circle had him seething with resentment, for he seemed the same impassive man.

At the far end of the Via Chiaia is a vast old movie theater that was once a bomb shelter, cut into the soft tufa of the hillside. Inside, it is always cool and damp, and the place smells of mildew and cats. Yet it has the virtue of being open most of the day and night, so that men like Bonner can do their peculiar business there. (Other men and women do other, also peculiar, business there.)

Bonner bought a ticket and climbed to the second level.

He passed the first men's room he came to and went on much farther than seemed sensible in a movie patron, finally stopping at a smaller, almost hidden toilet far around toward the screen. There, he pissed, then lingered by a basin, combing his flat hair, his bag guarded between his feet, until a fat man in a dirty T-shirt went out. The only other occupant was in a stall, stinking the place worse than the mildew and the cats. Bonner bent quickly and felt under the second basin from the wall and removed something that he found at the back, slipped it into his pocket, and went out. He did not stay to see the movie.

He checked into a hotel a block back from the tourist streets, a little place that was as plain and clean as a newly cut board. He had got it out of a tourist guide that promised to save you a hundred dollars a day. Bonner had lots of such guides; he made a little money on the ship renting them out—Naples, Monaco, Bahrain; it was well known that Bonner could tell you where to stay and where to eat for a minimum of rip-off.

He'd stayed here two other times, but they didn't remember him. Why should they? he asked himself. Better that they didn't.

The room was only big enough for the bed and a TV; the bathroom was no bigger than a closet, everything in it molded out of plastic, as if they'd just dropped the unit into place. Shower, no tub. No free shampoo or lotion or any of that shit. But *clean.*

Only when he was in the room with the door locked did he take out what he had collected in the men's room. He unfolded a sheet of paper. His lips moved a little as he read the instructions written there. His anger showed in his face now. He read it again, then tore it into bits and slammed into the tiny bathroom and flung the pieces into the toilet.

The message had said to burn the paper when he was done, but everything in the bathroom was plastic and he was afraid of what the flame would do. And who the fuck was going to glue the pieces back together in the Naples sewer? "Kiss my ass," he said aloud as he flushed the toilet.

Still, there was no question of his disobeying the message. He left his toilet kit on the sink and, seeing that he still had fifteen minutes, turned on the TV and watched an American horror film, dubbed into Italian. He'd seen it before, something about American kids saving the world from Dracula. In his experience, American kids couldn't save a gnat's ass from a spiderweb, but it probably sold movie tickets to tell them they were the hope of the world.

At five after ten, he went out.

Bonner knew the Galleria Umberto, but he'd forgotten how to get there, so he did some wandering and actually asked somebody for directions before he found it, then was astonished that he'd forgotten how easy it was to find. He went in, crossed the vast terrazzo floor under the vaulted glass ceiling, and found a chair at one of the cafés there. A waiter waved him to come closer, but he shook his head and stayed out there in the middle. Not that he liked it out there. What he liked was a corner, or at least a wall that he could put his back to. But the instructions were to sit in the middle. So they could check him out, he knew. He knew all that.

The Galleria was like a church, he thought. Like one of those big, overdecorated Italian churches you're supposed to fall down and vomit over because they're old. Still, the Galleria had its good points: you could get a coffee or a beer in there and stay dry; you got the feeling of being outdoors because of the glass ceiling; you could see everybody who came and went.

"Coffee," he said to the now angry waiter.

The waiter shot something at him in Italian. Of course the guy spoke English; they all had a little English, Bonner was sure. But he was making his point by speaking Italian because Bonner wouldn't sit close to the kitchen so he didn't have to carry anything so far. Instead, Bonner was sitting out here in Siberia, in the middle of the huge pavement.

"Can't understand you, sorry," Bonner said. "No capeesh."

The waiter hissed something.

"Coffee, I want coffee. just bring me coffee. Black, okay? A little sugar. What the hell. *Sugar-o.* Okay?"

The waiter spat some more words, of which Bonner understood "espresso."

"Sure espresso, fine, *molto benny.* And some sugar-o, okay?"

Surprisingly, it came with two packets of sugar, and it was very good. The waiter had decided to dazzle him with service. He even brought the *International Herald Tribune.* It was yesterday's, but what the hell? The news was just like home—bullshit. Bush was doing this, the Democrats were doing that, the economy was up or down or sideways; what the hell?

Bonner sat there for more than half an hour. He read the newspaper a little, but mostly he sat there with his hands folded over his belly, looking around the Galleria. There were several floors to it, and each one had a kind of arcade and places for people to look down to the vast floor where he sat. They had something interesting to look at, he thought—a few people coming in one entrance and going out another, using the Galleria like a street; him, sitting there, obviously an American; more people drifting in and taking tables, morning break time. The Italians, he thought, spent most of their lives on breaks; no wonder they were broke.

At nine minutes after eleven, he crossed the floor and went out a different entrance, as he was supposed to do. There was a pay phone. It rang.

"Across the street from you will be a taxi with flame painted on the hood. Get into it."

And there it was.

And he did as he was told, cursing them for making him do it.

•   •   •

She sighed. "See Naples and die."

"Jesus Christ!" Alan blew out his breath. "Wow."

She held him tighter. "I love you so much."

They lay silently together, timeless. "Say you love me," she said. He whispered it into her hair. "You need practice," she said. He could tell she was smiling. He raised his head and looked down at her. "It's true," he said. "I find it hard to say."

"It gets easier with time." She was still smiling. She kissed him. "Let's just stay in bed all week and when we're starved we'll tell them to bring us champagne."

"Not all week, Kim." He hadn't told her yet. He had thought there would be a good moment. "I've got to report to the boat day after tomorrow."

"No, you don't." Something steely, also new, sounded in her voice.

"Yeah, I do. There'll be a plane at Capodichino to take me. See, they started their liberty three days ago, while I was—"

"Well, you'll just have to be real sick. Or tell them you're doing charity work with an American woman who'll die otherwise."

He laughed. "Right! Compassionate leave. No, the Navy's understanding, but not that understanding."

"I won't let you go."

"Sweetie, they cut a set of orders for me. I have to get back to my own ship." He kissed her. "Be good. Please."

"I hate the Navy." A tear trickled down from the corner of her right eye. "No, don't—" She avoided another kiss and twisted aside under him, escaped, and ran to the bathroom for a tissue, with which she started to dab her eyes.

Naked, Kimberley Hoyt looked as if she had been put together from male fantasies. She was very large where men wanted size, very small where she was supposed to be small. She had honey-amber hair that she wore long, and it blazed around her face like a sunburst. She was, in fact, the very woman most of the men of the carrier hoped to meet in Naples, and only Alan would.

He rolled over on his back. "Let's have a great day together," he said. "Kim? Okay?"

She burst into tears.

He went to her and they clung together, naked. When she was quiet, she said into his shoulder, "I think I don't know you very well. It scares me, you going away and going away—I thought we'd have—time—"

"I have to."

"Why? *Why?*" She flung her head back and stared at him. "Is it your father?"

"I signed on. I'm committed."

She put a hand on his bare chest and began to move it back and forth, back and forth. She looked at the place as if she would learn something there. "I want you committed to me," she said.

The taxi driver said nothing the whole trip, which wound around Naples in an apparently incoherent way, first up toward the Vomero, then down again, then well out toward Mergellina, then back. Bonner did not try to make sense of it. He supposed they were being followed to make sure that Bonner hadn't brought a tag from the ship. He could have told them he hadn't. He'd checked. He supposed the taxi driver was one of them, and that if Bonner didn't check out he'd turn and he would have a silenced nine-millimeter and he'd go *pfft!* with it right into Bonner's chest.

Oddly, most of what Bonner thought he knew about this business he had got from movies. If he'd known that the taxi driver was really only a taxi driver, he'd have been deeply confused.

Finally, the driver turned back up toward the Vomero, and, halfway up, pulled over to the side and motioned for Bonner to get out. It was a road, not a street; there was a weedy verge and some trash, but nothing close by like a house or a café. Bonner got out and stood there. He was going to ask if he was supposed to pay, when the driver reached back and slammed his door and drove off.

Bonner found himself on a curve, from which he could look down over the rooftops and terraces of several apartment buildings. The other way, across the road, there was a wall, and, above it and set well back, more apartments. It was an isolated place in the midst of the city. He looked down the road and saw nothing; glancing up, he saw, where the road curved out of sight, a small bulge of green and a bench.

"That's it," he muttered aloud. He began to trudge toward it. The sun was brutal. Bonner did not like this uphill walking in the heat. His anger bubbled up again like heartburn, and he told himself again that he'd really let them have it for calling him in again so soon. *They'd had a deal!* Well, he'd give them an earful. He rehearsed the sullen speech he had been making up during the long taxi ride.

The sounds of the city came up to him—motorcycles, horns, a couple of women shouting. The view opened wider as he walked; he could see the palace, the Castel dell'Uovo, then the bay and the carrier riding out there at anchor. A civilian ferry was tied up next to it, taking on more liberty personnel. It looked like a toy next to the ship.

He walked on, sweating, hating this part of it, which always upset him and made his gut surge. He'd have a bad night, he was sure, up all the time with the crud. Nerves. He was breathing heavily, too, from the climb. At last he came to the bench, and he stood there, and up ahead about fifty yards he saw a car pulled over. The door opened and a man got out.

Bonner sat on the bench. There was a green metal railing around the little grassy bulge in the road. It was a wonderful viewpoint. He could see the carrier, Vesuvius, the castle, half the city, rolled out from his feet like a figured carpet. It was a great vantage point. But frankly, Bonner wouldn't give you the sweat off one ball for the greatest vantage point in the world.

He turned and looked at the man. He didn't try to hide his surprise. "Carl!" he muttered.

"A long time, Sheldon." The man sat down on the bench. He was small, nondescript, wore glasses that were only glasses and had no style. He was the only man in the world who called him "Sheldon." His courtesy seemed based on a respect that was, itself, almost more valuable to Bonner than money. No one called him "Sheldon."

"I didn't know it would be you, Carl." Already, he was apologizing, nervous; they always managed to do this to him, even though they must have had lots more to be nervous about than he did. How did they do that? It threw him off, to have Carl there. He had thought it would be some stranger.

"Please accept my apology for interrupting your liberty this way, Sheldon. I know how unfair it seems to you."

"Oh, hey—that's okay, Carl—" He had his speech rehearsed, even down to an explosion of anger. Now here Carl was, a really important man, apologizing for the whole thing.

"I wouldn't call you out except for something very important, Sheldon. I want you to believe that." Carl bent a little forward, his voice urgent. He was wearing warm-ups and a light nylon jacket and kept his right hand in the jacket pocket, but Sheldon didn't think anything about that, because Carl was the man who had recruited him and was a very high official and must have dozens of people to do dirty work if there was any to be done. Carl, in fact, was one of the two people in the world whom Bonner trusted. The other was his son.

"There have been some changes," the man called Carl said. He spoke in a flat, Americanized accent without any trace of his origins. "*I* have made a change. And so I wanted to share this with you and see if the change fits into your strategies. To see whether you would say yes or no to this change."

"What kind of change?" Bonner hated change.

"You see, Sheldon, we had a problem. A structural problem. I know, you see, that you feel you have not been paid well. I was trying to find money for you, I mean the kind of money that you deserve, in a place where there was no money to be had. What I mean is, there is no money there anymore. I am not immune to money myself." He smiled, as if this humanizing trait were a source of wonder. "I wasn't being paid enough, either, my friend. There seemed to be an assumption that I would work for love. Of what, I ask you? History? A corrupt system? It seemed to me contradictory that they impose the 'free-market economy' and then ask me to do without. So—" He turned more toward Bonner, his right hand still deep in his pocket. "I've changed employers, Sheldon. I want you to come with me." He smiled. "I'm afraid I must have a yes or no today."

"Changed to who?"

"Who has money?"

Bonner looked into his eyes. "The ragheads," he said. "Or the Japs, but you wouldn't go there. The ragheads?"

"They're very excited about you coming with me. 'What can you bring?' they asked me. I told them, some of my stars, like you. You most of all—my star of stars. My best!"

Bonner grinned, but his gut was churning. A change would mean relearning everything, he was sure. New people, new codes, all that shit he hardly understood as it was. "I dunno," he said.

"I hope you say yes," Carl murmured.

"Don't get me wrong, it isn't you, Carl. You're the best, you've never let me down. But jeez, this last two years—" Bonner made a face. Carl was the very one he had wanted to complain to, and now here he was and Bonner was tongue-tied. He tried to stare at the castle so he wouldn't see Carl's eyes, and he said quickly, "I think somebody's been skimming my money. There just hasn't been enough!" Bonner jerked his shoulders, then his head. He made a futile gesture with his left hand, the hand closest to Carl. He laughed nervously, then tried to rush at the prepared anger.

"They're nickel-and-diming me, I can't live on what I'm getting! It's insulting, is what it is. I'm taking the risk and they're paying me like minimum wage, like I'm bringing them goddam burgers or something instead of what I am." He had begun to stammer and he stopped, leaned back into the hard wood of the bench. He rubbed his forehead. "My taxes on my house are more than they paid me last year all put together. I told the guy in Norfolk, the pudgy guy, I need some things. They may not mean much to you; to me, they're important. I need a new boat. He as good as said I'd get one. Then, nothing!" He had actually worked himself up this time, and he let the anger burst out. "They're cheating me!"

"I'm glad we're having this talk, Sheldon."

"I think they're skimming my money, taking a lot for themselves. Can we go over the figures for last year? You may not know what—"

Carl held up a hand. "Precisely why I'm here, Shel. The very changes that I'm talking about! I can't tell you how glad I am to have this frank talk with you. It's exactly what I wanted."

They both looked up and down the road. Bonner then looked over his shoulder at the wall across the pavement. It was a well-chosen spot. They could see anybody coming a long way away; the car was nearby, and he supposed there were other watchers; and if they had to, they could go over the railing and down the hill in front of them. It was steep but not impossible and would lead to a maze of streets.

"This is a good place," Bonner said.

"I told my new employers what you did fourteen months ago. They were very excited. 'We must have him, we must have this man.' They'll pay."

"Ragheads?"

"Iran."

"Oil money." Bonner made a face. "The money'd have to be good. My expenses are enormous, Carl. I can't be nickel-and-dimed!"

"Precisely my point."

"How much?"

"They'll raise the regular amount to a thousand a month. But they are a different people from you and me. You must not be put off, Shel, if now and then their requests seem a little . . . quirky. The thing is, you know, they want to know everything and they don't know anything at all! For example, they asked me to get from you the liberty ports of your ship."

"For Christ's sake, it was in the fucking newspaper!"

Carl laughed. "But they don't know that! Humor them."

"They don't sound very professional."

"We will train them. And they will pay. Good money. They like to pay per delivery, bigger sums but for achievement. They are motivators." He leaned forward. "Yes or no, Sheldon?"

"I need big bucks, Carl. I'm in debt."

"I can get you twenty-five thousand for something good. They *want* to pay you that kind of money, believe me; they're dripping with oil, they like paying for quality. Persians are like that."

"I haven't got anything right now. We agreed, I'd lay low for a year! Christ, I risked my balls getting the IFF for you. And then your people nickel-and-dimed me. Why didn't you jump when you had the IFF?" IFF: identify friend or foe. It had taken him weeks to steal, and it had represented a new level of treason, a line being crossed.

"We think alike. No wonder I like you, Sheldon. As it happens, I brought the IFF out with me. I never turned it over in Moscow. It's what I'm taking to Tehran. My bona fides."

"Did you tell them I was the one delivered it?"

Carl nodded.

"They oughta pay me a bonus."

"They don't think that way." He smiled. "But I do. There'll be a little gift for you in your account this month. Out of my personal money."

"You don't have to do that—!"

"I insist. But I must have your answer. Yes or no?"

Bonner looked at the castle, not seeing it, thinking only of himself and his grievances and his money. Money. Well, if Carl could get him more money—"Sure, why not?"

Carl smiled. "I am so glad."

"Let's talk about the money."

"Good! Money." Carl relaxed. Bonner was flattered that his agreement seemed to mean so much to this important man. Carl's hand came a little out of his pocket. "I want to give you more money, my friend. Because you have done such good work. Now, I've told my—our—new employers that you must have more money or they'll lose you. But they would like something from you soon—a sign, a gesture. A commitment. Later, there will be something else. We will come to that. But for now, the short term, they think you can help them. What have you got? Unique to Iran, I mean."

This was new to Bonner. He didn't normally work in this way, being asked for specific things, right now; rather, he specialized in technology—not news but plans, models, parts, all things that took time. This new approach made him uneasy. "There's scuttlebutt we're on a joint ops with another carrier, it's up in Palma right now. We're going through the Canal first, to Mombasa then Bahrain. They follow in a month, then the word is we'll hit somebody. Some guys say Iran, revenge for that bomb in the German club."

"Yes? That's good. That's what they like. Can you confirm that?"

He shook his head. "I know the A-6 squadron's doing low-levels because I heard the pilots talk. Plus they're doing refueling with S-3s from the other carrier. So, you know, we could be way down the Gulf and still hit Iran."

"Or Iraq."

"Yeah, but there's no reason. Iran, everybody says we owe them one. For the German club." He wriggled on the bench. "Frankly, Carl, I think we owe the fucking ragheads one for that. That could've been me, sitting in that club when they bombed it."

"So, one A-6 squadron and refueling from the other carrier. And?"

"Cover, that's all. It's small."

"A surgical strike, then. You don't know where. But you will know—won't you, Sheldon?"

"I—I— That's not my—*modus operandi*. I don't like that shit. I'm a specialist."

"But, for once, I think we must work this way. The Iranians want a gesture. Between you and me, they would like to test the IFF before they surprise your Navy with it—specifically, they want to test using the IFF to target missiles. We have given them the system; they have the technology; what they will need is the frequency."

"We change it all the time."

"I know." Carl joined his hands. "But if you put a prearranged frequency into the aircraft, and the Iranians targeted their missiles for that frequency, then they should be able to shoot down the aircraft. Shouldn't they?"

Bonner's face became stubborn. "It wouldn't work."

"I insist it would."

Bonner turned his head toward Carl, daring him to contradict, angry again. "The first thing they're airborne, they make a test pass and flash IFF. If you put in a different frequency they go negative and they abort. Great idea! A whole squadron makes one pass around the carrier and lands. Brilliant."

Carl's face darkened and his hand slipped back into his pocket. "Think of something, then, Sheldon. Your future depends on it."

"What the hell!"

Carl shrugged. "They want results."

"They're Nazis. Fucking lot of Nazis!"

Carl merely looked at him. "Think of something."

Bonner looked up and down the road. It would be almost a relief to have some NCIS goon walk in on them.

No, it wouldn't. It would be the end of everything. Carl, he knew, was his only chance to make it big.

"*One* aircraft," he said. "One aircraft, you might get away with it. Some of these hotshots, they'll lie when they test the IFF, because they don't want to scrub. Especially a real mission. Some of these guys piss themselves they're so hot to go. Like—" He was thinking fast. "The skipper of the A-6 squadron. A fucking kamikaze. He wouldn't abort if the wings fell off his fucking aircraft." He shifted, began to get interested. "And if it was only one, see, they wouldn't trace it back to whoever put the codes in. A whole squadron, Christ, they'd know in three seconds it had to be something like the IFF, even if you could get around the test run. They'd put every sonofabitch who has access to the aircraft on a polygraph. Or they wouldn't even have to. They got us all on lists, computers. Big Brother is watching."

"Can you do it?"

"Me! Get some other sucker." Bonner folded his arms. "That's not my specialty. I've never *done* stuff."

"Can't you do it?" Carl's voice was soft and pleading, almost feminine. "Sheldon, I need you to do it. Only this once."

Bonner started to whine again. "I'd have to find out which *plane* he's gonna fly, and that can be tricky; then I gotta get *at* the plane, but I gotta nick the gun that inserts the codes and reset it. It's too much!"

"Twenty-five thousand dollars."

"I'm not a saboteur! I'm a—a—" He shrank into himself. "Specialist."

"I need you to do this for me, Sheldon. For both of us. The Iranians will be charmed to shoot down the CO of an attack squadron. They will love us! We will have years and years with them, Shel."

"I need more money."

Carl frowned. "I might get you thirty-five. I can try. I promise I will try."

"That's it? Tops?"

Carl nodded.

Actually, thirty-five was more than he'd dared think about. He owed about fifteen. Still, it would be a horrible effort. His gut would be a mess until it was over. He continued to object. "You'd have to get the frequency to me. So I'd know what to set in the plane. I'd try to give you the target. The timing's all wrong."

"I'll have a frequency for you when you put into Mombasa. Then you should know the rest by the time you reach Bahrain."

"What if we make the hit before we get to Bahrain?"

"We'll take that chance. These people understand that such a thing is not easy. They have a good idea what the potential targets are, anyway."

"I oughta get my money either way."

"That is understood. I think there will be a bonus for a confirmed kill. Yes, I think it is a very good idea, this one. They will be able to test their system and the Navy will have no idea it has happened. Then, the next time—" He fluttered his fingers in the air like disintegrating aircraft.

Bonner felt sweat trickling down his ribs. "I'll be shitting bricks until it's over," he said.

"Yes, but when it's over, think how good you'll feel. Money, Sheldon!"

They spent some time talking over the details, and the longer they talked, the more familiar it seemed to Bonner, therefore the more workable. This was a trick he would have to play on himself, making it familiar, so that after a few days he would not come to with a start and remember that he was going to do this thing, feeling his colon lurch. Actually, even now, once he got a little used to it and the chill of fear had passed, he liked the planning, and he liked sitting here with this important man, who had been a big gun in Moscow and now was going to be a big gun in Tehran. He liked being wanted. And he liked the money.

"How is your son?" Carl said when they were done.

"Good. He writes, like, once a month."

"He is still in the satellite communications school?"

"Yeah. Four months, he comes out, he's an E5, one bump down from his old man."

"Tehran are very interested in him. They are mad for communications technology. You will speak to him?"

"The time isn't right. When it's right, I will."

"Maybe, the slow approach, Sheldon—little by little—"

"Don't tell me how to handle my own son! *I'll* do it. In *my* time! He'll come around. I gotta put it to him just right—father and son, doing it together. He's very idealistic. He doesn't know I do this, I've told you that. I'll bring him around, but— Just don't tell me how to handle my own son."

"Well— Of course. It is a wise father who knows his child—eh?"

They walked up the hill to the car. Carl told him a taxi was waiting for him around the next curve.

They did not touch. Carl put on sunglasses, as if he were withdrawing his personality. "You must bring your son in, Sheldon. It will be worth—*lots* of money. Eh?"

The car pulled away, and Bonner was left feeling suddenly isolated on that sunny stretch of road, with the city close by but somehow unreal, as if it was unpopulated, as if he was the only man on earth. He had no idea how close he had come to dying.

He walked up the hill, sweating again, and found the taxi. On the backseat was a bottle of Jack Daniel's.

Bonner went back to his hotel and turned on the television and began to drink. It was only early afternoon, but he was content to sit there, watching the bright colors, hearing the language he did not understand, a man more comfortable with his loneliness than with any other companion the teeming city could offer.

He began to plan how he would turn his son into a spy.

1615 ZULU. MOSCOW.

Ouspenskaya slipped into the Director's office after a single knock. The receptionist was gone, the building quiet except for the duty crews on the second floor, and here and there some manager like the Director plugging away. He knew she was coming.

"Well? What is urgent?" His cold was worse.

"Efremov."

"Yes?"

She sat down. Her hands were trembling. She was truly wretched, for something monstrous had obtruded into this place, this idea she had of Moscow and being Russian, as if an obscene animal had dragged its slime across her foot. "Five days ago, a gang attacked an office in the Stitkin Building here in Moscow. Twenty-nine dead."

"I remember." He guessed at once; his voice showed it.

"The office was Efremov's latest front operation. Venux, Inc. To run the four agents I told you of."

"Oh, my God." He was breathing through his mouth like an adenoidal child, looking absurd and feeling dreadful. "My God," he said again as he saw it all. "They wiped out the entire operation."

She nodded. "A hired job. Ex-military all over it."

"Maybe it's a fake—"

She shook her head. "What do you think, the Army did it? No, no! It's just what we're doing to ourselves! Efremov disappears; somebody wipes out his best operation— every clerk, every computer operator; they burned the place out—files, disks, shredder, everything! We're already four days late; the police treated it as ordinary crime—'ordinary,' ah!—and our people didn't go in until I sent them an hour ago. There's already been looting of what's left. *What kind of people are we becoming?*"

"You think—the father of the girlfriend? Mafia?"

"I don't know. For what? Revenge?" She shrugged. "I'm having Papa Malenkov brought in. No pussyfooting. I've told them to rough him up and see what he says. Let him know we're not the Moscow police." She shook her head. "But it doesn't add up. If it's a message to us, why hit a disguised operation that we don't know about? If it's a message to Efremov, where is he? Is he dead? Then what's the point?" She wiped her cheeks, sank back. What she was suffering was grief, grief for a lost ideal. "Maybe he's dead. *But maybe he isn't.* And if he isn't—"

"If he isn't— Maybe *he* did it. Eh? You say this operation was new—a few months. Nine? Nine. So—maybe, that long ago, he was planning—something?"

"It seems far-fetched. But Efremov could be very cute if he wanted to. He liked to cover his tracks, even long before—mmm—current conditions."

The Director made a face. "Say it. Long before *perestroika.* My God! The good old days." He made a sound, something between a laugh and a groan. "My God, Ouspenskaya, what a ball of shit it's all turned into! Any idea where Efremov would go?"

"None."

"Out of the country?"

"I suppose."

"You've checked the various agencies that—of course you have. All right, he was clever, he was an old campaigner, he could have gone over any border he wanted. I'm only brainstorming, mind you—improvising; I'm sure he's dead, in fact. But let's say, for argument's sake, he isn't. Presumably he had money abroad. Well. So, he destroys the organization that handles his best agents. To deny us? Of course, a nice joke, one 'in your eye,' as they say. He never liked me, I might say. You, I always thought he had his eye on. No? Well, there you are. I'm a bureaucrat, not a human relations specialist. Presumably he plans to take himself to somebody else, with his star agents as his salesman's samples—eh? So he destroys everything and everybody who can track those agents. Well, that makes a grisly kind of sense. So who does he go to? The Americans? Not likely; he really despised the Americans. Notice I talk of him in the past tense, as if he were dead." He made the laughing groan again, trying to break through her mood. Failing, he said, "*Please,* Ouspenskaya!" He came around the desk, stood in front of her, patted her shoulder. He only made things worse: she began to weep. The Director poured a glass of water from his carafe (made in Sweden) and held it out to her.

"There's something else," she said.

"Oh, shit." He retreated behind his desk.

"I'm sure there's a discrepancy between his claims for eighty agents and the agents themselves. I haven't got proof yet, but there's too much organization, too much system manipulation, and not enough information. I think some of the eighty are dummies."

He leaned his forehead on one hand. "Not all of them. Efremov got wonderful information from real agents!"

"I have an idea, Director."

"Good, because I certainly don't."

"There is probably more in the computers than we can tease out. We need specialists. The computer was installed ages ago by East Germans who would not even be seen speaking to us now. Let's go to the Americans."

He paused, a tissue halfway to his nose.

"The Americans know everything about computers," she went on. She was more cheerful, talking about what could be done. "We tell them that Efremov has bolted and that one of his agents is American. That will make them hot, you know. Then we tell them there is more in the computer but we can't winkle it out. We will let their specialists into the computer if they will replace the system with IBM machines when they are done. And give us whatever they find of Efremov's. We lose nothing. And they will take care of Efremov for us."

He stared at her.

"I am sick of using low-end technology!" she shouted. "And I want a new telephone, too!"

He swiveled to look out the window. The rain was still streaming down. He balled a damp tissue between his palms, rolling it back and forth, back and forth, at last dropped it into the plastic bag, then got up and left the office. She heard the water run in his private bathroom. The toilet flushed. He came out wiping his hands on a handkerchief.

"Not yet," he said.

She hitched forward in her chair. "I was approached by an American at the Venice conference. A very obvious move—in fact, she said so. 'Now that the Cold War is over,' and so on. I know I could make the contact!"

"Of course you could make a contact; I could make a contact; who couldn't? You're not thinking clearly, Ouspenskaya. No, letting the Americans into Efremov's computer files would be obscene. Just now. Not that I wouldn't do it if I was absolutely sure he was alive and working for somebody else."

"He has been responsible for killing twenty-nine of his own people. And he is a traitor!"

"You don't know that! Did you report this approach at the Venice Conference?"

"Of course."

"Who was it?"

"A woman. It's all in my report."

He hesitated for that millisecond that betrays suspicion, then glanced at her almost apologetically. He was thinking *Those American women—you hear strange things—they do things with other women—* He moved uncomfortably; he felt out of place in this new and more dangerous world. He cleared his throat. "What did she offer you?"

"It wasn't an offer. An idea—a Soviet-American think tank. American money. I would participate at a high level."

"A little obvious, maybe?"

"She said as much—pointed out that three SVRR generals were touring U.S. military bases as we spoke."

He made a little throat-clearing sound, a sign of hesitation—this hint of possibly irregular sex embarrassed him—and said gently, "Who is she?"

"She works for George Shreed. She made that quite clear enough." She laughed, throatily. "*Quite* clear. What is it Americans call it—'name-pushing'?"

"Name-*dropping,* I believe. George Shreed. Well, well." Shreed was more or less his opposite number in the CIA, at least so placed that the Director looked upon him as almost a rival in the same bureaucracy. Competitiveness tingled, despite his cold. "People like Shreed never dared reach into my directorate before. It's a new world."

"One in which a colonel murders twenty-nine of his own people and betrays his country. For money! I know it! I feel it! The bastard!"

The Director groaned. He was sure that Ouspenskaya would resist any seduction from an immoral American woman. Wouldn't she? He had managed to clear one nostril. He breathed through it for some seconds. "Did I tell you Gronski left with twenty-four hours' notice 'to enter the private sector'? *What* private sector? Money—the new socialist ideal. Well. All right, renew the contact with Shreed's woman. Prepare the ground, but do nothing. File a report on everything you do. Put everything in writing for me. Get together with somebody who knows the computer and draft a plan for clearing it, then have them squeeze every drop of data out of it. I want every individual who has worked for Efremov in the last five years interviewed on polygraph—right down to the clerks. You run this, Ouspenskaya. If there are dummy agents he was taking money for, I want details. The individuals won't know about it; they'll think everything was straight. If they had suspicions, maybe he paid one or two off. But he was so good I'll bet nobody got suspicious. But somewhere in the records there will be glitches. You can't run ghosts and not have it show up."

She stood. "You go to bed."

He groaned. As she turned to go, he said, "Get what you can on the four agents who were being run out of the place that was attacked. You'll have to go back to before he compartmentalized them. Maybe even back before we computerized. A big job."

"I want to nail him like a new Christ."

"Yes, but don't want it so much that you overlook things that will exonerate him. Remember—maybe he's dead. Maybe he's under a new pouring of concrete somewhere. Maybe he's innocent."

"He isn't!"

He ignored that. "I want everything on those four agents. Especially the American. I think we can do something with that."

She didn't ask him what.

2010 ZULU. NAPLES.

Kim fed Alan a strawberry from her plate and pressed her leg against his. She had forgiven him, because he had wangled an extra day's liberty and because he had taken her to this elegant, expensive restaurant where Italian men looked at her as if she were the dessert cart. Then, Alan had pointed out three officers from the carrier, then Narc and two guys and a couple of women who wouldn't have dared look into the same mirror with Kim. Narc's eyes had bugged out, not only because Kim was such a woman, but because it was the Spy who had her. She giggled and pressed his leg and said she loved him so much.

"I hate the Navy," she said happily. Her tongue flicked at a dot of whipped cream at the corner of her mouth. "I'm going to make my father give you a job so you can get out of the Navy and we can stay in bed all the time."

He was not immune to being flattered. "You really believe your father's going to pay me to stay in bed with his daughter?"

"What Kimberley wants," she said, with a tiny smile, "Kimberley gets."

Her father was a big shot in Florida. The Hoyts had a huge house on the beach near Jacksonville; Alan had got lost in it, trying to find the head. Her brother had laughed at him for that. Alan hadn't liked him, a muscled twenty-year-old who spent his spare time on a jet ski and talked a lot about reverse discrimination. He had called Alan "admiral." Something in his posture, his aggressiveness, had challenged Alan, as if they were rivals. The father had looked on at this with a small smile.

"I don't think I could work for your father," Alan said now.

"Oh, if the price is right, I bet you could." She kissed him. "And the price will be right."

She smiled. She licked her lips. He thought she was about the most desirable thing he'd ever seen. He began to tell her the story of landing into the net.

5

Their first liberty ports behind them, the *Roosevelt* and the *Jefferson* moved down the Med in seemingly separate paths. The two great ships transited the Suez three weeks apart, then lingered briefly within a hundred miles of each other at the mouth of the Red Sea. *Roosevelt* docked at Mombasa; *Jefferson* forged eastward toward the Gulf, where Iran and Iraq, exhausted from their war, still lay spitting and snarling at each other like wounded cats. For Alan Craik, the carrier became his life. A meeting with Kim in Bahrain was dreamlike, quickly relegated to a vague background of fantasies and remembrance, against which his real world played. Real life was intelligence and flight, the CVIC and Christine. Now, he was like a hungry man let loose at a banquet table: he devoured and devoured and wanted more.

Over those three months, the two carriers approached each other and moved away, partners in a vast dance discernible only to their captains—never close enough to make a common nuclear target, never far enough apart to foreclose joint operations. Four months after they had passed Gibraltar, they reached designated points within range of the Iranian coast and began to brief their aircrews on the mission labeled KNIGHTHOOD.

On the scale of air warfare, the carrier is a siege engine; its target is a vast fortress of electronics and missiles. Night is the preferred environment, when men's eyes fail and the side with the best electronic vision wins.

On the night sea, the deck of the carrier is a vision from some ancient legend, lit by flashes like lightning, tense with the nervous movements of men, raucous with sounds like the forges of Vulcan. The senses are battered by the power of the thing, the urgency and vigor of its component parts. Planes land in a roar and flash of sparks or leap into the air from hidden catapults. All around, men labor in shifting, flickering light, while the deck vibrates with the power of the screws and the planes and the machinery, and you feel the vibration in your very bones. The smell of JP-5, the lifeblood of naval aviation, is everywhere.

Beneath this sensual assault is intellectual wonder that the engine works. Men scurry through the noise, the patches of light and blackness, the danger; mysterious instructions whisper down dozens of radio channels; planes are fueled, repaired, launched, recovered, given ordnance, checked for weight, preflighted, tied down, chocked, released, rolled, towed; alerts are set and manned; while high overhead those aloft conduct their missions, talk to the tower, talk to each other, refuel in the air, prepare to land, parts of the great engine even while distant from it. Below the flight deck, intelligence plans missions, reviews debriefings, plays off future against past; powerful computers trade immense quantities of information about the carrier, her friends, her enemies, and all the complex world that now falls between. Elsewhere within, her crew is fed, their clothes are washed, their spaces are kept clean and neat, their beds are made, their confessions are heard and their prayers are spoken, their frailties are punished and their successes are rewarded, all while the ship drives through the water, powered by her nuclear heart. Almost six thousand humans crew her and her brood of aircraft, and very few of them are sleeping now.

All of this marvel is directed toward a single goal: the extension of naval supremacy through the air to any target. Opposed to it this night is the modern technological fortress, the integrated air defense system—the IADS, sterile name for a citadel that might once have been called Ticonderoga or Krak des Chevaliers. Lay out this IADS on the map and you will see a many-layered fortress: the early-warning radars as the outer wall, spaced in rough terrain, bunched in smooth, surrounding clumps of smaller forts—missile sites—that defend potential targets; yet more sites defend the sector headquarters; at the center of all sits the air defense command, controlling all, ready to call up fighter aircraft the way Saladin once called up his cavalry.

The early-warning radars are the eyes of the system. They are everywhere—perimeter, SAM sites, defense areas, every attack corridor. The SAMs—surface-to-air missiles—are the archers; at each SAM center is a powerful, long-range missile site that must in its turn be protected by smaller SAMs and conventional antiaircraft (AAA). The AAA remains deadly against low-flying attackers; it is not tricked by chaff and flares—the electronic dust thrown into radar's eye. Each SAM site also has fire-control radars, a field of microwave dishes, landlines, cables, and communications devices: it is no small thing.

Communication is essential, because the radar horizon on our small planet is a measly twenty-two miles. Even from a mountain or a giant tower, a radar sees only thirty or forty miles—in the age of supersonic aircraft and big-stick (long-range) missiles, like being legally blind. Therefore, it is only at a headquarters controlling hundreds of EW radars that an incoming attack can be understood and that understanding passed to the SAM sites, usually by regions or sectors. At the center of all the sectors is the Air Defense Headquarters, resolving conflicts between sectors and controlling the fighter force.

This, then, is the siege warfare of the late twentieth century, when the besieger moves at hundreds of miles an hour, attempting to destroy EW radars and SAM sites to open safe routes to targets while fighting off the missiles and AAA and aircraft that the fortress deploys. It is fast and complex and seemingly clean, but, as in the days when warriors smashed steel visors with hammers, men die.

On both sides.

JULY 12, 1990. 0315 ZULU. OTTAWA, CANADA.

Most of the Royal Canadian Mounted Police building was quiet, but on the third floor a block of offices was alive with the sounds of day—voices, telephones, computer keys, music that boomed until a hoarse voice shouted to turn it down. A gray-haired man carried a computer printout along an uncarpeted corridor, turned a corner, started past a row of doors, and pulled up just after passing an open one. Thinking better of something, he leaned in.

"You interested in four Russians?"

"You got four for sale, eh?"

"Ha-ha, I'm laughing right out loud. I got a report from Vancouver about four Russians they're just processing through—tourist visas, very little luggage, at least one checks out as former Spetsnaz."

"Where they coming from?"

The man checked a sheet. "Vladivostok. Direct flight."

"They holding them?"

" 'Detained in the normal course of immigration procedure.' "

"Lemme see." The man at the desk took the printout. "Four hard cases," he said. "You read this, eh? All four Spetsnaz, would be my guess. Ages are right, descriptions. So what we may have is four nouveau-mafia types who think muscling in on Canadian rackets might be a nice way to go. The kind that give me the pip—right shits, thinking we're easy pieces." He held out the sheets. "Nice catch, Tony. Tell Vancouver to let them through but put a tail on them. Descriptions and photos throughout, middle priority, 'surveillance for information only.' Open a file, put it in your manor—stay on top of it, eh? Update every seventy-two hours. This one smells."

"Maybe it's four former Spetsnaz who like hockey."

"Wouldn't that be nice. And Tony, put together a grab team. Just in case we want to talk to them."

Tony looked a little piqued. "Some of us have lives, sir. And Senators tickets."

"Do it anyway. It's not like the Senators will win, eh? All our best guys are playing in the States."

JULY 23, 1990. 2113 ZULU. PERSIAN GULF.

Alan Craik lived in two worlds now. Squadron intelligence officers worked in the Carrier Intelligence Center (CVIC), planning routine missions, massaging raw intelligence. But aircrewmen flew with their squadron. And he was both. He had to balance the two, pretend that each of these prickly groups had his first priority.

But this night was different. He had finished his work as intelligence officer—forty hours of preparation and briefing—and he could take up his work as aircrewman without apology. If he was allowed.

He had been working to prepare the operation called KNIGHTHOOD. It was the reason for the doubling of the carrier presence in the Gulf, the reason for his father's boat's shadowing his own. Its generalities had been planned in Washington; its specifics were completed by men like Alan on the carriers; its execution would be done by men like his father.

An Iranian radar post was to be destroyed. KNIGHTHOOD would open a hole in the Iranian IADS by exploiting low-level coastal radar gaps, which would be used by two strike groups. Iranian casualties were meant to be light—casualties were bad press, even with a secret operation—but their military would learn how porous their fortress was. Perhaps a higher level would then understand how expensive terrorism could become.

Alan's work in CVIC gave him solid knowledge of what his own squadron would do, and he had begged his skipper and the ops officer to let him go. Christine was to be a mission tanker, fairly safe (he assured them) off the coast. He was a pretty good TACCO now, he had dared to say—ask Rafe, ask Senior Chief Craw. But they had put him off—because, he believed, he was Mick Craik's son and they didn't know how his father would take it.

He wanted to go more than he had ever wanted anything—more than he had wanted Kim, more than he had wanted that high school letter. He wanted the *reality* of it, and he knew that this want was different from the other wants, which seemed of another kind, even of another world. He wanted it, he thought, to be a man.

And, apparently, he wasn't to have it.

He knew every plane going out that night, every piece of the complex series of raids designed to peel the onion of the Iranian IADS and leave them to face the morning with a huge breach in their defenses. And he wasn't to be among them.

He sat with a cup of coffee before him, hurt as he thought he had never been hurt before. Around him, the level of voices was higher, somehow tighter, the ones who were going sounding too loud and too happy. A few who couldn't wait were already fiddling with their gear.

Maybe, he thought, *it's better in the long run not to get what you want.* Maybe disappointment makes you a man. Maybe the moon is made of green cheese.

"Been looking all over for you." The voice was right above his head. A hand fell on his shoulder. His skipper's.

Alan looked up. His heart lurched. The hand squeezed. The skipper was looking away from him, off to a group of pilots; he shouted, "Gilder, I gotta talk to you, pronto!" He turned back, looked down. Their eyes locked. "You're going. Get into your flight gear." The hand lifted and fell—a pat on the shoulder. And then the skipper was gone.

He was going.

Alan was only human. He longed to go back to CVIC and drop just a hint, to see the envy of the other IOs, that he was going on a real mission. *Cheap thrill,* he thought— but he almost did it anyway, saved from doing something tacky and small-minded and altogether satisfying because there just wasn't time. Instead, he bolted for his stateroom and started to twist himself into his flight suit.

His roommate looked up from a magazine, said with total conviction, "Lucky fuckin' prick!"

He already knew.

Surfer was a seasoned flyer, had taken him as a room-mate instead of another pilot so as to teach him some sub-stratum of ethics or manners that wasn't in the books.

"I wish it was you."

"Like hell." Surfer rolled the magazine in his hands. "Skipper asked me, I told him he goddam better let you go." He gestured with the magazine. "You deserve it."

"We'll probably go down on deck."

"You'll probably be the first Spy in history with a fuckin' Air Medal, you mean." Surfer nodded with sad conviction. "Get the fuck out of here."

Alan finally got his left foot into his boot and grabbed his helmet bag from his rack. "Don't wait up, dear." Surfer gave him the finger as he closed the hatch.

Mick Craik went over the details of his mission for the hundredth time while two para-riggers moved around him, squires to a knight in green armor. One part of his brain— the part that was squadron skipper—noted that Tiernan, the problem child of the rigger shop, was suddenly conscientious about his duties, made a mental note that maybe what Tiernan needed was more responsibility, not less. Another part of his mind—the NavAv part—noted that his helmet had finally been retaped; his personal coat of arms, a flu-orescent orange net catching a burning plane, glowed from the LPO's desk in the corner. The seasoned pilot in him noted that his young bombardier-navigator was having a more difficult time than usual getting his gear on. Kid was nervous.

Hell, he was nervous himself, and he was one of three people on this strike who had actually done it before. The difference was, he thought, that the boy was probably worried about intangibles: bravery, cowardice, the unknown. Craik was nervous because he didn't like the plan: not enough gas in the air, some of it too far forward; too much contempt for the Iranians, not enough worry about blue on blues over the target.

But that wasn't really it. What he really didn't like was that the targets had been set in Washington. He was leader for the whole strike, but he was an arrowhead on an arrow launched by politicians. He liked a different plan, his own plan, with a different target picked out here by the people on the spot: bomb the Iranian Navy base at Bandar Abbas. No chance of error, and a very direct message.

He patted the BN on the shoulder, gave him a reassuring smile. "Piece of cake," he said.

Miles away, his son ran down the main portside passageway toward the aviators' wardroom, the eatery known locally as the Dirty Shirt. His nose told him that chocolate-chip cookies had just been baked, and he meant to get some for his crew and fill his thermos with coffee. Rafe called him "the stewardess," but there was no barb to it; in fact, Alan believed that it was one of the things that the Spy did that made his crew think he might be a regular guy after all. He scooped twenty or so out of the cookie bucket with a practiced hand, ignored the mutters and shouts of the onlookers, and dumped them into his helmet bag. He filled his thermos (L.L. Bean, stainless, one of the few gifts from his mother that was right on target, considered so valuable by the crew that it had never been part of a practical joke) and bolted back down the passageway. He left behind a circle of indignant Tomcat RIOs, equally upset that he was flying while they sat on their asses and that he had taken two dozen cookies.

Can't take a joke, fuck 'em, as Rafe liked to say.

2120 ZULU. IRANIAN COAST.

It was dark along the Iranian coast. The noncom they called Franci was not a very willing soldier, but he was an able one. In fact, he made the decisions at his SAM battery, although the orders were given by an officer who had less real knowledge but a more reliable history.

Now, Franci was chewing his mustache and smoking. They had been ordered up to full alert every night for two weeks—missiles on the rails, radar warm and ready. The imams apparently believed the American demons were coming. Franci supposed they were—he had lived in America, knew the almost casual belief in exercising power. The reverence for the gunslinger, he thought.

So he sat in the command trailer and waited.

The box had arrived five nights before. It had been bolted on the main radar dish. The zealot who had brought it had said that it would see the infidels as they crossed into Iranian airspace. This was a story for children, in Franci's view; six years at the University of Buffalo, from which he had been forced home by threats to his family, convinced him that the box must somehow turn the dish into a (probably inefficient) passive detector. The zealot had sworn that when the blue-green light went on in the command van, the Americans would be coming.

And so they would be, Franci mused.

He had also seen the Revolutionary Guards bring in a missile launcher of their own, now standing well clear of the SAM battery. As usual, it looked like industrial scrap held together with string. The RGs loved toys, he thought—no, "Correction," as his American friends used to say, all Iranians loved toys—look at the outboard boats mounted with machine guns, the taxi-mounted rocket launchers. Gadgets for a preindustrial theocracy.

The missile, when he had been allowed to glance at it uncovered, had looked to him like an ancient I-Hawk with the front end tarted up. The electrical engineer in him had cringed. It had looked like trouble to him. Big Trouble. Things meant to go bang were always big trouble for some-body unless they were properly designed and engineered.

So he had approached his own officer about it, although coming at the matter circumspectly after the fashion of a stray dog approaching a kindly voice—sideways and ready for a kick.

"Ha, Rasi, and how is your wife?" he had said.

"She is well, soldier of the servants of God. Soldier, I am not to be addressed by name by you with, ah, hmm, *them* here." He had nodded toward the shrouded missile, as if it represented the Revolutionary Guards in all their power. And their narrow-mindedness.

"Rasi, may your name be blessed," Franci had said, not able entirely to suppress irony, "friend of all soldiers, I abase myself," and he had started to kneel, causing the of-ficer to wince and urge him to his feet. Enough was enough, obviously.

However, they had got to the real subject. "These Rev-olutionary Guards," Franci had said. He had nodded to-ward the missile. "*The Hour* is almost upon us, and their creation is, um, in the sun."

"What? Hour? What hour?"

Franci had got excited. He could deal with idiots only so long. "*The* Hour! Are you incapable? The Hour when our camouflage is supposed to be up! When everything must be covered! When—!" He had swallowed, flapped his arms up and down, and slapped his sides. Then, more calmly, "When Tehran tell us we must be invisible to the eyes the Americans have put in the heavens to circle the earth."

"You go far beyond yourself to shout at me. This is not proper. I will note it. Somewhere." The officer had pulled at his open collar as if he wished for a more formal, more dignified uniform. "The Guard take care of themselves.

Maybe they have their own camouflage. We do not tell them what to do. They are the Guard!"

Franci suspected they were shepherds who couldn't read a word of the Koran, but he didn't dare say so. Instead, he had said with the measured slowness of a man talking to a child, "They will give us away. They will give away the missile we are not supposed to see. They will get us all killed."

"It is the will of God."

Franci had sighed. He had not quite dared to say that the will of spy satellites worked no matter what God—or at least the Revolutionary Guard—might say.

So now, tonight, he sat in the command trailer and smoked his fifteenth Marlboro and watched the blue-green light that was supposed to come on when the Americans arrived.

And what would happen when it did?

2210 ZULU. PERSIAN GULF.

Skipper Craik walked slowly around his plane, looking into every opening, running his hand lovingly down her wings to her body, then crouching to look at her landing struts and gear. He never thought of the process as sexual, never saw the plane as a woman, although he would concede he had seen men run their hands over horses this way.

He glanced up to make sure that her chaff and flare cartridges were full, and as he did so was vaguely aware that the sailor coding his plane with an IFF gun was a stranger. Probably a recode, he thought; they changed IFF at the last minute, sometimes. Still, his BN had already got a sweet and sweet on deck, so why change it now? The question was an annoyance, low priority, not even a worry; he'd ask the kid what happened when they were on the cat.

He ran his hand up inside her jet intakes, checking for FOD or debris. Once in a while, some sailor with a grudge put a coin up there. He'd heard of a can of concrete, in another squadron. The fact that he had never found anything didn't stop him. It was part of his ritual. He checked his car the same way.

If he checked it himself, nothing could go wrong.

Alan was finally ready. The frontseaters had already walked to the plane, but Senior Chief Craw refused to be hurried, even seemed to be dawdling. The delay covered nicely for Alan's perpetual confusion about what order to put his flight gear on.

Master Chief Young, the senior enlisted maintenance man, met them at the back door to the ready room. He was kitted up for the flight deck.

"Got a present for you, sir," he said to Alan.

Alan looked around a little foolishly. Master Chief had a way of doing that to him. Going on the mission was all the present he wanted; what else could there be?

"On deck," the Master Chief said. They followed him down the passageway to the sponson, then up behind the tower.

All around them, the carrier was preparing for battle. Bombs were going by on carts; fuel lines were being laid out to planes; aircrews were checking them while last-minute maintenance was done. The heavy stink of kerosene filled the air.

Right at the elevator-deck edge sat Christine, long since repainted to cover the jokes left by their sister squadron on the *Roosevelt.* The face-lift made her seem young again, and, caught in the glare of the launch of an early-cycle F-14 on burner, she was the most beautiful plane Alan had ever seen—a tribute to his loyalty, to say the least. Bulbous, big, and awkward, she towered over them like a bad dream.

Alan belatedly switched on his blue light and bent to perform his own preflight responsibility, the chaff and flare pods; the Master Chief grabbed his shoulder, turning him up and toward the fuselage, instead. He pointed.

Alan had to look for some seconds, then found it just

below the TACCO's window. There, stenciled on the gray hull, it said: LTJG ALAN CRAIK.

His name on the plane.

It meant acceptance—more, approval. And permanence. And what's more, Rafe must have okayed it. *Or even suggested it?* Alan stumbled into the aircraft, knowing he was blushing and glad for the darkness, unable to speak. He almost forgot to preflight his seat.

Mick Craik sat on the cat, his eyes wandering over the instruments as he took his baby to full power. The earth moved, but the gauges were good; she was a goer. He and the kid began the priest-and-acolyte formula of prelaunch checks. He reached for his inner calm, found it, and pulled it over him like an old, loved coat. He wished he could do the same for the kid. If his boy were going, he'd want—

Where is Alan? he wondered. Surely Harry wouldn't let him go on a live one like this. *So you'd want him to treat your kid specially, and let somebody else's kid go?* he asked himself He was no good at self-doubt; he pushed the question away.

He thought the S-3 tankers were being put too close to the coast—big, fat, dumb grapes waiting for some Iranian MiG jock to bag them. He had made the objection to Staff; a lot of good it had done. At any rate, he didn't want Alan up in one of the tankers tonight. One Craik in the air was plenty. Anyway, Alan had a different future: he had a kind of smarts that his father felt he lacked, the kind that could take you to admiral. Mick Craik, he thought, would retire where he was.

Craik looked around. Planes crouched on every cat, and more waited behind every jet-blast deflector. Fire and light filled the darkness, and, as happened every time he saw it, he was filled with the power of it and moved by what he thought of as the glory. Not much glory left in war, he thought, but we still hear the tune.

This was the center of his life, the heart of his belief.

This is where we treat people fair, and a guy who works and plays the team can get ahead. This is where they respect competence instead of bullshit, because when the chips are down your bombs either hit the target or they don't. Skipper Craik had known some pretty weird types in naval aviation, but they all got measured by the same stick; either they could fly, or they couldn't. And this was his America, not abstractions like liberty, Western democracy, capitalism, but a place of no-bullshit that offered great cars, great women, great flyfishing, and the most beautiful mountains on earth. For that place, he would climb into his fiery chariot and ride like the wrath of God against people he had never seen.

The blast deflector came up behind him. A blur of green showed as the cat crew hooked on the bridle.

Mick Craik loved "The Ride of the Valkyries." It went with the noise and the thrill of this moment on the cat, the first seconds of launch. He wished they could play it as the cat blasted them forward.

He was The Old Man in squadron myth, skipper in fact, old by comparison with the kids, and he knew that this was his last cruise with a stick in his hand. Yet he was eager to go. He wanted to prove himself one more time.

This was what he lived for. No women's tears, no bill collectors, no bureaucrats. Just the stick and the target.

The cat officer crouched and began to extend his arm.

Dear God, he prayed silently, as he always did, make it a good one if it's the last.

He snapped his best salute and they began to move.

Alan was ready for the cat when it came. For once, the sickly dust/electrical/old sweat smell of naval aviation was not threatening him with instant airsickness. Airborne, Rafe got a good IFF check from the boat and they cheered; Christine's IFF was, according to legend, entirely constructed from chewing gum and old Slinkies. Rafe started her on the long, slow climb to their tanker station as Narc began cycling through volumes of kneeboard cards to figure out how he could talk to their fighter cover—the entire launch and deployment was being done EMCON. Senior Chief began inserting radar frequencies into a computer hit list. Alan, with the back end online and for once in his life way ahead of the mission, was wiping the inside of his oxygen mask with an alcohol swab stolen from sick bay. He figured they would be on oxygen if anything happened, and the taste of old pizza would not help his airsickness.

He thumbed the intercom switch and began his stewardess routine. He tried to keep elation out of his voice, suppressed the urge to burble his thanks to everybody as he said, "Folks, we're going to level off at Angels 23 and cruise there until someone needs gas, at which time Rafe will fart down the pipe. In the meantime, espresso and chocolate-chip cookies are being served by your flight attendant in the main cabin, and will remain available until we touch down at Cedar Rapids International. And thank you for flying Naval Air."

Rafe let out a whoop, and a flight-gloved hand reached down the tunnel. Alan pressed the thermos into the hand, balanced two cookies atop it.

He turned to his monitor. Their radar was off, but he could watch other, active radars with his system, picking up the Iranian EWs as they arrowed from the coast. He began to log each one for the future. *Someday,* he thought, *all of this will be done by a computer.* Christine, however, couldn't handle the math of multiple radar cuts.

Alan found that he didn't like what he saw. His divided self tossed the information back and forth, TACCO to IO to TACCO, and what they agreed on was that there was an unusual amount of Iranian radar activity. It indicated what they both saw as a very high degree of preparedness. Alan hadn't expected to surprise the Iranians; the Persian Gulf is too small for that. But he had watched the IADS from routine flights, and he knew what it looked like on an ordinary night—a lot of bored operators flicking on and off, some sites never coming online in a whole seven-hour hop. This looked more like a carnival; everybody was up. Everybody but the SAM sites; they were asleep, while the EW net seemed to have insomnia.

He looked at his watch. The strike was due to go feet-dry (over the coast) in two minutes.

Somewhere out there was his father, doing the glory thing. He knew his father well enough for that. He knew the slightly husky tone when he spoke that word, *glory,* the refusal to elaborate. Glory had magnetism for Alan now, too, although when he had been a teenager he had thought it was bullshit, something old men invented to get young ones to die for them. Now he lived with men who believed that glory was the goal of life: men of a certain kind— real men, they would have said—went where it drew them. He was not yet sure what kind of man he was, but he knew he felt that pull.

But you could think about glory and continue to massage data for only so long. Then something in the data fell together and you forgot about the glory. Now, a disquieting pattern showed: even in EMCON, one of the E-2C Hawkeyes was running the datalink, and a series of neat diamonds, denoting friendly aircraft and ships, lay over the screen like coarse mesh. What was now clear was that the activity of the IADS matched the diamonds. It did not take the intel half of his head to tell the TACCO that the Iranians had this raid pegged.

That's what the Nav gets paid for, he thought. Better equipment and better training ought to do the job. No sweat. Right?

PO1 Sheldon Bonner sat in the head and felt his entire gut shiver, as if there were ice there instead of the fire that seemed to explode under him. It had been getting worse for days, diarrhea like something you picked up in some god-awful liberty port where you couldn't drink the water or eat the fruit. Sick bay had given him pills. Christ, what a joke.

"Jeez, Boner," a voice said from the next stall. "What'd you do, swallow some of the ordnance? Christ, if I smelled like that I'd kill myself."

"Fuck off. I'm sick."

"I'd tell you to blow it out your ass, Boner, but that seems to be your specialty. Whoo-hoo! Jesus Christ, ask for a transfer, will you?"

His hands were still shaking. He had seen the pilot look at him and he had forced himself to go on setting the IFF code, when what he wanted to do was drop the gun and run. The guy had looked right at him. Fucking skipper of the squadron, helmet all fluorescent orange tape, one of the joyboys, guts and glory, all that shit. Fuck him. Let him see what it was like when he got to Iran.

He felt his bowels let go again. It would be like this for another week.

It's worth it, he told himself. He tried to see the boat he would buy. He had a mental picture he called up at night before he went to sleep, him and his boy on the new boat. Fishing on the St. John's. Beer in the cooler. Then he'd tell the boy about the scheme and the money and how they were going to be partners. Together. Just the two of them. It would be wonderful. It would.

His insides heaved and squirted and he groaned aloud.

2315 ZULU. IRANIAN COAST.

Franci worked with the intensity of a man at last able to do what he understood—tracking contacts, passing data, answering the telephone—using technology. He was one of the very few who understood how the electronic fortress works, and he had created his own informal phone link with others like him. For the duration of the raid, he was alive.

Now, he knew that a rain of antiradiation missiles had begun. To turn a radar on was to invite death; he did not.

Yet, through the eyes of a radar on a hill thirty miles behind him, he was able to watch the Americans come on.

The trailer door opened; a surprisingly courteous voice said, "Who is in charge, please?" It was a Revolutionary Guard full colonel. Everybody but Franci's officer pointed at Franci.

"I am in charge," the officer said.

"Show me the situation."

The officer turned smoothly to Franci. "Show the colonel the situation."

Franci didn't care who got the credit or what the pecking order was; he was caught up in the pleasure of doing the job. "They are coming in two strikes from the carriers, about forty miles apart. Northern strike will pass directly over us—unless we're the target, Allah forbid. Seven minutes to arrival."

The colonel handed him a cellular telephone. "Pass course and speed data to my shooter. No radar illumination until you are so ordered."

Franci was enthusiastic about not illuminating the radar: why make themselves a target?

The colonel left the trailer; Franci's officer teetered on his toes and watched the clock; Franci passed data and plotted vectors. Six minutes. Five minutes. Four. Three.

The Revolutionary Guard detachment fired their mysterious missile at six miles. Radar recorded one plane falling below the formation—an evident hit. Franci reported it on the cell phone.

"Illuminate your radar. Fire all missiles, whether targeted or not. This is a direct order from the colonel." It was like an order to commit suicide.

His fire-control radar stayed on for less than ten seconds before a HARM missile, launched minutes before, identified it as a first-priority target and zeroed in.

Franci felt the earth heave, and God reached for him.

• • •

2322 ZULU. PERSIAN GULF.

A new signal had just lanced out from the mainland. Alan hooked it and read its stats. Weird—not anything he remembered. He leafed through his notes and didn't find it. Then, too quickly, it disappeared and he was left to log it. *Somewhere in the parameters of a Chinese early-warning radar,* he thought. It had been on only eight seconds. Maybe somebody had shot it with a HARM. Maybe its operator had panicked at what he saw and shut down.

It had gone on within seconds of the feet-dry time and within four miles of the northern target group's route. It must have seen the whole northern strike package. Alan dialed up Strike Common, the radio frequency on which most chatter would occur when EMCON was dropped.

"Touchdown," a voice in his helmet said. EMCON was over.

"Packers!" another voice cried, and the plane seemed to drop out from under him.

Packers were unfriendly aircraft that had leaked through the forward screen. To four men riding a big, fat grape, the word meant danger. Alan had a brief recall of an argument in CVIC about whether the tankers would be too close to the coast. *We are, we are.*

Rafe had the plane in a dive for the surface.

Alan punched up his datalink display. Christine gave a faint whine.

The display died.

"Shit, Senior! We lost the back end," Alan groaned. Without conscious thought, he reached up, toggled the system switch off, counted ten, and toggled it on again.

Christine continued to dive.

As Alan tried to urge a glimmer from Christine's brain, he checked and rechecked the chaff and flare counters above his head.

"Dumped the load," he said into the mike. His anxiety showed in his voice. When you do a cold dump in an

S-3 you lose a lot—not least the ability to see if the Packer is after you.

Rafe came on the line. He had long since got his confidence back after the double bolter, and four months of flying had made his decisions crisper. He was busy just then, but this was what he was trained for, no bullshit, just flying. "Masks on. Spy, get that fucking computer up and tell me what's happening. Chaff and flare are armed."

Alan reached up and fired a chaff/flare sequence. The numbers counted down; three chaff, two flares down, plenty to go. "Chaff/flare checks good, Senior's got a reinit." Alan's fingers flew. He input the vital data—targets and known SAM sites—while Senior struggled to restore the datalink. Alan had to reinput his hotlist of radar contacts. When he hit the input button he saw that Senior had the datalink back up—and the news was bad.

Senior Chief Craw was drawling into the headset, "One bandit southeast nineteen NM and heading right at us. About 540 knots."

"Spy! What is it? MiG-29?"

If it is we're dead, he thought. *Where the hell is our CAP? We had an F-14 out here ten minutes ago; his wingman had a hydraulics failure, but—*

Alan found their missing CAP just as Narc did. "Fucking REO!" Narc shouted. Their protection had done his job and made a run at the intruder, but a nervous NFO and an inexperienced pilot had ended in a missed intercept and a bad shot. Narc had their Fighter Common on his comm and was trying to get the Tomcat back.

The intruder continued to bear down on them.

Why didn't he turn and engage the Tomcat? He didn't even seem to know that the fighter was there. Alan looked at his datalink and got a radar cut that ran like a sword through the unid box. The cut was rare; in effect, it was unknown, not present in the laundry list of radars and attached planes flown by threat countries. His head, however, unlike the datalink, was stuffed with such unconsidered trifles: he *knew* what it was.

"Chinese-built A-5 Fantan! Two Atoll AA missiles, shitty little radar. Rafe, get below eight hundred feet and he can't get a tone with his birds."

Rafe liked knowledge. He also liked certainty, and Alan sounded absolutely certain. And it was better than nice that it was a third-world pilot in a first-generation piece of shit chasing him, not some Russian merc in a MiG-29—an F-18 in drag—looking for a score.

"Okay, got it, we're going through two thousand and I'd really like to know his stall speed and has he got a gun?"

Alan had his kneeboard packet open and the A-5 card was glaring at him, printed for some reason on fluorescent orange card stock. "Two 20-millimeters. 165 knots clean. Worse for this guy, he's got to have a drop."

He looked at the screen; *Christ, he's close,* Alan thought, and all hell broke loose.

"Chaff flare!" shouted Narc, and he fired the sequence himself from the front. Narc's RAW gear showed a launch somewhere behind him. Alan leaned forward against the power of the dive and tried to read their altitude. "Below 1000!" he said, and Rafe pulled hard to the right, worse than the hardest break Alan had ever seen, and moonlit sea reached up hungrily toward the Senior's porthole to pull Christine down. The altimeter was now at two hundred feet: Christine did not believe in registering lower altitudes. Alan forced his arm up against the G force and put the chaff on automatic. He suddenly didn't trust all the data ingested at intel school. Had anybody ever actually fought an A-5? Fuck, what if all the intelligence was bullshit? Wasn't that the point Peretz had tried to make to him?

Rafe rolled the plane 180 degrees and started a more comfortable turn. A flash went by Alan's porthole. "Missiles timed out," Alan said, mostly sure that he was right. Craw was shouting on Strike Common, but nobody was going to save them; they were too far from the strike package and too far from the ship. In five minutes, every Tomcat and Hornet in naval aviation would be crisscrossing this airspace in search of air medals, but five minutes is an age in aerial combat and this was now.

"He's on top of us," Alan said.

Christine bucked savagely. He felt a slap at his left elbow, and a star-edged hole appeared in the windscreen.

They knew Christine had been hit by the 20-millimeter. They felt the rounds go into her and waited for disaster; at two hundred feet, any glitch and they were dead.

Rafe tightened his turn and dumped more speed. Christine was such a peculiar bird, he muttered, that he swore she flew better with the damage. "Nice shooting, Tex," Rafe murmured, and he eased off on the speed again and Christine was almost standing still in the air.

The last chaff pod emptied with a clunk. Another round hit Christine's wing and she started to leak fuel and pull to the right. The airspeed indicator registered 165. Rafe tilted the wings savagely and suddenly tightened his turn. His crew could not see the death's-head grin that clutched his face, an expression of vengeance and anguished hope and a desperate anxiety that came from seeing the white-caps, not so much below his window as next to it. He was muttering a fat-grape pilot's prayer: *Follow me, you mother, follow me, down and around and down and—*

A brief, violent flare lit the rearview mirror.

The silence of the cockpit seemed so profound to Alan that the whistle of air through the hole in the canopy was somehow outside it. He saw Christine's interior with un-earthly clarity—Craw's silhouette, the screens, the gleam of his thermos.

Then he knew they had leveled off and were starting to climb.

The radar cuts from the A-5's gun were gone.

Abruptly, Rafe punched his fist into the air over his head and gave a whoop. "Gotcha!"

Then, calmly, into the mike, he drawled, "Guardian, this is Gatoraid 2, splash one bandit, over," and he laughed. And laughed. "We got him. I mean, we fucking *got him!*" He couldn't seem to stop laughing.

Later, when he would tell this story to explain his Air Medal, he would lay his hand flat on the table and he would say, "You want to know how low I was? I was so low—I was so low that they had to scrape barnacles off Christine at the next maintenance check." And he would pause, and smile, and a little of this same delighted laughter would burble out. "And you wanta know how low that A-5 Fantan was? *On the bottom, ba-bee!*"

"That was beautiful!" Narc crowed. There was no fawning in his voice. "Fucking beautiful."

"What happened?" Senior Chief Craw asked. "Tomcat get him?"

"Rafe fuckin' dumped him in the water," Narc said. Rafe had managed to stop laughing. "He just went lower and slower till the raghead stalled."

Rafe chuckled—not the release of tension anymore, just amusement. "We got a kill," he murmured. "An S-3 got a kill!"

They all began to laugh. More, and louder, and then Alan was pounding on Craw's shoulder, and he realized what they had done. Rafe's flying, yes, but also his knowledge and Craw and Narc.

Christine climbed the night, bullet holes whistling, content that she had killed again.

2335 ZULU. PERSIAN GULF.

Strike Common was a tangle of voices. Southern Iran was covered in a net of radar cuts, AAA, and SAM radars coming on and off. The IADS had done well for the first few minutes; Alan had missed the climax, when their AAA and SAMs came online, but the HARMs and the jamming were beating them now. He saw no more hostile aircraft; their leaker had been a loony or a lone night patrol.

Millions of dollars were spent in seconds as he heard HARM shots called on Common and watched radar sites go off the air. Most of the strike package was still over the target, but some A-6s had already turned for home, and

Alan found one only twenty miles southeast of them. He hooked it and found that it was limping along at only a thousand feet.

"What's happening out there?" Rafe asked. He and Narc had assessed their damage and decided they could still give gas. That they were there, flying, doing routine, seemed an anticlimax; yet, astonishing as the attack and their survival had been, it was for the routine that they were there.

"We got one wounded bird coming in," Alan said, "eighteen miles out and wrong IFF, but he's low and slow and on his radial. Try and raise him on Common. Maybe needs gas to land."

Narc got the Hawkeye on comm. Alan's guess was confirmed: northern strike lead in a wounded bird, thought he could land it, needed gas at a low altitude. Rafe nodded; after going almost underwater to down the Fantan, he figured he could give gas while taxiing, and Christine's fuel leak didn't worry him. They rogered up and turned southeast, headed to intercept.

Alan was entranced with the electronic images of the raid, rapt, watching the Iranian IADS fall apart. The target EW sites and their protective SAMs went down under the strike packages and did not come back up as the strike came off target. There was a two-hundred-mile gap in the IADS. If they could get a plane that far, Alan thought, the Bahrainis could bomb Tehran now.

"Hey, Spy, get the FLIR online. I want to know how bad off this guy is. He doesn't have radio."

The FLIR is an infrared camera for watching surface targets, particularly surfaced submarines, at night. Bored S-3 crews on training hops use it to watch junior fighter jocks make fools of themselves trying to get their fuel probes into the basket at the end of the refueling hose. Now, Alan switched to it from the raid with regret. He couldn't watch the strike and FLIR at the same time; they both came up on the same screen.

Air-to-air refueling is an art at the best of times. Pilots try to perfect the technique against the day they really need the gas. Good aircrews practice no-comms refueling, using signals passed by flashlight and by aircraft lights. Yet, it is hard enough to maneuver a high-speed aircraft so that the attached fuel probe locks into the much slower tanker's basket; with the plane damaged, the pilot injured, it becomes torture.

Rafe made a good rendezvous with the wounded aircraft, an A-6 with a gash up the starboard side that went right through the cockpit.

Narc said, "He'll need about five thousand," and started to work the refueling computer. "Spy, have I got a basket out there?"

Alan got the basket dead center in the FLIR. "Bigger than life." He was still thinking of the raid. The urgency of the A-5 attack on them, the abrupt release, had left him unfocused.

He did not hear the change in Narc's voice as he cut the lights and said, "Oh, shit." Then, "He's hit bad. Losing power." His tone was odd, but Alan did not register it. Only later would he learn that both men in the front end had seen the injured aircraft's side number and knew who it was.

Rafe growled, "Soon as he's in the basket, we'll descend a little, give him some more airspeed, start a slowwww turn toward the boat. We'll get him home."

Poor sonofabitch, he was thinking. He meant Alan, not the wounded pilot.

Alan saw an infrared image of the A-6 pull into his field of view and realized that it was missing part of its canopy. The shock of it pulled him from his apathy, and he thought, *This guy is hurt bad,* and he began to function again. He was so intent then trying to figure out if the BN was still in the cockpit that seconds passed before he caught the glow of the pilot's helmet, the head bent far forward.

Volleyball net. A-6.

Dad.

The wounded bird plowed forward toward the basket but lost altitude. The probe missed, and the basket banged the A-6 windscreen. Invisible to Alan in the dark, Craw flipped on the camera attached to the FLIR.

Alan, cold, said, "He's losing it. He can't hold his altitude." The A-6's movements had a dreamlike quality now, too slow, silent, eerily altered by the FLIR's infrared. It seemed impossible that he was watching his father try to save himself. It seemed impossible that they were not back on the carrier, the mission over. Where was routine?

Rafe took Christine into a shallow dive. He was sure he could still save this one, get him his gas, get them all home. Fourteen hundred feet now; he had almost a minute to get him in the basket. He crawled. Surely bad things could not happen now.

Alan watched his father try again. In the slow dive, he came on straight and sure, but fifty feet from the basket something happened and the A-6 gave a shudder and disappeared from the screen again.

Alan whirled the FLIR back and forth until he found the aircraft again, now off to the left and right wing high. Slowly he tracked its attempts to try another pass.

Closer.

Seconds passed. The A-6 got a lineup and came on.

The probe was out. Alan's whole will tried to force the probe into the basket. The A-6 seemed to be flying through jelly, barely responsive, lazy. Slowly, slowly, the probe drifted closer.

Suddenly the probe was there there THERE and the basket sailed dead in front of it and it came on the last few feet and it was in.

"He's in!" Alan shouted, and he heard Craw call something at the same time. He tried to relax his grip on the seat. *It's okay,* he thought. *It's okay.* Then, as the fuel hit the wounded bird, triumph faded.

Christine gave a shudder. They were four hundred feet off the water and the A-6 had pulled the basket right off the hose. Fuel was raining down to the dark water, falling like blood from an artery, like lost opportunities, lost hopes.

He thought the A-6 started to fall away then, and that

would always be the image that he had of it—getting smaller, dropping slowly—but he would wonder later if that was only an image in his mind, the horror of a dream where the inevitable, the terrifying, takes form.

What Alan saw for sure, and knew he saw, knew that this really happened then, was his father raise his head and lift one hand in a gesture, half wave, half salute. *Does he know it's me? Does he know I'm here?* Then the head went down and the A-6 dropped like a stone.

An ejection seat fired, and a second later the plane hit the water.

"He's gone," he heard himself say. "He's gone."

He flipped back to the datalink.

Christine was silent. Then Narc began to report the downed bird.

6

Kim Hoyt had been doing small hits of coke since lunch and she wanted a party. It was pretty much a party already—her brother and two of his friends, her father, two business guys of his who had brought the coke as a sweetener for some deal they were making—but she wanted glitter and splash with it. She wanted to dress up and she wanted to strip naked; she wanted to be admired and she wanted to flirt; she wanted to be coveted and she wanted to be competed for. She wanted to be the center of something exciting, and that said to her a party.

Her father made deals. Mostly, his deals were in construction, condos and hotels, packaging and subcontracting, heavy in the part of the Cuban community where the money was. She admired her father. He was her model for a man: he could twist other men around each other, and he could make big money. Physically, he wasn't much—paunchy and soft-looking, smooth, barbered—but she had already learned what a lot of young men didn't know yet, that a middle-aged man like her father was more attractive than they were with their sun-bleached hair and their muscles, because he gave off signs of power. If all you wanted was to get fucked, they were okay. "Put a sock in their mouth, they're fine," as she said to her friends. But she knew there was more to life than that. She knew that unless you wanted to be some overweight slob with cellulite and three kids and a mortgage, you wanted power and you wanted money.

So Kim loved her father. Almost beyond what was allowed, but they never crossed that line.

She lay by the pool, loving the coke, loving herself, the smooth honey of her skin, the reflection of herself in all the others' eyes. Three other women were around the pool, too, but they weren't competition; they were playmates for the businessmen. She felt distanced from them by her promise to Alan. She was his. She'd be all his, only his. She loved her celibacy, all the more because she was the most desirable woman there. She loved their desire, even the other women's, their desire expressed as envy, but desire all the same.

"Telephone, mees."

Consuela was a black silhouette against the sky, bending toward her like an angel.

"Bring it out here."

She believed that she and Consuela were buddies. Consuela loved her, she believed.

"I teenk ees *heem,* mees. Maybe you want private?"

Him. Alan. Consuela knew all about him. (So did her father, for that matter, but in a different way, not the sex—at least not the intensity of it—which Consuela cleaned up after.) "Oh, my God—" The coke gave her tremendous focus, mostly on herself, her feelings (lust, loneliness), and she ran across the tiles, feeling her breasts move, feeling all the others' eyes on her. "In my bedroom, Consuela—"

She threw herself across the pink bed, grabbed the phone. "Yes?" Her heart was thumping.

"It's Alan."

"It *is* you! Oh, my God, I miss you so! You got my

vibes, you felt me missing you, didn't you! I thought I'd come in my—"

"Kim!" It was a new tone from him; maybe it was the telephone. He sounded uptight. As if he wasn't listening to her at all. "Kim, I'm coming home for a few days."

"You're not!" She shrieked the words. She rolled on her back. She crossed an ankle over a knee. "Oh, lover, when you—"

"Kim, my father's dead."

She felt herself go through three distinct stages in a fraction of a second; the coke let her see them clearly. First, annoyance that he would mention such a thing just then; next, fear that something was expected of her; then, heavy, conventional sadness of the kind she saw on television. She began to weep. "Oh—my darling—oh, poor you, I'm so sorry, oh God—"

"I have to settle his affairs. I've got compassionate leave. I'm flying commercial; can you meet my plane?"

She wanted to say that she'd be waiting with her legs spread, but that wasn't what he wanted to hear (she felt annoyance again, then something stronger than that), and she assured him she'd be there. She wrote the details on her pad, her writing too large, later hard to read. She was still weeping. The tears felt good, a letting-go. It was nice to cry for somebody's dead dad, she found.

"I've got to go."

"But you poor *thing*. Oh, your heart must be broken! The depth—I mean, this is just so sad. I wish I could tell you how I feel it. So—so—" She wept and wept. She couldn't stop, didn't want to stop, loved herself weeping.

But the more she tried to tell him how sad it was, the less he seemed to respond. She wanted him there with her, seeing her weep, making love, weeping and making love at the same time, and she tried to tell him this, tried to get him to see, but he said less and less and less.

Then she was holding a dead telephone.

It made her weep even more. She couldn't stop. Everything was just so sad.

Her brother's friend came into the room and shut the door. He was dumb as a stump but gorgeous, hardly eighteen. She told him how sad it was. He told her she had really deep feelings and began to unfasten her bikini top. That felt right to her.

JULY 26, 1990. 1322 ZULU. FLORIDA.

Alan Craik hadn't slept the three nights since he had watched his father's plane fall away. He was wound up tight with fatigue, his eyes too bright; he made quick movements that didn't quite do what they were supposed to do, stumbled sometimes. Yet he was alert, and when he lay down and closed his eyes, he remained awake, replaying the horror of it.

As the 747 dropped toward Orlando, he stared out the window, as if seeing Florida rise up to meet him was important. He was not seeing Florida at all, however; he was seeing meetings with his father, a last one when he had said goodbye in Bahrain. Death hadn't given them any premonition that it would be the last time. They had been casual, too quick; he had still been nursing resentment at his father's remarks about Kim, and his father had been anxious to deal with squadron business.

Alan Craik was confused. He had not known his father well, he decided; was that his own fault? His father had let his mother and stepfather raise him; what did he owe his father's memory, then? Had his father been a good man? A hero? A model? Where was Alan's responsibility to his memory? And where was Alan's part in his death?

"It wasn't your fault!" Rafehausen had shouted at him. Alan had stood on the flight deck, the warm air of the Gulf washing over him, babbling, "It was my fault. I killed him. They should have had a real aircrewman up there. I killed my father—" Until Rafehausen had grabbed him and bellowed at him, "It wasn't your fault! It wasn't your goddam fault! You did everything you could!"

He replayed the last moments of his father's life as the

747 put down. He saw the final gesture, that raised hand before the plane plunged to the water—had that been corny, or was it gallant? And what was he, Alan, in those moments? And where was grief, which, he thought, should have had him weeping, when actually he was alert and efficient and, after those moments of guilt, hard as a stone? Then he began to replay it all as a way of moving to the edge of his consciousness a question that wanted to intrude: *With him dead, why am I staying in the Navy?*

He was wearing civilian clothes and had only a knapsack. He came out into the arrival lounge, dodging other travelers who planted themselves wherever their welcomers waited, and Kim was standing at the far side, her back against a pillar, and he smiled automatically, as he did most things automatically just then. She was wearing a black dress and sunglasses and looked tragic and sexy, and it took him an instant to realize that he resented the way she looked, which seemed to require that he be Alan, Kim's Lover, and not Alan, Mick's Son. Or simply Alan.

"My poor love," she whispered in his ear. "I am so sorry." She held him just the right length of time and then let go. "Are you terribly hurt?" she murmured.

"I'm fine."

They walked all the way to her car before she spoke again. She held his hand very tight; he knew he was supposed to feel support, love, comfort flowing from her fingers. In fact, he felt nothing. He knew he should not tell her so.

"We're putting you in one of the cabanas," she said across the roof of her Mercedes. "We'll have to find someplace else for *us*."

"I'll be at my Dad's house a lot. All his stuff—"

She accepted it. Still, driving out of the airport, she said, "I am going to see you, aren't I?"

"Jesus, of course."

"I've missed you so."

"I've missed you, too."

He tried to blot the pictures from his mind and to think

of something to say to her, and he said, "Thanks for the letters. They really kept me going." She had sometimes sent him two a day, always short, not very literate, the envelopes stuffed with mementos—a scrap of black nylon, something cut from a newspaper, a joke. He had been charmed by them, often aroused, then grew a little weary of their relentless, one-note sexual cheerfulness. They were like directives ordering the world to be happy and start fucking.

He let one hand rest on her thigh as she drove. The black dress was very short; under it was a black slip, then her bare, golden thigh.

"Want to go somewhere?" she said.

"Where?" He had slipped into thinking of his father's death again.

"Don't you want me?"

"I want whatever you want."

She bit her lower lip. The sunglasses were as big as beer-can lids and hid half her face. After a long time, her voice level, she said, "I have something to tell you, when you're ready to talk. It's something wonderful, but you're not ready yet and I don't want to spoil it. Okay?"

"Okay." He had been thinking about Rafehausen's shouting at him.

She pulled into a motel, got them a room, and led him inside. Desire surprised him, its intensity like something that had been lying in wait. His lovemaking was humorless and driven, separate from his mind so that he was a kind of onlooker; yet there was physical relief, and the sense of pleasing her.

"You've changed," she said. She cradled his head. "My poor lover. Want to share it with me?"

"What?"

Tears filled her eyes. "Don't I mean anything to you?" She wept. "I can't get through to you!" He saw that he was supposed to comfort her, tried, turned it to sex, and became again humorless and driven.

1600 ZULU. TEHRAN.

Franci will not remember that he is awake sometimes. He will remember things after the sixth day; this is only the fourth day. Yet, he already knows that he has lost one leg. He does not know how he knows it. In fact, a doctor stood by his bed and told another doctor; he has forgotten the event, but his mind has seized the fact. Already, his brain is working on being a different person—no longer young, no longer whole, no longer full of life and promise. He is deadened with drugs and he seems unconscious, but his brain is working on the proposition that a few seconds at the radar post, the flipping of a switch, somebody else's callousness, have stolen his future. He has not yet been told that he is a eunuch.

1600 ZULU. FLORIDA.

His father owned a house near Five Points in Jacksonville. Alan remembered it from visits after the divorce. His mother had waited a year and then married a nice guy from Iowa, and Alan had visited his father during two humid Florida summers. Then his father had had other duty stations, but he liked Florida and kept the house.

Part of it was rented to a j.g. from another squadron. When Alan's father was there, they shared the house; when either was away, he locked his bedroom and that was that. A succession of such housemates had trooped through, leaving the house anonymous and male.

Alan saw a red Saab in the driveway and a lounge chair with one hairy leg hanging from it around the side. The grass looked a little scruffy, a pecan tree untended and dry. He walked to the side, said hello, and startled the j.g., who was mostly asleep with a beer can balanced on his hairy stomach.

"I'm Alan Craik. Mick's son."

"Oh, Jesus—hey, man, I'm so sorry, no kidding. Dingo Povick. Your dad was a great guy. It's a loss. What can I say?" He was burned brown, muscular, old for a j.g., probably a mustang, Alan thought. They shook hands. "I'm not good with words," Povick said. "He was a good guy and I miss him and I'm sorry for you, okay?"

"Sure."

"Go ahead on in. I guess it's your house, right?"

"You're welcome to stay here," Alan said. He had already seen the base lawyer to talk about his father's will. "It'll be mine, but I'm not changing anything. I might come back here to live when my tour's over. Okay?"

"Hey, suits me. Sounds great. I thought you might want to, you know, sell it?"

"I'm glad to have somebody in it."

He had been in enough Navy houses to recognize the slightly barren feel of the place, emphasized here by the lack of a woman. It was a house from which you could move on short notice, then return to months later and simply walk in and fall into bed. He tried several keys from his father's key ring (sent over with his personal effects from the *Roosevelt*) before he found the right one and stepped into the bedroom.

The blinds were closed, curtains drawn. The air was stale. He flipped on the window air conditioner and opened everything to let the light in, then stepped to the middle and slowly turned around.

What did he feel? He was asking himself that question as he looked at his father's private space. *What do I feel?* Not knowing that when you ask that question you are already masking your feelings. He thought, *I never knew him and this is my last chance.*

There was a surprising collection of opera music, mostly old vinyl LPs. He remembered now that his father sometimes whistled tunes; had they been from operas? Lots of Wagner. One Grateful Dead album with "Mick, I love these guys, I hope you do too" scrawled across it in red. *From a woman,* he thought. He felt a jerk of emotion over that one, almost an electric shock; he feared finding secrets he didn't want to know—something as tawdry as a porn collection, as pathetic as old love letters.

But there was nothing else like that. True, there was a nightgown in the wall-length closet, with the uniforms and civilian clothes and a lot of fishing gear and his medals and his sword. The sword made Alan pause—such a loaded symbol, such a peculiar object to find these days, causing him to imagine wearing his father's sword at one of those rare Navy ceremonies where one was required, the easy sentimentality of breaking down over that image (*Wearing his martyred father's sword, LTj.g. Alan Craik dedicated his life to*—). He cut the picture off, hating its easy emotion.

The nightgown, like the sword, was mostly symbolic, hardly more than a few inches of black lace. He wondered whose it was, what she was feeling now. Had she come here while the hairy j.g. was here, or did they have some system for giving each other the house sometimes? He could ask, but knew he wouldn't.

And who was she? A squadron-mate's wife? Somebody divorced from a Navy husband, still living in a Navy town? There were lots of those. Sea duty was hard on marriages.

He tried to imagine Kim here. The picture wouldn't form.

The civilian clothes were not very good and were, by Alan's standards, too loud. Alan's stepfather, a round little man who owned a men's clothing store in Iowa, had tried to teach him all about fabrics and cut, color matching, when to wear a tie and when to wear casual clothes. He had treated natural fabrics as a religion, artificials as the devil. It had amused Alan, therefore, to enter a profession where polyester was required. He had found he liked polyester. It had no status.

He began to make a pile for Goodwill, starting with the nightgown and three civilian sports coats, then all the shoes. (Not his size.) Then the uniforms, wondering if friends would want them for sentiment's sake, deciding against that. Would they fit him? No, he was bigger in the shoulders than his father had been, smaller in the waist. But the uniform hats fit him, and he kept them, really treasuring one with the old silver badge that must have gone back to the 1960s.

There were books, none of them remarkable, thrillers and how-tos and technical things about aircraft. A few other records. A small color television. Tourist knickknacks picked up on a wandering life, most of them destined for Goodwill. A high cherry bureau. He decided he would keep that for himself. He opened each drawer with hesitation, fearing what might be inside. Shirts, many shirts. A drawer full of socks: the Navy has three colors of uniforms. Underwear, sweaters, T-shirts. Nothing dreadful, nothing revealing.

He left the bedside table for last, fearing most what it might hold. When he slid the single drawer open, he unconsciously tipped his head back as if it might be struck by something springing out.

Inside were a three-month-old copy of *Time,* a small notebook, and a Browning P-35, a clipful of 9-millimeter cartridges next to it.

Why hadn't Mick Craik taken it to sea as his armpit gun? Every pilot carried one, some said to shoot sharks if you ejected, some said to signal for help, some said to shoot yourself. He must have had another, resting now under the warm waters of the Gulf. So this one was not his favorite—or was it, and so he had left it safe here?

Alan turned the Browning over and saw his father's name in gold. "From his fellow officers of VA-47. Nam tour, 1967." His father's first squadron.

He pushed the pistol into his tote bag.

He opened the black notebook. Only half of it had been written in, mostly single sentences separated by white space. Some of the entries were dated, many not.

The earliest was 1971. The latest was 1990.

Twenty years, barely thirty pages.

He sat on the bed and began to flip through. Most of it was too painful to read now, the attempts by a man not usually given to self-analysis to know his world and himself, to reduce that knowledge to one or two lines. Many about women, who seemed to have puzzled Mick Craik all his life. Alan skipped to the back and found that one of the last entries was about himself.

"Alan's commissioning today. I was moved. Tears in my eyes as those kids marched out—all those kids. There's a lot of b.s. about throwing hats and all that, but the bottom line is they have put themselves in harm's way and some will die. I felt closer to A. than ever in my life."

He put his hands over his eyes and began to cry.

There was dinner each night at the Hoyts', where he sat like a bad thought.

Kim's brother disliked him. When Alan first walked into the two-story-high entrance hall, Lance was there, in jammers and an oversized T-shirt that said SHIT HAPPENS. He stuck out his hand, grabbed Alan's, and said, "I'm really sorry, Admiral, really, really sorry, man."

"Don't call me that, okay?"

"What?"

"'Admiral.'"

Lance frowned. "Just a joke."

"Not to me. Okay?"

Lance shrugged. "Whatever."

Dinner at the Hoyts' was like a bad memory of the idea of formal dining, served by two Latino maids in a vast dining room, with Mr. Hoyt at one end of the table and Kim at the other. There was no Mrs. Hoyt. ("She was a drunk and Daddy threw her out," Kim had explained. There was no explanation of how a woman got thrown out of her own house.) Lance and his father wore sports jackets and open shirts; Kim wore dresses or dressy blouses and silk pants in white or black.

The first night, there were three other couples, as well, the women vastly overdressed, perfumed, false-eyelashed. Alan sat at Kim's end. The talk was all of money and its world—taxes, investments, salaries, winners and losers. Alan said nothing.

"Please be nice," Kim said to him when they were alone by the pool later.

"Wasn't I nice?"

"You don't say anything."

"There's nothing for me to say."

"It's very important to Daddy."

"What is?" The idea that her father even noticed him was a surprise. "What is? That I be nice?"

"These are his *friends*. His associates."

People used to go into mourning, he thought, and they didn't go out or have dinner with strangers, and being quiet by themselves was the right thing to do.

"I think I'll move to the base," he said.

"No!" She held his hands. "You can't do that. It's very important that you're here right now."

A few lights were on in the dark garden, and trees around the pool made lacy shadows on her face. Working it out, he said, "Were they here *because* of me?"

She wound her fingers around his. "Remember I said I had something I wanted to tell you?"

He didn't, but he said nothing.

"I wanted to wait for the right moment, but there isn't any right moment because you're so—so— You've gotten so distant, love. See, I went to Daddy and I told him how we're so much in love, and I said to him that we wanted to get married real soon but you were making this huge sacrifice for the country and you deserved better, and I put it really well, I really came on to him about it. And this is what I wanted to tell you, this is what's so just wonderful, sweetie, you're gonna die when you hear! Daddy will give us one of the condos at Silver Lagoon—I know the name sucks, but they're *won*derful—as a wedding present and he'll set me up in a business venture I have in mind and guarantee me a hundred thousand a year while you finish your Navy time and then he'll bring you into the company at a very high level. Isn't that wonderful? Christ, *say* something, Alan, I busted my ass for this!"

He opened his mouth and closed it and looked at her, watching the faint breeze move a shadow across her eyes.

"We can get *married*," she said. "Everything's *okay*."

"Kim, my father just died."

Something more than the shadow flashed across her eyes—anger?—and then was gone. She embraced him. "I know, I know." She kissed him. "But we've got to take Daddy's offer while it's good. My brother's going to be entering the business world in two years."

The father's love of rivalry, of course: Kim against Lance, to be replaced by Alan against Lance. It offended his father's death, offended that moment in his father's room when he had wept over the notebook; yet, because he thought he loved her, he said, "You want me in the business before Lance comes along."

"We have to make the playing field level. Lance is the fair-haired boy. The *boy*—get it? Once he's in, Kimberley can whistle for her fair share."

"Money."

"Mucho money."

"I don't think your father is about to give me a lot of money."

"He will if you're my husband. And the father of his grandchildren."

For the first time, he wondered if she, who used the word "love" so much, and who so bewitched him with a sexuality that he thought of as part of love, really knew what love was.

Anger is the hidden beast of grief. It surprises you, lies in wait for you, sometimes paces along on silent feet behind you and ponders its moment. You think that grief is tears and emptiness; anger seems wrong, something you should rise above. Worst of all, anger turns you against the person you are grieving, or so you think, and you feel disloyal, even unnatural.

Alan was just beginning to sense his anger.

The next day he went out to his father's house and sorted books. They seemed stupid to him today, the stupid pastimes of an uninteresting man. He started to make three piles—Goodwill, gifts to friends, books to keep—and contemptuously threw more and more into the Goodwill pile. He didn't know that this was part of grief: anger at his father for dying, for making trouble with Kim. Throwing his father into a discard pile as punishment. Abruptly, he kicked the books into one pile and stood by the window, hands in pockets, staring out at the scruffy side yard of the house next door.

My girl wants to get married, and all I can think about is my father! He was so fucking gung ho. He had to be such a fucking hero. Go, go, Dad! Way to go! Way to get killed! He felt something like hatred. It was a relief.

So stupid. So fucking stupid. Right at the front, leading them in, so that some wiseass Iranian teenager with a MANPAD—a shoulder-fired missile—knocked him off. One lucky shot—bang, your father's dead. Because he had to be a hero.

His face was dark; even in the washed-out reflection of the window, he could see its angry lines. Fatigue and anger made him look older. Used. And he felt used. Because it wasn't fair to have to sit and watch the final moments of your own father after he had been knocked out of the sky by a needle-in-the-haystack shot, then suffer guilt and loss and take it out on your girl.

He met his own eyes in the glass. Later, he would remember that he had thought the eyes looked like Peretz's, baggy and cynical, and that it was that moment of recognition that startled him into a new idea. Perhaps it was more complex than that, but that was the way he would remember it.

You're an intelligence officer: be intelligent.

He could hear Peretz as if he was in the room.

And he was thinking, Why do I believe my father was knocked down by a dumb-luck MANPAD?

The answer to that was that everybody said so. That was part of the consolation that people on the boat had given him: *Lousy luck.* Because, he thought, it was unthinkable to them that the ragheads could down a lead A-6 at night with anything but dumb luck.

But—

He leaned his forearms on the top bar of the window sash. His forehead contracted. One index finger moved back and forth along his jaw.

But what if it wasn't dumb luck? Just suppose—

He didn't see that he wanted to believe in cause, to disprove the idea of luck: because if there had been cause, careful thought, sophistication, then his father was not just a macho flyboy who'd taken one too many missions in middle age. And he, the flyboy's son, was not a jerk who would have to spend the rest of his life trying to accept the meaningless.

"Hey, Mr. Povick!" He had heard water running. He strode into the kitchen; there was the hairy j.g. in skivvies, running water into a kettle.

"Hey, man."

"Hey, listen—you know the A-6?"

Povick put the kettle on the stove with a bang. "I'm a chopper jock."

"I was just wondering something." He was not even sure what it was he was wondering—something about those minutes when his father had been going over the coast and Christine had been heading hell-bent for the surface. Things had happened too fast to remember, but something had happened then that he should think about.

"Let it go," Povick said.

"Not yet."

Povick rubbed his eyes. "Time'll fix it. Don't think about it too much, is my advice."

Alan stood looking at the kettle as if needing to see it boil, jingling change in his pants pocket. "What are the chances of hitting an A-6 with a MANPAD in the dark?" he said.

Povick shrugged. "Shit happens."

"So it does." That's what Lance's T-shirt had said, too. Consolation for the 1990s.

Povick pulled a chair out. "Siddown. Have a cuppa coffee, talk to me. Take your mind off of it."

Alan sat at the Formica table, mindful that his father must have sat here a hundred times, just like this, sharing a morning coffee with Povick. Yet mindful, too, that he had to stop thinking such things, the static gloom of grief. Much better to think about what might have happened out there in the dark of the Iranian coast. Something, something—he couldn't catch it. He wanted his kneeboard notes; he wanted the tapes of the flight. Maybe he had said something, or maybe Senior or Rafe had; maybe the computer had logged some anomaly.

"They knew we were coming," he said as Povick handed him a cup of instant coffee.

"No shit?"

"The whole coast lit up. They were on the attack from the get-go." He slurped boiling coffee. "It was no secret we were in the Gulf. You could say they put two and two together." He stared into the steam. *Maybe* you could say that.

Povick began to ask him questions about the flight, about his part in it and Christine. Povick was no fool. Maybe he didn't listen; maybe he let it wash over him while he thought about the Dolphins. But Alan talked for twenty-five minutes, and when he was done he felt better than he had since that night. He was acute enough to wonder why Kim never got him talking like that.

He went back to sorting the books, no longer so angry. And he was not simply replaying the scenes of that night; rather, he was remembering, and thinking, and asking questions. They all came down to one question: *Suppose it wasn't dumb luck?*

For the first time, he was able, late in the day, to sleep.

He lay on his father's bed. The venetian blind cast slits of light across the beige ceiling; he drifted in and out, seeing that pattern, watching it move, change, and at last he was fully asleep and dreaming repetitive and difficult dreams of the computer and the radar. He went over and over a meaningless set of calculations, finally woke with a jerk of his entire body, then fell asleep again at once and was wrestling. This, too, was repetitive, tedious, painful: he dreamed he was his own hand, searching for a hold on another body he could not see, could not identify, the fingers feeling over muscle, sweat, hair, trying to squeeze between limbs, an animal with touch its only sense. He felt an urgent need to know who this opponent was; the hand twisted, pushed, clutched; he tried to turn the opponent over, to find his head, turn his face. His fingers sought and sought and failed, and he woke in near-darkness feeling wrung-out, as if by a day's labor.

His anger, lying in the shadow, camouflaged, looked on and waited.

JULY 27, 1990. 2330 ZULU.
PEARSON INTERNATIONAL AIRPORT, TORONTO, CANADA.

Sergeant Kenneth McEachy picked up the pay phone and dialed the watch number. The duty sergeant knew him by voice. "Tony says take them. In the airport if it's absolutely safe, outside otherwise." McEachy walked carefully toward the Air Canada arrival area. It was empty, as well it might be.

"Ready?"

"One."

"Two."

"Three."

"Aye." That would be Sandy, blast him. McEachy leaned in studied calm against the ticket counter. He looked like most business travelers, although his shave was better. He hoped that Vancouver and Air Canada had done their bit. He listened to the dull static on his earpiece and watched the jet roll up to the gate. The bridge was quickly linked to the fuselage by unseen hands. After a moment, he heard a pop as someone jacked into the circuit.

"This is Callahan."

"Do you have them, then?"

"First four off the plane. No one will get off after."

One was under the fuselage, waiting to climb into the tunnel if he needed to. Two and three were behind him. Sandy was in the opposite passenger area.

"Ten seconds, Sergeant."

"Do it."

McEachy watched the monitor above the information desk and saw four very square, very solid men leave the fuselage and start up the tunnel. The last one looked back for a moment. Tough-looking customers. Probably Spetsnaz, indeed. The first one eyed the security camera, but they kept coming. The first three entered the passenger lounge and kept moving, looking for someone. The last was still in the tunnel. He shouted something.

Time began to slow; in a few seconds, the first three would be out of the cleared lounge and in a very busy airport. The last man called something again. The lead man stopped and barked an order. Their Russian sounded familiar, like the Ukrainian farmers with whom McEachy had grown up.

The last man emerged from the tunnel. He looked directly at McEachy as McEachy tapped his earpiece once, hard. A voice in his ear said, "Take them."

Sandy stepped in front of the lead Russian and held up a badge. "Lie down on the floor. You are under arrest. Royal Canadian Mounted Police."

Numbers two and three showed their H&K machine pistols. All four Russians hit the floor, like a squad of recruits. In seconds, they were handcuffed and back on their feet. Sandy took them past Sergeant McEachy, through the secured door to the flight line. A plain white panel van pulled up under the nose of the plane, invisible to the passengers and inconspicuous among the luggage carts. The four disappeared inside.

"Complete," McEachy said. Faintly, in the tunnel behind him, he heard other passengers emerging from the plane. One angry American passenger demanded to know why he had been kept on the plane when four Russians were let off early. No one else swore or complained. This was Canada, after all.

1605 ZULU. PERSIAN GULF.

Bonner figured he was home free. Thirty-five thousand bucks! He was so cheerful these days that Mattingly asked him if he'd found a new way to jerk off.

Dear Donnie, he wrote as he lay on his bunk. *We had an unhappy event that maybe you heard about on the news, it was unclassified and we saw it right on CNN, so you know what's going on here. Carrier life is not all fun and games. I am fine, never better, looking forward to the end of this tour and a new bass boat I hope to get when I hit the beach. Boy, have I got things to tell you.*

0015 ZULU. FLORIDA.

It was only the four of them at dinner that night. Alan and Lance sat opposite each other, Kim and her father at the ends. Lance and his father talked. Alan was deep in his own thoughts when he heard Lance say (for the second time, he was afraid), "What's your view on that, Admiral?"

He was about to say, *Don't call me that,* when he saw Kim's face and told himself it was the wrong time, the wrong place; instead, he said, "I'm afraid I lost the subject there, Lance."

"The military. That's not an easy one to forget. Huh?" Lance looked aside at his father, whose smooth face had opened in the small, eager smile that he saved for watching his children battle. "I was saying we oughta put these drug pushers and welfare fathers into the military. What's your view on that?"

"I suspect they couldn't cut it."

"But discipline would be good for them, wouldn't it?"

"I don't know much about it."

"But you're in the military!"

"We want the best now, not the problems."

"The *best?* Admiral, the best don't go near the military, no offense and present company excepted. The best make their own way. The military can't pay enough to attract the best—isn't that right, Dad?"

Mr. Hoyt smiled on his son. "Real winners don't get interested, in my experience, until you go over the hundred-thousand-per-annum benchmark."

Lance looked triumphant. "I and my friends wouldn't go near the military, to be perfectly honest."

Alan did not bother to wonder why he was being baited; this was part of this family's dynamic, a contest for Daddy's love—and money. He decided he wouldn't play. "Lots of people feel that way, I suppose," he said.

So Lance pushed harder. "You don't want your *best* people in the military, Admiral. You want your top men to lead the country, move it forward, keep the economy dynamic." When Alan still didn't rise, he said, "The military's a good holding pool for your also-rans, am I right, Dad?"

Mr. Hoyt was smooth as oil. "A well-organized military is essential to the defense of freedom. However, it's a known fact that the current American military organization is at base socialistic. Socialized medicine, socialized pensions, guaranteed promotion. It may be a necessary evil. We keep our eyes on it."

Imagine spending the rest of your life with these two, Alan thought.

Then Lance began to talk about athletics and teamwork and competition, and Alan thought how much more they'd like Narc for a son-in-law than him. "Competition brings out the best," Lance said. "I'm really competitive. Can't help it, I guess. Just the way I am. How about you, Admiral?"

Kim said, "Daddy's a shadow member of the Council on Competitiveness," and she gave Alan a very bright smile that said if he didn't join the conversation she'd be an unhappy woman.

Alan cleared his throat and said, "Just what do you compete in, Lance?"

"Golf." Lance flexed his muscles. "I'm a member of the golf team."

Alan heard a sound and realized he had made it. It was something like a bark, then more like a strangled groan. Then he realized it was laughter. It was the first laugh he'd given since his father's plane had gone down, and it oozed from him, then erupted and poured, and he held his white napkin over his face and laughed until it drained out of him and left him wet-eyed, tears on his cheeks, and he saw from their faces that he had done something terrible, and he smiled at Lance and said in a strangled tenor, "Just kidding," and exploded into laughter again.

After dinner, he and Kim had a fight.

He gravitated back to his father's. Povick was on nights; the empty house suited Alan, a kind of neutral ground where he could think. He sat in a chair and stared. When Povick came in a little after four, he was still awake and had coffee made. Povick looked at him, took the cup that was offered, said, "Wanna talk to an old man about it?"

"What?"

"Cummon, you look like dog food. Look, don't eat your heart out trying to make sense of it. Shit happens."

"I wasn't thinking about him." He began to babble about Kim, her brother, her father. He surprised himself with the strength of his feelings. "She wants me to go to work for him!"

"Leave the Navy?"

"Of course."

"You wanna do that?"

He stared into his empty cup. "When I got here, I thought maybe I did. With him gone—what was the point? Now—"

"Cute girl?"

"Beautiful. Incredible."

"Most guys, they've got something good going with a woman can make them rich, they're not gonna sit on their thumb. How come you don't jump at the chance?"

He turned the cup in a circle between his hands. "The more I see her brother and her father—" He shook his head. "Money-money-money-money-money!" He hunched over his cup, his eyes like stones. "I know it's bullshit, but I like once in a while to hear words like, like—honor—duty—" He looked at Povick. "I should trade my father for her father?"

Povick clapped him on the shoulder. "I hear what you're saying. You think you might wanta be your own man for a change."

"I was sure I loved her. Now— Maybe it was just great sex."

Povick nodded slowly, got up, and washed his cup at the sink. Drying his hands on a filthy towel, he said, smiling, "You don't know how much like your dad you are."

1926 ZULU. TEHRAN.

Yuri Efremov stood on the terrace of his new house. In his hand was the day's note card, ready to be burned. It recorded a meeting with the head of Iranian intelligence, two ideas for recruitment, and a reminder about Bonner's payment. Bonner had done superbly well—an American squadron commander dead, a high-tech aircraft down. Now, the aircraft lay at the bottom of the Gulf, and Efremov was wondering if they could raise it. The Americans had made no move to raise it themselves, a good sign that they had no suspicions. It would be a coup to bring it to Iran, but the military told him it was beyond them. Anyway, the Americans would know.

Efremov wondered what they were thinking in Moscow. That pathetic noodle, the Director, would be suffering from his spastic colon. He would put Ouspenskaya on Efremov's disappearance, he supposed. She would file a nicely written report that said nothing.

He touched a flame to the corner of the card and put the burning paper in a flowerpot. His house was elegant, the terraces rich with flowers and fruit trees; they had given him, he thought, a little Muslim paradise.

And they were already demanding more product to pay for it. Soon, he would have to tell Bonner what they really wanted from him. And his son.

JULY 27, 1990. 1630 ZULU. FLORIDA.

On Friday, they held a memorial service at his father's church. He sat with Kim, he in choker whites and she in black, and he knew that people looked at them and thought they were a perfect and beautiful couple. Afterward, she slipped away, murmuring, "I'm no good at this," and he stood alone and received the people, literally hundreds of them, down to an E2 and up to two captains and a one-star. They all said half-unintelligible, nice things, and he said thank you, thank you, thank you. At the end of the line because he had to move so slowly, a gray-haired civilian on metal canes hobbled to him, tall enough to look straight into Alan's eyes despite a stoop; his face was, he thought, prematurely old, gaunt, deeply lined down the hollow cheeks.

"My name is George Shreed; you don't know me, but I'm an old friend of your father's. I am so sorry. He was one of the best."

Alan thanked him. He waited for the man to move on, but he lingered; maybe it was his difficulty walking. Alan had time to think that Shreed could afford very good suits and Italian shoes before the man said, "We were very old friends. I hadn't seen a lot of him in recent years, but when you've been through hell with somebody, the friendship never leaves you. I'm so sorry."

"Were you in the Navy, sir?" Alan regretted saying it as soon as the words were out; he flushed deeply, embarrassed by the gleaming canes.

"I was your father's wingman. That's how I got these. If it hadn't been for him, I wouldn't be here at all." He murmured something more and hobbled away, moving almost quickly but with a painful difficulty, like a disintegrating machine. Alan remembered him then, not the name but the story, a child's vague memory of it. At the door, waiting for somebody else to go out, Shreed turned and looked at him. Meeting his eyes, he raised the tip of one cane in a kind of salute. He was still a good-looking man.

Afterward, Alan went out with Povick and some friends of his father's and drank a little and ran down, and he found himself thinking that he was comfortable with them in a way he never was at the Hoyts'.

Still, the idea that the death had been caused, part of some kind of plan, filled his mind. He wanted to talk to Senior and Rafe; he wanted the tapes and his notes. There would be other records, too, some on his father's carrier. He wanted to get to work on them. And he wanted Kim back in that nice little box, The Girl He Left Behind Him.

2050 ZULU. LANGLEY, VIRGINIA.

A low-level analyst in a cubicle deep in the bowels of CIA headquarters was trying to make sense of two widely separated, apparently unconnected terrorist attacks by a Kurdish offshoot of the PKK. He was trying to identify Turkish incidents beyond the borders of Turkey. He got a hit on a murder in Amsterdam five months before: Lisbet Stroeher, found with her throat slashed in an Amsterdam park, was believed to have had "a private relationship" with the assistant to the Turkish military attaché.

Nothing about it suggested a Kurdish connection, so he didn't bother to copy it.

JULY 28, 1990. 0230 ZULU. FLORIDA.

That night, there was a party at the Hoyts', noisy, meaningless; he wandered from room to room until he went into what Kim called The Game Room and saw one of Hoyt's business pals and Lance and a number of people he didn't know, snorting coke. He had never done coke, but he knew what the white lines on the inlaid poker table were. Just then Kim came up behind him and his anger burst out, and he said, "What the hell have you got me into?"

"Oh, come *on!*" She tried to laugh it off.

"For Christ's sake, do you know what would happen to my clearance if the Navy saw this?"

"Who *cares?*" She pulled him back into the room by an arm. He jerked free.

"I care."

"Don't be so fucking stupid!" She tried to back him away from the others; she was whispering. "It'd be *good* for you. You're so stiff. You're a fucking zombie, sweetie. Come on, get out of yourself for once."

She was beautiful, he saw, and soon she would want to go to bed. She would be wonderful. Everything a man could want.

"I'll see you tomorrow," he said. "I can't stay here."

Her face closed up. She did something with her body that seemed to turn it off. "Suit yourself. You stupid prick."

He went to his father's and lay on the bed. Povick was on duty. Cars on the street shone their lights on the ceiling as they came near, and he watched each bright cone form and be cut off. It began to rain, soft, hissing Florida rain.

The television said that Iraq was massing troops along its border with Kuwait, as if anybody in America cared where either Iraq or Kuwait was.

He turned his head and looked at the television. The

spot was over but would come again. CNN—intelligence for Everyman, Peretz had said. Alan had been storing away bits from the dailies about Iraq, because it was an enemy of Iran and because it had been an Iraqi aircraft that had thrown a missile at the *Stark* and killed thirty men. But Kuwait?

He fiddled with the channels, getting nothing else, thinking about Iranian radars coming on like flashbulbs as the raid had started.

Then he found CNN again and got the report on Kuwait, and later another channel had an expert they had dug up somewhere who said Iraq would never invade Kuwait; this was saber-rattling, and we had the assurances of the Iraqi president, Saddam Hussein, that he respected the territorial integrity of Kuwait.

Alan knew quite a lot about Saddam Hussein. Saddam wouldn't respect the territorial integrity of Lucifer and his angels, was his view. An almost joyful excitement surged: something was going to happen.

He threw himself into the car and screamed through Orange Park in the blackness of the morning. *Be intelligent,* he thought. *Use the tools.* He rolled up to the gate at Cecil Field and drove carefully, exactly at the speed limit to avoid attention from the base police until he pulled up at the intel center, a drab little bunker protected mostly by its anonymity.

A sleepy IS3 let him in. Alan shoved his ID forward, waited until the IS3 was satisfied, and stalked back to where the message traffic was kept. He picked up the board labeled CENTCOM. It was heavy—more than a hundred messages. He scanned them. He nodded to the absent shade of Peretz. There really was going to be a war.

He grabbed a secure phone and punched up his father's air wing office at Oceana. While he bullied the overwhelmed ensign on the other end, he noted that whoever usually sat at this desk had a wife who was both beautiful and comfortable-looking, and apparently thousands of children. Their drawings from school littered the walls. CDR

KARL, the nameplate said. Lucky man. The family thing—
At that point, the ensign got it, and Alan had himself a
ride from Philadelphia to the Gulf. Now he had to get himself to Philly.

Alan signed out and roared back to his father's house.
He packed his own few clothes and some things of his
father's, piled all the Goodwill stuff in the car and dumped
it at a Goodwill box in a still-closed shopping center. There
were other things he had meant to do, but he knew they
could wait. Suddenly, nothing seemed as important as getting back to the ship.

He left a message about the will on the lawyer's phone.
He dropped his car back at the house, with a note for
Povick, then picked up his father's uniform hat with the
silver crest and took a taxi to Cecil Field.

There, he humped his gear on foot across the field to
the MAT terminal, an unglamorous shed that didn't provide VIP lounges or satellite parking. What it did have was
a wizened senior chief with a face like an old apple who
said there were no flights and if there were any, he had a
dozen people ahead of him, sir.

"I *have* to get to Philadelphia, Chief. I got a flight to
Bahrain."

"You do, eh, sir?" You could almost smell the tar on
him, hear the seagulls in his rigging. "Late for duty?"

"There's going to be a war."

That set the Ancient Mariner back a little. He studied
Alan's papers, stared into Alan's face, studied the papers
some more. "The *Jefferson*," he said. "I might get you as
far as Pax River."

"Great!"

Davy Jones was looking at a computer terminal. "Well,
I could send you as aircrew on an admiral's plane—have
to wear whites, mind you—then—mmm—Jeez, there is
a lot of traffic up there today, really a lot. Mmmm—
Philly—"

"I'll walk from Pax River!"

"Well-l— You get yourself over to Jax by noon, there's

a P-3 going straight to Andrews, VIP flight so wear uniform of the day. If I can persuade Andrews to put you on this unsked I see here to Philly—or take the goddam Amtrak—"

By ten, he had the itinerary and an authorization. He changed into polyester whites—short sleeves, shoulder boards, his father's hat with a new cover—and caught a taxi to the Hoyts'. "Wait for me," he said, tossing a ten-dollar bill.

Consuela led him out to the pool, told him that Kim was awake and would start dressing soon. "You like sompeen to drink?"

"Tell her I have twenty minutes," he said. He was back in his grim mode, he thought, hearing the voice that came out. He had hoped that he would seem brighter, even happier now; certainly he felt that way. Action should have lightened him. He did not know that his anger was just hitting its stride.

"Hey, Admiral!"

A gate on the far side of the pool led to the beach. Lance and a friend were just coming through it, red and windblown from jet skiing.

"Hey, Admiral, I understand you didn't like the party last night! Jeez, that's some uniform. You do valet parking on the side?"

Alan thought Lance was still at least a little drunk. He was carrying a beer. Lance dropped his life vest in the shade.

Alan had put his father's hat, upside down, on a glass-topped table near the end of the pool, and then he had changed his mind about where to sit and had picked a lounge chair some feet away in the shade. Now, Lance headed toward the hat.

"This yours, Admiral?"

"Don't call me that, I told you."

Lance, brilliant in a pink-and-purple muscle shirt, was looking down into the hat. "I always wondered if these things were waterproof. Hey, Jack, what d'you think?"

Jack, who was a little younger and a little soft in the upper arms, said, "Waterproof or beerproof?"

"Good thinking!"

Alan was sitting very straight. "Don't do that," he said. He sounded unmoved, although his anger was ready, switching its tail like a cat.

Lance tipped the beer can and the beer ran out in a yellow stream. It landed in the hat. Lance moved the can in a circle like a chef finishing a dish. He looked at Alan and laughed.

Alan was aware of somebody at the edge of his vision. Mr. Hoyt. He would be smiling, he thought.

Alan stood. He felt calm. It was too bad it was going to take this turn, he was thinking. Things were about to get complicated. Or were they at last going to get simple?

"Okay," he said. "You've been on me since I got home—make your move."

Lance was surprised, recovered quickly. He glanced at his father and said, "How about that, Dad?"

Mr. Hoyt's smile broadened.

"If you're going to do something," Alan said, "do it. I'm in a hurry."

Lance came at him with a nervous grin on his face that he tried to change to a Mike Tyson imitation as he got close. Alan was thinking that he shouldn't be doing this in uniform, but the skipper would understand, Rafe would understand; and his anger snarled and leaped; and he moved away from a fat punch and pulled the hand on past him, did a hip throw and a takedown and pushed Lance's right arm up behind his head as he lay facedown on the tiles. Lance began to scream.

The friend named Jack made a move, and Alan said, "Come near me and I'll break his fucking arm!" He wanted to break the arm. The violent action felt good.

Blood splattered the figured blue tiles. Mr. Hoyt shouted for Consuela to get the police; and Alan said, "Yeah, do that, and we'll have a chat about the coke dust in the game-room carpet." Hoyt screamed at Consuela to stay where she was; then he shouted at Jack to do something, and then he bellowed for the gardener.

Alan ratcheted up the pressure on Lance's arm; he screamed, and Alan said into his ear, "Say you're sorry, you little shit. Say it!"

"I'm *sorry!*"

He let go and stood, noted that his uniform was still clean and unwrinkled except for one tiny blood spot, and he walked to the table where the hat lay. He dumped out the beer and then went to the pool and knelt and swished the hat through the blue water. The three men watched him, frightened looks on their faces. The sound of the hat moving in the water seemed very loud.

He stood.

Lance was sitting up, holding his arm. Tears were running down his face, smearing and thinning out the blood below his nose. Jack was in some version of a karate stance. Mr. Hoyt was leaning backward, plump palms out.

Alan had turned to go, trying to think of a message to leave for Kim, when she appeared in the doorway. She was flushed, one eye not yet made up; she was buttoning the back of one of her little dresses and pushing a foot into a shoe.

Seeing her, Jack found his courage. "I fucked Kimberley!" he shouted. Then, as if shocked by what he had said, he retreated a step and jerked into the karate posture like a puppet whose strings had been pulled.

Alan looked at her, then at the boy. It was true, he saw. He walked toward Jack.

"Don't—" Jack started to say.

Alan flicked the water from the hat at him. Jack put his hands up over his face and Alan kicked him in the groin, doing it with the savagery they had taught him at Quantico, and then he put his hand on the suddenly bent head and pushed him backward into the pool.

"He could drown!" Mr. Hoyt cried.

"Good."

Alan walked past him to Kim. The two different eyes

looked at him, like two women pasted together in the middle of the face. She was breathing heavily. He leaned toward her.

"You have to make up your mind, right now. Money or me. This or the Navy. I've made my decision, Kim."

She hit him across his left eye and nose, as hard a slap as she could manage.

It set him back for a moment. He looked at her rage-flushed face, couldn't help thinking of her in bed.

"Have a nice life, Kim," he said.

He went out to his taxi and started to dry his father's hat on a shirt from his knapsack, looking forward to the boat and Christine.

7

The haze-gray helicopter appeared black in the hot, rainy night, moving only a few feet off the water toward the darkened aircraft carrier ahead. Despite the heat and the oppressive humidity, the heavy noise of the blades and the vibration of the fuselage lulled Alan to a semisleep that was shot through with brief, fleeting dreams. It seemed the same as the last flight in Christine; no wonder he kept seeing his father's gesture as his A-6 began the short plunge to this same ocean. Again and again, in fragmented dreams, Alan relived that moment. Then, as his father's plane hit the water for another nightmare repetition, his own body felt impact, and he snapped awake. The chopper was on the deck; he could feel the change in the pitch of the engines. He looked out the small porthole and saw the folded wings of an S-3 in the dim, red light.

The aircrewman came over to help him out of the rig that took the place of a crash seat. No luxury for military passengers, not even for the sake of safety. Alan fumbled with the seat belt and the aircrewman tugged it free; Alan stood, tried to straighten, felt his body as a clumsy machine, heavy with fatigue. Groggily, he noted the pilot coming back into the main cabin; a woman. She glanced at him with unconcealed interest. He picked up his sea bag and a helmet bag: his father's helmet. She nodded to him as he passed.

"Nice landing," he said.

"Heard you slept through it." She had night-vision goggles flipped up on her helmet, only the mouth and the swell of hips suggesting a woman. Her voice, however, was distinctly female despite a huskiness that should have made it seem masculine but certainly didn't.

"That's a nice landing in my book," he shouted, although he trailed away at the end, failing to reach her over the flight-deck noise.

A petty officer from Air Ops poked his head into the fuselage.

"Lieutenant Craik?"

"That's me."

"Follow me, sir."

What was the protocol for saying goodbye to a female COD pilot? No matter; she was already gone. Alan stepped from the chopper and became any new arrival; he needed help to cross the deck at night. He followed around the S-3, waited in a rush of heat as an F-18 powered toward the waiting catapult, and followed his guide briskly down a catwalk to a hatch in the O-3 level, where he could see nothing in the darkness until the petty officer opened the inner hatch.

He could smell JP-5, and unwashed bodies, and fresh food. Back to his father's world. Back to work. Home.

And to a war, it seemed.

SEPTEMBER 10, 1990. 1100 ZULU. PARIS.

Ouspenskaya liked the room. She liked quality; she liked luxury. She had been raised in luxury, a child of the nomenklatura, and she in fact felt that luxury was her due. This sitting room in a hotel suite whose windows looked over the Place Vendôme was precisely what her sense of worth required.

"I am so pleased," she said to the man who stood waiting for her. She crossed a figured carpet of admirable thickness to take his outstretched hand, her eyes carefully avoiding the steel canes on which he supported himself. "Mister Shreed. Such a vast pleasure."

She wished she hadn't said "vast." Her English was rusty; the proper word was "great," of course. On the other hand, a little comic opera "Russianness" tended to disarm Americans, as if anyone who spoke poor English couldn't really be a threat. Shreed made no sign; he smiled, made proper sounds about sitting and all that, and she had time to think he was a good-looking man and it was unfortunate about the canes, and then to think that perhaps the misfortune was in her own head because he was said to be successfully married with several children, so the accident hadn't affected his sexuality. Not that she was interested in that; anything with Shreed would be counterproductive for both of them. Perhaps the woman with him was his mistress, although there was nothing about such a relationship in the file. She was his deputy, a rather formidable intelligence professional (although no more formidable than Ouspenskaya herself, she thought with some satisfaction).

"May I introduce Mrs. Baranowski," Shreed said. The woman leaned forward and they smiled at each other. Each probably had the same thought: they looked as if they had been turned out by the same fashion house, both in rather severe, skirted suits, both with a silk scarf adorning neck and one shoulder. (Indeed, Sally Baranowski was thinking, *Frick and Frack.*)

There was some casual talk, coffee, a few informal remarks about the arrangement that was to be made. Sally Baranowski talked about what a "virtual think tank" was; she was careful never to make the Russian feel that she was *nyetkulturnyi* for not understanding the Internet. "We will be funding an office here with an executive director

and a facilitator—actually an expert in computer communications—and when it's useful, maybe once a year or so,
we'll actually gather here face-to-face. Paris is such a swell
place for that! But mostly, we'll be meeting in a place that
doesn't exist." She smiled.

Shreed leaned toward her. "We'll supply the hardware
and the expertise. We laid the figures out in the contract."
He waved a hand. He was like many Americans, she
thought, as arrogant as a stage magician: wave a hand, and
things appeared—rabbits, colored scarves, computer networks. "Now—as for the classified protocol."

There was a little silence. They had finally got down to
business. Ouspenskaya could not restrain a smile; seeing
it, Sally Baranowski smiled, too. Ouspenskaya thought, *No,
my dear, you are wrong; I am not tipping my hand. I want
you to know how this pleases me. I have nothing to hide,
in fact.*

"It's understood," Shreed said, "that one of our people
is to dismantle—'rebuild'—Efremov's computer and bring
the drive and some other parts back to Langley. Our tech-
nicians are also to have access to your mainframe dump
under what I think are stupidly narrow limitations, but your
boss won't budge. Am I right, he won't budge?"

She nodded. Actually, it wasn't the poor Director, it was
Internal Affairs.

"That almost certainly means we won't find anything.
Your people will purge the mainframe before we ever see
it. That's really stupid. Tell your boss I used that word—
'stupid.' He can pass it along to Internal Affairs." They
smiled at each other.

"We want you to find everything," Ouspenskaya said.
"We want Efremov."

"So do we. Let's talk about that. The think tank business is okay, is it—do we agree how that works? No problem with the protocol?"

"None whatsoever."

"Okay. So, Efremov—that's why we're here. Let me tell

you what we've got; then you tell me what you've got. Okay?"

"Okay." She giggled. She had never used the word before.

Shreed went through it very quickly because in fact the Americans knew very little. It went without saying that they knew who and what Efremov was; what they didn't know was what he had been doing over the last year, or where he had disappeared to, or where he was now. "But we wonder if he had a connection with the Stitkin Building massacre a couple of months ago." He looked a question at her.

"No question of it," Ouspenskaya said. "But we don't know what the connection was."

Shreed's eyes narrowed. He was ready to suspect her. Well, of course, they would always be ready to suspect each other.

Ouspenskaya told them of Efremov's false agents (a slightly edited version; there were real agents to be protected), the dummy corporation, the four real agents run from the office in the Stitkin Building. "The attack was very professional and very thorough. We still entertain the idea that it was aimed at Efremov by an enemy." She told them about Malenkov, the gangster father of his mistress. "We pulled him in and put the screws to him."

Sally Baranowski smiled. "The car bomb in Platinka? We thought that might be government work."

"It was excessive; truly, we didn't intend all that. But you put out a request, it gets misinterpreted—" They all agreed that they knew how those things happened. "At any rate, Papa Malenkov was suitfully—*suitably,* forgive me— suitably impressed. He insisted the massacre was not his work. Gave us some proofs. Fairly persuasive. We're keeping him on the ice, still."

Shreed held out a plate of wickedly delicious chocolates and said, "How deep is your so-called mafia into intelligence matters, anyway? I'll be blunt; we had a feeler from

Malenkov about the time the massacre happened. Is he into SVRR?"

"God forbid he or any like him should be. What did he offer you?"

"He never got a chance; the attack happened, then the car bomb, and we figured you were after him. That's partly what made us curious about Efremov and the massacre." He wouldn't say what else had made them curious. She supposed—as they wanted her to, and as she knew they wanted her to—that they had a mole inside SVRR. She took two chocolates and smiled the plate away. Shreed passed the plate to Mrs. Baranowski and said, "Okay. I interrupted you. Efremov—the massacre—?"

"He had disappeared a few days before. You know that? Dropped out of sight—'off the screen,' as I heard it said. We have procedures, as you well know, to monitor movements—exits from the country, and so on—but they are not what they once were, and Efremov is a master. We have not found him. Most certainly, he was not killed in the massacre; we have identified all those. Nothing of his has been touched—bank accounts, flat, friends, a personal sort of safe house he maintained in London. Nothing. It is as if he is dead."

"But no body."

"Exactly."

"We had a report he was seen in the Sudan," Sally Baranowski said. It was a probe, less a statement than a question.

"We have that one, too!" Ouspenskaya countered. The two women smiled at each other. Was it never possible, Ouspenskaya wondered, to eradicate this faint whiff of gender—the two women in their identical costumes, the man between them like a judge? "We have also reports from North Korea, Kinshasa, Damascus, Baghdad, Tehran, and God knows where else. None verifiable, none top reliability."

"The Khartoum sighting was given a B-plus," Mrs. Baranowski said. "We think he's alive."

"So do I." She made a face. "Without evidence, I think he is alive. He is either running from whoever made the massacre, or he made it himself."

"Okay, let's talk turkey," Shreed said. (Ouspenskaya spent some seconds contemplating *talk turkey.*) "Why would he destroy his own front company?"

"Two possibilities: somebody is onto his fiddle—do you say 'fiddle' or is that British?—to his trick, his—"

"Scam," Sally Baranowski said.

"Scam, thank you. Somebody is onto his scam, and he is destroying the evidence, or—he has some great scheme to be a traitor to his country and go elsewhere. For money. For money and nothing else, because Efremov had no political ideals, I assure you, one of those good communists so long as communism was in power, then not so good. And, after all, we know he was on the scam—a vast number, I insist, of false agents, for whom he had collected money for up to nine years, but mostly since *perestroika.*"

Shreed looked down at his joined hands; he might have been reading from them. "He sees the end of communism coming; he decides it's going to be every man for himself—the Soviet idea of capitalism—and he builds an escape mechanism. He needs money to do it; he gets the money by creating fake agents. I suppose you've checked his movements over the last five years or so? Okay. Nothing suggestive? No meets with a new nationality or a new kind of person?"

Ouspenskaya spread her hands. "Most of his agents were run at long distance, many through cutouts. Of course he went abroad sometimes, but a senior officer of his kind has great leeway. Even in the old Soviet Union. Well, he was surveilled sometimes, of course. Nothing was reported. Nothing. And you—?"

"He didn't make contact with us. If it was just money, you'd think he'd come to us. He didn't. Absolutely. You have to take this one on faith."

She smiled. "He hated Americans."

"Oh. Mmp. Well, some people do. Okay, so let's say he

put himself on the market and he found a buyer without you knowing it. Or us, for that matter. Sally, we checked the whole shooting match, didn't we? Yeah. Our surveillance gave us nothing; we made him when he was posted in Belgium years ago, if I remember, and a couple of times in France and Italy, but we didn't get zip."

Zip, she thought. *What is zip?*

"So, let's say he found a buyer. What did the buyer buy? Intelligence? Sure, why not; he must have had stuff he could lay his hands on, either transmit or just carry out. No problem. But he wants to go, really cash in, so what he's going to take is potential—future intelligence. Am I right? Sally?"

"He'd have to turn his own agents."

"Hmm. That is not unthinkable," Ouspenskaya said. "From the beginning, I am struck by the isolation of the four agents—now I will tell you this; this is why we have met, to share this—four agents who were isolated away from all the others. From the other real ones and from the other fakes. He took four agents and ran them through the dummy corporation that was the object of the massacre. And they were the only agents run through this dummy corporation."

"And so," Sally Baranowski said, "he could have engineered the massacre himself to hide the four he meant to take with him to his new bosses."

Shreed threw his head back. "Yeah, but do the agents know? How does he do it? We haven't made him out of Russia in the last year. Mrs. Ouspenskaya—"

"Darya, please."

"Had he been out?"

"Only once, and as it happened he was surveilled—a trip to Italy, several cutouts we know about, all authentic and still in place."

Shreed's eyes widened. It was like being looked at by a hawk, the effect emphasized by his eyebrows, his raptor's nose. "In fact, what you describe is a demonstration trip. He knows he's under surveillance, so he does everything by the book and says, 'See what a good boy am I!" In fact—who ordered the surveillance on him?"

"The usual, I suppose."

"Check it out. I bet he ordered it himself. He'd do it through an office, hide his identity, but it might be in his computer. Sally, note that for the tech people. Okay! Yes, I see it! Out he comes—he's got a cache somewhere, money and documents; he gets out of Russia without leaving a trail—difficult but not impossible. Bribes, et cetera. Then he's out and—? And what?"

"He turns his four agents," Ouspenskaya said.

"Just like that?"

Sally Baranowski turned toward Shreed but leaned a little toward Ouspenskaya; it was the first time that she had hinted that she and Ouspenskaya were allies. "The important thing is he has to *try* to turn the agents; Darya's right. Whether he did or not is beside the point. He has to travel and he has to get in touch."

"No—" Shreed was looking at the ceiling again. "Don't get ahead of me. I grant you he has to try to turn his agents. But what if they say no?" He looked at her, then at Ouspenskaya. "Huh? What do you do with an agent you've been running for years and you want to turn him and he says no?"

Ouspenskaya was shaking her head slowly. "You cannot go back."

"No, you sure can't! You can't just turn around and say, Oh, well, if you won't change bosses, then I guess this won't work, so I'm going home. No way. And you can't say, Oh, well, I'm sorry you won't join me, but keep this to yourself, will you, please? Uh-uh. If he says no, you go black."

They all thought about that. Sally Baranowski said, "I suppose we don't know who the agents were?"

Ouspenskaya made a scandalized sound. "You think we are infants? No. We have a few tantalizing bits. Nothing to identify them." She took a dramatic pause. "One was an American."

To her surprise, Shreed only nodded. "You are not surprised," she said.

"Nothing surprises me. No, I thought it might be the case because you came to us so fast. Well, that's interesting, See, a thing like this you'd have to do all at once—you say he dropped off the screen four days before the massacre. That says to me that the massacre came at the end, not the beginning—he did it when he was committed. He already knew that he couldn't go back. So what does that tell us? That his agents would go with him to the new boss. Or some of them would. Sally?"

"It could be that he wasn't interested in the agents."

"No, no," Ouspenskaya cried, "why else set up the false corporation for them?"

"But he had to be willing to go without them—if there was no going back, he had to be ready for all four to turn him down."

"Willing, yes—but what he desired was to have them all turn. Absolutely, I think this." She reached for her coffee cup, saw that it was empty. "But perhaps it is not so certain that the massacre waited for the agents' response. Maybe it was all beforehand."

"We'll pretend it wasn't." Shreed grinned; the effect was somehow wolfish. "The massacre gives us a date certain for the approach to the agents—assuming he waited for their response, anyway. Sally, we want to put AB on deaths in the days before the massacre. How many days had he been missing? Six. Okay. In his area of operations, which we take to be the old Western Europe—a hell of a big area, I must say." He looked at Ouspenskaya.

"He had several reassignments but kept some, um, contacts. He became quite a powerful man, quite a selfish one, too, always. Vain, you would say."

"Okay, so we scan for deaths with any sort of security or intelligence connection—any rumor, any liaison, anything. What we're looking for are possible agents who said no to him and got eliminated. If nothing reads, expand the search. If we get a hit, I want air passenger manifests and immigration databases scanned for names he's known to have used—Darya, you'll supply those?—plus scan for all incoming traffic from the Soviet Union. Maybe we'll get lucky."

"Efremov never let luck happen."

Shreed grinned again. "We're all trained that way. But resources are finite—even his. What's on our side is that he was probably acting alone. That's awful hard to do. Awful hard."

Ouspenskaya repressed a happy shiver. Not because of Efremov—to hell with Efremov, she thought. She was happy because for once she was on the side of luxury— endless computer networks, databases of unimaginable complexity, Paris hotel suites with deep carpets. She wondered if she should get herself a Paris flat.

"Will you lunch with us?" Shreed was saying. "The hotel brasserie is really quite good."

"I should be enchanted." And she was.

SEPTEMBER – OCTOBER 1990. INDIAN OCEAN.

Alan made himself busy, sought work to make himself busy; when he wasn't busy, he brooded, and the depression scared him, like standing in a doorway that opened on an abyss. He had become, he discovered, silent, even in this closed world of five thousand men, and only work would fill the silence. The silence hid a secret, however— depression—and it made him unwelcome: a silent man is a trouble to his shipmates.

There is no sorrow at sea; only work, or light conversation, or sleep. First encounters with Rafe and the rest of the squadron had shocked him because they had no place for his grief or his silence. Indeed, Rafe went right at him at the beginning of the first tanker flight after he got back. Rafe's approach was direct and crude—vintage Rafe: "Don't start bawling about your father, Spy; we need our oxygen." Alan spent the rest of the flight stewing over it, appalled by the brutality. But his silences were resented even among his friends, he found; even the skipper took him aside to say something. "Everybody knows what happened, Craik. Everybody feels for you. But you can't show it—know what I mean? It's sand in the gears, you follow me? Lighten up. Give them a break—give yourself a break."

Lighten up. Humor is the oil of civilization in a closed world like a ship at sea. Grief is self-indulgence; self-indulgence is grit in the machine. Alan tried to help the machine go. Mostly, he worked.

Around him, the imminence of war was palpable, a new tension in the ship its harbinger. The battle group sailed back and forth between the Red Sea and the Persian Gulf, transiting the Strait of Hormuz, with the Iranians and their Silkworm missile launchers thirteen nautical miles away. Then they bored holes in the Indian Ocean. Alan had to limit his air time; not really a conscious decision, but he was now too busy to fly while the strike-planning teams, of which he was now by definition a part, sweated in the mission-planning area, often laboring all night on a target that the Pentagon would take off the official target list the next morning. The skipper had asked the ops officer to put him in a tanker any night he asked, but the fact was that now his job was in the intel center, not the air; if he was not in mission planning, he was making another intel officer lose sleep. Better that Alan lose the sleep; his dreams were bad, anyway. Not that he remembered them: only the bitterness they left behind, a waking sadness to greet another day. It had to be his father's death, he knew, yet he could pull no details from the dreams, no explanations from his depression; even most of that mission in Christine was blank now, gone from his memory. He remembered the enemy aircraft, the attack on Christine and the triumph as Rafe caused the bandit to splash. Then there was nothing, until he was on the FLIR, watching his father's last salute. Was this healing? Or was it withdrawal? Was something hiding from him in those missing minutes?

The life of the ship became familiar again, its size and

its intricate complex of spaces so normal he might have been walking the streets of a hometown. He found himself eating more often in the wardroom—the Clean Shirt, as it was called, because khakis were required there, as compared to the Dirty Shirt, where a flight suit was acceptable—and spending more time with the nonaviators, even making some friends in the ship's company. To his surprise, he found that he could eat at the Captain's table, although the Captain himself was rarely there; more surprisingly, there were always spaces at the Captain's because of some misplaced awe. (To be sure, he was the only j.g. who chose it; that kind of awe no longer scared him.)

Mission planning became a welcome change. Lives depended on what was done there. As a squadron intel officer, his role was often limited to sharpening pencils and making coffee, because, although he had ideas about tactics, he had enough sense to realize that he did not have the experience to give the ideas credibility. Still, after a couple of weeks, he began to see that even some of the most senior officers believed too easily the information that splashy, graphics-heavy computers gave them about threat envelopes and enemy SAM site locations. Yet, he knew, some of the information in the computers had to be months, even years out of date. He began to check this flashy information, not from any need to push himself forward, but to fill the silences of his waking mind: the dread of time to think pushed him to work when there seemed no more work to do. Now and then, he flew.

He read and read; old pubs on Iraq, put together back when the Iraqis were allies, not enemies; every message that he could find, even releases on how intelligence databases had been generated. It was dull work, but it required concentration, and Alan poured that concentration over his grief the way another man might pour alcohol. He slept little, moved in a fog of fatigue.

He never found any shortage of data; pages and pages

of new SAM sites discovered or deleted by various means; estimates of enemy strength at airfields; changes to the target list: it went on and on. He began to listen to other AIs and to his seniors, to note that some data was held in higher esteem than other; some information was discounted; some went unread from day to day. Why? Time, he found, and laziness and ignorance. And excess itself—too much data, so that you had to look for reasons to deep-six some of it. Some data conflicted with other data; shit-can it. Some data explained its own derivation and so was more suspect or more solid; ignore the suspect. Some simply appeared like the voice of God, and so was taken on faith or heard as mere noise. Some AIs, he found, read all the traffic and tried to make sense of it, while others simply adopted a single source—usually CIA or CNO—and used it as their bible and convenient filter.

Alan spent weeks, after hours, comparing these externally produced bits of data with his own "ground truth," which he extracted from those systems within the battle group that had the capability to sense enemy radars and installations without aid from outside intelligence. If, for example, a SAM site in southern Iraq lit up an EA-6B Prowler, the Prowler would fly along the border, attempting to take as many cuts off the enemy radar as possible. With a little work, and a bit of computer support, the intelligence officer for the Prowler squadron would reconstruct the site's location within a few hundred meters. *That* was ground truth—not last year's truth; not Washington's truth; the truth, now—ground truth.

Alan made himself a big chart. He listed, in erasable marker, every SAM site. He color-coded them by source of information: red was a site identified by units of the battle group itself, like the Prowlers; CIA information was black; DIA blue. Every agency and producer of intelligence received a color, so many sources that Alan ran out of markers. Then he noted which producers tallied with the ground truth of the red marker. He kept score.

The Prowler AI noted that Alan had become his best

customer—indeed, virtually his disciple for EA-6B electronic intelligence (ELINT)—and so they became acquaintances, like businessmen in the same trade. Harry O'Neill was a tall, heavily built black intellectual from Massachusetts who spoke like a Kennedy and thought like a Reagan Republican. In the strange, insular logic of shipboard life, he was called "Creole," a nickname he never commented on, but he had a number of mocking voices and personae, one African, one a rip-off of a *Saturday Night Live* character ("Isn't that *special!*") that suggested comedy used as a defense. Early on, he said to Alan in the African character, "What you do with all this good data, Bwana?"

"I put it on a chart, Kemosabe."

"Chart? Bwana make chart?"

"Come on."

Alan led him to the squadron intel space, where he kept his masterwork turned face to the wall. He whipped it around and explained the color coding.

"You mean, old chap," Creole said, shifting abruptly into 1930s-movie Brit, "all the red ones are *mine?*"

"Well, they're based on your Prowler data, yeah."

"Isn't that *special!*" Creole grinned down at him. "*Our* chart, old chap. My data, your Magic Markers. Mmmm?"

Creole had the respect of his squadron; his minute and technical knowledge of electronic warfare stood out even in a squadron of EW professionals. He had neither the need nor the urge to fly; he had earned his place, and he knew it. Alan suspected that life would be a living hell for his replacement unless he had the same math and computer science degrees that made Creole so formidable. But Creole also had a surprising grounding in both Alternative (which Alan liked) and Gangsta Rap (which Alan despised) and an extensive collection of CDs that he was quick to lend. Many of them were signed; Creole admitted a little hesitantly that he had a sister in the biz. The New Orleans/Seattle/LA music scene got very real as Creole opened up and began to trust him.

After two weeks, they had plotted the consistency of several sources of information, and at the same time proven the worth of the battle group's own efforts to collect the locations of enemy radars and SAMs. Alan found himself able to speak with more assurance to his strike team; he explained to them why certain sites were known facts and others merely suspected. Alan took Creole to the CAG AI to explain "their chart." They hauled the now rainbow-colored chart to the office and, after a brief speech from Creole—no funny voices, no characterizations—announced that they had begun to doubt some of the outside sources of intelligence.

The CAG AI was sitting at his desk with a single light turned up on its gooseneck to illuminate the chart. "You two just *decided* to do this?"

"Yes, sir."

"Because in your many years as strike planners, you had learned how much smarter you are than the Office of Naval Intelligence and CIA?"

Alan looked at Creole, saw that Creole was looking for a way to bail out, and said in a joking voice, "Not *much* smarter, sir."

The CAG AI looked at the chart—weeks of ESM cuts, triangulations, message-traffic data comparisons. Now, CAG AIs are the senior intel officers in an airwing, and they are therefore busy people. They run the airwing's mission-planning effort, and they manage the very junior AIs and act as staff officers to their airwing COs. They have to review every completed strike package, monitor the performance of eleven young officers and thirty very smart enlisted intelligence troops, and play airwing staff politics, all at the same time. Very little of their time is taken up with the "business" of intelligence—including comparing data flows.

Lars Nordheim was thirty-nine, overweight, and exhausted. He knew he was going to stay exhausted until they turned for home. During this planning phase for a real war, it took most of his day and part of his night just to review and critique the airwing's intel products; the last thing he needed was to hear from two j.g.s about a huge, man-hour-intensive project that they had created without his permission. But— He looked at their chart. *But.*

"You guys not have enough to do?" he muttered.

Alan glanced at Creole. Creole made an Ollie face: *Look at the fine mess you've got us into!* "It was—spare time. Sir," Alan said.

"Spare time!" Nordheim rolled his puffy eyes toward Alan. "You're the one who flies, am I right?"

"When I can. Not so much now that we're so, ah, busy."

Nordheim muttered, as if to himself, "Not so much now we're so busy, Jesus H. Christ!" He looked up at Creole. "You're the Prowler AI, right? This is your data. Right? You're the unimpeachable source?"

Alan was sure Creole was going to bag it then, but Creole surprised him by saying, "That's good data, sir! My guys get good stuff. I *believe* in what's on that chart."

Nordheim rolled back. The light was on the chart and the two junior officers; only Nordheim's hands were lighted, the rest of him in shadow. "Boys," he said quietly, "boys, so do I. This is good. This is really good." As if for himself, he switched to a Bogart imitation; Alan had the giddy sense that he had caught it somehow from Creole. "Really, really good, Shweetheart." And then out again into the no-nonsense voice of the CAG AI. "It shows dedication, and it shows a basic understanding of what intelligence is all about. The awful truth is, fellows, I like it so much that I'm going to take the credit for it." His face was invisible to them, but Alan sensed that the man was grinning. "I'm going to march into CAG with that chart and tell him that I ordered the study done and that all of our strike groups will use these data sets from now on, and that two officers and two enlisted will be assigned to periodically check the data." He rolled his body forward and his face came into the light—weary, puffy, excited. "See, boys, you don't need credit with the CAG, and I do. You, on the other hand, need credit with me, and with your skippers, and I'll see to that. Any problems?"

Something about a man who told you to your face that he was stealing your project made Alan smile. Creole looked more relieved than anything else; he later admitted that he had dreaded the whole thing. They all shook hands. Still, before he left the office, Creole said to Nordheim, "*O'Neill,* sir. Prowler AI. My skipper is Commander Santana. Credit where credit is due, old chap." He grinned. Nordheim grinned. Alan was startled by the crassness of it: *So that's how you do that.*

OCTOBER 11, 1990. 0017 ZULU. INDIAN OCEAN.

PO1 Sheldon Bonner slouched along the passages to his bunk. Air ops were still going on, so people were awake in many of the spaces, but it wasn't like daytime; the heads were pretty empty, the snack bar quiet, with the depressed and sour air of a bus station somewhere in the goddam Midwest at about two in the morning. Bonner had been drinking coffee the whole watch; the idea of more of it made him feel as if his bodily fluids had all turned to vinegar. He bought a Coke from a machine and sipped it, leaning against the bulkhead.

"Hey, Bonner," a chief named Fink grunted.

"Fink."

"You finish that beach stuff?" Fink was senior to him in the photo lab, always on edge about getting done, having the officers get on him, not having done something just right.

"It's drying."

"How'd it look?"

"It looked like a beach. I'm not a fucking PI."

Fink went away, frowning. Bonner shook his head and drank more Coke. Fink was a perfect example, he thought, of why you didn't want to make chief. All the problems and none of the excuses of the rest of us.

He lay on his bunk and leafed through a catalog for

bass boats. Page after page gleamed at him—boats with metallic flecks in their paint, boats with seats that went up and down, boats with two motors, boats with three. He could picture them all on the St. John's. In his fantasy, he was at the wheel, his son in the other seat. They'd be jump-fishing—hopping from patch to patch of screaming gulls, casting into the roiled water where baitfish were being gobbled by big fish, hooking one or two, then hopping to the next. He smiled. It would be great.

He was spreading the word about the bass boat he was going to buy. He was spreading the word about how hard it would be to make the payments, about maybe having to settle for a secondhand boat, about maybe taking a second job on the beach to pay for it. The word would get around. If NCIS ever checked on Sheldon Bonner, they'd hear that he barely got by, and the boat was a luxury he really had to save for.

The truth was, of course, that the boat would be bought with cash from a guy in Delray who handled funny deals for a price and didn't talk about it. He'd draw up a dummy contract, even give Bonner a dummy coupon book for dummy payments. Dummies for dummies, was Bonner's way of looking at it.

Life had been quiet since the Iran raid. Bonner had hit the beach in Dubai and Bahrain; there had been no sign for him either place. *Lay low,* he told himself. *A job well done.* Carl would have deposited his money in Switzerland, direct; meanwhile, his monthly payments would be piling up in Florida in cash, ready for him when he got home. He dealt strictly in cash at home. He had nearly forty thousand dollars hidden in his house. Nobody would ever find it. Nobody, he was pretty sure, would ever look. Life was good.

Just now, beyond the photographs of gleaming boats throwing rooster tails of bow wave, he was seeing the words *offshore investment.* He was a traditionalist, thoroughly locked into an admiration for the Swiss and the secrecy of Swiss banking. Still, he had seen a lot of enthusiastic crap about *offshore investment* in this English newspaper somebody had. *Offshore* meant the Bahamas, Turks and Caicos, one of those funny-money places where half the government were drug dealers. If they were as good at secrecy as the Swiss; if they'd deal in cash; if they'd *deal*— He fell asleep.

OCTOBER 31. 1817 ZULU. INDIAN OCEAN.

Lars Nordheim found himself eating a slice of really decent pumpkin pie in the Dirty Shirt with Alan's skipper.

"Special occasion?" Nordheim said, holding up a forkful of the pie.

"Halloween, Lars," the skipper said.

"Oh, yeah," Lars said. "Halloween. I remember Halloween, back on earth."

"How's my boy doing?" the skipper asked after two minutes of companionable silence. "Craik."

"Works like a sonofabitch."

"He hasn't had a hop in two weeks."

"Isn't his job," Lars said.

"You tell him to quit?" the skipper asked.

"No, sir. I told him to remember what his designator is."

"How'd he take it?"

"He's a smart kid. I think he finds intelligence a little dull."

"Let him go flying tomorrow?"

"Sure, sure, he's earned it. Besides, we're out of range of our targets, right? CAG intends to call off all strike planning at noon and give everybody thirty-six hours."

"Subplot tells me there's a Russian Viktor II in the area," the skipper said. "Maybe within two hundred miles, maybe on the moon. Sir, you know how that can work."

"I got a hunch, Lars. I'm going to take my smart boy on a real live submarine hunt. Ain't that many white whales left since the wall went down. Craik thinks all we do is give gas to F-18s and carry ELINT pods. I want to show him what we really do. He flies tomorrow, okay?"

Nordheim shrugged.

"Thanks, Lars."

NOVEMBER 1, 1990. 1230 ZULU. LANGLEY, VIRGINIA.

Every morning at seven-thirty, George Shreed had a half-hour meeting with his deputy. It was the best part of his day—coffee, a cigarette, complete mutual trust. Sally Baranowski would undoubtedly be happy to take his job someday, but she was devoted to getting it on her own achievement. He sensed no rivalry; rather, a shared ambition: the tide would raise both boats.

"Whatcha got?" he said.

"You look wrung out," she said. "You okay?"

"Didn't sleep very well." In fact, he hadn't slept at all, a frequent experience. His legs had been smashed almost thirty years ago; they could still feel great pain. He lit his first cigarette.

"Those things'll kill you," she said.

"Let's hope so."

She dropped into her chair with papers, appointment book, and the morning briefing on her lap. In a field that was not yet really comfortable with women, no matter what the men said, she was a success, he thought. He wondered what it had cost her. Something in the more overt kind of femininity, he supposed. Sometimes she seemed false, too bright, too *on*, as if she had to show she could take it.

"How's your little girl?" he said.

"Do I have a little girl? Is that the one whose picture's on my desk?" She laughed too briskly. "She's fine. Or so John tells me." Another laugh. She caught his eye, sobered. "Tell me I'm not a shitty mother."

"You know you're not." They stared at each other. "Anyway. Whatcha got?"

"Efremov. Yuri Efremov, the Russian who—"

"I remember."

"AB thinks they got a match on his agents. Not one, but two deaths the night before the Moscow massacre. You remember, the Stitkin—?"

"I remember this one pretty well, Sally; just give me the top."

"Okay. Brussels, the body of Émile Clanwaert turned up in the city trash; he was a facilities maintenance foreman at NATO HQ. Location of the body suggests he had been in a Dumpster from the airport. Body probably dead more than twenty-four hours when found." She shifted her legs, sipped coffee. "Then, in Amsterdam, a woman was found in a park, throat slashed. Oh, Clanwaert had been garroted, by the way, professional job. The woman is in our files as probable sexual connection with the naval attaché at the Turkish embassy; I did a check with the Amsterdam resident and in fact she was carrying the Turk's child, no question. She was a buyer for a textile company, so the intelligence connection has to be the boyfriend. That's it."

"Same night?"

"Well, the woman in Amsterdam is certain; she was found about four a.m. but the body had been dead some hours, no question. Clanwaert—Brussels—could have been plus or minus, but if you accept the best guesstimate, he was killed the same night. But plenty sufficient hours apart for somebody to fly from one to the other, probably. Maybe even drive."

"Okay, good." He swilled coffee. "That's good. Scan all incoming flights in both—"

"They're on it. I expect a report today."

He smiled, put his hands behind his head. "What can I say? You're making me superfluous."

NOVEMBER 2, 1990. 0900 ZULU. INDIAN OCEAN.

Alan awoke. There was a sense of something wrong. No, not wrong. Different. What? *No bad dreams.* On the contrary, a good dream. Of what? Nothing left of it now, but a feeling of great pleasure. Yes, a bit—fishing. He had been fishing. And—It was gone. *But he had waked up happy!*

"Woooo, big Spy!" Somebody was shaking him. "Time to rise and shine, dude. Rise and fly, man!"

He opened one eye. The pilot they called Surfer was leaning over him. Alan growled, "If you kiss me, I'll scream."

"Fuck you, Spy man. This is ASW. AY ESS DOUBLE YOU. Real subs for real people, okay? A Russian Viktor II is somewhere to the southeast, and we are going to beat the P-3 pukes on station, drop a million dollars' worth of sonobuoys in the water, and tag his ass. Me pilot, Skipper copilot, Senior Chief Craw SENSO—you TACCO, dig?"

Alan threw on a flight suit for the first time in two weeks and wandered toward the Dirty Shirt. He ordered a big breakfast, poured a full mug of coffee, and upended a packet of cocoa mix into the coffee. "All the sugar and twice the caffeine," he murmured happily. *I'm happy! Sonofabitch!* He was wolfing down pancakes loaded with syrup and part of a runny egg when a shadow fell across his plate, and a voice said, "Hey."

"Hey, Rafe." His mood collapsed. He was still pissed at Rafehausen.

"Thanks, yeah, I will sit down next to you." Rafehausen plunked himself into the chair and banged his coffee cup on the table. "Heard the news?"

"There's going to be a war, right?"

"The *big* news, shithead! Flag's passed on our medals. Air Medal for Narc and me, goodies for you and Craw. For downing the Fantan, asshole!"

"Good. Nice. Congratulations." He couldn't make himself sound enthusiastic.

Silence. Rafe hated silence. Alan waited for him to leave. Instead, Rafe said, "Hey." It was a sound that meant something more, the way other people might say, "May I ask you something?" or "By the way—"

"Hey, Rafe."

"Uh—Narc says I was too rough on you that first flight

when you got back." This was an apology, remarkable in itself, yet still not enough for Alan; he should have said, "No problem," and that would have been that; instead, he said, "Yes, you were." Exactly the wrong thing to say. And when he said it, he turned his head and looked Rafe in the eyes. "Yes, you were."

"Hey, man—" Rafe winced. "I was trying to pull you out of it."

"Well—" Alan thought about it. "Well, you didn't." Then he laughed. The buoyant mood returned. "But something has. I feel great! The first time in— Forget it, Rafe; no problem. You did the right thing, maybe a little overkill in the frankness department, okay? All is forgiven. Congratulations on the Air Medal." They shook hands. Rafe should have left then; it was a natural stopping place, a cue for him to leave. He lingered that moment too long that means you've lost your opportunity; Alan offered him a cigarette, and both lit up and blew smoke and Rafe, to his surprise, said, "You ever think about that night?"

"Oh, yeah. Except I've lost it. I'm blank from the time the Fantan went in until my old man went in." There. He had said it. The first time. And to Rafehausen, of all people. "You don't want to hear this."

"I don't mind. No, no shit, I don't—so long as there's no, you know, heavy stuff."

"It bothers me."

"Naturally, he was your old man."

"No, no, no, no, not that part. What *happened* bothers me. I mean—*what happened?* What are the chances of an A-6 getting hit with a MANPAD? And don't tell me 'shit happens.' I've heard that so many fucking times I think it's Navy doctrine."

"Well, I'm not a suspicious type, Spy. But I'll tell you something." Rafe blew smoke sideways and turned his head away. "They knew we were coming. That bothers even me. They knew we were coming." He mashed his cigarette. "You flying today?"

"ASW run,"

He whacked Alan's shoulder. "Git 'em, tiger."

Five minutes later, he was poring over the latest ASW data in the tiny, smoky ASW module, a cell ruled by two warrant officers who smoked without pause, drank fifty cups of coffee a day, and had grown so alike, as if they were a long-married couple, that Alan had trouble telling them apart. No AI before Alan had really ever set foot in their space that either could remember; he, however, had found it a quiet haven, was willing to put up with comments about "this kid who bums my smokes." It was also a good place to pick up the wisdom of ASW work along with the technical skills. Like learning how to fish from two old fishermen.

Now, he looked at the day's picture until it made sense, then looked at the grams coming in from an S-3 currently on station, until he felt he had the main shaft and auxiliary lines down. Only then did he accept a cigarette. It went very nicely with the end of his coffee.

The watch officer (Erskine? John?), without ever taking his eyes off the displays, growled, "A Russian Viktor II. Screaming loud—bad bearing in his drive shaft, I'd say, although some people are coming up with theories about auxiliary power units, pumps, and the Kennedy assassination, I have no doubt. Anyway, the poor bastard should have gone home a long time ago."

Alan finished the smoke. He didn't say thanks; that never seemed to get him anywhere. Instead he said he'd get the buoys on datalink once he had contact. The watch officer (John? Erskine?) said he better. "Easiest sub that ever swam, young man. Just get her and send her to me."

Alan knew damn well that this was aviator-speak; getting submarine contact from a plane was never all that easy—his back end could go down off the cat or his tape could be bad or his datalink could dump and he would have nothing to show. He also knew that (John? no, he thought this one was surely Erskine) probably was telling him that even with all that, this was comparatively easy and there would be no excuses.

"I picked you two tapes from my 'no fuckups' library," the warrant said.

"Thanks, um, Erskine."

"Fuck, you *do* know my name. I bet John a beer you didn't!"

NOVEMBER 2, 1990. 1220 ZULU. LANGLEY, VIRGINIA.

"Got a minute?" Sally looked better this morning, not as tense. She was leaning in George Shreed's doorway with an unusual nonchalance.

"One minute, exactly; I have to go scold an asshole at State. What's up?"

"We got a hit on the Efremov thing. The passenger manifests, Amsterdam and—"

"I remember; cut the crap."

Sally said, "A man listed as P. Kazinski flew into Amsterdam two hours before the woman was believed killed. He flew out of Brussels sixteen hours later."

"Into Amsterdam, out of Brussels. Car between? Let's hope not. Four agents he had to contact—Amsterdam, Brussels—where did he fly to after Brussels?"

"Naples."

"Naples! Holy shit. Naples. God, there's a NATO facility there, too—Christ, all sorts of things— That would be three. There were four. How much time between Amsterdam and Brussels?" Shreed was utterly involved now; State was forgotten.

"We don't know when Clanwaert was murdered. But if—"

"Find out when the trash was picked up."

"I have them checking."

"You're good, kid, you're really good!" He struggled toward the door. "Let's pretend he had some time. Start checking air manifests to see if you can match a name outgoing Amsterdam with somebody incoming Brussels. He can't have had too many fake passports—right?"

"Why not?"

"Because we're fucked if he did."

NOVEMBER 2, 1990. 1220 ZULU. INDIAN OCEAN.

He was at the top of his game during prebrief: relaxed, prepared, and, thanks to Erskine, ready to talk lines and tapes and convergence zones and isothermic layers. Surfer gave him a little thumbs-up at the end, and he gulped a last cup of coffee, forced a piss, and headed for the flight deck. Only on the ladder to the O-3 level did his failure hit him— a full bowel. He was going to be in an ejection seat for seven hours. The Aircrew No-Dump Two-Step. *Oh, shit.*

The flight deck was quiet. Only the Vikings and helos were flying today. And the day was breathtaking. There was the lightest of haze, right out in the corners of the distant horizon; the sea was a rich dark blue with perfect whitecaps, and the sky was a high arch of pale blue more suitable to upstate New York in deer season than the Indian Ocean in autumn. The low humidity, rare as water in the desert, made the day seem a holiday to every man on deck. Alan breathed the pleasant salt air deep and decided, as every sailor does three or four times a year, that life at sea was the only life for him.

Senior Chief Craw was inside the plane, preflighting his seat and making sure that he had a spreader pin and that the seat would function if it was needed as a parachute. Alan leaned in and looked quickly through his seat, stowed his bag and thermos, looked one more time in the bag for his tapes, and showed them to Craw, who nodded amicably. A spare tape almost certainly nestled in the Senior's bag, too, a pet that never went bad. Alan leaned over and said, "Erskine says they're both good," and Craw nodded emphatically.

Alan began to go through checkoff without thinking about it: he taped the day's frequencies and datalink info above his computer console, went down his mental checklist for the flight, and returned to the glare of the sun out-side the plane with relief. It was stifling in the cockpit until the APU came on, and with it the air-conditioning. He began to look at the control surfaces, the wings and stabi-lizers, then looked under the plane for the telltale pink of leaking hydraulic fluid. He checked the alignment of the landing gear piston, where Rafe had shown him; it had something to do with the possibility that the maintenance guys could put the part in backward or upside down, so you always checked to make sure that two black lines and a grease fitting lined up. Alan wasn't sure that he had the whole story right, but he had a clear idea what it ought to look like, and Christine was up to the mark today. Alan was aware that a real TACCO would be checking about ten times as many things as he knew to check, but he also knew that this was really the pilot's game and all he could do was contribute a little extra attention.

The sight of his name, stenciled under the TACCO win-dow on Christine's starboard side, caused a small response somewhere below his stomach; so did the schematized Fan-tan up near the nose—Christine's kill.

It was the TACCO's job to count the chaff and flare rounds that were loaded like bloated shotgun shells in the belly of the plane. From that perspective he could see that they had a full load of sonobuoys and a torpedo, as well. Craw stuck his head under the plane and yelled against the jet noise of the deck. "Sir? Can you tell me what we have in what hole, since you're already down there?"

Sonobuoys come in two flavors—passive/active, which actually get down there and find a sub, and environmen-tal, which test salinity and temperature and all the demons that affect sound in water. Kneeling on the painful nonskid decking, Alan gave Craw a succinct count and saw him tick off his calls on a plastic sheet. Clearly, Craw already knew the answers; that was cool with Alan.

Alan climbed out from under the plane on sore knees. He contorted himself up the ladder and into his seat, then went back in the tunnel and installed a tape in the box, seated it firmly home, and strapped it in. Then he rapped his knuckles sharply against the housing. *Luck. Drive the electromagnetic demons away. Whatever.* He went back to his seat and wrote two strings of numbers on his screen in grease pencil.

And he was done. Ready to fly.

Craw poked his head up. "All set, sir?" he asked.

"Have we got time to go back down to ASW and get the final picture, Senior?"

Craw smiled. "Ayuh." The skipper arrived just then and started his walkaround, and they nodded and shouted their errand as they passed. He waved. They ran. Through a hatch, down a ladder; Craw ducked through the ASW door, grabbed a mug of coffee, and lit a cigarette. Alan took one from Craw without a thought. He was on edge with a very pleasurable set of nerves suddenly. He was ready. The coffee was great. He smiled. Warrant Officer Erskine frowned.

"P-3 lost the fucking Viktor II. P-3 won't take advice or order. P-3 thinks the Viktor's still on the same course, going flat out at thirty-two knots due west, keeps running ahead and dropping buoys, the stupid shithead. All in the last hour."

Where had Alan's easy sub gone? Everyone packed into the little space looked grim. Alan knew Erskine's rant about "straight-line ASW officers" who always kept looking ahead when subs might have turned. Alan read the status board; the P-3 was using up her gas and buoys fast, for nothing. He peered over Erskine's shoulder, looked at the red and blue lines drawn on the chart, picked up a compass, ticked off a distance on the chart, put the needle where the carrier's position had been marked at 0900 and put the other end down on the sub track. It neatly matched the lost contact position.

Alan caught Craw's eye. Craw had been watching him. Erskine was dealing with the TAO—the Tactical Action Officer—a god who had drifted over to check on the sub and who now went back to his own domain, not a happy man. He wanted the Viktor II caught. Craw had caught Alan's idea by professional telepathy.

Craw put a hand on Erskine's shoulder.

"My Spy says Viktor turned when he detected the battle group. My Spy thinks he turned *toward* us. I say, Viktor's got a fucking loud shaft, and we'll get him, and I've a bottle of Irish Mist to back my man." He shifted into a Leslie-Howard-as-Scarlet-Pimpernel voice. *Christ, everybody's doing it!* "What say you?"

Erskine looked at Craw. He looked at Alan. "No bet. I already lost a beer on this guy." He looked back at Alan. "My theory, too. TAO isn't buying it. You go fly on our theory, and if you find the sub I'll buy a round at the Highlander." The Highlander was in Dubai; they were in the Indian Ocean. Well—

Alan felt a sudden urgency in his gut. He smiled. "One stop at the head, and I'm good to go!"

Then he was ready, strapped and plugged and taped and numbered. They were number two to go on cat three, the one over his stateroom. A KA-6 tanker powered up for the roll to the cat, and the cockpit temperature climbed again, going through one hundred and twenty degrees. Alan knew that this affected his chances of getting a good load from the computer, without which their only hope of ASW detection was spotting the Viktor on the surface. The jet-blast deflector went up, protecting them from the worst of it, but as the KA-6 went to full power the heat seemed to rock the S-3 right through her skin. Alan was wearing a turtleneck, knowing that it would be cold when the aircon kicked in. Right now he was soaked.

The boat jerked under them; then a noise like a hockey puck on a wooden table, for a three count; then the hockey puck fell on the floor—thud—and the KA-6 was airborne. Alan sat back, watched the interplay between the skipper in the copilot seat and Surfer in the pilot seat. Then they were rolling forward. Punk—they stopped. Clank—the stirrup was linked up. They rolled about an inch and the nose went down. Like a cat, AG 707 prepared to spring, head down and hindquarters high. Surfer turned his head, all business, gave a crisp salute, and the Lady Christine flung herself down the deck and leaped into the air. She sagged off the cat, gave a little growl and stretched herself, then rose heavily, gravid with sonobuoys and torpedoes.

As the auxiliary power unit was shut down, he clicked the keyboard out of its up-and-locked position down across his knees, reached up for the big toggle over his head (right next to the big, Lucite-covered red weapons-release switch), cycled it up, and watched the screen. Right on schedule, Christine told him that, like him, she was in a good mood today. He counted to sixty while looking at his watch for time, and just on the last tick of the second hand he brought the toggle sharply down. Counted to five. And up she came. No jilting little alphanumerics, just a solid read and a good system. In two more minutes, he knew he had a good back end.

He heard Surfer check in with the E-2 and get a sweet and sweet on his IFF, and Alan felt a jolt of awareness, a feeling of something uncompleted—Rafe, that morning, his father: what?—and then Craw said over the intercom, "Good to go, sir. Hey, Skipper, Mr. Spy has seduced Christine and she's being a real little lady. Ayuh. Good back end." The skipper and Craw started a long and fairly technical ASW discussion, and he forgot whatever it was that had jolted him; he was hand-feeding data to Christine so she would show the right symbols, recognize distances, tie up with computers aboard the carrier. Only gradually did he realize that Craw was explaining Alan's own theory of where the Viktor II had gone.

Skipper gave it a hearing. "This is from John? Or Erskine?"

Craw paused.

"From Mr. Craik, sir. But I see it as likely, my own self. Erskine likes it too."

"Alan?"

"Sir?"

"What's up?"

"When the P-3 lost contact, the Viktor was at the edge of the battle group's passive-detection range, sir. Group makes a lot of noise for him to hide in. I think he turned in, not out."

"And you two believe that this ex-commie is going to head for the BG? Like, swing north and get ahead? What, just to be macho?"

"That's about it, Skipper. I'll stake my nonexistent reputation that he turned when he heard the BG. Okay, so he was already headed like, what, 160 relative to the BG. So if he wanted to run, he just keeps going. Plus, the P-3 is passive on him, so maybe he doesn't even know he's detected. And even if he does, what's smarter than heading the other way, real slow? Skipper, I hadn't thought about getting ahead, but that Viktor's got to know we're headed back to Hormuz, right? Predictable. So he heads north at three knots—that would make even *his* shaft fairly quiet. And he's 170 off access from the search. That would place him right—here." Alan keyed a far-on circle, timed it out with a heading, and dropped a puck on the computer for the skipper to read in front. Craw looked over his shoulder and started to set up a V-shaped sonobuoy pattern at a very wide dispersion.

The skipper studied his screen. "Okay, I like it. But it's your ass if you're wrong. *Both* of you." He turned his head to give Craw a look, then Alan. The skipper had had a little chat from the TAO before he had come to the flight deck.

"TAO wants the sub found. Right now. Thinks the sub just might pass our location to the locals." If we can find him, and keep him, the skipper thought, we prove ourselves again. If you flew S-3s, you spent a lot of time proving your worth. "And if we can, we'll ping him. Alan, you've never done this. If we go active, we humiliate them, and they'll go away, for a while. Till the next time."

Alan thought that this was the longest speech he'd ever

heard from the skipper. He finished the datalink setup. Skipper had the link set up in front. Buttons were pushed, data transferred; in five minutes Alan had a picture of every sonobuoy field that the P-3 had dropped. Off by fifteen miles or so, he thought; aloud, he said, "Deep?" and got a big grin from Craw in return. A grin? From Craw? In fact, Craw's grin was constant now: he was loving it, a game, a sport, like fishing. Like his dream.

In the front, the skipper was whistling.

Surfer turned his head, brilliant Indian Ocean sky repeated in his visor and sunglasses—cyberpunk surfer boy—and raised his chin at Alan. "Hey, Spy?"

"Yeah, Surfer?"

"I hear you dole out decent coffee and cookies when you fly with Rafe."

So, back to Alan the Stewardess, except nobody made the joke today. Craw took his, gulped coffee, said, "Wicked," and never took his eyes from the screen. He was getting ready to drop his pattern.

"Beautiful," the skipper said to Surfer. "Hold it for the drop."

Craw had it set to manual. Most SENSOs, and almost all TACCOs, would drop a pattern on auto—unless it mattered. This mattered. Craw dropped each buoy as the skipper chanted the litany of time and distance and altitude. Alan, following them, managed to get each buoy up on the link as it dropped. Surfer crisscrossed the ocean as if the waves had lines engraved on them, powering into turns at low altitude so that he left the turn at exactly the same altitude as he entered.

"Gotcha!" Craw muttered, and then he cursed. The module agreed that they had had the sub just as the buoy hit the water. Then gone. Right at the east end of the V, the bearing muddy but looking north. Alan felt a surge of relief and then exhilaration; he laid a far-on circle and a track and shouted, "Go for it!" Craw pumped out more buoys, this time in a line, a straight barrier; and the Viktor, like a trout with the fly in its mouth, sprinted off downstream at high speed, right through the heart of the pattern and—and out of it again.

"Shit!" the skipper muttered. Craw said, "Sonofabitch."

Ten minutes working. Fast or slow? Did he turn, or didn't he? Does he want his periscope picture of an American carrier—A Souvenir of My Cruise, *komrad*. Look how close I got to the great Americans—or doesn't he?

Alan balanced the probabilities and took his best shot: he tried having Viktor turn in the last stage of his sprint, and he put an L 4000 yards away where the Viktor would turn back toward the battle group—a macho Russian who was going to show these American pricks how vulnerable they really were. Craw accepted this with a nod; the skipper accepted it; John and Erskine back on the carrier, following their moves over the datalink, accepted it. The P-3, still flying and no smarter than before, late on the contour and surly from its lost contact, did not accept it and rained buoys on the IO, on the theory that the sub had gone straight after the sprint.

Craw laid an L-shaped ambush pattern that allowed some margin for error on Alan's part. The minutes ticked away. *Not enough margin if it was a big, big error.* Alan chewed on a knuckle. Craw reached across and took the thermos and poured himself coffee without ever taking his eyes from the screen. Eight minutes. *Where the fuck was he?* Two minutes more, and it was a bath; the Viktor would either hit the line or he was miles away.

Eleven minutes from Craw's last drop, the Viktor drove right through the middle of the ambush. Craw chuckled; the skipper turned and flashed a thumbs-up; Alan cheered. Surfer rocked to music only he could hear.

Craw kept the contact for five hours, playing his big fish with finesse. The carrier, its driver warned by John and Erskine, sprinted away, denying the Viktor his periscope photo for another thirty minutes.

ASW called them. Erskine (or John—it really ought to be John's watch by now) said that he had the TAO standing by. The TAO, that god whom Alan had seen pass before him in the ASW office, spoke direct to the skipper, who opened the channel for everybody to hear.

"A-number-one job, 707. Let's put the icing on the cake. Permission for active prosecution if he comes to periscope depth. We're going to turn right into him. If he wants to pass underneath, let him go, it's a free ocean. If he comes up to take pictures, give him a ping." He meant, *They're not our enemy any longer, so don't shoot—but remind them that we could if we wanted to.*

Alan watched Craw set it up. It was clearly a simulated torpedo run, and the Viktor would know it. As the sub began to rise, Surfer turned cleanly and ran right up the invisible wake at 140 knots. Alan leaned forward, trying to see. Down there the great shape would appear suddenly, as if the water itself were going solid. Then, if they didn't scare the shit out of the sub's captain, the periscope would cut a V and the sub would take the photo—and Alan and Craw and the skipper and Surfer would have lost the game. In the last second.

"Right *now!*" Craw said.

At point-blank range, ten seconds after the Russian sub reached periscope depth, the sonobuoy splashed into the water.

The talk on board the CV later claimed that the sonobuoy actually struck the Viktor, but that was exaggeration. That buoy was at least fifty meters from the sub when it let loose its banshee screech, and seventy-five Russian submariners held their ears and cursed the sky, and the captain shouted, "Dive! Dive!", or whatever unhappy Russians shout, and the Viktor went down like a rock—without its souvenir.

AG 707 one, Viktor zero.

The sun was setting over the Empty Quarter in a spectacular fireball as Surfer took a three wire and taxied to the edge. Alan cleaned up, a little smile on his face and his fingers no longer trembling (much), wiped the grease pencil off his screen, stowed his junk, found a missing pen, and retrieved a very loyal tape from the tunnel. He shut

Christine down, unhooked, stretched, and felt again that he was happy. So was the skipper. The squadron had two more planes on the Viktor now, and the squadron's contact hours were spiraling up.

Surfer shut the plane down and said, loud in the silence, "Sliders for all. Come on, subhunters!"

"Subhunters, hell! Let the P-3 pukes hunt subs. I'll have a slider with my sub*finders*," the skipper barked. He actually said stuff like that. Like a football coach. And they loved it.

Crossing the deck, he put a hand on Alan's back. "You done good, kiddo. I mean, *good*. Anything I can do for you?"

Alan stopped at the catwalk. "Give me a day on the *Roosevelt* before she goes home?" Their carrier had had its tour extended; *Roosevelt* was going home on schedule.

Alan wanted to talk to Peretz.

The hot wind on the flight deck blew their hair and whipped the fabric of their flight suits. The skipper looked at him for a moment. "Let me talk to Nordheim. We may need to find a cover-your-ass reason." He started for the ladder, then turned back, put his fingertips against Alan's chest to stop him. "I want you to think about changing your designator to aircrew. Think about it." He grinned. "Anyhow—today was great. You seem to have got hold of yourself. Run with it."

They went down into the ship.

8

It took him nearly two weeks to get enough free time, plus Nordheim's permission, plus the availability of a COD, to visit the *Roosevelt*. As it was, he barely made it; *Roosevelt* was turning for home three days after, its replacement already transiting Suez. His ostensible excuse was the pickup of classified tactical stuff—viewgraphs, templates, lists, notes, debriefs—that *Roosevelt* would no longer need (and that *Jefferson* would not, either, but they could pull the few good items and dump the rest on the new carrier).

His real reason for going, of course, was to get Peretz's support for a theory about his father's death. He had reached the point where he could think of it without his heart racing, without even the dread of something forgotten and the sudden memory that he would never see the man again. His father was gone. Alan did not believe in ghosts. But out behind him in the deep, too far from the coast of Iran for any land smells ever to come, his father lay encased in his plane like—Creole was right; he was a romantic— a dead warrior in his armor. Alan was increasingly sure that that armor held secrets, and that he had to persuade the Navy to raise it.

The helo winnowed above the *Roosevelt*'s pad and hung there long enough for him to stare into the flight ops bubble, where a yellow jersey was staring at something with binoculars. No air ops were under way; somebody had probably seen a dhow, or a school of flying fish. He felt a wrench of envy: they were going home.

The chopper settled. He began to rehearse his arguments for Peretz. *I've studied the FLIR film of his attempt to refuel*—kept under his rack, in his stateroom, since August; only last week had he been able to face it—*eleven seconds* (and no wave; just his father, head down, trying to get his wounded plane to the basket)—*the missile crippled his aircraft but didn't destroy it. All of the visible damage to his plane*—as seen on the pathetically few seconds Alan had shot on infrared before the film had snapped, but he couldn't say that; it made his case weak—*showed around the leading edge of one wing and forward of the wing on the fuselage. Not a heat-seeking missile, or the damage would be near the engines.*

"So?" Peretz, friendly, supportive, was nonetheless professionally skeptical.

"It wasn't a heat-seeking missile."

"You said that. So?"

Alan went into his be-very-very-patient voice, the one he used on really slow aircrews; Peretz smiled even more. "Heat-seekers are normal. This was abnormal."

Peretz put his feet up, hands behind head. "Okay, I'm a senior investigative administrator. Here you are, outlining a possible case to me. I'm a natural skeptic; that's how I got to be where I am. I'm also aware that there's a budget cut coming, I'm already short on personnel, and my boss doesn't really like me and so is inclined to say no rather than yes. Okay. You tell me that heat-seekers are normal, this wasn't normal. Well, I'm not an aviator, so I'll take your word for now. Okay—so what's so important about abnormal?"

"Only my dad took a missile. Nobody else even saw a missile—I've asked other people on the strike. Zip. So, one missile, and it's not the usual. That's what's important about abnormal. Get it?" Peretz smiled—sadly now—and shook his head. Alan leaned toward him and began to gesture with a half-closed fist. "The Iranians like to adapt, rebuild, scratch-build weapons. That's what this was—some weird, one-time-only, Iranian wet dream."

"Says who?"

Alan shrugged and stood up. "Okay. Bad idea. Thanks for your time."

"Hey, hey—"

"No. I won't waste more of your morning. Bad idea."

"Jesus, you've got short-tempered. We all have, but holy shit, Alan! Come on, siddown. I'm trying to help you. Really." Peretz shoved the chair toward Alan with a foot. "Come on. Make nice, as they say." Peretz was tired too—everybody was tired, what the hell?—but it made him nicer. Maybe knowing that he was leaving the Navy made him nicer, too, some wisdom gained from failure. "Look," the older man said, "if you follow through on this, you're going to have to make a case *in writing* for people whose lives are dedicated to being cynical. You can't do it on hope and spit; you gotta have facts. Give me *facts.*"

Alan sat down, suppressed his irritation. Peretz was right, of course. *The world is full of assholes,* he thought. "Okay. Fact: most of the Iranian air defense network was down; the proof is in my computer tapes. Okay?"

"Okay. Noted."

"Fact: no other missile was fired. Source, my computer tapes, debriefs with other flyers; I can pull them up if need be."

"Good."

"Fact: the Iranians are tinkerers, blue-skiers. Source, intelligence community country briefs."

Peretz made a face. "Weak, but okay. That's Agency psychobabble, say I—in my role as skeptical administrator, I mean."

"Okay. Not fact, but educated guess: I think Mick Craik wasn't squawking IFF that night, but he went anyway—a typical act. We couldn't read his IFF when he tried to gas; I know that could be because it had been knocked out, but I've talked to other guys who said they didn't read him, either, but earlier. One source did a query and it had been bad, or wrong, he didn't remember which. This is where I need some help—it's not too hard to follow up on if you can put me onto the E-2 people who flew the strike from *Roosevelt*."

"This isn't fact."

"Not yet. I'm asking for help to prove it."

Peretz looked at the ceiling. "The kid who was with him and ejected was medevacked to Hamburg next day. Somebody did a debrief and probably filed it; I can get that, but it'll be a couple weeks, anyway." He sniffed his right index finger, that bizarre, slightly unpleasant habit of his. "I can get the E-2 tapes for that night, I guess. They'll piss and moan and say they're stored in the bottom of the boat or they're written over or something. Would you pop for a bottle of Scotch for the guys there? It might ease the ways a little." He was thinking out loud. "Do that on the way home—everybody's running down, have a little happy hit-the-beach in Monaco or someplace, yeah that'll work."

Alan was irritated again. "I want to wrap this up, if I can."

Peretz merely looked bland.

"Can't I get this stuff today?" Alan said.

Peretz smiled. "You know what investigative people need the most of, even more than money? Time. You know why? Because the world is a goddam slow place, and everybody else has better things to do. You know why it's worth waiting for? Because real investigators want to be super-sure. Copper-bottomed, end-of-the-world, bedrock sure. Go-to-court sure. That takes time." He got them both coffee without asking; Alan knew he was slowing him down, forcing him to be patient. When he held the cup out, Peretz said, "Give me your theory and tell me where you're going with it."

So Alan told him: he believed that Mick Craik had been squawking a wrong IFF code. This by itself would be remarkable; normally, if IFF got screwed up, it didn't read wrong; it just didn't read. Then, his had been the only plane shot down. Alan put these things together and suggested (*knew in his heart, believed, wanted to believe*) that Mick Craik's plane had somehow been targeted by the missile on its IFF.

He explained that over the past months he had used spare moments to study his own records of the source of that missile, Site 112, until frustration or priorities had forced him back to other tasks. Site 112 had behaved differently from the other Iranian sites. It had played possum, bided its time, then at the last minute let loose a momentary sweep from an oddball radar and almost instantly taken a HARM. But too late for CDR Craik. And 112 was nearly on the track of the strike—and it hadn't been there ten days before.

"And where is this leading you? What do you want, Alan?"

"I want them to raise my dad's aircraft. To prove that the IFF was set on a different frequency and the damage is not heat-seeker damage."

Peretz doodled with a pencil, made little *tck-tck-tck* sounds with his tongue, and at last said, "And then—then if you prove those things—" He stared hard into Alan's eyes. "You're saying that there's an Iranian agent on the *Roosevelt.*"

Alan nodded. That was the inescapable conclusion he had come to, too.

Peretz blew up. Did Alan know what he was saying? Did he understand what sort of charge that was? Did he really believe ship's security would roll over and play dead while some j.g. with a personal grievance said they'd blown it? What world did Alan think he was living in, anyway?

Alan stared at the floor. It was all Mickey Mouse, he thought. Why couldn't things go straight ahead—and fast?

"Look here, young man." Peretz's voice was suddenly kind. Alan looked up; their eyes met. "I'm getting out of this business. I don't care. But if you push on this, it's going to push back. Other people will resist. That's the way the system works. I'll get you the stuff I said; you build your case with it. Make it airtight. Then write it out, logically and clearly; get your skipper or somebody else with clout to endorse it and send it up the line to NCIS. *But don't expect much.* Understand?"

"But it'll be proven! Then all they have to do is raise the plane."

"That's not the way the world works." Peretz fiddled with the pencil, sipped coffee. He was frowning. "What's your next assignment?"

"I don't know."

Peretz stared, an overdone look of mock astonishment on his plain face. "You don't know! What happened to career planning?"

Alan shrugged.

"Jesus Christ. Look—you need to get yourself someplace good; don't make the mistake I did, thinking you're going to be picked out because of your genius. It doesn't work that way. I was going to say, you need to get yourself closer to the investigative process so you can keep an eye on this business with your dad—oh, yeah, don't look so unhappy; it's going to run into next year, into your next assignment, at least—but you also need to get yourself someplace where you demonstrate other skills, get on a career path. You know what information management is?"

He said he thought he did. He didn't want to hear about careers. Creole was always going on about his career, which he had planned for the next three tours—one in each "int"—electronic, ELINT; communications, COMMINT; human, HUMINT—"learn the ropes, and then run them."

Alan laughed. "I'm six months from rotation, and I don't have a clue what I want in my next tour."

Peretz wagged a finger at him, half teacher, half surrogate parent, both rather exasperated. "There's a collection manager job opening in Norfolk. It's a liaison office with the branches and it'd put you near some strategic thinking. Also, you'd make contact with NCIS and get some sense of how their world works—how to make a case for them. And you could do a little travel, find adventure, glamor, romance—all that good stuff. Interested?"

He wanted to say that the trout fishing was lousy around Norfolk, and he wanted to point out that a major war was imminent and he was a little busy right now, but he didn't dare, and he said, "Sure."

"Lemme send a couple messages. It's really a senior lieutenant position, but you've got credentials and your detailer will feel he owes you one. Understand? No? Here's how it works: war makes careers. You're in a war. The detailer knows he has to push you, because ten or fifteen years from now, the Navy wants itself to be run by people who were in a war. Mm? You don't get it. Never mind—you will." Peretz stared at him. "God, there's a lot your dad didn't teach you." He smiled. "Lucky for you." He whacked Alan's knee. "You're okay as you are, kid. A little naive, but okay. You're not him. No offense, but that's a good thing. Just keep doing what you're doing." He smiled again. "How does a Naval criminal investigation work? *Ver-y slow-ly.*"

A month later, Alan had everything the E-2 people from the *Roosevelt* had to offer. They had sent cassette tapes of all their contacts with Mick Craik the night he died. They had answered Alan's questions: his father had probably gone flying that night with a different IFF code from every other plane on the mission—a code well separated in frequency from the real code. The 161 skipper agreed with Alan and Rafe, too: off the record, it appeared that the Iranians had known where the strike would come ashore.

Still, Alan did not have proof; he had a pile of circumstantial evidence, and a suspicion: Someone, some American on the *Roosevelt*, had betrayed the mission. Someone on the *Roosevelt*, probably the same person, had altered his father's IFF.

Peretz was right. He needed proof—and the proof was lying at the bottom of the Persian Gulf. He needed to approach Naval Investigative Service with a request to raise his father's aircraft. And war was imminent.

He began to write it all out, *ver-y slow-ly.*

When he had a draft, he ran it past Creole. Creole checked his EW logic, his triangulations, his conclusions based on what the *Roosevelt* E-2 had given him. "Not too shabby," he said—high praise from Creole.

"What d'you make of the radar sweep just before the HARM took out Site 112?"

"I don't. It makes no sense, old chap. If things don't make sense, I let them lie there."

"It's got to make sense somehow. Crazy sense, maybe. Iranian sense."

"Suicidal sense, old chap. You turn on a new radar just when the local vicinity's full of HARMs, you're putting a gun to your head."

Which made no sense to Creole, but suddenly made dazzling sense to Alan: the Iranians had blue-skied a missile, and, the moment it was launched, they had made sure that an American HARM would destroy the evidence— Site 112. And the witnesses. He could see some Iranian drudge leaning over a console, waiting with unknowing eagerness to destroy himself: *When you get the signal, turn on the new Chinese radar.* Blam.

He was sure that was the way it had been. But, like so much of the rest of the affair, he couldn't prove it. Yet.

NOVEMBER 27, 1990. 1350 ZULU. LANGLEY, VIRGINIA.

Sally Baranowski read a message on her computer screen and then forwarded it to George Shreed marked "Priority," with her own comment to introduce it: *AB found a Yevgen*

Tzadzik flying Amsterdam–London then London–Brussels, stopover London three hours. Quick work, but double. It looks like the same Tzadzik who flew Rome–Libya the day after our man flew Brussels–Naples. Bingo.

9

The war wasn't on yet, but the old expression "phony war" kept recurring. From Alan's perspective, most of the work needed to be done before the real war started. While aviators slept and talked, Alan planned contingency targets. The complex process of putting together a mission against an enemy facility, a task that easily ate three hundred man-hours during peacetime, became codified and routine. Where once twenty men had spent days creating both a plan and the most elegant viewgraphs to support it with the flag staff, now each plan was reduced to its bare bones. The only aspect of planning that actually grew was their part—intelligence. Now that the plans involved flying against real targets with real defenses, every strike team demanded the latest and most accurate information. The aviators learned to doubt the messages and to question authority, but they also learned that the AIs were their allies in the struggle for ground truth. Alan and Creole continued to massage the numbers and judge the traffic against the BG's own ground truth, but Nordheim had his own team on the chart now.

Alan found a line in his father's black book that made him laugh—one of his father's few comments about intel. *The doughnut is the greatest source of reliable intelligence.* That was all. But he knew what it meant—conning a tray of fresh-made doughnuts from the enlisted mess and prowling the squadron and intel spaces, handing out goodies and getting crumbs of local truth in return. He had heard his father make a joke about it. He laughed again.

"I got a trick they didn't teach at intel school," he said to Creole.

Creole's eyebrows went up and down. "Babes?" he said in a movie-gangster voice.

"Doughnuts. Come on."

The two of them would then roam the darkened ship, dropping off a couple of fresh doughnuts at selected cubicles and modules: ASW, EW, Air Ops, and the TAO, often Subplot and their respective ready rooms, Meteorology. *Hi, Petty Officer Shmucketelly, have a doughnut, hey, how's it hanging? Any word on the Air Tasking Order? The 2100 strike off target yet? Can I pull up a screen? Show me how to look at Bandar Abbas on the radar. What's the weather tomorrow?*

Creole was not a people person, both too private and, inside his joking mask, too elitist, but, once he relaxed, Alan was. Creole was practiced at protective coloration, however; he caught on fast. TAD—Truth According to Doughnuts—became another ground truth, source of new wisdom in mission planning. A little to Alan's surprise, Creole gave Alan credit.

"That was nice of you. I mean it, Creole—I thought getting credit was a big thing with you."

"Never give a sucker an even break, but never fuck a buddy. Right? Anyway, I owed you one for the chart."

"Creole, you have a heart."

"You mean it shows? Aw, shit."

There came a time, however, when a young j.g. could have too much truth, and it led to his and Creole's inflicting hurts on each other. Combat conditions were not kind to uncertainty or guesswork, so Alan took to cutting the crap, as he came to think of debate not founded on hard data; sometimes thoughtless with other AIs, he turned knowledge into a kind of useful arrogance. Nordheim encouraged him; Nordheim, always weary, always harried, liked speed and hard facts, didn't care about manner. His planning sessions were often harsh give-and-takes, Alan often the harshest because he had the most to give.

Then the admiral and the N2—the admiral's intel staffer, a full commander with a very fine idea of his own worth—sat in for a briefing on Iraqi ground forces. The usual stuff was batted around; TAD was much in evidence, Alan very up-to-date on all sorts of trivia, what the more literary Creole called "unconsidered trifles," and everything would have gone off just fine if the N2 hadn't decided to give them a little impromptu chat of his own. And then Alan said—absolutely correctly and utterly ungraciously— "That isn't quite right, if you'll excuse me, sir. I think the Seventieth is about twenty miles closer to the border than that by now, but I don't think you mean the Seventieth, anyway, but the Al Bacquar Battalion, which is really a bunch of little boys and old men with pitchforks." He had missed some sort of signal Nordheim was trying to flash him, for he had gone on as if it was one of his peers to whom he was giving this lesson in intelligence. "This whole idea that the Iraqi army is huge and modern is bullshit. You've got to think of them as a glorified World War II home guard! They're gonna roll up like a cheap carpet. The problem will be keeping up with current data for our own forces; this is postmodern war! We need—" And on and on.

Afterward, Creole had simply shaken his head. "Craik, I knew you were naive, but today's performance takes the pickle-dish. Man, you're lucky they don't keelhaul people anymore."

Alan was bone-weary and therefore irritable. "Everything I said was true."

"What's truth got to do with it? He's a fucking admiral's staffer. You got the political smarts of a pet rock! You shot him down in front of the admiral!"

"He was wrong." Seeing that this argument was unconvincing, the reason why not yet clear to him, he said grumpily, "Lars stood by me."

"You watch the admiral's face?"

"I was busy."

"I saw him be mad at the N2 for being a prick, and just as mad at a certain j.g. for dissing an O5. Okay? I look for this shit. That's what being black is all about. You learn to watch."

"It hasn't got anything to do with being black, for Christ's sake," Alan lashed out. "The world doesn't revolve around being black!"

"My world does." Creole hadn't risen to his anger; instead, he was ironic, superior. "Whites make it that way."

"Oh, tell me about your slave name and how your people built the pyramids!"

It was as if Creole welcomed this, perhaps in a perverse way did; they had discussed race before, but never like this. Perhaps Creole was ready to prove to Alan that he, too, was merely another white. "Your racism's showing," he purred.

"Don't you use that word to me!" Alan shouted. He put his index finger just below Creole's nose. "You're a goddam elitist snob and you know it, and this race bullshit is a cop-out! Get out of my face!"

The extent of Alan's anger shocked Creole, left him for the first time speechless; Alan walked away. His face was red and felt hot. Instantly, he was ashamed of himself. Creole had been right, of course: he had made a fool of himself in front of the admiral, and he had known he was doing so, he had to admit now. He was tired of the tiptoeing that went on around the admiral and his staff, even to the extent of letting falsehood be prized more than truth. The admiral himself was all right, a rather tense man not quite accustomed to his flag but without pretension, nonetheless. His staff were something else: courtiers. Perhaps it was in the nature of the job. He hated that it was in the nature of *his* job to let their positions redefine his truth.

That night, he stopped by Creole's stateroom. The big black man was sitting with his earphones on. He must have detected Alan's shadow, for his head turned. He slowly pushed the earphones up on his head.

"You come to apologize?"

"Yeah."

Creole nodded.

"You were right about the N2. I made an asshole of myself."

Creole nodded. He started to pull the earphones back down, then stopped, not looking at Alan. "I was glad. Thought it would take you down a peg. I'm jealous of you, all the stuff you can do. I'm sorry." He flashed a hesitant grin. "Love is never having to say you're sorry. I guess this can't be love."

He pulled the earphones down and retreated into the music.

DECEMBER 26, 1990. 1915 ZULU. ST. JOHN'S RIVER, FLORIDA.

The bass boat rocked slowly in its own wake, gleaming metallic blue in the hazy winter sunshine. Bonner yanked a handle and the anchor went down; he flipped a switch and the twin 120s stopped their throaty idling and fell silent. Bonner took his beer from the padded holder and drank.

"Well, what d'you think of your old man's boat?"

"I'm impressed. No kidding, I'm really impressed!"

"Really? No shit?"

"Really. God, Dad."

Bonner popped another beer and offered it to his son, but the boy—man, Bonner had to start thinking of him as a man—shook his head and instead touched the padded dash, the windshield, the incredible smoothness of the side.

"Nice?" Bonner said. He had got the reaction he sought,

but he wanted more—more of his son's praise, more of his admiration, more of his desire for what he desired.

"In-credible. Unbelievable. Man."

Donnie was twenty and a good-looking kid, was Bonner's view, although he was prejudiced. Straight-arrow, not a kid who had given him much trouble, unlike his sisters, the hell with them. *Little whores,* he thought. He never lost the bitterness. *Putting out at twelve, pregnant at fifteen, one of them anyway; where were they now? Who cares?* He cared, actually. All that hell of being their father—cops, counselors, psychologists, the Navy's pet family adviser—bullshit! And he had tried. He had really tried. And got—what? *Got shit on. By them and their mother. Fine. Okay. Suits me. Where are they now? In some double-wide with their bastards and their welfare checks and their HIV. Fine. So what?*

"Don't think about it," his son said.

"What, you're a mind reader now?"

"You're thinking about Chris and Barb. You get that look." He was a good kid, a kind kid—too kind, probably, but Bonner loved him for it just then. "That's over, Dad."

"I still get mad."

"Yeah." The boy wriggled in the contoured seat. "Hey, some boat!" He slapped the dash. He was trying to cheer the old man up. A *good* kid. "God, Dad, how do you save the money for a thing like this?"

"I got a deal."

"You and your deals." Donnie chuckled. "You always got a deal."

"It's the way the world works: how many times I gotta tell you that? Everybody's got something going, Donnie."

"Not me." He made a face, an apology.

"Time you grew up."

"Well—" Donnie shrugged. He pulled the bill of his baseball cap low over his eyes. "I'm no good at that stuff. Donnie the Nerd."

"You could be. You and me, we could do things—you know, together. I could teach you."

The boy grinned at him. "Remember when you tried to teach me to pitch?"

"Well, this'd be different from pitching. This'd be—intellectual. Right? You gotta use your brain to get by in the world, not your muscle. We could be in business together, you and me. Hey?"

"Be great."

"Bonner and Donnie? Bonner and Son? Hey?"

Donnie grinned again, the grin perfectly genuine, maybe pumped up by the day and the boat, but still an honest expression of affection. "Be great, Dad. You're owed something. No, really—I know life has kind of dumped on you. Mom—the girls—"

Bonner waved a hand. He didn't want to hear about that, he meant; that was history, he meant. He belched into the back of a hand and reached for another beer. "Merry Christmas," he said. He meant it, but it came out with a kind of sneer, like so much of what he said. He tried to change the subject. "How's Sheila?"

"Fine. Fine."

"What's that mean?"

"She's fine, Dad. We're a little—" He rocked one hand back and forth. "It'll be okay."

"That's what I used to say. Then the bitch ran off with Chief Petty Officer Milton Marengo, USN." He shouldn't have said that. Donnie didn't like to hear him talk about his mother that way, even though it was true. Bonner decided he was a little drunk. What the hell, it was Christmas. He punched Donnie's thigh. "Hey! How about the business idea. Bonner and Son. You buy it?"

"Sure, great. What're we gonna sell, empty beer cans?" Smiling, but it was his way of saying the old man was drinking too much.

Bonner belched again and tasted heartburn. It was because he was approaching the moment, the subject, like driving to the top of a hill where there's a drop-off on the other side. His heart began to hammer. He couldn't face it yet; he veered off. "Did I show you how the autobailer works?"

"Yeah. Great."

Bonner finished the beer in a long, head-back guzzle, and carefully put the empty in a plastic trash sack that swung in a special holder next to him. Donnie was right; there were a lot of cans in there. Well, it was Christmas. "I don't throw the cans in the river. Pollution," he said.

"You told me, Dad."

"I'm telling you again. So, I'm a little happy. It's Christmas! Loosen up, Donnie. Christ. It's like I'm the kid and you're the old man. It's that bitch you married, isn't it? I told you you were too young. The same mistake I made. How many of your old man's mistakes you gonna make? She doing dope? I took one look at her, at that shithouse she grew up in—Christ, talk about your white trash—I was gonna say something, where was I?"

"Give it a rest, okay, Dad?"

Bonner heard the seriousness in that—a man talking, not a boy. It hurt. "I'm sorry."

"No reason to be. You're my father, you've got—a right—to say anything. But, just now—Sheila and me—"

"Your old man's an asshole. I'm sorry, Donnie." Bonner took a tray out of his tackle box and found the pint bottle down there. "Wild Turkey! Christmas bourbon, the best. Okay? Come on, a Christmas toast. Donnie? A toast— Bonner and Son?"

"You're drinking kind of a lot, Dad."

"It's Christmas! Tell you what, you drive the boat home. Designated driver. Okay? Merry Christmas." Bonner tilted the bottle and drank off a quarter of it and passed it to his son. Donnie shook his head, smiling, then gave a little laugh, lifted the bottle an inch as a toast, and drank. He grinned, and his eyebrows went up and down.

"I got something I want to talk to you about," Bonner said. "Out here—we're alone, private—just you and me." He took the bottle back and drank and held it against his chest, looking at the haze and the flat water, the trees along the bank a faded green in the thin sunshine. "I want to tell you where I get the money from. But you gotta promise to keep it to yourself. Secret. Promise?"

"Sure." And he meant it, a straight-arrow kid with a troubled marriage, decent, confused.

"I'm not an honest man, Donnie." He waited. He looked aside at his son. "You already knew that, right?"

"Well— Jeez, that's a little strong, Dad. You cut some corners, I know."

"I got something going. Long-term. Good money. I want you to come in with me." Bonner drank again and again held the bottle, warm from his touch and the sun, against his chest. His heart was pounding and seemed to rise in a crescendo, as if it meant to explode. He looked over the lifeless water at a dead tree near the bank, and a water turkey motionless on the top. He tried to keep the panic out of his voice. "You do things in this life you know aren't right. You do them to get back, to make up for other things. It's the money, sure. Basically, it's the money. But the money is the way out of a hole, or the way of getting back. When your mother ran out on me, what I worried about, I mean stayed awake nights and sweated about, went crazy over is the truth of it, was money—how was I going to afford somebody to take care of kids, run things when I was at sea, what they call make a home, all that. This isn't an excuse. I just mean it's what my mind was going through. Money, see? So—" Bonner squinted at the bird. It never moved. His heart seemed to fill his whole body: it was wanting to convince his son, to make him understand, to make him part of it. "Now, it's just the money. It's my scam. General Motors has a scam, McDonald's has a scam, the U.S. government has a scam. My scam is a little piece of shit that doesn't even show up under a microscope compared to what the big guys are getting away with. It's nothing. Well, it's something. You'd say it's something. I know you. You're a straight-arrow kid, naive, you don't get it. But—you're the best—" He had lost the thread. What was it? The water turkey had gone, taken off when he wasn't looking, as if he had blinked and it had flown and carried his line of thought with it. He drank and saw how low the bottle was and passed it over and said, "Finish it," but the younger man waved it away. Bonner finished it and dropped the bottle into the trash sack.

"I work for a guy who sells things to other countries. I sell him what are called secrets." He turned his reddened eyes to his son. "I want you to get in it with me. It'd mean the world to me, Donnie. You're all I got. See?" Tears formed in his eyes. *"Please."*

10

That was the winter he gave up kid stuff, Alan would say
afterward. He learned that failure was a better teacher than
success, although success was more fun. He learned what
it was like to have the responsibility of other people—three
intel ratings, at first only nominally his but then really so—
not only their work but also their private grievances and
failings. He learned to work, to budget time, to accept
boredom and loneliness, to find pleasure in small and surprising things—the soft air of the fantail at night; phos-
phorescence and moonwake; the surge of the ship; the cool
smoothness of a clean sheet against hot skin.

War bore very little resemblance to his expectations. It
was either very far away or very close, never in good perspective; vital and dramatic moments passed him by while
he read Air Tasking Orders or helped plan raids on targets;
overall strategy and the big picture vanished as he flew
bombing missions and got shot at. He was two people,
with two wars. Creole called him the Amazing Alternative-
Universe Man. Alan and Creole had made it up, and they
were closer after that, but in the way men are, not boys,

the friendship touched by the inevitable sadness of self-knowledge.

He was in Mission Planning three days after the real shooting started when the squadron ops officer stuck his head in and shouted, "Craik!"

"Sir."

"You're on the flight schedule. 1300."

Alan glanced at his watch. Two hours. He was working on a target list revision. "We're up to our ass here, sir. Can I pass on this one?" It hurt to say that; he hadn't flown in days.

"Negative. Narc's sick. Rafe wants to cruise for those goddam Iraqi missile boats—make sure you're current."

He was gone.

Alan looked at his watch again, rubbed his eyes, and explained the change to Nordheim, who winced and muttered something about *just what I needed.* "Okay, let Ensign Cohen earn his keep. Show him where you left off and get out of here."

Ensign Cohen was a late addition to the AIs, a replacement for an experienced j.g. who had had an emergency; without a clue, basically a nice young man without too much brain, Cohen had so far been carried by Alan and Creole and another AI. Not this time, however. "You got it," Alan said. "It's due at 1330. Lars likes to review it first, so give him fifteen minutes. Don't hit Shift F7 or you'll wipe the lot. Got it?"

"Jesus. Look, I'm not too—"

"Neither am I. Real world, guy. See you."

His mind was already on the Iraqi missile-patrol boat. These were usually targets of opportunity but in the last several days a more pressing target as they had become problems for people working the inshore islands and the Kuwait landing zones. Rafe would go after it with a Harpoon, Alan knew. Okay; he could do that. He had ridden along on enough practice runs; hell, one crew he flew with did a practice Harpoon shoot every time they went up, even on a night tanker, if they could arrange for simulator plugs.

And Alan had played with the Harpoon simulator in the back of the ready room for hours; it made a pretty good game, and it meant that he could take a Block 1 Charlie through all the little wickets of waypoint planning and shooting in his sleep. *Been there, done that.* Was he getting cocky? *Yes, you bet your ass.* He was also scared.

He looked in on several stations, noted that the target was a big Thornycraft PG and pulled out a Jane's, then did a freehand sketch of what it ought to look like on ISAR. He checked his watch. Time for a second breakfast before prebrief.

"Flyin today, Mr. Craik?" Carson asked. Carson was an ex-admiral's cook who ran the Dirty Shirt like a gourmet greasy spoon.

"I only get to wear this fashionable garage-mechanic suit when I actually fly, unlike some aviators I could mention," with a nod to Rafe, who was just entering the line, "who haven't been seen in khakis since we left Jax. Hey, Rafe, how's it going?"

"What you want, Mr. Rafe?" Clearly, Carson and Rafe got along, which seemed unfair to anybody who had heard Rafe's repertoire of nigger jokes and knew how Carson—a self-described Watts badass—felt about such things. "Waffles, sir?"

"I just eat your food, Jumper, I don't ask it questions. Hey, Spy, the Jumpin' cook here wants to come to the squadron for his next tour. Despite what this says about his mental capacity, I think we could build a pretty mean B-ball team on him and Wilson. What do you say?"

Alan could have said what Creole had said to him, that basketball was the "they sure got rhythm" of the 1990s, but he put on his frat-house face and said, "For what, Rafe? Get Jacksonville an NBA franchise? Who do you play?"

"I just want to play. I'm getting fat."

"That's just age. And Carson's food."

"Fuck you, Spy."

Alan sat down and Rafe joined him, a rare event.

"Ready for today, Spy?"

"Sure."

"How ready?"

"I know where the Iraqis are, I've read the message traffic, I know how to shoot, and I plan to use the same lo-lo-pop-shoot profile that you used in your mission-commander test."

"How long a stick does this missile boat have?"

"About twenty-five miles. Give it plenty of room, though: find them at one-fifty, shoot at forty-five."

"As usual, Spy, you *sound* like you know what you're talking about. I hope you do, because these fuckers shoot back." Rafe actually smiled. "You want to ride in front?"

"I know the rules."

"Fuck the rules, I'm mission commander now. I don't want you in front on the cat; I don't want to run the checklist alone today. So when we get off and level, we'll switch you for Surfer."

"What's the matter with Narc?"

"Head cold, the wimp. No, forget I said that. I saw a guy blow a sinus, grossest thing I ever saw. Cured me for life of lying to flight surgeons."

"I'd like to stay in back until I lock my boat up on ISAR. I did a mock-up of how he'll look."

Rafe looked at him with his head back at a curious angle. "Good call." He stood. "See you in the ready room."

Alan moved through the boat quickly, checking in each of the combat spaces for signs of his target. In EW he got the freqs on the Iraqi's surface-search and air-search radars; in the Anti-Surface Module he got its last location, its bearing from the ship, and its course and speed. He checked that info in Subplot to make sure that ASUW were tracking the right ship. They weren't. The Anti-Surface watch officer was a squadron-mate, and Alan hopped back and forth between ASUW and Subplot until the problem was resolved. When the TAO saw the puck jump on his big central screen, he flashed out "What's up on JOTS? Where did our allies go?" A Subplot petty officer stepped in, muttered something about operator error, and promised the TAO that the new plot was correct. The TAO looked mollified, and the watch officer, sweating slightly over in the ASUW module, raised his eyes to heaven and gave Alan an okay sign as he left the space.

The ready room was mostly deserted. The high-backed mock ejection seats stood in neat, plastic-covered rows, the squadron emblem embroidered in silk on a silk flag at the front of the room. The skipper was invisible behind his seat back up there near the flag. He punched out some twisted and devious "what if?" questions at Alan and Rafe. Alan stumbled once, but Rafe was no help, so Alan flipped through his abbreviated stack of kneeboard cards, found a possible answer, gave it. Silence fell for a moment. The skipper leaped from his chair, walked over to the little huddle in the back of the ready room; Alan, Rafe, Surfer, and Senior Chief Craw, who seemed to fly whenever Alan did. Craw was asleep. The skipper leaned over Alan's seat back and said, "Good brief. Don't fuck up," and marched out of the room.

Alan had hoped to beat Rafe to the plane, but whatever his other failings, Rafe was a conscientious pilot. Alan did his walkaround in the opposite direction from Rafe's, then clambered under the airframe to count the chaff and flare canisters; Rafe nodded his approval. Alan ached to notice something really useful as he prowled under the struts of the landing gear and duckwalked back along the underside of the fuselage, but AG 710 appeared as clean and bright as a new coin. This was one of his rare flights in an aircraft other than Christine—a pleasure because 710 was a sweet plane with a solid, workhorse reputation.

He sat, bored and sleepy, until Craw nudged him as the plane began to taxi. They rolled straight on the cat, hooked in, crouched, and leaped; 710 was light, as S-3s go, and responded cleanly off the deck, Aside from the usual "hoover" noises, she acted like a much prettier plane.

To a TACCO, 710 seemed smarter than Christine; the

screens were crisper; even the smell seemed different. Alan worked the toggle, read the numbers, and announced that he had a good load. He began setting up a rough map, feeding the datalink numbers, and feeding data; then he set up a routine for the ESM suite to start looking for the parameters associated with the Thornycraft. This was the wrinkle that he had not briefed and had no intention of mentioning, his own private challenge. He intended to locate and target the Iraqi on ESM (passive radar detection) and do one single-sweep, active-radar check just before Harpoon launch to increase surprise and lower the possibility of a response.

When they were a hundred and twenty miles out, he requested that Rafe fly a descending spiral to a thousand feet. A little below a thousand, Alan found the duct he had expected and started getting ESM cuts on the Iraqi radars, both air-search and surface-search. After five minutes, he requested that Rafe go sixty miles north, and Rafe obligingly pointed the plane that way. This all made perfect sense to Rafe, first because he felt they should maneuver for a broadside shot, and second because he expected that the Spy would try to do the whole thing on ESM, which, if it worked (and give the Spy his due, he was a whiz at ESM), would be a nasty surprise for the Iraqis and a feather in everyone's cap.

After another quarter hour, Alan had numerous cuts and a solid plot on the screen with a range, a bearing, and a course and speed. They were still a hundred and twenty miles out from the target. Alan got out his kneeboard, looked up the mast height of the Iraqi, calculated his radar horizon for an aircraft of a given altitude, and asked Rafe to take them up to 1250 feet. Rafe laughed.

"Not 1247, Spy?" but he did his bit. As soon as Rafe called the altitude, Alan did a single sweep with the radar. He found four banana-shaped blips about a mile apart under his cursor. He chose the largest, switched to image mode, and generated another single sweep, then asked Rafe to dive to five hundred feet and head south.

"South? That's a bow shot, Spy. Let's take it broadside. Higher odds of a center-of-mass hit if there's more mass visible."

"Point taken, Rafe, but I'll put in a waypoint to handle that, and it makes us all the spookier."

"Roger" was Rafe's only comment. A glance suggested that the tilt of Rafe's head might be a little grim.

Alan went back to the screen and brought up the results of his second sweep. Senior Chief Craw gave him an almost imperceptible nod and settled back in his seat. He had the image up on his screen. On Alan's it looked good; slightly different from his sketch, but the right length and not a tanker or a cruise ship. In fact, it was a damn good picture. He passed it to Surfer in the front seat, who came up on the intercom and said, "Nice."

Alan set up the shot. Rafe flew to the launch point. For the first and last time, Alan lifted the Lucite cover on the big WEAPONS RELEASE switch.

"No sim plugs, Rafe?" He was mostly joking.

Rafe actually looked left and right. He nodded.

Alan pressed the button and called, "Missile away," and Rafe popped briefly before descending below five hundred feet. Alan watched the water, seemingly only a few yards away. He tried not to think of the Iraqi Thornycraft, the people.

"Hit," came a message from the *Jefferson* over the datalink.

"Sonofabitch." Rafe was grinning at him. "You got yourself one. Goddam, Spy, you come a long way."

To his surprise, there were women in the Dirty Shirt. Two of them, in fact. They wore flight suits, both attractive, both pilots. Probably brought a helo out from Bahrain or Dubai, he thought. The blonde was an LCDR, the brunette an LT. Rafe looked them over frankly, took his slider and fries, and sat across from them as if he were taking his seat at a ball game. Alan joined the trio more slowly.

The women didn't appear talkative. In fact, the LCDR looked withdrawn, perhaps angry, certainly pale. Rafe was attempting to tease the other woman about life in Bahrain; she mostly looked bored and murmured to the LCDR. Alan, too, was quiet. He really wanted to talk to Rafe about the flight, but that was history. Rafe had a short attention span; the women were now.

Alan thought about women. *Women.* How long since he had been this close to one? *Sexual harassment.* Just looking.

The LCDR put her forehead on the cool plastic of the wardroom table.

Alan meant to be helpful. He meant to make a connection. He was still wired from the flight. "Is your friend okay?" he said. It was a stupid question, but innocently meant. It was not innocently taken.

"No, j.g., I feel like shit, okay?" The lieutenant commander answered for herself without lifting her head from the table. "My head is spinning, I want to barf, my mouth is full of salt, and my life sucks. Fucking food."

Alan spoke without malice but without caution. "You're seasick, ma'am."

Rafe let out a belly laugh. Rafe went on laughing while the LCDR glared at both of them. The younger woman scowled.

"Nice shot, asshole, but I'm pretty sure Clare has about six thousand more hours than—wait—fuck, are you a fucking *groundpounder?*" Alan thought she might actually hit him. He was thinking about the consequences of that—officers got into a lot of trouble for hitting each other, especially in the wardroom; but this one was a woman; she could claim harassment; the court-martial would say— "Get out of our face!" the lieutenant snarled at him. She hated him. "Clear out and leave us alone. You groundpounding asshole!" She had a slightly rough voice, as if she had spent a good part of her life shouting; and even as he felt himself flush and heard himself start to stammer some sort of apology, he knew he'd heard the voice before, and he remembered—the COD pilot that day a million years ago when he'd returned to the carrier from Florida. She'd seemed so nice then. What a tiger!

"And don't make wiseass seasick jokes to somebody who happens to be female, asshole. The joke might be on you."

"Look, lieutenant, uh, lady, whatever. Your friend *is* seasick. Everybody gets seasick on the boat."

"Everybody female, you mean, right? I'm so sick of you guys and your macho shit I could be sick, myself, right in your slider."

The lieutenant commander waved a hand, her head still down. "Just get the fuck out of our sight." Alan looked at Rafe. Rafe opened his mouth for another laugh. The lieutenant commander raised her head far enough to look at him and say, "If you make one sound, I'll report you for harassment and—and—" She put her head down again. "Conduct unbecoming. Oh, gross. Oh—" She got up and headed for the door, the back of a hand pressed to her mouth.

Lying in his bunk that night, he leafed through his dad's black book, found what he was looking for: *Women can't be friends. They can't be friends with each other and they can't be friends with us. You always have to have the romance shit or the sex shit.* He wondered if his father would have done better with the seasick LCDR than he had. Or, just conceivably, worse?

JANUARY 21, 1991. 1535 ZULU. KENSINGTON, MARYLAND.

The committee officially called Joint Tasking and Interchange Review, known in the community as Jitter from its acronym, met usually in the basement of this building in a Washington suburb. Slapped up in Washington's expansion of the 1970s, the structure looked like a cheap motel extended upward for seven stories, its oxidized aluminum façade the color of lead and now depressingly dated. The building correctly represented the committee's lack of status.

Sally Baranowski chaired. She sat on thirteen committees, chaired four of them; this was the least important. It was, nevertheless, a useful place to dump low-level information into an interagency puddle so that the appearance of cooperation could be maintained. (*Well, God, we copied you guys on this two years ago at a Jitter meeting; here's the minutes!*)

They had been at it for two hours. Her head ached. She had skipped breakfast to get here from her house in Virginia; even so, she had been late. One of the FBI men was droning on and on about international operations. The female member from State was asleep. An Air Force major was rolling his eyes and making faces at his opposite number from the Army. When the FBI bore paused, Sally jumped in.

"Jack, could we take the rest as read? Could you circulate a printed version? I've still got four items to get through. I'm really sorry. Okay?"

Jack said he would just summarize, then, and went right back to the same plodding discussion of trivia. She hated to stop him again. That was the point of this committee, after all—to let each agency feel it had made a gesture, however empty, toward sharing information. This was where good little bureaucrats covered their bosses' asses. Still, she was about to risk insulting him—suffering bores gladly has its limits, even in government—when abruptly he stopped, folded his papers, and said that that was it, but he'd be happy to go over any of it again if they wanted.

"Discussion?" she said; and, before anybody could speak, "No discussion. Okay, agenda item fourteen. This is my agency's." She looked around. People were rubbing their eyes, checking watches. The end was in sight.

"I've inserted a page in each standalone concerning a former Russian officer who's believed to have gone over to another government. This is purely for information, no action. No details available and questions are not appropriate at this time. One point of information, please flag it, we have reason to believe this officer had or has an American asset, possibly located in London, England, or Naples, Italy. Please keep this page current by informing the addressees on the attached list if you get anything relevant. Yes, Bernie?"

A surprisingly young-looking Navy lieutenant commander was waving a pen as a means of attracting attention. "The Navy's got a lot of personnel in and around Naples, needless to say. You got any reason to believe this so-called asset is military?"

Before she could answer, the Air Force major was saying that Shit, Bernie, so had they, and he was starting to enumerate Air Force entities within five hundred miles of Naples when she said, rolling right over his voice with her own, which could be remarkably powerful when needed, "We have no reason to believe the asset is military and no reason to believe it is not. We have an ascription and two locations and that is all. Please, no more questions, because I do not have answers."

The Army officer growled, "In other words, Same Old Shit: you ain't got nuthin', so you're happy to share it with us. Thank you, thank you, thank you."

She thought of making nasty noises but suppressed the notion. Jitter existed to spread sweetness and light—or sweetness and darkness, at least.

"Item fifteen? NIS, New Policy on Interaction with Civilian Police, Azerbaijan and Kazakhstan." They all had the same thought: *Get a life!*

JANUARY 27, 1991. 1300 ZULU.
60 KM NORTHWEST OF TEHRAN, IRAN.

Franci looked through the eyepiece with the incomprehension of fatigue. He had painstakingly opened the envelope; he had avoided touching the pages of the typed letter. With time, effort, and a little luck, he had used the cheap Chinese two-power loupe to locate the tiny raised dot masquerading as a period. Franci worked the tiny dot clear of the paper's surface. He transferred it to a slide and kept it in place with a dot of oil. He placed the slide in a battered microscope marked "Bausch and Lomb, Rochester, New York." From the days when the Great Satan had been the Great Ally.

Franci had thought himself saved from the bleak life of a cripple when the Russian had asked him to join his spy service. Franci had imagined a gleaming, highly technical facility with sliding automatic doors and the quiet, Western brush of air-conditioning. He had imagined working directly with the Russian, whom he admired.

None of that had come true. First, he had received an excellent short course of physiotherapy that had enormously improved his ability to function with his replacement leg. He had also received a first-class artificial leg of Japanese manufacture. But the dream had ended when he was faced with the reality of the training camp. They had taught him to shoot a pistol, and then they had made it clear that he would never be issued with a pistol. They had taught him map-reading and tactics of escape and evasion, and then admitted that a man with one leg would neither escape nor evade. Now this idiocy with the microdot. Franci was pretty sure that the microdot had been in use during the First World War, possibly in the Second, certainly not now.

He stared through the microscope and began copying the long columns of numbers. They were in Arabic, like, but not truly like, the Western digits. Franci noted with resignation that the fictional American general in this exercise wrote in fairly fluent English about his affair with another officer's wife but wrote code in Arabic.

At the end of an hour, Franci had copied all of the numbers and checked them against the slide. Then he compared them to his copy of the Koran. Two hours later, he had the supposed time of launch of a dastardly missile strike against Tehran, no doubt using missiles from the 1940s.

Franci pulled a slip of paper from his pocket—the answer to the test, given him by the instructor. He suspected that neither the fiery young Saudi to his left nor the two very dark Sudanese in front of him had been given the paper. It was clear to him that the training camp was simply one of those experiences that were meant to convince him of his own worth, not to teach him much. In other words, the Russian had felt sorry for him.

11

MARCH 28, 1991. 1700 ZULU. DUBAI, UNITED ARAB EMIRATES.

The war ended; Kuwait was liberated; medals were handed out by the fistful; life for the AIs became boring again. After learning to do all their peacetime duties and get in sixteen hours of strike planning every day, they suddenly had too much time. Alan went on making doughnut runs alone, unable yet to let go of the paradoxical wartime high of stress and little sleep. Creole, basically a more sensible man, made up for lost rack time.

Saw the movie Patton, his father had written in the black book. *"God forgive me but I love war so."* Do I really love war? His father had never answered that question for himself, apparently; Alan, now with his own small war behind him—knowing terror, exhilaration, deep weariness, the guilt and joy of dealing death—wrote, *Not war, but ourselves in war, the men we become. A kind of personal best.* He thanked God he was not an infantryman.

They made a port call at Dubai, their last before going home. That was all most of them wanted, to go home. He wanted something more.

Even from the ship, anchored almost a mile from the long, golden peninsula of the city and its surprisingly modern skyline, he believed he could smell the Orient. It was a rich smell, laden with the sea but utterly different from the deep water where the carrier had lived. The smell had brought him to the giant picture window of elevator number two on the hangar deck. Neatly framed by the armored doors, the whole expanse of the city lay there, from the modern port that appeared to be paved with neatly parked automobiles to the distant rise of a Western-style hotel. A land breeze brought that odor of spice and fish, car exhaust and Eastern cooking. He inhaled it, the sailor smelling port.

He had two days of liberty and he meant to make the most of his first taste of Arabia after four months at sea. He found Creole still in bed, puffy-eyed. After hearing Alan's enthusiastic description of the Dubai skyline, he said, "Man, you're crazy! We're going home!"

"I want something more."

Creole stared.

Alan rode ashore in a private ferry, with two decks, and his obvious "officer" civilian clothes earned him a spot on the upper deck, forward, where he could watch the early-afternoon sun beat like a hammer on the golden city. They raced past a dhow, fully laden, her high sides working visibly, her sail out to catch the breeze. Two men, naked to the waist save for loosely wound, flapping headcloths, hauled at a line. A black man stood at the tiller. They might have sailed from Iran or Oman or Pakistan or Kenya, somewhere far down the trade winds that bound the old Islamic sea empire together.

His heart lifted. They might have sailed from another time entirely, but they were sailors, just as much as those who went down to the sea in nuclear aircraft carriers. *This is what I came for.*

Alan waved; the black man at the tiller waved back.

The ferry landed him a hundred yards from a British frigate tied up pier-side. He walked down a short accommodation ladder, and the reality of the heat hit him, the sun threatening to crush him. He moved quickly through security, took a taxi to a "safe," Navy-approved Western hotel, and for ten dollars got the concierge to tell him what to do next. The concierge, a somewhat superior Oriental gentleman with a towering British accent, made a determined effort to size up his customer and asked him if he liked a little adventure. Alan allowed that he did. The concierge suggested the souk. *The souk!* "Souk" was a ten-dollar word, surely; he dropped his luggage and left the air-conditioned West for the heart of the Middle East: the market.

Two hours of searching took him to every corner of the souk, searching, searching for that *something*—a sign? An end? Something that would say, *The voyage is over; you were here; you once sailed the sea.* He passed perfumes, spices, vegetables, meat, cameras; every gadget of the decadent West, posters of Madonna, pirated cassette tapes from Singapore and pirated computer programs from Hong Kong. Veiled women walked arm in arm; children in Western clothes ambled freely through the press of bodies; men argued in high-pitched voices over the price of a sheep's head or a pound of gold.

At last, in a tiny, crooked alley off the main thoroughfare, Alan found the shop he had been seeking. He had not known he had been seeking it; he only knew he recognized it when he saw it. The window was dusty, crammed. Above the littered counter hung a huge, heavy, cross-hilted sword.

He entered and stood by the heavily carved wooden counter, which appeared to be as old as the sword. He was standing with his back to the door, staring about, asking himself, *What? Which thing?,* when the door was thrown open behind him with such force that it bounced against the stone wall.

Alan whirled and saw a tall man wrapped in black and gray, one corner of a head scarf pulled over his face. Only his eyes showed, old, fierce. He was magnificent, and he stank. In later years when he would tell the story he would always say, *He was like Sean Connery rolled in goatshit.*

The figure ignored him. He walked to the counter and crashed something on it. The thing rang as it bounced, and Alan, wincing at the violence of that sound, saw that it was a sword, the blade broken near the hilt. The figure did not speak. One hand pointed imperiously at the sword above the counter. The wrinkled shopkeeper jumped and placed the good sword on the counter next to its broken twin. The gaunt figure lifted it, inspected its blade, then slammed it home in the scabbard by his side. One hand reached into his robe and produced coins, threw them on the counter.

Only then did the man look at Alan, and the eyes seemed to smile; a gentle inclination of the head, almost imperceptible—saying what? We have both been in war?—and he was gone.

On the counter were two large gold coins and some silver. None was currently legal tender anywhere in the world—a krugerrand and a worn British sovereign. One of the silver coins was so worn its pattern was indecipherable. Alan covered it and the hilt of the broken sword with his hand and looked the shopkeeper in the eye and saw that, remarkably, the old man was trembling.

"Bedouin," the shopkeeper stammered. He tried to smile, then shrugged. "Bedouin," almost to himself, as a frightened man might say, *A ghost.* Bedouin—the savage sailor of the ocean of sand.

Alan placed ten American dollars on the counter, took the coin and the hilt, and left the old man salaaming behind him. The hilt was still warm from the Bedouin's hand.

Alan clenched the coin in his fist. The sun was just beginning to set, gilding the streets of the city. He had touched something, been touched by something. Had been allowed to look through a windowless wall.

Now more, he thought. *More.* He continued to walk until he found an old, walled section he had passed earlier. This, too, had shops inside; he could see them. It was guarded, however, by military sentries with machine pistols.

"Can I go in here?"

The sentry hesitated. Then, "Yuus, syur."

An Arabian fairy tale: tiny lights, mostly candle lanterns, lit displays of richness; piles of black and colored silk; perfumes; toys, lingerie. In the dark, the heavy scent of musk. Everyone, absolutely everyone but Alan and a few children, was swathed in black. He poked from stall to stall, captivated. Again and again, however, when something interested him, he could not catch the attention of the stallkeeper. Finally, he realized he was being followed by a crowd of veiled, giggling, teenaged girls. He stopped at the richest of the stalls, a wide expanse under a fringed black silk awning that looked as if its wares had only a moment before spilled off Ali Baba's camels. He picked up several items, finally located a magnificent silk scarf whose colors changed as he moved it in the candlelight. He tried to get the attention of the merchant, who, like the others here, ignored him.

A hand fell lightly on his shoulder.

"He won't sell to you, Lieutenant Craik."

It was the female pilot from the boat. The one who looked great in the flight suit. The one who had read him out.

"This is the women's souk, Lieutenant."

He felt himself go red, was instantly grateful for the darkness. He began to babble: "Hey, I owe you an apology—God, I was such— This was really stupid, of course it's the women's souk, I just didn't— Call me Alan."

"I'm Rose. It's really beautiful!" The merchant now showed interest, even enthusiasm.

"Women's souk, by God."

"Women come here so that no man sees them. You got in because you're foreign, I guess."

Alan looked at her and smiled. It was a good smile; not brash, just there. "Can I explain about what happened on the boat?"

"You were right, she was seasick. I thought it was, you know, aviator b.s. Although you didn't seem the type."

They were still squatting in front of the booth. A boy came with tea. The merchant, sensing that all this might be a prelude to business, smiled. Alan took a cup and handed it to her. She was very beautiful, there in the candlelight with the air full of perfume and his scarf in her lap. He showed her the sword hilt, and she understood.

"You want the scarf?" she said. "I've got to go soon."

Alan wanted to say *Don't go,* but instead nodded and handed her a wad of Dubai cash. She laughed. "I've been here six months. Watch." There was some haggling, very polite at first, then strident. Mostly it was in Arabic, although Rose spoke in English with occasional Arabic and a few Italian words, and some very Italian gestures; the merchant threw in a little French just to show his willingness. Alan was entranced. The merchant and Rose knew each other, was his impression; there was a certain amount of theatricalizing, some laughter from her. Finally the man bowed; Rose smiled widely, and even Alan bowed.

"Nine dollars U.S. Not bad! About a hundred, stateside." She handed him the scarf. He caught her fingers.

"Do you really have to go?"

"If I hurry, I can just get a shower before a brief."

"No time even for coffee?"

"I'm sorry." And she did sound sorry.

"If you've been here six months, you must be about to rotate." They walked out of the souk.

"Three weeks. Then thirty days' leave, and—I'm hoping."

"I rotate in twenty-nine—not that I'm counting."

She smiled and stuck out her hand. This was where they parted, she meant. "Somebody told me about your father. I'm sorry. My bird brought you back to the boat after the funeral, maybe you don't remember? I recognized you when my friend was sick, but it didn't seem quite the time to mention it."

"I recognized you, too." He grasped her hand, then

kissed her on the cheek. It hadn't been premeditated. She kissed the air near his cheek and laughed in her throat.

"Could I have your leave phone number?" There, not so hard.

She looked at him, measuring, probably thinking of all the people who had asked for her number in six months. "Got a pen?"

A minute later, she was gone. *Rose. The rose and the sword.* He had got what he had come ashore for. And more?

He headed toward the lights of the western section, where his friends were, and left the darkness behind him.

His war was over.

12

Leaving the squadron defined a period of his life, not immediately perceived because, despite two parties and many
individual goodbyes, there was no real end, only a day
when all the paper-signing was done and he had no job to
go to. He took a month's leave, which blurred the margin
between the old and new. The skipper called him in the
day before he was to leave and said warming things, things
Alan was sure he meant. "Stay in touch!" were his final
words—the words many had spoken—and he said he
would, meant what he said; but in two weeks, the outlines
of those people were dimming. Yet he missed them. *Really*
missed them.

He spent a few days with his mother and stepfather and
found them almost strangers, two pleasant, baffled people
who seemed not to understand that he now had his own
tastes and his own ideas. Unaware, they kept telling him
what to do; he left earlier than he had intended. He spent
an evening with Peretz, now a civilian trying to finish a
doctoral dissertation; he seemed too cheerful, said he was
confident he would "knock it in a couple more months."

His wife was loud and bossy, big, outspoken. Behind her jokes was anxiety, Alan thought. After dinner, Peretz told his wife to "go do female things, wash the dishes or something; this is guy stuff," clearly a joke; she roared at him and bellowed with laughter. But she left them alone.

"So," Peretz said when they had settled in his living room. "Anything new?" He didn't have to say that he meant Mick Craik's death.

Alan laughed, a bad, cynic's laugh. "I wrote up my facts and my proof and my conclusions, and I got some endorsements, and I sent it up the line, and Admiral Dickhead Fuckface said, 'Insufficient evidence. Request to raise Commander Craik's aircraft denied.' You were right."

Peretz looked embarrassed. He shook his head, said he was sorry. They both looked for another subject. "You get that job in information management at Norfolk?"

But Alan returned to the old subject. "I wish my dad was buried someplace. I never understood visiting graves. Now I wish I could. My mother used to take me to put flowers on her mother's grave on Sundays after church; I was a kid, I hated it. Now I see you do it to give yourself some relief." He still couldn't talk about it very well. "Maybe the admiral is right. Maybe I just want his body so it can be buried someplace."

Then, to change the subject, he said, with a laugh, "My new duty station! Funny you should ask. My detailer had me down for a different job he thought I'd much rather have, a flag staff at the Pentagon."

"Did you take it?"

Alan shook his head. "God no! I'd checked out the Norfolk job; it looked great, just what I need right now. I've seen staff people; I'm not like that. But the detailer said somebody had pulled strings to get me there."

"I sense the fine Italian hand of George Shreed. CIA? You said he came to your dad's memorial service."

"But why?"

Peretz bobbed his head from side to side, lips pushed out, eyes smiling. "Shreed's a gunner. He's also a funny guy—funny sense of obligation. Everything is personal for him. I'd think it would hurt him as an intel officer, always seeing the other side as somebody in particular. 'My enemy.' "

"Why do something for me? Because of Dad?"

"Sure. Shreed was your dad's wingman in Nam; Shreed took a hit and ESCAPAC'd, and your father stayed in the area until the choppers came. That's when Shreed was crippled up; it ended his career, but your dad saved his life." He smiled a little apologetically. "There was also a little more than that. Shreed had, um, what we used to call 'bird-dogged' your father's girl before the deployment. In fact there was a fight, at least a lot of shouting; I missed the good part. They were both a few sheets to the wind. Anyway, your dad risked his life for Shreed, so I suppose Shreed carries some guilt as well as some gratitude. Now, here you are—he sees a chance to make amends."

"Kind of late."

"Well, Shreed isn't a simple character, by any manner of means. I suspect he's not unaware that there's a party in DoD wants a military HUMINT capability. Having a probe into that community would suit his purposes—I mean, CIA doesn't like competition."

"I would have been the probe?"

"Now, now—probably Shreed doesn't put it like that. He probably saw this chance to do something to pay an old debt; at the same time, he's thinking that DoD would profit from having somebody with a new slant and Gulf War experience."

"What new slant?"

Peretz grinned. "Shreed would supply that. Anyway, I'm glad you didn't do it. You'd be dead meat the next time there was a shakeup. Shreed would tell himself that was okay, he'd just pull you over into CIA when the Navy dropped you. He means well. Everybody means well, right? From Shreed's point of view, he'd be doing you this enormous favor. Getting into the Agency is getting into Heaven, right? See, George was in the Agency for a couple of years before he joined the Navy; I've always had some doubts about that, whether he ever really severed those ties. Not the personal ones, certainly. They took him back quick enough. And he's grateful—I told you, things are personal for George. He must be going through hell with the Cold War over, his old personal enemies now good guys. I suspect he's desperate for reasons to make them bad guys again." He laughed. "Woe betide the old Soviet spook who runs afoul of George Shreed in the New World Order!"

Bea Peretz came in then, and there was a lot of noisy chatter and a diatribe about the Democratic candidate. When Alan left, his head ached from shouting over other people's shouting, much of it in laughter, and he wondered that Peretz, the quietest man he knew, had such a high-decibel home life. On the doorstep, the Virginia night warm and blissfully silent around them, he said to Peretz, "Should I do anything about Shreed? Thank him?"

"Sure. Not over the phone. You'll be up there sometime, ask to see him. Thank him, explain. He's a good guy to have on your side."

After that, he spent two days in New York, trying to recover something with an old girlfriend. That having failed, he spent a day in Boston with a college friend who was at Harvard Business School. They still liked each other, but they were in different worlds. Alan realized he wished he had work to do; he thought of reporting to his new assignment two weeks early. What good was leave, if there was nothing to do? At last, bored with trying to entertain himself, he flew to Jacksonville and the house he had inherited.

MAY 25, 1991. MOMBASA, KENYA.

Boredom is international, neither a cultural nor an ethnic specialty. Franci, leaning down from his high wood perch, was bored, too. Around him were the shelves of Bash-O-Vision, now his personal kingdom; on the shelves were rather thin scatterings of cheap radios and clocks, plastic beach toys, sunglasses, umbrellas, cat food (an error), battery-powered toy cars, and, in the camping department, eighteen plastic air mattresses. Behind him and the high gray wall that separated him from his customers were four television sets and a computer already obsolete in Europe and America.

Franci was bored. So bored he did not recognize the vast abyss as boredom; he thought it was depression or impending madness. He had been in Mombasa a month and had had seventeen customers, five of whom had talked to him. Although he spoke excellent Swahili, they had insisted on English, and they had said nothing of any interest to him. "Hey, man, you got the batteries?" "What size?" "For make the ra-dee-oh go." "Big, little?" "I try other place."

The stock was—like his wife, Risa—not of his choosing. The stock was meant to be more or less unsaleable, thus to make him invisible to the police, who were known to take too much notice of success and wish a share. Still, he gathered that the stock was even shabbier than it need have been. The fourth day, a Chinese (a competitor from down the street, he later learned) had come in, looked around, said with a lot of laughter, "You oughta try inland, man!"

"Nairobi?" he had said.

The Chinese had laughed and laughed. "Little town, man—some little town!" Because Bash-O-Vision was clearly going to be no competition, he had come to like Franci and dropped in almost every day; for his part, Franci found the Chinese bored him even more than silence did. As for Risa, his wife—she really was his wife, wed in the presence of a mullah at the training camp—he hardly spoke to her. She was there to spy on him, he was sure, although he had not yet found how she reported. She did her job; he did his; they slept in different beds, alternated sitting in the shop. She cooked, screamed at the black servant and the yard boy, a forty-year-old who had appeared at the door the morning after they had moved in and insisted he came with the house.

Franci sighed, thinking about it. There was a lot he didn't know about life and a lot they hadn't thought to teach him in the camp. The yard boy was an example. Now he came twice a week, tore at the rocklike soil behind the house, often with tools that weren't Franci's, probably borrowed from other houses to which he had also said he belonged; it was apparent that in fact he more or less ran the backside of the street through a brilliant mixture of bullying and helplessness. That morning he had asked to borrow a hundred shillings "against wages." What wages?

Franci sighed again. It was boring, too, being a eunuch. Harem eunuchs were shown as fat, he thought, because they were bored and ate for lack of anything better. Ditto their supposed love of gossip. For his part, he couldn't eat, because the explosion had also taken part of his gut and now nothing sat well, besides which Risa was a poor cook (another thing they had forgotten to teach in the camp). She was a sullen young woman (*no wonder,* he thought, *married to a eunuch*), rather pretty but always scowling (*and why not?*). Soon they would have to acquire a baby or two, he thought idly; already, the Chinese was asking why two such fine young people didn't have children.

Tuesdays and Fridays he made his rounds, checking five message sites and a dead drop. The trips were the most exciting parts of his life; it was a little like fishing, he thought, hoping for a bite. Once, there had been a sign; his hands were trembling with excitement when he had made the telephone call that would alert someone to deal with it. But that was the end of his involvement. He was a middleman, a pass-through. He would never know whether the message was some secret of deep importance or a request for a new pencil.

He sighed. He thought of Iran, of the mountains and his farewell to his father, who had wept. The family believed he was living in Zehedan, working at the Institute of Engineering. They sent letters to him there; the letters were read, then passed to him under other covers. He replied to a box in Beirut, where, he supposed, his letters were read, edited as necessary, and sent to the family. At least one, he knew, had been retyped on the letterhead of the Institute of Engineering, because his father had been greatly impressed by the paper.

He had lost his family, he thought. Lost them as he had lost his testicles, boom, everything gone. Now he was Lebanese, injured in the shelling years ago of Beirut, one of those good businessmen who had fled from the end of the Mediterranean all over the world to bring the joys of entrepreneur capitalism to nations that could not afford it.

Franci sighed and seemed, on this hot day in that black city, calm, resigned, and bored. Deep inside his skull, what was left of the young man who had once been a student at the University of Buffalo screamed and screamed.

MAY 25, 1991. JACKSONVILLE, FLORIDA.

"Hey, my man!" Povick said. He was right where Alan had first seen him, in a chair beside the house. "How's my roomie?"

"Been busy cutting the grass, I see," Alan said, glancing at the unkempt lawn.

"Get yourself a beer, and bring me one while you're at it. Yeah, I just this minute put the lawn mower away, glad you noticed."

"What do we do about the grass, anyway?" Alan said when he came back with the beers. He had some idea that cutting it would take up a few hours.

"Some kid'll come around. Hey, man, you here for good?"

"No. I got some leave. I'm on my way to a new job."

"Me, too, pretty soon." They talked about what to do with the house if they were both gone. The talk ran down. Alan realized the beer, undrunk, was warm to his hand. He drank a little. He looked at Povick, laughed. "I'm bored out of my skull," he said.

"Get laid."

Alan laughed.

"What about that girl you had? Call her up. She's probably waiting with open legs. No shit—women love that on-off stuff." He told a story about some woman he had known; Alan lost the thread. Povick laughed at his own story. "See what I mean?" he said. "Hey, lighten up. You didn't hear a word I said, did you. My best story, too. So, you're bored, you say? Want to jump off the fantail? Welcome to the U.S. Navy. We offer three alternatives—booze, women, and television. There's also family values, to be followed by divorce, with alimony to come. Get yourself a girl. That's what leave is for."

Alan thought about that. "Ever meet a chopper pilot named Rose Siciliano?"

"Nah. Cute?"

"VH-22."

"Nah, man, that's *Maine*. I'm a Florida kind of guy. Also, I'm gun-shy when it comes to female pilots. They intimidate me. I like fairly stupid women, really stacked, no morals—you know. I don't believe women oughta be able to do what I can do, and I don't believe they oughta be allowed to. Especially at sea. Women at sea! Holy shit! What's her name?"

"Rose Siciliano."

"Chinese girl? Well, go for it. You meet her on the boat?"

"And in Dubai. No, no, not a date. I bumped into her. But she seemed—"

"Call her. Go on, call her! You got her number, right? Of course you have! She gave it to you; it's like a request, for God's sake! You don't know much about women, for a guy was going with a heavy number. Go on, call her. I'll even pay for the call." Alan was laughing; Povick kept telling him to go on, asking for a beer when he came back, and after a couple of minutes, Alan was sitting on his father's bed with the telephone in his hand, and a female voice on the other end was telling him that Rose was still in Maine for three days before her leave started.

"Are you a friend of hers?"

"Yes, ma'am. From the Navy."

"Then it would be all right if I gave you her number at work?"

Alan took a deep breath, thought of abandoning ship, and drove on. "Sure."

He placed another call. This time, somebody droned through a dreary, duty-officer routine. "VH-22 Duty Office. This is not a secure line. May I help you, sir or ma'am?"

"May I speak to Lieutenant Siciliano?"

Lieutenant Siciliano would be right there. And she was.

"Siciliano."

"Uh— My name's Alan Craik. We—"

"Oh, hi!"

"Hey, you remember."

She chuckled. She had a great chuckle, not quite a laugh, something like a bubble pipe at work. "Of course I do." She had a great voice, too, husky, now and then breaking.

An hour later, he was headed for Maine.

13

"No!"

She actually pushed him away. When he tried to hold her, thinking this was some residual part of foreplay, she said *No* again and stood up. "You want to get laid, find another bimbo," she said.

"Oh, Christ, Rose—"

"You hit it on the head. Christ, Rose. Yes." She crossed the room and sat in a narrow chair. "Rose is a Catholic, Alan. Rose isn't a virgin, but she sure wishes she was. For you, you sonofabitch."

"Maybe we got here too fast," he said. It had been a remarkable two days: like falling in love when you were a teenager, moon-eyed. He tried a bad joke: "I think it was running through that field of daisies in slow motion that did it."

"Alan." She leaned toward him. She started to cry.

"Don't—"

"Oh, just let me." She turned to look through the slit in the venetian blind, tears oozing. She gave a single chuckle, wept some more. "I thought I was going to do it." She chuckled again and blew her nose. "I was sure we were going to do it!" She closed the tissue into her fist. "But—" Her voice was thin, strangled. "I've fallen in love with you." She laughed, looked at him. "In two days!" She started crying in earnest.

"Rose." He tried to kneel in front of her; it was no good, awkward because of the narrow chair, which had arms that were in his way no matter how he tried to hold her. He had to stand again and then bend way over and hold her face. "Rose. I love you, too."

"Not in two days!" she wailed.

"Yes—yes—"

"You just want to get my clothes off!"

"Yes, I do—no, not just that—yes, I want to go to bed, have sex, whatever you call it— But not if you don't want to."

She was holding his hands by then; now she used them to push him off a little. "I do want to. I've never wanted to so much in my life."

Her eyes shimmered with tears. She blinked to rid herself of them, then laughed. The laugh touched him more even than the tears, and he said, "What do we do?"

She shook her head.

"No, tell me, Rose! Tell me—what happens? What happens next?"

Three times she started to speak, until finally she shook her head, stood up, and kissed him. "Let's get some coffee," she said.

Four hours later, holding hands across a plastic tabletop, she said, "I'm going to go home and talk to somebody. That's what I have to do next. Then I'll tell you what I think we do."

"I love you, Rose."

She nodded slowly. "Yeah. I really believe you do."

• • •

St. Rose's is a bastion of the Italian community of that part of Utica, New York. A few people in the neighborhood still speak Italian, although most families have been there for generations. There is an Italian museum; there are Italian bakeries; Italian restaurants are strung along Bleecker Street like beads. The first generation came to work on the canal and the railroads, then in the heavy industries that sprang up. Now the factories are empty, but the neighborhood goes on, and the little church seems eternal.

Opening the door to the sanctuary, Rose was carried back fifteen years: dampness and incense, furniture polish and flowers. Two women were ahead of her by the confessional. One glanced around and recognized her: a friend of her mother's. She pulled a scarf over her head and sat down, away from them.

She thought about Alan.

One woman came out of the confessional and was praying.

Sin. It was impossible to keep from thinking about sin, being what she was, raised as she was; the Navy was not a very encouraging atmosphere for spirituality, and she had almost certainly thought more about altitude and approach angles than about sin, the last several years, but the idea was always there, like the earth when you flew. She envied people who had no religion; they would be in bed with him now, right this moment. Joy.

The other woman came out, waddled to the front of the church.

"Forgive me, Father—" Her sins were hardly spectacular—anger, envy, impiety.

"Can I talk to you, Father? A personal thing."

"Wait after."

Father Amato had been her priest all her childhood and adolescence. Confirmation, first communion. Old women loved him; young women practiced birth control and didn't tell him and said privately he was a pompous asshole, and then took communion from him; men rolled their eyes.

Still, if he walked into a restaurant on Bleecker Street, the whole place fell silent.

"So, Rose." He had got older, fatter. His cassock still sounded like sandpaper on wood when he moved. He took her hand. "Have you come home?"

"Only for the weekend, Father."

He sat next to her. "Your mother wants you should come home. I saw her last week. She misses you."

"Father, I want some advice. I've met a guy. A man. Another officer. I love him. And no, he isn't a Catholic, so don't ask."

"Did you make a complete confession?"

"Of course I did."

He smiled. "Then you haven't sinned that way, even though you say there's love."

"Not yet."

"Rose!"

"What can I do?"

"You can marry him. After he has taken instruction." He started to dither about conversion, souls. She wanted to scream. It was all the old bullshit.

"You are planning to have children, I hope."

"Yes." Not planning, *wanting.* Yes.

"Then we must plan where you will live, how you will have children, with God's grace, while he is at sea."

"Father, I'm in the Navy, too."

"Yes, yes, yes, but that ends when you marry. To have a child—"

"It will not end when I marry! I love the Navy. It's my career! I mean to be a success in it!"

"Rose, Rose, this is foolishness. Women are meant to be—"

"It is not foolishness, you—!" She stood. "I'll have babies when I'm on shore duty. It can be done. I can do it!"

"Sit down." He would have made a great senior chief, she thought—real authority. "Rose, sit down!"

She sat.

"Apologize to me."

"I'm sorry, Father."

"Have you told your mother?" He didn't acknowledge her father's existence: Father Amato and her father weren't on speaking terms.

"Not yet."

"My advice is, tell her tonight, then get your young man here. Does he know?"

"That I love him? I think so."

"Does he know he's going to marry you and be the father of your children, I mean."

"Uh—not exactly."

"Then you better propose to him real soon. That's the way you women's-libbers do it, isn't it?" He tittered.

APRIL 11, 1991. THE HOMEPLACE MOTEL,
BOWLING GREEN, KENTUCKY.

"How do you make a secure call?"

"I call on a pay phone, ring twice, hang up." Donnie Marengo's voice was a singsong. "I wait twenty seconds and I call again. Then I go to the phone at Arbutus and Pflaegler and wait at twenty minutes before each even hour. Jeez, Dad, we been over and over it!"

"And we'll go over and over it until it's like fucking breathing. This could be your life, Donnie."

Donnie scowled. He as much as said, *It isn't what I want my life to be;* it was in his posture, his set mouth.

Bonner put his hand on his son's T-shirted shoulder. "You with me, kiddo?"

The young man nodded.

"Okay. We see each other and something's wrong. How do you tell me?"

"I'm wearing a hat backward. Dad, for Christ's sake, everybody wears his hat backward these days."

"*Not you or me.* I'm wearing my old Orioles cap backward. What's it mean?"

"You're warning me off. Something's wrong." The young

man made a face. "Dad, have you ever really done any of this Mickey Mouse bullshit?"

Bonner, who was proud of the possession of such secrets, which made him feel like a special sort of man, said that of course he had, lots, Christ! He opened a beer and handed it to his son. "Okay?"

Donnie shrugged.

"What now?"

"This stuff makes me—" Donnie shrugged. "I'm not comfortable with it, Dad."

"It makes you feel like a creep or something, right?"

"You said it, I didn't."

"Donnie— I told you and told you. It's all right. It's like our own people we're working for." He had told his son that they were working for the Israelis. It was an honest lie, he thought, made for the kid's own good. Donnie didn't understand about countries and world affairs, that it was all bullshit, one was just like another. To Donnie, Israel was a good place, almost American. Well, let him think so.

"It's just such bullshit," the boy said. He smiled. "It's a lot of stuff to memorize, Dad." He made a face, laughed, swigged beer. "I'll think every guy I see with a camera for the rest of my life is goddam James Bond. I'm either gonna laugh out loud or shit my pants if I ever have to do any of this stuff."

"You just get it all straight in your head and do as your old man tells you."

"I know, I know. Little joke. Okay? Little joke."

"Okay, Athens. Tell me about Athens."

"Oh, jeez—!"

"Come on, go through Athens and then we'll hit the Corvette show. That's why we're here, right?"

Donnie looked disgusted and said something about its being bullshit if you needed cover to meet your own father.

"Athens," Bonner said.

"Okay, okay." His tone was that used by teenagers to express their sense of oppression by such burdens as being on time or eating nutritious food. "Athens. Kritikiou Street. I approach it from the north on Maimonides Street. Mind you, I don't read Greek and I've never been to this place, but I'm supposed to find these streets somehow. Okay. Sure! Oh, yeah!"

"You take a taxi, and you got a Greek alphabet so you can puzzle out the street signs. I told you, next tour I'll take some photos so you'll have some help. Go on."

Donnie mumbled very fast to himself, going over what he had just done, then said louder, "Maimonides Street. Okay. I turn right on to Kritikiou. Straight ahead I see a church about a block away, it looks like it's in the middle of the street, actually a traffic island. I walk toward the church. Third building on my right there's a stone, no a metal *thing* out in front near the curb, it's like an old gatepost— What if they've torn it out by the time we use it?"

"They won't. Keep going."

"Keep the faith, baby. They won't. Okay. This *thing*. I go to the street side of it, cars parked along the curb, I put a square in white adhesive tape at shoulder height. What if somebody sees me?"

"They never see you."

"What if they do?"

"They think you know what you're doing and they don't."

"Dad, if I saw a guy making a white square on a mailbox or something in Philly, I'd think it was really weird."

"Yeah? What would you do?"

"I'd think it was weird."

"So, big deal! They think it's weird. You're on a street in Athens, you think some Greek is going to come up to you and say, 'Hey, asshole, wotta you do on my city? *Come on.*"

"I'd tell him it's a joke."

"You'd tell him nothing."

"I'd tell him it was a secret sign to my girl, that's what I'd do."

Bonner looked angry, and then he looked resigned. He told himself Donnie's attitude would change, in time. "Whatever," he said. "Okay, you're fine; you're right on the location, you got the route and the sign. What does the sign mean?"

" 'Meet me.' "

"Where?"

"The—Adonai Café in Piraeus."

"What's Piraeus?"

"The port for Athens, about nine miles from downtown. I take a cab, but I tell him to take me to the Perikles Superbar; it's two blocks away. I walk. I walk *west* and turn one street toward the water, which I can see, then left and there's the Adonai Café. I sit outside."

"When?"

"From quarter of seven p.m. to quarter after."

"What if I don't show?"

"I come back next day, same time."

"What if I don't come then?"

"I do it again the third day."

"What if I don't show then?"

"We meet at the next place on the list, depending on what the liberty ports are."

Bonner nodded. He smiled. "That's pretty good. You're smart, Donnie. You got it a hell of a lot faster than I did. Now cut a groove in your brain for it, you know? Over and over, over and over. Hey?" He held his son's shoulder, and Donnie, seeing them in the cheap motel mirror as if he were having a glimpse of a future, saw a suddenly old man leaning on him, and he was deeply touched. "Let's go look at Vettes."

14

By August, Alan was used to the new surroundings, and the new people were used to him and to the fact that every Friday he raced out the door to pick up Rose at the airport. The cost was killing her, she said, and she had thoughts some weekends of driving both ways, but it would have taken too much time. She had time and he didn't, she had decided; she was a short-timer in her squadron, readying to move on. He, on the other hand, was trying to learn a new job. They spent their waking weekend hours together, slept apart.

Rose had become the center of his life. He couldn't believe it. He simply wanted to be with her all the time. Nothing like it had ever happened to him before. It was not like the times with Kim, not at all; those had been a blaze of sex, little more, as he understood only now. Yet in a way the Kim kind of relationship was much easier.

The new job was a little dull, a little mysterious at first, then slightly more interesting as he caught on. He was nominally an intelligence analyst, more often a kind of talking head who briefed outgoing carrier crews and squadrons; but already, a month into the job, he was impatient with that side of it and eager for more. As a result, his written briefs got longer and more in-depth: they went to a central command, then were filtered and went to other agencies if they were thought useful.

"Welcome aboard," his new boss, a stringy-looking commander named Reicher, had said to him. "We're going to make an analyst of you."

"Good. That sounds good."

"You're taking Africa."

"Does it matter that I don't know anything about Africa?"

"Not a bit."

So now he read everything he could lay his hands on about Africa, pored over classified CIA estimates and ONI reports, filled his attaché case with books to read over the weekend, even listened to African music in his room. He tried to learn Swahili from a Berlitz tourist aid. The squadron was a wonderful but fading memory. Africa and Rose were his life.

"Hey, Craik, know anything about diamonds in Sierra Leone?"

"Uh—a little—"

"Take care of this, will you?"

A low-priority message would be dropped on his desk. It would turn out actually to be about the Russian–South African diamond cartel and its effect on Sierra Leone, but he would follow it up, anyway.

"Al, Mombasa's in Africa, right?"

"Kenya."

"Handle this, okay?"

"But—" Too late. It was actually about Islamic evangelism in several areas, most of all the old Soviet Union, but there was something in there about Kenya and Uganda; anyway, it became his. So did Iranian terrorist-training camps in Libya, France's relations with old colonies, UN internal reform (because the new SG was an African, if you thought of Egypt as Africa), the upsurge in high-tech mercenary war as a business (its most spectacular examples in England and

South Africa). He devoured everything he could find, took it home with him, got up early to devour more. It was just as well he did.

"Craik!"

"Sir."

He was passing the boss's door; he pivoted back, was waved in.

"Siddown." The commander stared at him. "You pretty well up to speed on Africa?"

"I'm running as fast as I can just to stay in place."

"Jaeckel tells me you're doing okay. In fact he said you're, quote, the smartest goddam kid he's ever had on Africa, unquote. That's a compliment." Jaeckel was a civilian analyst.

"Thank you, sir."

"Think you can do a half-hour briefing on the Navy's concerns in Africa and possible U.S. intervention?" Before Alan could answer, he said, "You're going to, anyway. Next Thursday, 1300, House Office Building. Some goddam subcommittee. Uniform up there is whites for something like this, not chokers, you know. Wear every medal you got. Normally, Jaeckel'd do it himself, but he's booked. Okay?"

"Who, who—what's the audience?"

"Couple congressmen, staffs, probably some other briefers from the community. Nothing classified. The idea is you save them the trouble of looking it up in the encyclopedia, okay? You don't have to be profound." He cleared his throat. "You still got that girl?"

"Utica, New York, this weekend. Her parents want to meet me."

"Good for you! Get married, settle down; you won't look like something the cat dragged in every Monday around here." Alan stood up, started out. "Hey!"

"Sir?"

"The word is, you're going to be up for early lieutenant. Don't get your hopes up, but, you know—"

"Thanks. Right."

He talked to Rose every night. His telephone bill was

enormous. That night, he told her about maybe coming up for lieutenant a year early, and there was the slightest pause before she said something. She was complimentary, happy for him; still, there had been a moment when, he now realized, she had been thinking that she was two years ahead of him in rank and he might catch up. Nothing between people was ever easy, he was learning, even when there was apparently limitless love. Yes, being with Kim had been easier.

"I love you," he said. It was instinct: when there were obstacles, reaffirm what worked.

"Yeah." She sounded pleased. They talked about what they were doing, their problems with their superiors. She was coming up for reassignment and had heard of an opening at Pax River. It was too far; he wanted her to come to Norfolk. On and on.

"I love you," she said.

He laughed, hearing her do what he had done. "We do keep coming back to that," he said.

"You're damned right. That's all there is, finally."

"That isn't all there is. Just listen to us."

"Well— You going to marry me?"

"You bet."

"When?"

"Isn't that what I'm meeting your folks for?"

They were silent. She said, "After they meet you, I'm ready. More than ready. I want you."

For a moment, it frightened him, the imminence of a great change, even danger; it was like something that had happened in Christine, the precise event escaping him; then it came to him—trying to evade the A-5 Fantan's attack.

"Let's do it," he said.

She picked him up on a warm September day at the Syracuse airport and they drove through the early-evening traffic with a kind of shared joy. She was a good driver—why not? she was a good pilot—and she looked happy, even excited. They were going to "the lake," she said, not Utica; the weather was going to be warm, so her father wanted to spend it at their cottage. Her mother was outraged. All the good silver, the good dishes, the good tablecloths, her good clothes were in Utica. Rose thought all this highly entertaining. "You'll see!" she said. "You'll see!" That rich chuckle rose and fell.

And he saw: her mother was angry and disliked him on sight. She was short—both parents were short, in fact—big-hipped, gray; if she was an example of how Rose would look one day, he was not unhappy. But she made no secret of her outrage. She made it clear that they had waited up to meet him, and he and Rose should have arrived hours earlier. She had no real bedroom to offer him, only the sunporch, which was cold this time of year; this was her husband's fault, but, ultimately, Alan's, no reason given. She put out enough food for eight or a dozen people and disappeared with a headache.

None of this bothered her father. He was a dapper little man, narrow-headed, his hair still mostly black. He chatted with Rose, kept eyeing Alan; like his wife, he spoke with a local accent that Rose had lost and that grated on Alan's ears—"ditn't" for didn't, a nasal A. After half an hour of talk about the neighborhood and baseball and her job, he put on an old vinyl LP and danced with Rose to old swing tunes.

"We always do this," Rose said. She was flushed and laughing.

"She's my sweetie," her father said, looking at Alan.

The next morning Alan and Rose walked along the highway by the little lake. Some kind of hunting season was open (bear, he learned later), and a few cars went by, but mostly they had the quiet of the morning. A kind of town had grown up, scruffy and, along the road, apparently dying. A number of the cottages were boarded up and collapsing in on themselves. The real life was a hundred yards away along the water, invisible from the highway.

"I spent every summer here until I was seventeen," she

said. "I knew everybody. It was like the neighborhood in Utica—blue-collar, I guess. What people could afford. It's sad, these places falling down. I kissed a guy whose family owned that one over there with the paint gone."

"Don't tell me about that part."

"I was thirteen."

"That makes it worse."

She held his arm. "My dad is going to take you out in the boat. That's when you talk."

"It's on the schedule?"

She chuckled. "Don't mind my mother. You scare her."

"Well, that makes it mutual; she terrifies me."

"It's all she knows to do. You're upper-class to her— WASP, educated. You know—class."

He was astonished.

"She thinks she ought to put out all her best because she has to impress you. Just go with it. Finally, she'll do what my father wants. She's the queen, he's the boss."

"What happens if I kiss you right here on the road?"

"Let's find out."

Her father took him out in the boat, just as she'd said—an ancient sixteen-footer with an outboard that looked big enough to power the *QEII*. Alan had expected a rowboat and was ready to offer to man the oars; instead, he slumped down out of the wind while they put up big rooster tails and went right across the little lake in about four minutes. Her father kept up a chatter about the great weather, the World Series, big fish he'd caught right *here*. He stopped the boat without warning, and, as they bobbed on their own wake, handed Alan a fishing rod and a coffee can that proved to be full of night crawlers.

"I don't have a license," Alan said.

"Well . . . I don't see no game wardens." He pretended to search the sky. "Unless they're gonna do one of those surprise airdrops. Anyway, the fine is about two-fifty, which is cheap to find out are you gonna marry my daughter."

Alan laughed and opened the bail; the sinker slupped into the water and line ran out. "What are we fishing for?"

"Privacy."

They sat there. The September sun was thin but warm, yet a breeze from the west was now and then surprisingly cold.

"That's an osprey," her father said. "See? The white, top of the spruce tree on the point? They're a beautiful bird, like a white eagle, and they fold their wings and drop right into the water, bam, and come up with a fish. We got everything here. Deer, bear. Rosie's crazy about you."

The change of subject caught him off guard. He was nervous, he realized. "Yes, sir," he said. "And I'm crazy about her."

"Call me Bobby." He jerked his rod tip up and down and looked over the side as if he could see what the fish were up to. "When I went to work at the metal-processing plant, they said, 'What's your name?' So I told them. They say, 'We already got an Angelo Siciliano.' I thought they meant I had to go home. I was sixteen. I didn't know no better. They said, 'Call yourself something else.' So I said, 'Bobby,' after a ballplayer who was very big then. So I been Bobby ever since." He looked at Alan appraisingly, the way he had looked at him last night. "You and me are different. You come from people who go to college, am I right? What they call white-collar. Me, I'm blue-collar. Rosie says that makes no difference and I think she's right. You got any thoughts about that?"

"I don't think it's a problem."

"Between you and me, it's a problem for Rosie's mother, but she'll get over it. She thinks she's entertaining Prince Charles, it makes her jumpy. Pretend not to notice."

He jerked his rod again. Alan jerked his rod, supposing it might tip the balance for some undecided fish down there. Nothing happened.

"Where I worked," Bobby said, this time in a lower, contemplative voice, "it was all Italians and some Pollocks then. I'm talking the end of World War II—one more year and

I'd've gone in. I went in anyway in Korea, drafted; a whole lot of nothing. Rosie says you been in combat and got medals. More power to you. I spent two years counting GI underwear. Then I come back, right back into the metal-works. Good jobs then. Everybody doing the same thing, year in year out, fathers and sons, whole families, you know? There goes a pine siskin, what the hell is he doing out over the lake? We had a union, a good contract— Life was good. Now—I'll take you down along the tracks in Utica. Gone. Everything gone. Where I worked thirty-two years, a lot of weeds. I picked up a brick, I put it on my shelf, it was from the factory where I worked. Maybe I looked at that brick for thirty-two years. Now, nothing. There was a brewery down there—a shell. A leatherworks. Everything gone. All of a sudden, it seemed, this city where I'd spent my whole life fell apart. People out of a job, people leaving. Then kids like Rosie going away. Everybody's kids going away! I tell you!" He shook his head. "Thirty-two years, one day they come around and go, 'We're sorry as hell, boys, we can't do it no more,' and they close it down. They opened up in Alabama, what the hell. I wasn't going to move to Alabama, no sir."

"What did you do?"

"What do you do? You pull up your socks and find something else. I and a buddy, we opened a kind of machine shop. It pays the bills. What the hell. I get by. But it isn't like it was. The old days, a kid like Rosie wouldn't't've gone away, she wouldn't't've come back with a guy like you. No offense." He studied the end of his rod. "Rosie's my favorite." He started to sing, in a husky, surprisingly well-pitched voice. "*Rosie, She is my posy; Rosie, She is my joy*— You hear that one? Jolson sang that. She is my posy. You want to marry her?"

"I sure do."

"Then do it. Just understand, if you hurt her, if you let her down, I'll come after you myself. Okay? We got a deal? Just remember, I mean what I say. Okay?"

"Okay."

"Yeah, and about that damn priest and the church and all that, you do what you want. Rosie's mother goes on, 'Oh, what about Father Joe?' 'Oh, what about his catechism, oh, the children—!' I tell you, boy, women in black and old men in skirts, what a way to run a religion! I believe in God, don't get me wrong, but I don't believe I need that no-balls jackass, you should pardon the expression, to tell me how to act. You agree?"

Alan was saved from having to commit himself by a tremendous tug on his line; he reeled in, and Bobby started shouting, almost tipping the boat while he got the net, and in time a big jackperch came over the gunwale.

"Nice! Nice! Get your hook back in the water, for Christ's sake! Come on, you're gonna break the law, you might as well do it right." Alan caught two more and Bobby caught one; then the fish stopped biting, and Bobby pointed out a great blue heron going slowly across the sky. "They fish down there where it's shallow; they nest up there someplace, where he's going." He stood up to watch the bird. "God, I love this place! I just love it. I dunno what you see when you look at it—lot of cottages, I suppose, nothing really wild. Not like it's some private fancy lake. But I just love it. You know, you work all week, busting your ass, pardon me, you come up here—have a beer, sit in the boat, listen to people's radios a mile away, or they're singing or just talking— And you know what it all comes down to? I'll tell you: a job. That's what it's all about. A man's got to have a job." He reeled up his line. "I like you. You're a good listener."

They turned in the rental car at the Syracuse airport and she waited with him, because his plane was leaving first. After the tension of the weekend, they were both quiet, both saddened. As his plane taxied in toward the boarding walkway, he said, "Let's do it."

She hugged him.

•   •   •

The Thursday briefing brought out a so-far hidden talent for making trouble. On the Monday, he reviewed the Agency's estimates for selected African countries and began to suspect that they represented a blend of wishful thinking and false assumption. It was, he thought, part of the numbness of the Cold War's slow death that caused informed people not to think that their withdrawal of attention and money would itself become a factor; and so far as he could see, the same informed people seemed not to have noticed that their client in central Africa had got old and their clients in the Horn had never really liked them—or anybody else, for that matter.

He tried to tell Rose all this and more over the phone; she told him to shut up and save it for the congressmen. So he blundered on, stayed up long after he had said good night to her. It was already morning in Africa; there were people there quite ready to talk to him. By Wednesday, he was asking classified questions over a scrambler phone of people in Washington, one of whom finally told him he was an arrogant shithead and banged down the phone. A couple of others, less tied to the past, said pleasantly that his surmises were absolutely right but would not be well received, especially with an election coming. And anyway, Americans didn't care about Africa and we had no interest there.

"Americans care about starving kids."

"Not if they don't know about them."

"But they do know about them. They're on the tube."

"Bubba doesn't make policy."

On Thursday, he walked into the congressional hearing room feeling as if his skin had been split and stitched up after a piece had been cut out, so that it all fit too tight. He even had a slight tremor in his fingers, from tension and fatigue; yet he felt entirely ready. He had his hat (white cover) tucked under his left arm, his wings and his ribbons marching down his chest over his heart, his black briefcase in his right hand. A woman stopped him just inside the door. "Yes?" she challenged.

"Lieutenant Craik. Fleet Analysis?" He grinned. "They cleared the bench."

She wasn't amused. "Sit there. When the chairman calls you, sit at the center by the microphone and start right in; we're running behind, so don't try to charm us, okay?" She shouted something at a man with a pile of papers and he scooted, red-faced, to the other end of a long table.

It was not Alan's idea of a congressional hearing—no lights, no television cameras. Not even C-SPAN. *This is it?* he thought. Relief and disappointment mixed. *What was all that worry for?*

Only three actual congresspersons appeared. Only one of them looked at him, a red-eyed septuagenarian with the distrustful look of a prison guard. The woman who had challenged him at the door whispered in the old geezer's ear and kept glancing at Alan. *What's she got, a file on me?*

He laid it out for them as if he were briefing a roomful of enlisted personnel—no bullshit, no big words, no pandering. He came out within twenty seconds of the assigned time, ending with a summary that was not a warning but that put his serious reservations in one little package: ethnicity and the African center, meaning Rwanda-Burundi and Zaire; the Horn, meaning Somalia; the long-term problem of poverty in South Africa. Then he said thank you, and he sat back.

The old man fixed him with his prison-guard stare. "Are you aware of this body's position on interference in sub-Saharan Africa?"

"That was not my subject, sir."

"Are you aware of our position?"

"If you mean HR 3901, yes, sir." He had got that from the Congressional Research Service.

"That's what I mean, that's exactly what I mean. You are aware of it. Well, you surprise me. Do you mean to sit there and tell us that the United States Navy ought to be moving into Somalia? Is that what I understood you to say?"

"No, sir, that's not what I said. I said that if—"

"I don't want to hear 'if'! Are you trying to tell us the Navy has a place, a role, an—involvement—in Africa?"

"Under certain conditions, it might have."

He got a lecture on quagmires and no-win situations, and he felt for the first time the sting of that old saying about the messenger and the message. The congressman then moved into an area that Alan knew was classified, and the woman all but put her hand over his mouth. He listened for some seconds and stared at Alan with what seemed to be hatred. "No more questions," he said sullenly. Alan looked at the woman, and to his astonishment she winked.

He slipped away during a recess but got only to the corridor when she came after him. "That was swell," she said. "You really surprised me! Your first time?"

"Afraid so."

"You're going to do okay here. You touched a nerve, you know that, don't you? It's okay, but next time, check out the politics and save yourself some grief."

"I didn't think what I said was political."

She smiled wanly. "You'll know better next time."

Another woman came out of the hearing room and walked toward them, her heels striking the marble floor like small hammers. She looked rather elegant, hard, practiced—a lawyer, he would have said. Thirties, not pretty but well put together, always prepared. The congressional aide seemed to know her, and they exchanged a kind of greeting, subtle in its shadings, like two animals who didn't want to fight but would if they had to. After a few seconds, Alan was alone with the newcomer.

"I'm Sally Baranowski," she said.

"Alan Craik."

"That was impressive." She was amused by something but wasn't sharing it with him. Finally, she decided to take pity on him, and she said, "I work with George Shreed."

"Ah." *Aha!* "That must have sounded really simple-minded to you."

"Not at all. You handled the congressman well, thank

God. He's one of our supporters." She laughed. "He doesn't like to hear people disagree with us."

"I didn't disagree with you."

She smiled. "Don't be cute."

"Hey—hey! Wait a minute—"

"Is this a message from ONI or something? I'm on a committee where we try to head these things off. I wish I'd known." She said it with that tone of regret that parents use for the follies of their older children. "We could have dealt with it."

"Look, I'm an analyst. There was no message. I didn't say anything here that I haven't sent out in daily briefs. There was no policy, for God's sake. I simply tried to show where the present situation might lead."

"We have estimates on all that. We expect you people to profit from them."

"Not if they don't follow from the facts. I was told to come here and do a job, and I did it. If I stepped on your toes, sue me." He leaned back. "I'm sorry; I was wound up. I want to get in touch with Mr. Shreed; how do I do that?"

"You can't just now; he'll be back in a week." She started to burrow in a shoulder bag.

"It's something personal—not what happened in there."

"I know." She was writing in tiny letters on a business card. She handed it to him, smiling. "About the job you didn't take."

"Oh, you know about that. Was he mad?"

"Oh, sure. But he got over it. Still, you should apologize."

"I know he meant well."

"Yes, he did." She was still smiling; it was not a smile that was for him, but rather was about him. Or at him. "You're so bright-eyed and bushy-tailed!" she said. She turned away and laughed. "You'll learn!"

What the hell was that supposed to mean?

Friday afternoon, a strong memo of protest from the CIA reached his boss's desk.

Saturday, he married Rose.

15

OCTOBER 14, 1991. MOMBASA, KENYA.

The warm reek of the sea lay over the Kilindini harbor, over the whole coast, even as far inland as the mangrove swamps and the malarial belt that had once been a barrier to traffic inland. Franci thought he had got used to it, but now and again it would surprise him, like the faint stink of rotten fish somewhere, an air so thick it seemed liquid, a wet breeze. Clouds gathered overhead; the morning's blue sky became white, then gray, then charcoal, and the rains fell so heavily that it was hard to breathe, the nose taking in water that gave the astringent feel far back of a swimming pool. He hated the coast, too reminiscent of the place where his life had been ruined, where his life had ended. He wanted mountains, cold, harshness—not this soft stench, this wet heat, these limp palms and downpours.

How long? he wondered. He had thought, in the camp, that it might be a release, this living a secret life in a new place. Secrecy can be a kind of revenge, if not on one's real enemies, then on strangers, surrogates. But what sort of revenge was it to sit behind the barricaded desk of Bash-O-Vision, to listen to his shrew of a wife? She had started to embroider her role, to behave like a real wife. She was wretched, too, he knew; her cooking had got even worse, and she served the food with spitefulness. He thought she might have taken a lover, and to his astonishment *this* infuriated him! Why? Why could he not let the poor woman have whatever comfort she could take in this alien place? But he actually spied on her now, tried to find excuses to go home at unpredictable times, leaving Bash-O-Vision in the care of the Chinese while he skulked through backstreets to enter his own house silently, expecting to find her on the bed, twined with some stranger whose hairy ass greeted him above her nakedness.

He had never seen her naked. He found that he wanted to. He wondered if he really was going mad. There was nothing he could do with a woman, his poor stump of a member an outrage, a joke, and then—well. But he thought of her, of things he could do. Of her pleasure. If he might give her pleasure, perhaps then—what, he would be more of a man? No. Perhaps he would be more alive. Risa was no beauty, but she was a woman; she had a certain lushness; she was *there*. She was his wife!

He had hinted at something. She had scowled. He had gone into her bedroom last night on the pretext of asking if the mosquitoes bothered her; she had pulled up the bedclothes and hidden herself. But why?

He supposed he would come to commanding her. She was, after all, his wife. She must obey; she was a religious woman, one who always covered her head, who would have gone covered head to foot if she had not been ordered, as a special duty to God, to pretend to be a secularized Lebanese. Well, he would come to that, he thought. Ordering her to accept his caresses. What a contradiction, to order somebody to accept pleasure. What a parody of marriage.

He rode his bicycle along the trolley track toward Kilindini, where he had a meeting with a woman who was supposed to pass something from the German consul's trash. Riding a bicycle had become a real pleasure, not least because he hadn't thought he could do it with only one leg; yet, with the good foot in a racer's clamp so he could pull the pedal up as well as push down, he got along quite well. His good leg, he thought, would be oversized in a year or two.

Oh, the stink of Mombasa. Now he could smell the mud. The harbor was full of ships, one a gleaming cruise liner. Oh, to get on it, just go with this little crowd of elderly South Africans, sail somewhere nice! Somewhere magical, where there were mountains, an oasis, his real self recovered.

NOVEMBER 10, 1991. NEAR JACKSONVILLE, FLORIDA.

Bernie and Bea Peretz were in bed, drifting toward sleep. He held her big body in his right arm; her buttocks were pushed into his belly.

"You awake?" he murmured.

"Sure."

"I sort of came to a decision. I'm shit-canning the dissertation."

"You're not!" She rolled on her back in one move, then pushed herself up and loomed over him.

"I've already done it, babe."

"You stupid *idiot!* All you've been talking about—"

"So I'm a shithead. Don't be mad." He slipped a hand under her pajama top.

"Don't try to distract me."

"It was no good, Bea. I tried it and it was no good. Anyway, you hate what *you're* doing."

"So it's going to be my fault?" She did hate what she was doing, teaching in an elementary school while he supposedly finished this degree that he had been working on for years. "I can stand it, Bernie."

"I already put my name in for a job at FBI."

"You're *sure?* I don't want to hear about this for the next forty years, there you'll be in the senior citizens' center, bitching about how I kept you from getting your Ph.D. I don't want to be the Wicked Witch of the—stop that!"

"Why?"

"Bernie—" She giggled and hoisted herself on top of him, and they were soon lost in another of the activities of good marriage.

FEBRUARY 20, 1992. NEAR NORFOLK, VIRGINIA.

"I love to dance with you."

"I'd be better in top hat and tails."

"No, you wouldn't."

The room was dark. The glow from the nearby strip mall lighted the ceiling, but they had blocked out most of it with the curtains and a blanket. Neither of them wore a stitch.

"I've got something to tell you," she said as they moved slowly around the little room to a dead composer's love song.

"Shall I guess?"

"The stick turned pink."

He chuckled. "We didn't lose much time." They danced until the song ended and then stood together, wrapped around each other, waiting for the next cut. When it started and he began to move, she said, "You know what I think two people could do while they danced?"

"You think?"

"Mmmm."

"You're a flaming prevert."

"Mmm-*hm*."

She was right. Two people can do that while they dance.

16

They lived like that for another month, Rose coming down
on weekends so they could be together in a ratty apartment he rented in the great sprawl of exploitation that sur-
rounds all naval facilities. His one consolation was that he
was renting by the month and could get out as soon as
Rose got an assignment to the area.

He had learned to live with his new role as in-house
whiz kid, the one assigned to him by his boss and the other
analysts. Commander Reicher had referred to him in a meeting as the Genius, and the name, not necessarily well intended, had stuck, along with the idea that he was too smart
for his own good. He was not, he thought; what they took
for insight was only a willingness to rethink their received
wisdom, but Somalia had done exactly as he had said it
would, and he was proven more correct than a young j.g.
should be. It did not help that he had a friend in a high
place—Shreed, with whom he had made up his ingrati-
tude—who now got him placed on a committee that nobody but Commander Reicher had even heard of.

"I've been told to assign you to Ad Hoc," Reicher said one day when they were discussing some business.

"Where's that?" It sounded like Southeast Asia.

"It's not a where, it's a what. The Ad Hoc Committee. It's a kind of offshoot of a subset of a subset of NFIB." He pushed over some papers. "Don't commit us to anything. And don't make waves, okay? There's supposed to be somebody from a NIPPSA unit there, ditto NIS; mostly, they don't bother. We want to keep up appearances."

The Ad Hoc—actually the Ad Hoc Sub-Committee on Inter-Agency Discrepancies and Standards Resolution—was supposed to be an offshoot of something called Jitter (which, he discovered only weeks later, Sally Baranowski chaired), but it had a life of its own and rolled on, as deaf to calls to stop as a stone wheel in its rolling. When he walked into the first meeting, he saw an empty chair, next to it a black officer, and he had sat down before he realized the man was Creole O'Neill, who was laughing softly to himself at Alan's failure to recognize him.

"Don't tell me you've forgotten what we meant to each other in the Gulf," O'Neill said. " 'Old chap.' "

"God, Creole! It's just that I didn't expect to see you. It's like a hundred years ago. Hey, man, it's great to see you!"

"Yeah, I been through that, too—you see somebody, you go, 'Hey, that guy looks familiar,' and it turns out you spent six months with him. But it was another world, right? 'And besides, the bitch is dead.' Which leads me to the O'Neill theory of incognito—the best disguise is context. Change the setting, everybody looks different. Which reminds me, I'm not 'Creole' here. That was flyboy shit. Okay?"

Alan grinned. He wasn't "Spy" anymore, to be sure. "Context?" he said. They laughed. O'Neill would have said something more, but the meeting started.

On a break, he asked O'Neill what Ad Hoc meant, anyway.

" 'For This Only,' meaning it's supposed to die when its task is completed. This is Washington; nothing ever dies.

The Ad Hoc is almost as old as the tea-tasters board. Still, it's a place to get seen. How'd you get yourself appointed?" He seemed just faintly put off. It occurred to Alan that they had exchanged roles: O'Neill was now in his element, Alan a neophyte, even an interloper. To his surprise, O'Neill suddenly abandoned him and hurried to chat up the Ad Hoc's permanent chair, an overweight white man in his thirties who seemed to have been squeezed into his clothes from a pastry tube. He was from the CIA, looked like the class nerd: thick glasses, tiny eyes, a porcine nose, yet he wore a suit that Alan knew was more expensive than he could afford, and O'Neill respected him. His name was Hadley. His voice—and Alan heard it a lot, as Hadley was a vocal chair—was pushed up into his nose so that it was both adenoidal and accented, and he sounded, as somebody said, like William F. Buckley with the flu.

"Hadley's an asshole," O'Neill said as they left the meeting together. "But don't underestimate him. He's one of those guys who works twenty hours a day and weekends, plus he's a brown-nose without any shame. But he's important."

"His voice sounds—I think of Harvard."

"Get real! *I* went to Harvard. I think Hadley went to some school in Detroit or someplace. That isn't important."

This was a new way of thinking about people, utterly unlike the squadron. Hadley wouldn't have lasted a day in the squadron, he thought; people would have been merciless with his nerdishness. But out here in the world of power, Hadley was somebody—and O'Neill buttered him up.

He told Rose. He wanted her to meet O'Neill, wanted her to like him. Still, he felt imposed upon by assignment to the committee, which, he learned only weeks later, he was supposed to make his lowest priority, anyway.

"Don't let it swamp you," Rose said. "Interagency, interservice—none of that will do you any good career-wise. They don't write your fitness reports."

"Yeah, but Reicher does, and he's the one who sent me."

"To take you down a peg, it sounds like. Are you sure you aren't too smart for your own good?"

He couldn't say that the subcommittee was as close as he came to operational intelligence, and that he thought analysis was unrewarding. "Like pouring water from one glass into another," O'Neill said to him offhandedly at a meeting; Alan cringed at the image (and didn't realize O'Neill had swiped it from Chekhov).

So he worked at his briefings and his reports; he went on board carriers and missile cruisers; he flew to Quantico and briefed Marines on potential trouble spots. One evening a week, he spent two hours with a Tanzanian graduate student who mostly made fun of his bad Swahili rather than teaching him a better. And he waited for Rose to get her new assignment, so that they could find a real place to live.

And then she did.

She came down on a Friday. He picked her up at the airport as he always did, and they had kissed and murmured things as they always did, and he was driving through near-sleet when she said, "I've got something to tell you."

"You're pregnant, right?"

"No, I think I already told you that." She put her hand on his thigh, squeezed. "I saw my detailer. I've been offered a really great job. Plus one not so great."

"Wonderful!"

"The detailer's got no problem about keeping us together; that's policy. Plus there's no problem about me being pregnant for either job. One is in Norfolk, practically next door to you. Fuels Officer with a LantFleet office."

"Great!" He could see them in an apartment near the base, a blissfully short commute. Commuting, he had found, was a very important thing.

"The other is at Little Creek."

"Oh, bummer." Little Creek was more than an hour away. Too far for her to drive, he was thinking.

"Air wing staff."

When she didn't say more than that, he felt himself

pulled up, as if she'd jerked a leash. *Air wing staff.* Well, yes, that was a good career move. But surely, she wouldn't sacrifice him, his—his what? his (he avoided the word *comfort,* much less *convenience*), let's say, responsibility—to her own convenience? Or was it her comfort?

"Well, love—God, that's a long way."

"I'd split the difference. We'd find a place halfway between."

He didn't say that commuting to Little Creek was a breeze and commuting into Norfolk was hell. Instead, he said, "I just hope you'll consider both our needs."

She started to get angry. She had been waiting to get angry, he realized, since she had got in the car. He was just thinking that it was going to be their first fight when she went right to the top, no intermediate stages, and began to shout at him. *"I'm up for lieutenant commander! I'm in a fight! You're a j.g., for Christ's sake!"*

"Wait a minute! God, I have a stake in this, too!"

"You're not going to interfere in my life!"

"Rose, Rose, listen to what you're—"

"Fuck you! I've already taken the Little Creek job!"

Then he was angry. It was the rawness of her ambition that offended him. She had made the decision without telling him, without even consulting him. It was so one-sided. It was so heartless. It was so *unfair.*

They drove to the apartment without speaking, another fifteen minutes of hairy driving (so that he felt put upon as well as angry). She got out of the car as soon as he stopped and stood by the apartment door, fumbling in her shoulder bag for the key, muttering obscenities. He got out more slowly, ready for her to say something really outrageous so that he could offer to drive her back to the airport, *right then*—and he saw her, bent, hurried, rain sparkling on her shoulder and her hair, somehow the beautiful stranger in the souk in Dubai, and he remembered what she was to him.

"Rose," he said softly. The car was still between them. She turned and stared at him.

"Rose, it's *me*," he said. "Congratulations on the job. Whatever you want is fine with me."

He came around the car and they more or less fell against each other. She muttered something about "Rose, the Bad Girl." She kept saying she was so sorry, and he kept saying he was so stupid. "Next time it's your turn," she said. "Honest. I have to have this one. Honest!"

"I know you do. You're absolutely right. Only—next time—can't we talk about it?"

"I was afraid you'd argue."

"Well—" He thought of the long commute each way. "You're right, I would have argued."

"See?"

"What's wrong with arguing? Or talking, anyway."

"In my family, everybody gets mad and screams. Which is what I did."

"This isn't your family. This is our family. Let's go inside; it's raining."

She held him back. "Love me?"

"There's nobody else in the world I'd do that drive twice a day for. It must be love." He pulled her inside. "Anyway, I'm the father of your child."

APRIL 1, 1992. 2153 ZULU. NAVAL COMMUNICATIONS RE-SEARCH CENTER, PHILADELPHIA.

Donnie Marengo made space in his black shoulder bag with his left hand between the remains of his lunch and his copy of *Wired* and began to feed papers in with his right: an office copy of *Aviation News,* stamped with the office stamp and chosen for that reason, so it would be clear that he took office stuff home; two diagrams of the proposed U.S.-Russian space station, photocopied on the office machine from pop magazines; then eleven sheets photocopied from a classified report on message scrambling for satellite transmission. Last, he put in a copy of a long poem about bureaucracy, a lot of bad jokes and workplace humor.

He had picked the classified report after a lot of thought. It was old, for one thing. For another, its classification had recently been downgraded, but the Israelis wouldn't know that. Would they? He wished he knew more about how all this stuff worked. Did the Israelis have other people who also got them the same stuff, so they could cross-check? Or was he supposed to be the one getting stuff so they could check on somebody else? The thought that there might be somebody else in the same office doing the same thing made him sad and then angry. He didn't want to give anybody, not even the Israelis, anything important, so he had dug out this outdated stuff and was going to pass it along. It was the first batch he'd ever lifted; he believed he could string them along with stuff like this until—maybe until his dad gave it up, or got out of the Navy, or—something. On the other hand, the Israelis, they were *Jews,* and it was hardly a secret that Jews were smart. Wouldn't they catch on?

He looked, with his tongue slightly sideways between his front teeth, like a young man doing something absorbing but not unpleasant, not like somebody stealing outdated state secrets. He might have been packing for a day off somewhere, wondering if he needed a toothbrush or a condom. He did not look as if what he was doing involved any moral qualms. Still—

It isn't right, he told himself for the (dozenth? hundredth?) time. He didn't blame his father. His father was a man with a lot of problems, not born with some of the things that made it possible for other people to put up with their problems. Donnie Marengo knew, somewhat murkily—knowing the result, not the mechanism—that his father had somehow driven his own wife away—probably with his anger and his boozing and his distrust; he knew that his father had had a lot to do with the mess his sisters had made of their lives. Yet he loved his father and knew his father loved him (*in his way,* always that forgiving qualification), so that his father should have been capable of not driving away his wife and messing up his daughters, having succeeded in both with his son. He knew that he had been treated specially, on the other hand, not like either his mother or his sisters; his father had somehow protected him from that part of himself. Even when his mother had taken him away and changed his name to that of her new husband, the man for whom she had left his father, his father had forgiven him. Now, in return, he felt he owed his father love—even though his father already had his love, got proofs of it; one always wants *more*. He also, like almost all sons, wanted his father to approve of him. To like him. He wanted his father to, what? be compensated for all the shit he'd taken. And given.

Donnie Marengo was smart without being wise, because he was still very young. "Marengo's going places, once he—" his division and commanding officers said, their voices trailing off to mean *once he grows up*. They didn't know that his father had presented him with a dilemma that gave him no time to grow up.

Donnie zipped the bag, but not all the way.

Going down in the elevator, he checked himself for signs. He thought he had a slight headache. He made himself breathe slowly, the way he had read about in a book. He told himself to move slowly, too, but he didn't seem to be moving too fast, so that was just excessive caution. At the outer lobby, he got in line with all the other office geeks to go through security, not even Navy personnel but some rent-a-cop outfit. The guy tonight, a young black man, was joking with the guy who was checking the other line, riffling through people's bags, his eyes flicking up and down, up and down, to the other guy and then down to the bags, talking all the time.

Donnie unzipped his bag and held it out, open. His fingers trembled, but not bad enough to cause the bag to tremble. The rent-a-cop glanced in and waved his hand.

Donnie walked out.

It wouldn't always be that easy, he thought. He would sew a false bottom into the nylon shoulder bag. Maybe some sort of pocket in the raincoat. They never checked coats. He'd use his wife's sewing machine. She would make fun of him; the more stoned she was, the crueler fun she'd make.

Life was a bitch.

17

They bought a house, rather than renting an apartment; and
it was closer to Little Creek, not Norfolk. The seeming
enormity of buying something scared him, but Rose was
impressively practical, and she showed him figures that
made all that debt seem a positive benefit. He already
owned a house, he said, but of course it was in Florida.
He rented that one—Povick was gone, somewhere in the
Med—and, cleaning out his few things on a weekend visit,
felt a pang of guilt for evicting his father's ghost.

   They had a housewarming party. Rose had lots of Navy
friends; so did he, once he thought about it. The Peretzes
came, and late in the evening he saw Rose and Bea Peretz
with their heads together, like two dark sisters. Harry
O'Neill (he was Harry now, Creole rigorously banned)
brought his wife, a pretty, sullen woman who was ill at
ease and who, from a single remark he overheard, thought
of herself as slumming. His new skipper came for a few
minutes. When they were all gone and he and Rose were
cleaning up, she said, "I liked Bea Peretz."

"That's a side of her I hadn't seen. I always thought of her as very noisy."

"She's going to take me someplace baby clothes are cheap." She piled a tray with glasses. "I didn't like your friend O'Neill's wife, I'm afraid. She's a snob."

"Oh, come on." Of course, Harry O'Neill's wife was a snob, but he didn't want her saying so.

"I know when I'm being patronized. I may be a hick dago from upstate New York, but I know when I'm being patronized."

"Well—" Alan felt defensive. "He went to Harvard."

Rose laughed. "That's what my mother calls *you*—'the Harvard man.'" She came out of the kitchen and fell backward into a chair. "I'm bummed out. But it was pretty good, yes?"

"Pretty good, yes." He was opening windows. "Too much smoke. Bad for the kid. How is the kid, anyway?"

"I'm starting to show. I've got to get some bigger clothes."

"Do they make pregnancy uniforms?"

"They better."

The long drive at first appalled him, gradually became normal, a time to think, prepare for the day. He was often early as a result of his fear of being held up; he used the time to review message traffic, clear his pile of reports, glance over the summaries, his equivalent of the morning paper. He would listen to NPR's *Morning Edition* on the drive down; he would check CNN, then, if he had time, hit several Internet addresses, mostly universities, where interesting African ideas popped up.

One morning, he turned from his computer to find Commander Reicher standing behind him.

"I thought you were married, Craik."

"Yessir."

"Are you here every morning this early?"

"I beat the traffic."

"If you'd like to move in, I could give you Europe and

maybe Japan along with Africa. We could use some genius in the other areas."

"Uh—sir, I'd really rather you'd stop making that joke, if you don't mind."

"Lieutenant, I'd really rather you didn't talk to me like that, and I do mind. I'll say any goddam thing to you I want. You may walk on water but you're still a j.g., and you've got a lot to learn."

The African analysis became automatic; so, after a few weeks, did the Ad Hoc. Without realizing it, he came to think of himself as going nowhere, a squirrel in a cage. The excitement of the squadron had given way to white-collar routine, and, despite wearing a uniform, standing inspections, saluting, he thought of himself as a kind of decorated civilian. Alan realized that he had adapted to the squadron too well. All this analysis, this was what intel guys dreamed of. Alan wondered if he missed flying. Face facts, he thought—it made you feel airsick and you were always second best. What Alan missed was the squadron itself, the solid feel of a job well done, and the people.

Rose, on the other hand, was excited about her work, about her contacts, about her career; as the fetus grew, so did her sense of place and purpose. He admitted to himself a deep disappointment, not least because the unfinished business of his father's death was fading to nothing. He thought of asking his detailer about a transfer, even thought about leaving the Navy. He had talked to somebody who was in Counterintelligence; he thought there might be a place there. Counterintelligence sounded like real life.

Which was why, when the time for his fitness report came, he approached it with a kind of defiant shrug. If it was bad enough, he would have an excuse to find something else (and the Band-Aid that his CO didn't like him).

He walked into Reicher's office at the appointed time, sat down as he was bid, made polite talk with the man about how he liked it there, how he liked analysis, what his personal problems were. (He didn't have any, he said.)

Reicher was in his shirtsleeves; he leaned back in his swivel chair, his cheek on one hand, seeming to study Alan as if he were an exotic, and unattractive, specimen. Finally, he rolled forward and skittered a sheet of paper across the desk.

"Draft fitrep," he said.

Alan picked it up and read *One of the two best officers in my command.* He felt himself blush.

"You're surprised," Reicher said.

"Yessir."

"Why is that? Inferiority complex?"

"I, uh—didn't think you liked me, sir."

"I don't. What's that got to do with it?" He seemed to spring at Alan merely by bringing the chair still farther forward with a rasp of its mechanism. "Notice I said one of the best two. I said the same thing about the other guy. Why? I want you to get better. How do you get better? Get older. Get wiser. You're already lucky, so I won't say, 'Get luckier.' You're a hell of a briefer. You're a great instinctive analyst. You're not as good a plodder. I want you to learn to plod, like the rest of us. We all shovel shit, tons of it; that's how you find the diamonds, right? I'm not talking about work. You work like a fucking slave; in fact, I intend to say you work too hard. I mean just putting up with the boring, day-after-day, uninteresting crap. The dumb ideas. The other guy's bad analysis. The stupid estimates. Your own dumb ideas; we all have them, even you. You miss flying, Craik?"

"Sometimes. The esprit de corps."

"The goosing. Yeah. The glamor, am I right?" Reicher was not a flyer (he had never heard of Mick Craik, Alan supposed, had no concept of Mick Craik's son—a relief) but had, of course, a similar experience somewhere in his Navy past. "You don't seem a very happy young man to me, and that concerns me. You're just married; you got a great wife; she's gonna have a baby—what's the matter?"

He suppressed the notion of talking about the spy who had caused his father's death—the spy nobody else believed in—and said, "I guess I wish I was in something more—active."

"You want the Navy to provide you with excitement, along with everything else? How do you see yourself— Clint Eastwood? Tom Cruise?" He leaned back again with his hands behind his head. Reicher had a planed look, as if his face had been cut from some hard wood, and he wore his sandy hair very short. Seeing him, Alan abruptly saw that Reicher, too, was often bored here, perhaps equally unsure of the value of what he did. He wondered why he knew so little about the man, realized it was because he had never asked.

"There's going to be a SNIE on Africa asked for." SNIE—Special National Intelligence Estimate. A big deal. "I can feel it. Well, it's all over the tube—famine, corruption, this clicking around in Somalia. It's an election year, too; those people up in Washington are up to their ass in polls, and what a few of them will have the good sense to ask for is a special estimate. You'll be involved." Again, he rolled forward, and again his chair moaned. "You want a change, here's your chance. There's a port-appraisal team going from DDS's side, a couple of agents and somebody in AT; I'm going to ask to have you tacked on." He punched an index finger on the desk to emphasize certain words. "I want you to *go;* I want you to *watch* and *listen;* and I want you to soak up *everything* you can. *No collection.* You understand what that means? Don't pay anybody; don't offer anybody anything; don't even take anybody to lunch. Look but don't touch. We're not tasked with collection; that's what ops is for. Can you hold the horsepower down that much?"

Alan smiled. "I think so."

"Okay. Port-appraisal group is going to Mombasa. No country clearances—that means they're glorified tourists. They fix something up with State for the visas; I don't do that part. They'll liaise with local police—that oughta be fun—and make their peace with the CIA resident, who won't give a shit because he doesn't care whether Mombasa's a good liberty port or not. They're going to be a couple weeks." He looked a little aside at Alan. "Somalia. Two questions: (a) What's going down in those refugee camps? And (b) How is it affecting Mombasa? Go out. Talk to people. You'll go under the wing of a senior NCIS agent."

"That sounds like collection."

"Be that as it may, you're going to stand on the sidelines of that and watch the process. At some point, you can take off and visit any three other destinations to talk with our people in-country. Look around. There will be three products—the port-appraisal report; a classified Somalia receptivity estimate, mostly for the Marines; and your 'What I Did on My Summer Vacation' report of your own impressions. You speak any of the language yet?"

"Some Swahili. What destinations?"

"You tell me. Come on, you're the African hotshot— what cities do you want to see?"

"Kinshasa, Johannesburg—Pretoria, if I'm seeing the attaché—either Kigali or Kampala. You mean, I really get to do this?"

"Orders will be cut next week if there're no glitches. Back when we had money during the Cold War, every analyst did a whistle-stop through his area. If you're going to talk to big guns at the Senate, you had better be able to say you've actually been to Africa. Run over to Quantico before then and get checked out on Fleet Marine panic about Africa. They think that if we go in, they're the point. Don't make any predictions; they're likely to ask you to go along. And I won't let you. And get Top Salter to give you a firearms qual." He pointed a pencil at Alan's nose. "You're not going to be an ops officer. I've got you for three years, and you're an analyst, and by Christ you're going to get a fitrep that says you're the best, not one of the best two, before I leave here. I have high standards. Don't you screw up." He gave a kind of smile, more a parting of the lips. "That's all."

• • •

"It's only a few days each place," he said to Rose. "I'll be home before you even miss me."

"It's not a good time. I'm pregnant, for Christ's sake!"

"You've got months yet, Rose."

"But you said yourself, it's not required."

"I'm an Africa analyst and I've never been to Africa. It's a great chance."

"Great chance, my ass; Reicher hates your guts, you tell me one minute, now he loves you and it's a great chance? Bull. I think he's blowing the money in his budget before the year ends."

"You're cranky."

"I sure am."

"You *love* your job."

"I want my husband."

"Now you talk like a Navy wife."

"I do, don't I!" She threw an arm around his neck and held him. "Be careful over there; no playing around, everybody's got AIDS. Stay out of the jungle. Where is it you're going, exactly?"

"Mombasa."

"Why the hell do they care about it as a liberty port?"

"Somalia. Maybe some other things that are shaping up. All we do is spend a few days looking around, talking to some people, then they write a sort of tour guide."

"What sort of people?"

"Oh—cops, storekeepers, you know—prostitutes—"

"You let somebody else do that part."

Later, they lay in bed; the house, still so new to them that in the dark he had to feel his way from room to room, made small, domestic sounds: the furnace, a drip. She nestled into him. "I know it hasn't been so swell recently for you. Has it?" He said nothing. "What is it you want, anyway?"

"I think I miss the squadron. All that activity. It isn't anything."

She kissed him, one of those feather-light touches of the lips that become a means of communication between real lovers; not the false lip-brush of public fashion. "Is it your dad?"

He had told her about his father—told her all of it, the attempt at docking, the last gesture, the dead end. Tears sprang to his eyes. He turned his face away from hers to hide them; she turned it back, kissed him. "I miss—*doing* things," he rasped. Doing things to make sense of his father's death, he meant. She understood. He felt grief—astonishingly fresh—like a stranglehold on his throat. He tried to smile. "So, I go to Mombasa instead."

He was walking along the Dulles airport ticket counters toward the international departure end when he heard a voice shouting something; he paid no attention, but it shouted even louder, "Hey, Spy!" He turned; it was Rafe-hausen. Alan's reality wavered for an instant.

"Hey, Spy! What are you, deaf? I been calling for a couple minutes, man!" Rafe stepped over the barrier rope. "I got about thirty seconds before I gotta run for a plane. You're lookin' good. I heard you got married."

They traded news; Alan asked about Tailhook, and Rafe winced. "You at Tailhook, Rafe?" Alan was so far from aviation now that he was surprised at the reaction.

"No, I fucking was *not*. But the witch hunt is on. You were one of us at sea, Spy, you know how it is—a different world. Some stupid shits took it off the boat and brought it to Vegas, that's all. Everything in its place."

Alan thought about sea time; nicknames, practical jokes. Flying. His father saluting, Christine falling out of the sky. A different world with its own rules for keeping everyone sane. No sand in the gears. Rafe clearly wanted to change the subject. "Hey, you heard about Christine?"

Alan had not.

"Went down. In the water. Took all four crew. Drug interdiction for some asshole country down south. Well, she was a classy old slut, in her way. I gotta run, Spy." He was teaching at Pensacola. "How about you?"

"I'm headed for Africa."

Rafe said that was really too bad. "Ever miss flying, Alan?"

Alan couldn't remember being addressed by his name by Rafe.

"Yes. Often."

Rafe laughed. "Glad to know it even bites geniuses."

"Call me if you're ever in Norfolk?"

"Will do. Stay safe in Africa, Alan." Rafe walked away. Alan stood there for a moment. Rafe had called him Alan twice. Tailhook must be a sore subject.

Alan met his "partner" (in reality, his chaperone), a civilian NCIS agent, in London. Mike Dukas was older, tough, stocky. A Navy cop. After several beers in London pubs and a quick tour of Piccadilly, Dukas shepherded Alan out to Gatwick for their flight. Zipping out of Victoria on the express, Dukas laid down the law. "Stop acting like a Navy guy. Your rank, my rank, not important. I'm a pushy Greek who likes to talk; you're going to talk some, too. You don't call me sir, you call me Mike. Okay?"

Thirty thousand feet over the Med, Mike gave his opinion of their destination.

"Great town, Mombasa. Cops are brutal and corrupt and fairly untrained, but there are a few really good ones there. We'll meet both kinds. I'll try to take a few out and get to know them. You can come if you want. But I want you to play tourist a bit. I want you to hit Old Town, talk to the locals. I want a head count on Lebanese merchants in the city. We'll look through the phone book, hit as many as we can. Look at their shops, see what they sell, how they react."

Alan was seldom baffled, but this baffled him. He wondered if Rose was right: this was punishment, and Mike was ditching him with a made-up job. It must have showed in his face.

"Al, look; scratch a Lebanese and find an Iranian. Those merchants are the support network the ragheads would use to pop a bunch of sailors in Mombasa. Dull job, but folks at HQ want to know."

"Mike, I don't want to annoy you, but it sounds pretty, um—"

"Dull? Sorry, Mr. Bond." Dukas pulled his ball cap down over his eyes.

18

Franci scowled at the European who was staring in the shop window.

From his high, walled desk in Bash-O-Vision, Franci scowled at everybody. He had more customers now, some who even came back. He wished they wouldn't and was quite rude to them. The shop had dropped into some niche in local needs, but it no longer interested him as an enterprise. He had amused himself once with a shop-wide sale; the Chinese, frowning, had stood outside and shaken his head. Risa had looked frightened, then angry; she was afraid they would be returned to Iran and hanged for embezzling the difference between the assigned price and his sale prices—"Half Off! *Starehe* Powerful Bargain!" *Stupid woman,* he had thought and gone ahead with it. Then, one morning, he had ripped the sign down for no better reason than that he was tired of it.

He had given up his notions about her and now lived in his own part of the house, even cooking for himself much of the time. They hardly spoke, except when she shouted at him to shut up, and he realized he was talking to himself. He never seemed to sleep. At night, he prowled his part of the house and the street outside. He noticed that his hands had begun to tremble; fearing some disease, he kept them closed into fists and hid them from himself. Even though it was probably too late, he disinfected everything he might have to touch, wiping the surfaces again and again. He always smelled of disinfectant.

Now, seeing this European outside his cluttered window, he felt outraged. The man would be a tourist who had wandered into the wrong street; shortly, having satisfied himself that the shop represented a typical god-awful Third World hole, he would head back toward the affluent part of the city. *Go go,* Franci thought, *Go to hell, in fact.*

At which point, the man walked in. He was young, tall, dark, obviously American. He smiled. "*Salaam alekkem,*" he said.

"And to you," Franci growled in English. "What do you want?"

"I'm looking for some batteries."

Franci nodded at the wall behind the man. "No American batteries."

"I need double-A."

Franci knew he wouldn't buy the batteries. He was an American; he wanted good batteries, not this Chinese shit that his supplier in Aden provided him. "Tiger Brand is all I carry."

"Well, they'll have to do then, won't they?" He took two packs and laid them on the high desk.

"They won't last," Franci said. He was angry that the man had proven unpredictable. "Chinese—no good. They don't last."

"You speak very good English. I keep trying my bad Swahili, and people keep speaking English to me."

"British colony," Franci said as, reluctantly, he took his money.

"You sound more like an American, yourself."

"I learned from Americans. Forty shillings your change."

"In the U.S.?"

"I have never been to the U.S.!" The lie was presented too strongly. "Beirut. I am Lebanese." What if the American were an Iranian spy, there to check up on him? "Where are you from in the U.S.?"

"Virginia. About four hundred miles south of New York. East Coast."

"Yes, yes, yes." Franci could have said that he had been to Williamsburg once. A wave of longing swept over him: he had gone toWilliamsburg with an American woman who had been crazy about him. Oh, the missed opportunities! He felt intensely sorry for himself. "I remember Virginia on the map in school," Franci muttered. "George Washington." He stared at the other man, hoping to trip him up.

"Right. Mount Vernon." He slipped the batteries into a shoulder bag. "Can I get tea around here?"

"Tea? I do not carry tea."

"Tea to drink, I mean—a cup of tea. *Chai na asali.* I really like it, the way they drink it here."

"Better you go back toward the hotels. Better-quality places."

"Well, crazy as it sounds, I don't like the better-quality places. A *hoteli.*"

It did not sound crazy, because Franci remembered what young Americans were like. A taste of adventure, a little Third World slumming, then back to the Hilton. He decided the young man really was an American. He thought of what had disgusted him about America—the materialism, the waste, the narcissism, the racist hatred of Ay-rabs. "To the right out the door," he said, "first street, make right, then— I will show you."

The young man protested, but Franci got off his stool and limped to the end of the partition that separated him from his customers. He watched, with sour satisfaction, the American's face change as he understood the missing leg. Then, of course, the American began to protest; Franci insisted even more strongly, leading him out of the shop and along the street. At the corner, he watched his own doorway for thieves but pointed the other way, giving directions.

"Would you join me?" the young man said.

"What?"

"Would you have tea with me? It's almost closing time."

"Why?"

He smiled. "Courtesy."

Franci, for whom courtesy was only a memory, felt enraged all over again; what was the man trying to do, humiliate him? He started to say it was quite impossible, and then he saw that probably the American was trying to trick him. The correct answer, of course, was no; therefore, rather nastily, he said yes. Now let us see what the young ruler of the world would do with an Ay-rab on his hands for tea.

He locked the shop door and limped back down the street, and they made their way together through the streams of people. He never felt comfortable among them, for all they were Muslims, too, in their caps and white *kanzus* like nightshirts. "Not your kind of people," he said to the American with some satisfaction.

"How long have you been here?"

"Oh, a long time." Personal questions annoyed him; on top of that, there was all the paranoia they had taught him at the camp. In fact, he thought this American was merely arrogant, like all his kind, not a threat. His wife might threaten him; the Mombasa police might threaten him; he did not believe a young American could threaten him. "You are a tourist?" he said.

"Vacation, yes—sort of. I'm in the Navy."

"You are a military man?" Momentarily, the camp's warnings returned. "Oh, yes, the Navy and, and so on. The Marines were in Beirut, you know. A tragic business." He hazarded a more elaborate lie. "I, too—my leg, you know, also in Beirut. It was a war. A hideous explosion, like, like—looking into the sun. When I woke up, I was—" That was too close to the truth. Tears formed in his eyes. This was happening to him more and more now, he thought, this loss of control. "You have been in war?" he said.

"Not like that."

They sat in the shadow and drank their tea. The American was not forthcoming about the military life but was not offensive, either; he seemed to ask questions quite honestly. Had Franci been on safari? Where was it best to see animals? How did he get along with the Africans? Were they friendly to him? Did he have friends among them?

Franci began to talk, slowly, then more rapidly, words rushing over each other to get out so that he stumbled sometimes. He even found himself laughing, too loud, not always appropriately. "Oh, these people!" he said. "These people—really!" He told several of his comical experiences at the shop—the Chinese; a beggar who regularly appeared; the yard man. "He calls me bwana and expects I will help in his scrapes! It is colonialism all over again—me, a colonial!" He giggled.

"You're Muslim, aren't you?" the young man, who by then had told him his name was Alan, said. "Isn't that a bond with the people here?"

"Yes, yes, but they are a different sect. You know the Aga Khan?"

"Not personally."

That tickled Franci. It had been so long since anybody had made a joke around him that he screamed and spilled his tea. "Here, they are followers of the Aga Khan. Quite different. Of course, we all go to mosque; we all go to Mecca. You know Mecca? Of course. I have not been there, of course, I am not a *haj,* a pilgrim, but it is the same. Even American black Muslims go to Mecca."

"Malcolm X. He was *El-Hajj Malik.*"

"How do you know that, Alan? You know a great deal. How did you know to say *salaam alekkem* when you came into my shop?"

"I read a book."

"Aha, my friend, that explains your pronunciation. It was very bad. You must say 'alekkem' this way." He made a guttural sound, and Alan repeated it until it was really quite good. "That is good. You are quite intelligent, actually."

"For an American."

They both laughed. Franci, in fact, laughed until tears came.

When they walked back to the shop, Franci found that he had swung from acute dislike for the American to a feeling of disproportionate loss that he was going away. "Please forgive me," he babbled. "I cannot respond—return your hospitality. The tea, I mean. My house is—quite impossible." It was a terrible thing for a Muslim man to have to admit. "I have had such a good time. So enjoyable. Like—having a friend. I am not—" After some seconds of silence, he realized that he was moving his lips but making no sound. Had he been rehearsing what to say?

"That's okay."

"Well, you said—courtesy. Yes. That was a very nice courtesy. I do not meet much courtesy here. I should want to return this one example of it. But I cannot. I, ah—my house—" His lips moved; again, no sound came out. *I am a madman,* he thought. The idea, entirely new, explained much.

"Well, you can buy me a cup of tea sometime, how's that?"

But there would be no "sometime," Franci knew. Even so, he said, "You come back, then. Good. This was a most enjoyable afternoon, my friend Alan." They shook hands.

After Alan was gone, Franci looked at the shop, the tawdry goods, the beetle lying on its back on the unswept floor, and he began to talk aloud to himself.

I've met a funny Lebanese, Alan wrote to Rose. He wrote her every night, never at a loss for things to say, even though they also talked on the telephone every few days. *Only he isn't funny, He's kind of sad. Certainly in some kind of emotional state. Maybe a bad marriage, poor guy, from what he said about home. Plus he lost a leg in the civil war. Hard for a young guy to have that. Still, he's bright as hell, and full of information about all sorts of things. I liked him. And he speaks good English, which is a real plus here.*

The little man with one leg really did interest him. He was a good source. And Commander Reicher to the contrary, conversation over tea wasn't collection. *I think if we lived here he would become a friend, and you'd like him, too.* He wrote about other things—weather; the food; an NCIS guy on the team he liked, Mike Dukas, now his roommate—and closed the letter.

Alan loved Mombasa. He loved the smells and the swirl of the place; he loved it the way tourists love it—an actual dhow seen in the harbor; carved antique doors in a narrow street; *kanzus* and striped *kikois*—but loved it also for something deeper. He was trying not to lose his objectivity over it.

He wanted to go to a mosque. He wasn't sure if the rules were different here, and he stuck out even more in Mombasa then he had in Dubai. *Naval Officer Sparks Riot,* he thought. That wouldn't do. And so, next morning, he was on the way back to Franci's squalid store. He had met a number of people in Mombasa who might have helped him, most of them local cops, one a woman of consummate elegance whom he had spoken to at the hotel pool, but none would do as a guide to the mosque. Franci might.

He put his head in the door. It was gloomy inside, as he remembered from the first time; his sun-dazzled eyes narrowed, trying to find a human being. He could hear a voice but couldn't see anybody. "Hello?" The voice stopped. Now able to see his way, Alan stepped inside. "Hello!" The place reeked of something like Lysol.

Franci rose from behind the barrier, spectral to Alan's still-dim vision. "Friend Alan!" he shrieked. He held a rag and a bottle with "Dettol" slanted down it.

"Hi. I can't see you very well. The sun."

"I was only cleaning. Filthy places. How nice to see you!"

They shook hands over the partition. Alan put his proposition: would Franci take him to the mosque?

"You want to go to the mosque?"

"Can I?"

"Yes, yes, no problem. You have to take off your shoes. You must cover your head."

Alan produced a cloth cap, bought that morning at a stall.

"Yes!" Franci giggled. Abruptly, he seemed to swing to intense suspicion; he said, "You will not mock?"

"Of course not."

"We do not want to be looked at. We are not animals. Zoo."

"No, no."

Then, Franci as abruptly swung back. "I can repay your courtesy! I buy us tea, and I will teach you the regimen of the mosque. Yes? That would be very friendly. Yes? Maybe—" He giggled. "Maybe you will be converted to Islam, might Allah be praised. Then we could be true friends."

Alan smiled. He was thinking that this young man desperately needed a true friend. Maybe he needed much more than that.

Next day, Alan flew to Kampala, the first of three African capitals he would visit that week. He tried to remember every sight and sound, to see everything, talk to everybody, taste the food, smell the air. He returned worn out but excited—a new world, *his* world. His notes were a hodgepodge—Zaire—potholes! Uganda—bicycles—charcoal—bullet holes—but they called up for him an exoticism as intense as Dubai and the Bedouin.

He had only three days left before they flew home. He spent the day after the whirlwind tour walking the waterfront, going everywhere now, wearing his Muslim cap and not caring about people's sometimes startled looks, then their smiles. Some of them even began to recognize him. He went out along Makadara Road and had another look at the old Portuguese fort, which was supposed to interest him but didn't much; he was too drawn by the people and the swirl of life. So he turned into the old town. If he hesitated, a shopkeeper would be at his side; if he murmured one of his words of Swahili or, better yet, Arabic (he had learned to say *Maharaba* from Franci), he was invited inside for coffee. *Why not?* he thought, his time drawing short, and so he had two tiny cups of the wonderful, bitter brew before he reached the old harbor. Boatmen surrounded him, wanting to take him somewhere—to the actual dhow that was moored out there. He was tempted. He almost said yes.

And then a shrill voice shouted, "Friend Alan!"

He turned, and there was Franci across the road, waving with a manic vigor as cars and bicycles whizzed between them. Alan waved, not entirely pleased.

"My friend Alan!" Franci scolded at the boatmen in Swahili and they backed off, grumbling as Franci took charge of him. "These people are uncouth, probably criminals; you must not associate with them. Pocket-pickers, some. Alan, I thought you were gone back to U.S.!"

Alan regretted the disappearance of the boatmen. "I had to come back to Mombasa with my tour." Franci's intensity annoyed him this morning; he was enjoying being on his own, stumbling through with his bad Swahili. "I don't want to keep you," he said.

"Oh—I am on an errand. Out toward—" Franci waved a hand. "I would say, let us chat, but I have an appointment." He looked at his watch. They could meet for lunch, maybe. Alan said no. For tea, then. Alan lied and claimed another appointment. Dinner, Franci urged; he knew an authentic coast-Arab place where tourists never went, upstairs, Alan would never find it without him. Alan was tempted, tired of meals with the NCIS agents in the safe, fake-American confines of the International Superba Beach Hotel.

"Sounds good. Dutch, though."

"Dutch?" Franci frowned.

"I pay for my own. No, no—I'm not allowed. Truly. It's against my, um, orders. Unethical." He thought of what Reicher would say if he got a free meal. *What the hell do you think we're giving you all that per diem for, to work up an obligation to some raghead?* "I'd really like to, Franci, but I can't let you pay."

Franci's lips were moving. Finally sound came out. "I do not understand. Not a good way. But—yes, well— You will meet me there?" He borrowed Alan's pen and notebook and drew a map. "Perfectly safe," he muttered. He kept muttering it as he drew. "Perfectly safe. No problem. Okay." He held out the pen. "Upstairs over the hardware, okay?"

Alan regretted it, off and on, for the rest of the day. He liked Franci but thought he was cracking up, and he was tired from the flights and the tour. When he called the hotel to tell the others he wouldn't be there for dinner, Dukas said, "You're crazy. Mombasa Old Town is a zoo."

"I'll be okay, Mom."

"You're gonna wind up in a harem in the Saudi outback, Craik, I kid you not. They cut your wazoo off and stick it in your ear for a decoration, no shit. What are they going to feed you, fried goat turd or something? Eat American."

"I'll be fine, Mom. Don't wait up."

"Where do you want the remains sent?"

For a moment, he was ready to say he'd eat at the hotel, after all; Franci would show up at the restaurant, realize at last he wasn't coming.

No, he couldn't do that.

And he knew, within minutes of entering the dark, spice-scented upper room, that if he had backed out he would have missed one of the great meals of his life. Course after course came, subtle foods, outrageous foods, strange and familiar foods. Franci's craziness was put aside. He was teacher, entertainer, friend. They laughed a lot. The black waiter padded back and forth, bringing tray after tray; only one other table had customers. The meal went on for hours.

"I may never move," Alan said at the end.

"It was good, Alan?"

"It was magnificent."

"I am made happy. When I find this place, I thought, to

bring someone here is also a happiness. I thought of my father, back in—Lebanon. A man who loves food. How he would appreciate this! Your father is living, Alan?"

"No. He died. About a year and a half ago."

"Ah, I am sorry. Truly sorry. The father is—the source. No, what is the word—the cause. Of understanding of God. Yes?"

They had tiny cups of black coffee. He sipped. "To have the father die is to feel the deepest loss, I think. I fear it with my father. Every letter that comes, I fear that this time— He was old, your father?"

"No."

"Worse. My father is old. I am a late child, many sisters and four brothers. You have brothers, Alan?"

He was not quite paying attention, thinking instead of Christine and death and his father's aircraft. "I saw him go down," he said. "He was a pilot. I saw his plane go down."

Franci's breath drew in harshly, shocked. His overreaction was a sign that he was swinging back toward his fragility; Alan did not notice.

"He was a Navy pilot."

"I am so sorry. How terrible, my friend. You *saw*—this?"

Alan began to tell the story. He had been over it so many times in his mind, had told it so often to Rose and Peretz and others, that the details were sharp and practiced. It was not a story to him but a present reality; Franci was more or less forgotten, although he was aware of Franci's hands, trembling as they tried to pick up the coffee cup. Once, he glanced up and saw Franci's lips moving. He had reached the moment when he had recognized his father's helmet. He went on—the attempts to refuel, the failures, that last gesture—the aircraft dropping away—

And he became aware that the man opposite him was sobbing and was starting to babble.

19

He woke Dukas in the hotel room. It was past midnight. The NCIS man had drunk too much and was heavily asleep, and he woke grudgingly, resentfully. Blinking at the light, he said, "What the hell?"

"I've got to talk to you, Mike. You sober?"

"I'm not even sure I'm alive. Jesus Christ, what time is it? God, what a taste! My mouth is like dogshit."

"Mike, come on. Make sense."

"Okay, okay, okay." He staggered into the bathroom. He was a heavy, hairy man who still wore white boxer shorts to sleep in. When he came back, his hair was wet and combed back, his face red from rubbing. "Okay, whatcha got?"

"Is the room secure?"

"Of course it is! Jesus."

"When did you check?"

"This morning. Okay, okay." He opened his attaché case and took out a dark device, walked around the walls and back and forth with it. "Nada. Satisfied? What's the big deal?"

"I had a contact with an Iranian."

"So what?"

"I think he's an agent."

"Oh, bummer. Well, cover your ass. Report it to your security officer."

"That isn't it. This guy is willing to give me stuff."

"Uh-unh, don't do that! That's trouble, *big* trouble. Contact is one thing, recruitment is another." He was fully awake now, pulling on a cotton robe and then adding a pair of black calf-high socks; the gap between was pale and hairy. "What d'you mean, 'give you stuff'?"

"There was an operation just before the Gulf War; this guy was in it, on their side. I was in it, too. There've always been some questions about what happened. *He has the answers.* He gave me some of them. I couldn't stop him, honest to God; the stuff just poured out. The guy's a basket case, right on the edge or maybe over it."

"You sure he's the real thing?"

"I'm not sure of anything. I don't want to screw up; what do I do? Before you answer, I have to say I want to be in on it; I *have* to be in on it. There's a personal angle. It's— I'll tell you later; it's not part of my problem right now. This guy is going to change his mind or run away or just clam up if we don't move on him right now—debrief him, make him feel good, give him some sense of, of— security. He says he won't talk to anybody but me."

"That won't fly."

"Why not?"

Dukas sighed. "Because this is the real world. Because this is Kenya, not the U.S. Because there are people at the embassy who are fucking misers about everything like recruitment that goes on here. You can't just say, 'I'm an intelligence guy so I'm going to recruit an asset.' You gotta have a team—a comm guy, a security guy, a debriefer, maybe a psych expert, maybe a lawyer; maybe you want people with guns and stuff like that. Has this guy got a watcher?"

"I think his wife. He wasn't very clear."

"If he's an Iranian asset and he's got a watcher and he or she is onto your meeting, you can be looking at some very rough play. You can't just land in a foreign country on a tourist visa and think you're James Bond. You *gotta* have a team, and they gotta have country clearances, and those come through the Agency and State. At the very least, you can quickly get yourself in deep shit with the Kenyans for playing spy here. They'd love to find an Iranian asset, you can just bet; they wouldn't be too nice about pushing you out of the way to get to him. You ever been inside a Kenyan jail? You know what 'human rights' means here? Jesus H. Christ, Al, we've dropped money around on the Kenyan cops like fucking rain, and they still barely let us talk to the Somalis about stuff that isn't even going on in Kenya! You think they're gonna play nice while you turn on a tape recorder and debrief a maybe Iranian asset? Get real."

"What do I do?"

"Report it to your security officer and go home."

"I can't abandon this guy. I can't—lose him."

"What is this, up close and personal? *You* can't lose him? You work for the U.S. government, boyo."

"It's very important to me."

"If you try to recruit and debrief a foreign intelligence asset *yourself,* you're going to face a court-martial. Or at least a reprimand that will be like a kick in the ass right out of the Navy. I'm a civilian, but I know how this works. I can tell you exactly how it would go if I had to investigate it. You'd be crucified, buddy! You gotta use the system!"

"Okay, okay; I'm not asking to go it alone. I'm asking what I do so I can be part of it. Mike, the guy won't talk to anybody else!"

"I can't tell you how often agents say that. They recruit somebody, they think they've given birth to them. Then they get rotated out of the job, somebody new comes along—surprise, surprise, the contact is just as happy with the new guy. So long as the money flows."

"This guy doesn't want money."

"Ha, ha."

"Mike— All right. What do I do? I'll call Carol Schuler in the morning, our security officer. It better be a secure line, right?"

"Better, yeah."

"Who's got a secure line?"

"The embassy."

"Uh-unh."

"You're afraid they'll take it away from you?"

"I sure am."

"You're right. Well, we don't got one. What you need is a STU-III, which I'd have if I was here on an investigation, but I ain't. So, who's got a STU? There's a British ship in the harbor. Try 'em."

"Just go and ask?"

"Yeah. All they can say is no. Tell the intel guy you have a classified message, tell him he can listen in if he wants. The Brits are okay about shit like that."

"Okay, I tell Carol. Then—? Who does our asset recruitment?"

Dukas smiled. "Nobody. The Navy doesn't do HUMINT, sweetheart. *We* don't do it. You guys don't do it."

Alan remembered something that he had said once to Peretz about HUMINT and its uselessness. The remark had come back to haunt him.

HMS *Agile* lay well out in Kilindini roads. Alan saw no boats out and so hired the same sort of boatman he had been tempted by the day before, when Franci had interrupted him. Now, at barely half past seven in the morning, he was rowed across the oily water in a brightly painted wooden skiff, hardly what he would have chosen to approach a British ship. Yet there was no comment when he clambered up her ladder, saluted the after flag, and told the bosun's mate at the gangway that he had business with the intelligence officer.

"If you'll wait one moment, sir—" A certain amount of electronic communication followed; then Alan was led along the deck and down a level. He was wired by lack of sleep and anxiety over Franci, yet he had the sensitivity still to feel nostalgia: small as the ship was, it reminded him of the carrier.

"Leftenant Houlting will take care of you, sir."

Houlting was an absurdly young-looking lieutenant who immediately offered him coffee, made remarks about early risers, and glanced at Alan's credentials with admirable quickness. When Alan had explained what he wanted, he said, "That's really Trevor's program, but I see why you came to me. Come along, then. You're intel, are you? I'm mostly a ship's officer, you know; nothing so grand as a dedicated intelligence officer on a little thing like *Agile*."

They ducked through a watertight doorway and Alan, meaning to be sociable despite having lain awake all night, stewing, said something about tight quarters and destroyers. Houlting stopped dead and turned around and said with mock severity—at least Alan hoped it was mock—"HMS *Agile* is a frigate, sir, not a destroyer. Rather Patrick O'Brian, serving on a frigate, eh?" He saw Alan's lack of comprehension. "You do read Patrick O'Brian? Oh, dear." Off he went again, up ladders, along narrow passageways, darting finally into a space filled with electronic gear and apparently bored other ranks. "Trevor! Where's Leftenant Monck?" A rating jerked his head without even looking up. Off they went again. "Trevor! Aha. Trevor, this is Leftenant Craik of the American Navy who has serious business with you, he says, but seems not to have heard of Patrick O'Brian. Only a Russian spy could make a mistake like that; what d'you think?"

"I think you don't have enough to do, and I have too much." He gripped Alan's hand and then spent far longer over Alan's documents than Houlting had, then disappeared for five minutes while Alan cooled his heels—Houlting had disappeared—and then came back saying that, well, he thought that was all right; and a minute later, Alan was sitting next to a STU-III and dialing the U.S. country code.

"You want to listen in?" he said while the tones chirped in his ear.

"I haven't time. Don't feel offended, please, if I put a rating in here just for form's sake."

It was midnight in Norfolk. He raised his unit's duty officer in clear, found she had no access to a secure line, and got the security officer's home number from her and made sure the DO logged his call and his purpose. The security officer didn't answer her phone; he left a message. He had gone back and forth all night on calling either Peretz or Rose; neither would have a secure line, and he would have to risk calling them from a pay phone somewhere. That would be his last resort. Now, disappointed but not surprised at the failure to get his own security officer, he called George Shreed's private number. A little to his surprise, it was answered on the second ring.

"This is Alan Craik. Do you have the means to go secure from a STU-III?"

Pause. "Sure."

Moments later, he was listening to the slightly tinny, slightly delayed but understandable result of satellite transmission and scrambling-unscrambling.

"Where are you?"

"I'm aboard a British ship in Mombasa harbor. Sir, something important has happened and I have to know how to move on it fast."

Shreed was a good listener. Alan gave him an edited version of the encounter with Franci, the result of the night's thinking and rethinking it—no specifics, no name, but the all-important tie-in with his father's death. "So I think this is a breakthrough. This is very important. To me."

"Who else knows?"

"I'm trying to tell my unit security officer. One of the NCIS guys here knows. I had to ask advice."

"Right. Well, don't do anything yourself. You understand that?"

"Yes, sir. Dukas gave me a lecture."

"Okay. Just stay out of it. I'll handle it from here. You been in touch with the embassy?"

"I don't want to stay out of it, Mr. Shreed. I have to be part of it. The contact won't talk to anybody but me."

"Well— Be that as it may, don't do ánything alone. For one thing, it may be dangerous. You sure this isn't a trap? You can't be sure. Think about that. This is a tough business. Will you trust me on this?"

"I have a responsibility to the Navy."

"Yeah, yeah, we'll take care of that. They'll understand. Just keep the guy at a distance for twenty-four hours. Can you do that?"

Alan thought of Franci when they parted, in tears, shaking. "I promised him I'd see him today. He needs support. I'm really afraid he's going over the edge."

"Stay out of it. How do you meet him?"

"Oh, a kind of cops-and-robbers telephone thing. At ten after eleven I—"

"Don't tell me; I know how it works. He's doing it right; it isn't cops and robbers. When you call him, play him along, give him support and comfort, but don't make a date. Tell him something—you're sick, you've got a commitment—just don't make direct contact."

"Why?"

There was the slightest pause, as if Shreed might have been about to blow up, perhaps to say something like *Because I say so.* "Just do it. Do it my way, okay? I'm the professional here, Alan. You've got to trust me. We'll work this out. It's all about catching the guy who set up your dad, isn't it? That's what matters to me, too. Trust me."

He knew then how Franci felt—the lure of trust, of somebody else to carry that burden. "Yes, sir," he said.

"Good boy." He asked for some details about where Alan was staying, his schedule, his plans. He said that everything would be fine.

Later, when Alan was standing by the ladder waiting to go down to one of the ship's boats, Houlting appeared at his side. He held out a tattered paperback book. "We carry these in case we have a chance to convert the heathen. Read, and be saved, brother." Alan looked at the cover, which had a painting of a sailing ship. *Master and Commander* by Patrick O'Brian.

"Can intel officers be saved?" he said.

"Even we will ascend into the rigging." He grinned. "O'Brian's awfully good, actually. He makes you see why we're all proud to be sailors."

He called Franci at the appointed time from a pay phone up the beach from the hotel; it rang twice, and Franci answered. To Alan's surprise, he seemed better, but he was dashed by Alan's refusal to meet him. "You will not give me up?" he said.

"No, no— Something's happened. It's only today. It will be all right, Franci. I'm glad you told me what you did— last night. It will be all right."

"You are still my friend?"

"Yes."

"I feel better than in a long time, Alan, but I am worried. I am not well, you know. Sometimes— You will call me tonight? Call me at ten minutes before eleven. I give you a different number. If no answer at four rings, hang up—don't let ring five, hang up—then call again, *this* number, ten after. You see how this works? Maybe I answer at the first phone, depending. You see? If I don't answer, if they— Never mind. If I don't answer, then subtract one and add one, you understand? One hour, I mean. Each day, one hour each way from eleven, night and morning. Alan?" He went over it again. When he rang off, it was with the reluctance of a lover saying good night.

As if to turn his lie to Franci about "something coming up" to truth, Dukas was waiting for him at the hotel.

Alan wanted only to go to bed, but one look at Dukas's face and he knew he was not going to have that luxury.

"We're wanted," Dukas said. "Plane leaves in an hour."

"What the hell!"

"Just what I said, only worse. We'll be back tonight."

"Who says?"

"Make nice, that's the message. We report to the embassy. If we don't, the whole project's in trouble. Come on. Shit happens."

All the way there, he kept asking how the embassy knew. And why they wanted Dukas. There were no answers.

They were very nice at the embassy. They provided good coffee and comfortable chairs, the overall impression very much that of the hotel where they had been staying. This was not the embassy of some rinky-dink nation, was what it all said. Alan, weary to his bones, was grateful. He didn't want to fight grunge just now.

They had been met at the airport by a couple of pleasant young men who had chatted about football with Dukas on the way into town. At the embassy, they had turned Alan over to a pretty black woman who had led him back through cubicles and corridors—all like an American office complex, lots of potted plants and bulletin boards covered with photos and kids' drawings—to an office with a view of a courtyard where people were sitting on the grass.

"Hi! I'm Bob White!"

He was chipper, bright, and eager; he wore aviator glasses and a short-sleeved shirt with a power tie. He had his wife's picture on the desk, and on the wall a number and photo of himself from a road race.

"I'm going to debrief you," Bob White said.

Through his fatigue, Alan saw a problem and said, "You Navy?"

"Uh-unh. State. Same government, though." He looked over his glasses and smiled. "You're wiped, aren't you?"

"Pretty much."

"This won't take long. Then maybe we can find a place for you to catch a nap."

"I have to go right back to Mombasa."

"Five minutes is better than nothing. So. Let's start at the beginning. You've been contacted by a foreign national."

"Who told you?"

Bob White spread his hands. "My boss. I don't know the background. I just do the debrief. Okay?"

He began to lead Alan through it. He seemed to think that Alan had been contacted by Franci, not that he had stumbled into Franci's by accident. Was he *sure* there had been no enticement? Maybe somebody had mentioned the shop? Pointed it out? The second time he had met the man, then—had he been invited back? Maybe there had been a telephone call, a message. Had he been followed? What had he said? Had he said anything compromising? Had there been a sexual overtone to any of the meetings?

"You've got it wrong, all wrong," Alan said wearily. They had been at it for thirty minutes. "It was coincidence. Luck."

"I see."

Bob White was taking notes, even though he had turned on a tape recorder, telling Alan he was doing so. He looked over his notes. "And you believe this man was somehow involved in the death of your father. Let me get this straight, now: you and your father were both in an air operation—"

Like most civilians, he had no real idea of what combat was like. To explain it all to him was tedious beyond bearing. Alan was irritable and flared up at him. Bob White was patient.

"Look, Alan, I know this is painful, but we have to get it right. Look at it from our point of view. You are saying that by sheer coincidence you happened on the one man who could tell you how your father's plane was shot down—"

"That isn't what I said."

"Well, then tell me again."

"I don't want to tell you again! I've told you; you've got it on tape! He isn't the one man who *can* anything; he's one of probably a thousand! He happens to be the one I met. And my father's plane wasn't shot down. Jesus!"

"But it crashed."

"It ran out of fuel and crashed."

"Well— Okay. This must be hell for you. You want to take a break?"

"No. Get it over with."

"O-ka-a-ay. See, the chances of you meeting somebody like this by accident are—well, one in millions. You may be biased in favor of finding somebody to solve this mystery about your father. Isn't that likely?"

"Everybody's biased."

"Exactly! We don't want you involved in something that may be a setup."

Alan sighed. "How could it be a setup if I walked into the guy's shop of my own free will?"

"Well—we don't know that's what you did."

"*I* know."

Bob White looked over his notes and glanced at a wall clock. "When did he reveal himself?"

"He didn't 'reveal himself.' He broke down. He started to babble. We were in a restaurant; I thought I was going to have to get him out before there was some sort of scene. Then he quieted down, and I got him out to the street, and he started again."

"Started what?"

"Babbling. Talking a mile a minute. Not making sense, a lot of the time."

"What *exactly* did he say?"

"How would I remember exactly what he said? I only got part of it. It came in spurts, all mixed up. He has this thing about his wife, about sex—"

"Gay?"

"Oh—! I told you, he has no sex. He's obsessed with

it. Then he'd switch all of a sudden to his family, his father; he felt a bond with me because of his father. My father. Then he'd be back to that night. He kept talking about a blue light and a missile. Somebody named Ravi. Stuff I didn't get about the Revolutionary Guard, some sort of joke. What the hell are you grilling me for anyway? If you people want to know all this, send a team back to Mombasa with me and let them listen in while he talks to me!"

Bob White chewed on his pencil. "Did you ever think you were being followed?"

"Only by the Mombasa cops, and they called it off when Dukas bitched to them."

"Why did they follow you?"

"Because we looked like Persian-rug thieves! Jesus Christ, do you think they like having a Navy team swoop in and start writing up their city?"

"How come you guys didn't have country clearances?"

"We didn't need them. Who told you that?"

"How do you know the Mombasa police weren't in it with this foreign national? How do you know—?"

Alan stood up. "If you don't stop asking me stupid questions, I'm walking. Fuck off."

Bob White talked him back into the chair; he was a patient young man, essentially pleasant, not really very assertive. He was just being careful, he said. After all, he was answerable to his boss. Alan was tired, wasn't he? and his perceptions were skewed, weren't they? And then they went over the whole thing again—what Franci looked like, what he sounded like, what he had said, what Alan had said, on and on. Alan again went over the instructions Franci had given him for telephoning.

"And doesn't that sound to you like the caution of a trained professional?" Bob White said.

"What if it is?"

Bob White leaned across the desk and said with utter sincerity, "Alan— I think you've been had."

Then he said he thought he was done and he would only be a minute, and he left the office; Alan sank down, noting that it was past four o'clock; he slept in bursts, waking abruptly, dozing for bare seconds; and he had been doing that for eleven minutes by the clock when somebody he had never seen before was looking at him from Bob White's chair.

"All right, let's go over this again," he said.

"Who're you?"

"That's none of your business, Lieutenant. I want to hear your story. Shoot." He was older than Bob White and a little going to pudge, with some of the disillusioned-cop look of Dukas.

Alan sat up. Their eyes met. "What's going on?"

"You've made contact with a foreign national under suspicious circumstances; you're in no position to ask what's going on. Give."

"Show me ID."

"You shithead." The man pointed a finger. "You give me what I want or I'll come over this desk and rip your head off."

"Try it." Alan felt suddenly alert and rested. "I can take you."

The man stared at him and then chuckled and picked up a telephone. "Get Lieutenant Commander Huff over here, will you? I know he's in the other building." He looked at Alan. "We'll wait." And they did. Ten minutes later, a worried-looking black man came in and showed Alan his ID. He was the naval attaché. "You do what this man wants, Lieutenant. You hear me? That's an order."

"Sir, I feel out on a limb here. I'd like to contact my unit commander or my security officer."

"Well, you can't."

"Sir, I don't think this is in the best interest of the Navy, and I'm pretty sure that the embassy has absolutely no legal jurisdiction over the Navy, and I am goddam sure that this is heading toward an investigation. I want a lawyer and a representative of NCIS or I am walking out. Sir."

"That's not for you to decide."

"Then I want to file a formal complaint."

"You can do that through your chain of command at the appropriate time."

Alan started to say he had a plane to catch, but he was told to do as he was ordered, and then he and the questioner went back and forth for another hour, and he watched the clock with increasing anxiety, knowing that the last plane to Mombasa left just after seven. He could call Franci from here or from the airport if he had to; if this went on and on, he thought, he could call him long distance. Maybe that was better. He so needed sleep he would have to crash somewhere soon, anyway.

Then the pudgy man was done with his questions, and Alan was alone with the clock and his fatigue. It was almost five-thirty. He heaved himself up and opened the office door. The corridor was silent. He saw nobody in either direction. He could walk out, he thought. But that would get him in a lot of trouble, he suspected.

At ten minutes to six, three people came down the corridor toward him. One was the naval attaché; one was a man in a suit; and one was Bob White. Bob White looked unhappy.

They stopped a few feet from him. The man in the suit drew himself up, as if getting more height would help him do whatever came next. He didn't bother to introduce himself.

"I'm sure you're very tired, Lieutenant," he said, in the voice of a man who had no ability whatever to empathize with other people's troubles. "We won't keep you any further." He produced a folded paper from an inner pocket. "These are your orders returning you to the United States." He produced an envelope from the same pocket. "Here's your ticket. The aircraft leaves at nine-forty. Mr. White will drive you there."

"I have a meeting in Mombasa," Alan said.

"You are finished here, Lieutenant. You are going home." He pushed the papers toward Alan. Alan took only the orders. His fingers, he noticed, trembled with fatigue. He thought of Franci. The orders were drawn in the name of a captain in the Naval Intelligence Command and ordered him "at once" to travel to CONUS by "earliest available commercial air" and to report to his own unit upon arrival. They had been signed true copies by the attaché.

"What the hell is going on?"

The official, late for his drinks somewhere, turned impatiently to Bob White and handed him the tickets and said, "Get him on that airplane." He walked off down the corridor.

Alan started to argue that he had to contact Franci. The man was depending on him. He had to go to Mombasa. Where was Dukas? All his stuff was still in Mombasa. What the hell were they doing to him? The lieutenant commander read him out—briefly, because he was also late for drinks—and said he would write a letter to his commanding officer, and then he, too, walked down the corridor and into the night, and Alan was left with Bob White.

"Don't take it wrong," Bob White said. "We all work for Uncle, right?"

20

He had had only a few hours of sleep when he stumbled out of the aircraft in Washington. He had spent five hours at Schiphol airport in Amsterdam, where they have flat, padded benches, but tourists kept sitting nearby and jabbering and slamming their luggage on the floor. When he got to Washington, it was thirty hours after he had left Africa, but he felt as disoriented as if it had been years. The cycle of hours to call Franci had come up twice, but both times he had been in the air. All he could do, he thought, was try to telephone him from home at two the next morning.

They were rebuilding the international arrivals gate at Dulles. The plywood corridor seemed to go on forever, at last ejecting passengers into a long hall with a railing along their left side, where welcomers leaned in and stared at every face, curiously hostile, as if they were spectators at some fascinating, perhaps dangerous, sport. Other people slowed to look for friends; he charged on, thinking he would have to find his way home.

Until he saw Rose at the very end of the barrier. She was in uniform. She smiled and held out her arms.

"Was it awful?" she said as she clutched him.

He was conscious of not having shaved, of needing a toothbrush, of loving her. "How did you know where I'd be?"

She touched his face. "Are you okay?"

Somebody bumped into him from behind and he almost fell, and he realized he was blocking the corridor. "Come on." He moved them both aside and around a corner, and there was Commander Reicher. He and Alan looked at each other; to Alan's surprise, Reicher showed no anger, no condemnation. There was something there, to be sure—a fixed somberness, but not aimed at Alan, he thought.

Reicher came toward him with his hand out. When their hands touched and began to grasp each other, Reicher said, "Your man is dead. They think he killed himself." He held on to Alan's hand. "I'm sorry. I'm sorry."

Waking in his own bed, he felt a comforting, still-drowsy warmth. A man who has been on a journey and come safely home feels a specific satisfaction; perhaps it is a holdover from the hunting apes. This lasted a few seconds, and then he remembered Franci and the rest of it, and cold anger drove the satisfaction out.

Rose was already gone. He ate sparingly, almost austerely, a kind of monkishness imposing itself on him unbidden. He dressed with care in his best uniform.

Reicher called him in as soon as he had arrived.

"The shit's hit the fan," he said, less with anger than a kind of ferocious cheerfulness. "The admiral wants to see us tomorrow. You're to go over to NIS and get debriefed. Tell them everything, take your time, get it right. These are our guys. What's happening is, CIA are waffling on involvement in your man's death, like they'd like us to believe they never got near him. It's your fault, is the line they're going to take. You didn't cooperate; you tried to go it alone. Did you?"

"I volunteered the whole business to George Shreed. I wouldn't have called him if I'd been going it alone."

"You got a record of the call?"

"I made it from a British ship. They'll have a record."

Reicher wrote it all down. "We'll get it. How about the asset? You absolutely certain you didn't recruit him? No offers, no enticement? Okay. You keep a diary, appointment book, anything with the meetings in it?"

"I reported the last one to security. I have a kind of bunch of notes— Plus letters I wrote to Rose—"

Reicher wrote it all down. "Your buddy Dukas called me from Mombasa. Actually, he called his office because he wanted to cover his ass; then he called me because he wanted to protect yours. You must have already been on the way home by the time we talked. He thinks they were putting a team together at the embassy when you guys got there; he saw something in an office, heard something— anyway, he thought they had people on-site in Mombasa before you ever got sent home. It sounds to me like they stiffed you, then walled you off and went after your man."

"And killed him."

"Not literally. Or didn't you mean that?"

"Are you sure it was suicide?"

"One witness saw him walk in front of a freight train. Granted, you can bribe a witness, but in this case suicide is the simple explanation. If it was his own people, I don't think they'd have moved that fast to kill him. Whisk him off someplace, sure. Not kill him. It sounds as if they didn't have a clue. Anyway, that isn't the issue. CIA is sitting on whatever its people did in Mombasa—'internal investigation,' which means they'll keep it to themselves until they hope everybody forgets. Meanwhile, they're going to make it your fault. We're not going to let that happen." He looked at a notepad. "I'm supposed to get a copy of the letter you wrote when you asked to have your father's plane raised; you got one?"

"I didn't think you knew about that."

"I know lots of things you don't know, surprising as that may seem. You got a copy?"

"Yes, sir."

"Make it available, please—today, if possible. The admiral wants to see it, along with the orders I wrote you for the Mombasa trip and some other stuff. I'll take care of that." He leaned back. "Concentrate on this until the admiral is through with us. You won't be worth much as an analyst, anyway."

"I'd like to make a trip into Washington."

"Why?"

"George Shreed."

Relcher thought about that. "I'm not going to stop you," he said slowly. "But I think you're making a mistake."

Shreed kept him waiting for forty-five minutes, a fine way to make an angry man incoherent, and when Alan finally was allowed in, Shreed was on the telephone and waved Alan to a seat as casually as if he had come for a chat.

"Okay," Shreed said finally. He looked up at Alan. "I hear you screwed up."

Alan let that pass. "Sir," he said, "I want to know why you lied to me."

"*Lied* to you! What the hell—?"

"I want to know why you lied to me."

"I didn't lie to you. I gave you good advice; clearly, you didn't take it. Now the whole thing is wrecked."

"I would like an explanation of why you said 'Trust me,' and then betrayed my trust."

Shreed stared at him and then laughed. He picked up the phone and asked somebody to come in here, and within seconds, Sally Baranowski was there. "Sit down," Shreed said. "This young man is here to talk to us about trust."

Alan knew he wanted a witness. He was to get no satisfaction, then, or only the sour satisfaction of speaking his mind and seeing the words have no effect. "Sir, a man is dead, and it's your fault."

"Sally, what do you say to somebody like this?" He pointed a finger at Alan. "You're going to get yourself into deep shit."

"You told me to trust you, and I did, and a man is dead. You should be ashamed."

Perhaps that word had never been spoken there before. Certainly, it set off odd echoes. Shreed seemed to swell. "Get your ass out of here!"

Alan stood his ground. "What you did was contemptible. You are a disgrace to this Agency." He turned slightly to look at Sally Baranowski. She tried to smile, then went very red, and her eyes flickered to Shreed. Alan turned and left the office, hearing, behind him, a hoot of laughter.

After he was gone, Shreed's laughter died; unsupported by any from his deputy, it didn't have much staying power. Shreed twisted a ballpoint pen, then threw it on the desk and cried, "Little shit!"

A very red-faced captain came out of the admiral's office, and Reicher winked at Alan as the man walked between them, looking neither right nor left and moving with as much speed as an aging man can without breaking into a run. To be a naval captain, and a fairly pompous one at that, and to be royally read out by an admiral is a remarkable thing.

Then Reicher went in, and in another ten minutes he, too, came out, a little red but not so bad that he couldn't give Alan a small, wry smile and say, "Your turn." Alan's head was as empty as his hat as he started for the door: too much had happened, he had done too much, expended too much anxiety; now he felt a little cold, nothing more.

The office was finer than the typical Navy office, which has little to recommend it. There were leather chairs with brass nails, pictures of the President and the CNO, and one of a sailing ship; there was the usual Navy smell of coffee, and a smell of cigars that was not naval but that apparently emanated from the admiral's well-cut uniform. Alan presented himself in front of the admiral, who was a small man with the sort of glasses that made him look slightly like Harry S. Truman. He had a reputation for some of Truman's hardheadedness, too. He was in his fifties, immaculate, framed by American and Navy flags. He wore an Academy ring.

"Well, Lieutenant, this is quite a can of worms." His voice was harsh and his words came briskly, as if he hadn't a moment to spare. "Have you made any mistakes in all this, do you think?"

"Yes, sir."

"What?"

"I let something personal affect my judgment. And I trusted somebody I shouldn't have."

"The Navy has procedures to prevent mistakes. How come you didn't follow them?"

"Sir, I believe I did, as far as I could. I thought that time was of the essence."

"So you got yourself involved with people outside the Navy who screwed you. That was *stupid.* It was not what I expect of my officers. Is that clear?"

Alan mumbled that it was.

"That said, let me add that you seem to have been on the verge of a breakthrough, and you and the Navy have been abused by people with far more power than you were in any position to fight. Now—" He pushed forward a piece of paper. "I have had an e-mail from an official of the Central Intelligence Agency who demands that you be reprimanded for entering his office and 'reviling him with inappropriate language and accusations.' Have you reviled anybody over there with inappropriate language and accusations, Lieutenant?"

Alan sat very straight and looked the older man in the eye. On this point, he was absolutely sure of himself. "I don't think the language was inappropriate, sir, and I didn't make any accusations, although I did ask George Shreed why he had lied to me. And I stated what is a fact, that he was responsible for the death of a man."

"Do you remember what you said—*exactly?*"

Alan did, and could repeat it verbatim.

" 'Contemptible'—you actually said *contemptible?* I don't think I've ever heard that word used. Contemptible. Well, I can see how that might fit. And you're sure you didn't swear or shout—no obscenity? Well, your explanation seems okay to me, Lieutenant. I think we'll send a message back to the Agency and suggest that if they'd thought about their behavior before they did certain things, people would not be calling them 'contemptible' now. How does that sound?" He studied Alan through his steel-rimmed glasses. "Commander Reicher thinks very highly of you. So did your squadron CO. You're a bright young man with a good future if you don't make too many stupid mistakes. But you need some education in how the operational side of intelligence works; we'll give you some—not down at their place; you've made an enemy there—and then give you a taste of it if that's what you want. I've been through the files; I know how important the matter of your father is to you. I'm going to do something about that, because I think you're right, I think there could be an agent inside the Navy, and that just makes me sick inside. In fact, what's saved you from a real reaming is that I think you've been right all along. I think you were right a year ago, and if I'd been making that decision, I'd have had your dad's plane raised then." He screwed his mouth up in an almost petulant way and shook his head. "What you have to learn, Mr. Craik, is that Naval intelligence is a very complicated and not very rational universe. To make it work, you have to know it upside down and backward—and you don't! You're like a . . . pup that's thrown into a field trial. Well, it isn't the pup's fault if he puts the birds up too soon, but people get mighty damn mad at the pup, all the same." He glared at Alan with eyes as hard as marbles. "Don't you *ever* go direct to the CIA again!"

"No, sir."

"But don't lose your initiative, either. The Navy needs men who are willing to use a word like 'contemptible' when it applies. The way I see it, you're going to be a fine young admiral, if we can ever get you through being a j.g. That's all, Mr. Craik."

Outside, Reicher was waiting. He was happy; he had got only a tongue-lashing for sending Alan to Africa without clear guidelines, but he had already wheedled from somebody on the admiral's staff the fact that the captain who had, at George Shreed's behest, ordered Alan home from Nairobi had got a letter of reprimand in his folder.

"Myself, I think we made out like bandits," Reicher said after he had heard Alan's account of what had happened in the admiral's office. "You a drinking man, Craik?"

"I wouldn't turn down a beer, sir."

"How about two beers?" He hurried them toward a bar. "You know, Craik, you're beginning to grow on me."

MAY 2, 1992. ATLANTIC FLEET HQ.

A message landed on a lieutenant commander's desk and was dutifully delayed by other matters in the stack. When she got to it, she read it and noted it and moved it to another tray, then turned to a computer terminal and scrolled through lists of ships and their current positions. Finding USS *Lifter,* she clicked on the name and pulled up details of its orders and next destination. It was now in the eastern Mediterranean, salvaging oil from a small tanker that had broken up in the 1960s and was now leaking. It would be free in two weeks.

She began to draft orders for the ship to proceed to the Persian Gulf to raise an A-6 from the bottom; she entered the plane's last known position, in this case a very accurate one because it had been logged when the plane went down. Sonar records were to be sought.

JUNE 6, 1992. PERSIAN GULF.

Petty Officer First Class Norman Boardman directed his headlamp toward the dimly seen shape and took two slow steps. The brilliant beam picked out part of a wing, already encrusted with small marine life; in places, the metal surface, corroded now, showed like patches of leprous skin. Bubbles rose from his helmet, fish moving around them in darting motions like hummingbirds.

He moved carefully around the site. The plane had broken up, and he was wary of jagged metal. Wire, like the tendrils of undersea plants, twisted all around him, some as fine as grape tendrils, some as thick as rope. The fuselage was recognizable. The wings had come off, and the after section of the body. Yet the forward part was more or less intact, and he could even see a jagged hole made by the missile that had brought the aircraft down.

Boardman described the site and the remains of the aircraft. He read off numbers from a flat section, perhaps part of a wing, then more numbers from forward on the fuselage. As they checked topside, he moved as close as he dared in the tangle of cables and shone his light at the cockpit.

"Boardman?"

"Yo."

"That's the one. Numbers check."

"Okay. Affirmative on human remains inside, too. Yo?"

On a Friday, with the sun sparkling through haze, *Lifter* raised what remained of Mick Craik's aircraft. Her deck was already piled with wreckage from the site; more had been stowed below, and a small crane was moving more of it to the hold that day. In Kuwait City, an empty warehouse was waiting; a team flown in from the States—manufacturer's reps, squadron mechanics, an NCIS agent, various specialists in EW, damage, crash analysis—were waiting to lay the wreckage out, every piece of jagged metal, every inch of cable, until the whole aircraft would lie, like an expanded drawing, on the warehouse floor,

"Ready to raise, sir."

"Clear divers."

The salvage ops officer was himself a diver, as well as an engineer. Glancing at the main crane's cable, he was seeing the dive team in the gloom below, the rig that would bring the main piece of fuselage up. A worrier, he was calculating strain and dive time and water pressure and Murphy's Law, and a personal piece of pessimistic theory he called the Rule of Foreseen Consequences: if you predict everything that can possibly go wrong and work hard enough to avoid it, a piece of space junk will fall out of orbit and set your pants on fire.

"Divers clear."

He flashed the con. "Preparing to lift Piece Seven."

"Steady and ready."

"Okay, this is the big one." He eyed a thin bank of gray cloud on the horizon, considered saying something about the possibility of bad weather (about two percent), and thought better of it.

"Crane Three, are you ready to raise?"

"Ready, sir."

He eyeballed his board, got a nod from the Dive Officer and a hand wave from the deck lookout.

"Make it so."

The sound was like a tightening fist—first a whine, then a growl, disconcertingly smooth and almost quiet. Only the tension of the cables, and that visible only to an experienced eye, showed what was happening.

He licked his lips. The ops clock was running. He figured about seventy minutes if nothing went wrong (*right, yeah, that'll be the day*). Sweat trickled down his temples. It was already well above a hundred degrees. *Take me back to old Australia,* he thought. They had done a job there recently. Wonderful weather. Great bars. Nice women.

An arm went up on the deck; the crane stopped.

"What is it? Deck?"

"Looked like a bad spot in the cable, but it's only some green crap from down below. Like jelly. Yuck."

They had to stop three more times, and the total was not seventy minutes but almost a hundred and thirteen. A twist set in; a diver had to have a look. The load shifted, only a few inches, but the operator was concerned. And so on.

Then the last color code of the main cable broke the surface and climbed steadily up past the ship's side and up, up to the end of the crane and along and on toward the master drum. The ops officer stepped down to the deck to watch the end, always somehow exciting and disturbing, the emergence of these secrets taken back from the ocean. Davy Jones's Locker, the sea bottom used to be called. Now the locker had a key.

The water around the cables seemed to seethe, as if it was close to boiling. It darkened. The top connections of the rig appeared, then a gray-green mass; he could see the aircraft shape, a stub of wing. It broke free of the waves and rode again in air, water streaming from it, from holes in the fuselage, from the gape where the tail had been, from the nose, the broken wings. Broken and torn metal hung down as if trying to return to the water. Electrical wiring spilled from the shattered wing like entrails. Some of the water was almost white with mud and sand.

He made himself look down into what had been the cockpit while the plane was still below him, coming more slowly now, soon to be swung on board, long cables guiding it to the secondary winches on the deck; forced himself to look into the cockpit because it was what he thought they owed the dead, terrible as they were—that bad moment when you made the surface with a body, something in the water for a while, and the stench of it hit you—and saw the top of a flight helmet, tape markings still intact, tipped against the side as if the pilot were resting his head, and then, separate from it, a smudge that might have been a flight-suited arm or even a leg, wire, foam rubber, mud, metal, a bone. . . .

JUNE 9, 1992. NORFOLK.

Alan had been staring at a place on their living-room wall for so long that he had forgotten where he was or what he was doing. He had been "decorating"—Rose's word for trying to fill the blank expanses of the walls—and he had, many minutes ago, pulled a straight chair to the middle of the room and sat on it, backward. Now, his chin resting on his forearms, which in turn rested on the chairback, he dangled the broken Bedouin sword from his right hand and stared at nothing.

Rose came in with sacks of groceries, started to ask him to help her, then smiled and shrugged and went back out to the car. When she came in again, she put the bulging plastic sacks on the kitchen floor and came to him and put a hand on his hair.

He smiled. He looked sideways at her.

"Thinking about him?"

He stirred. The broken sword swung in his hand. "I suppose. Him and Franci. And this guy." He held up the broken sword. "Remember?"

She smiled.

"He was so—"

" 'Ferocious.' That's what you said last time."

"Boring, huh?" He jumped up. "I'm going to put this goddam thing on the wall if it harelips me, as they say Down South."

"They don't!"

"Yeah, they do. 'If it harelips me.' Pretty graphic." He began to pound nails into the drywall.

"I think we ought to get a dog," she said.

He laughed. "First a baby, now a dog—what's next, goldfish?"

"You need something to talk to."

"I got you." He grabbed her. "Anyway, dogs don't live very long."

"You've got to stop thinking like that! Nothing lives forever, honey."

"You will. Yes, you will. Forever." He squeezed her.

She put her hand over his mouth. "That's bad luck. Don't even say it. Don't tempt—whatever. Don't—"

The telephone rang. He answered as if he were at the office, military and correct, and she saw him stand there muttering monosyllables—*When? None?*—his eyes on the broken sword that was now up on the wall. He put down the telephone, picked up his father's naval sword, and grinned at her shyly.

"They raised the plane. They're sending his body back here for burial. The crash team is going to pull the IFF and start the analysis."

He banged nails into the wall and put the naval sword on them, slanted upward so that, if both swords had had complete blades, they would have crossed.

"And then I'm going to catch that sonofabitch and see he pays!"

21

Alan felt older, no longer somebody to be thought of as a kid, least of all as "Mick Craik's kid," rather a man at the end of one of life's pulses and the beginning of another, the change marked by a first gray hair, fatherhood, the two lieutenant's rings on the sleeve. By the end of the eighteen months after his father's plane was raised, he was this older man. Others changed around him, too: O'Neill's marriage fell apart and his wife left; Bea Peretz found a lump in one breast, then found it to be a benign cyst; Mike Dukas fell in love with Rose, turned it into friendship.

"Five years," Mike had said, the week after his father's plane had been raised. "It'll take five years."

They had gathered at Alan's and Rose's, a Saturday evening that would become the pattern for all the Saturday evenings for the next eighteen months—Alan and Rose, Dukas, the Peretzes, O'Neill and his sullen, soon-to-split wife.

"They gave me your dad's case," Mike said. They had been skeet-shooting, a novelty to Alan, dismaying to the rest because he was good at it the first time he picked up a gun.

Alan offered wine. "My dad has a case?"

"Yeah, well the possible-spy thing. I'm putting a team together." Mike looked like a wary schoolboy. They didn't know each other so well then; only the fiasco in Mombasa connected them.

"I've heard fuck-all since they brought the plane up. They're going to bury him at Arlington."

"Damage was right where the FLIR showed, up by the IFF, and the codes were set, by gun and not by hand; 180 out from the codes everyone else had. So: you were right: somebody tagged your dad's plane to get hit by some rag-head Rube Goldberg missile. Somebody on the boat."

"How long?"

Mike had looked at him and laughed with embarrassment. They had been cleaning the shotguns, which lay on a metal table by the backyard barbecue. The air smelled of charcoal and meat and gun oil. Dukas had picked up a shotgun, thrown it forward, snapping the breech closed against his hand and raising it to his shoulder in one motion. He squinted down the barrel at a streetlight.

"Five years."

In the event, it was eighteen months, but you can't predict the irrational, and without it Dukas would have been right.

Only to Rose did Alan admit his disgust. But he remembered what Reicher had said about learning to plod, and he saw that that was what he would have to do. He lay awake in their bed, knowing she lay awake beside him. He said, "It's tempting just to let it go. Just to let it happen. Just—be a guy with a job and a wife."

"But you can't."

He put his hand on her bare hip, moved it slowly up and down the smooth, soft skin. "On the boat, there was all that stuff to do. And here, too—you can always find things to do. Skeet-shooting, for Christ's sake. And meanwhile, all the time you're doing it, there's a guy who caused your father's death and betrayed his country. And behind him, there's some foreign control who ran him. And there was Franci, losing a leg, going crazy. And you can ignore all that and pretend it didn't happen and just live your little life as if that's all another world. *But it isn't!*"

"But if Mike says it'll take five years, you just have to learn to wait."

"Plod. Yeah. But I don't have to do it with my head under a rock. I'm going to get myself put on Mike's case team."

She didn't say he had enough to do as it was. She was working six days a week, herself, trying to justify the time to have the baby.

The next Saturday they shot skeet again, and the Saturday after. By then, Alan had his own shotgun, a flea-market buy that turned out to be a British Purdey 20-gauge, a sweet, small gun that pointed like a compass needle and that caused Dukas to go off on a long, droll attempt to convince Alan that the gun was worthless. And Alan was almost convinced, until O'Neill clattered down the stairs and shouted, "Oh, my God, a Purdey!" and Dukas swore. Dukas was a gun collector. Alan's luck seemed to oppress him. "Do you know what that thing is *worth?*" he groaned several times during the day. Alan grinned each time. "Forty-five dollars. That's what I paid for it."

Peretz couldn't hit the broad side of a barn; his occasional lucky hits gained even more comment than Alan's rare misses. Nonetheless, it was Peretz to whom Alan turned for assurance that he was doing the right thing—Peretz the old pro, the intellect. What he got, however, was not reassurance, but advice.

Alan left his Purdey with Mike and O'Neill and went back behind the firing line, to where Peretz was staring out at the horizon toward North Carolina. The heat was heavy; just walking outside caused all of them to sweat. Two coolers, mostly full of water, sat on the ground behind them. The two of them watched the distant breakers for several long seconds.

"Mike says it will take five years to catch the bastard."

"Your friend Mike's an optimist." Peretz didn't show even the ghost of a smile. "Could be never."

Alan thought about never. His voice shook slightly. "I've asked to be put on the team. My admiral's behind it."

Peretz looked at him, hard. He shrugged in his Hawaiian shirt, seeming to become smaller, older. "Revenge ends ugly, Alan. Mike wants to catch this guy because it's his job. You just want him dead. I understand that you loved your dad, and I'm sorry to talk tough with you, but your dad died with a lot of issues unresolved with his only son, and you're turning all that emotion into hate for a man you never met. That man, whoever he is, is probably small and gray, twisted, greedy, crass. Not a worthy enemy for you, or for your dad. Let Mike catch him."

"I don't want him dead. I just want him—ended."

"One last chance to prove yourself to the old man."

Alan realized that the shooting had stopped; Mike and O'Neill were a little too busy with a cleaning rod to be convincing. Alan didn't care.

Peretz looked him in the eye for a couple of seconds. "I say again—give it up. If you make this thing a part of your life, it will eat you, your marriage, your time, your friends. One day, if you're lucky, you or someone from our side will catch the bastard, and there you'll be, a man who has spent his youth on revenge. I can see in your face what a great reception this lecture is getting. Fine; blow me off. But don't show your admiral the naked eagerness you're showing me or he'll make the right call and tell you not to worry and read the papers like any other citizen."

"If I don't worry and all I do is read the papers like any other citizen, I might as well be out of the Navy."

Peretz flushed, because he *was* out of the Navy, then tried to control his mouth, which had started to turn down at the corners. "Excuse me," he murmured. He walked past Alan and picked his gun off the table and walked away.

That was what he had meant about losing his friends, Alan thought. Except that he didn't lose Peretz. Rose and Bea wouldn't let it happen. Afterward, they were closer.

JULY 1992.

Mike Dukas, rare among special agents, liked analysts; he enjoyed listening to their long-winded arguments about theology and black holes and baseball, and he valued their unique, if often narrow, realms of knowledge. Even so, his big question about each one on the Mick Craik case was, *Has he or she got the stamina?* Because they were in for a long haul together.

They came to be known in the community as Mike's Kids, because most of them were young, new hires not long out of college. Melissa, a Latino woman, was the oldest; a single working mother with a hard-won education, she had made E6 in the Navy before heading off to college. Jimbo was a tall, very shy kid with some esoteric advanced degree from a big university; he lacked any pretense to interpersonal skills but seldom missed the mark in ideas, was at his best in misspelled e-mail. Carla was a black woman whose youth and inexperience rarely showed, and who wore her blackness like a very cool body makeup that favored her highly colored clothes. Mike attempted to sell her on the office dress code one slow Friday afternoon, but she just smiled and pointed at Jimbo. Mike saw her point; Jimbo would be a nerd in Brooks Brothers; Carla would be a society hostess in a burlap sack. And he seriously doubted that anyone on the floor had the nerve to consider harassing her. Roger was a young Navy officer who reveled in the freedom to wear civilian clothes and clearly wanted to be an agent; as the only one who had actually served on a carrier, he was a vital member of the team. Some essential members were not located with Mike's Kids; some were country analysts for Russia or Iran, and they were far off with their branch chiefs, a few even located in the old building.

After a month of letting them find their pace and read the basic documents, Dukas gathered the Kids and the essential loaners into an office where he had installed the case "break room."

"Everybody caught up?" he asked. Mostly, they looked bored, occupying various nooks and crannies in the furniture, almost twenty people crammed into a one-man office.

"Right. Here's how I see it." He looked around at them, noting the folded arms, the lowered heads, the covert looks. This was the real beginning, and they were waiting to see if it would fly. "One guy did it." No surprise there; they all knew that. "He was on the carrier. That limits us to 5,287 men. No women. We have the names of every man aboard. Right. Somebody paid him. Russia, Iran, France, somebody. So there's too much money somewhere. Carla, that's you." Everybody looked at Carla. "Look for money. Task the Norfolk office to do some interviews; that might get us a lead. Somebody recruited and trained him. Maybe blackmailed him. So look for a weird guy, somebody who fucked up somewhere and won't get promoted or has a secret. Alcoholic, gay, ethnic. Jimbo, you take that one." Jimbo frowned and wrinkled his nose. "Make up some questions, get Norfolk on it whenever they do a routine interview onboard, plus their memory of anyone who might fit that bill from the NCIS agents onboard at the time. Find 'em and interview them, Jimbo." Jimbo looked scared—interview somebody? In person?

Mike looked around the room. Most of them were more interested now, but with analysts, it was hard to tell who was daydreaming and who had just had a great idea. "What else? Yeah, interagency crap. Melissa, you seem to know every damn analyst in DC. Start looking around for cases that match. Time, type, mission; oh yeah, try to run up an MO with some crim guys. Get a Psych guy to do a personality profile on the subject. Circulate it. Everybody else, just watch the ground. We'll break this case because somebody sees something in message traffic or evidence and puts two and two together and makes five and a half."

Everyone was now taking notes—on what, he would never know. What had he said that was worth writing down? Mike felt more like a professor than a cop, not a role he had ever really fancied. "This is an analyst's investigation. Now, what I'm going to do, besides management and paperwork, is simple. I'll go over every existing counterintel case we have and try to make a fit. When that fails, and it will, because life is never so easy, then Melissa and I will tour other agencies and try to look at their cases. Roger, you're my XO. You make up a pretty brief on the case and keep it current; everybody do a 'copy to' for Roger on any significant data you send me, That's our dog-and-pony show. We'll go around the community, show the brief, look at their cases, and discover that they have all kinds of CI crap that should have been ours in the first place." He leaned back, hands behind his head.

"In one year, I want to eliminate five thousand of our suspects. That is our first goal: year one, knock off five thousand names. So everybody put on your thinking caps and start knocking out every damn sailor who can be proven not to be involved. Everybody think. Who can't go on a flight deck? Who can't get access to a coding gun for the IFF? Who can? Were there ever any missing? We probably need to interview as many of the flight-deck guys as we can find—Roger, make a note for Norfolk to get us a list of all personnel with flight-deck access, present rank or rate, address, etc." He stood up and stretched.

"Folks, one final note. This will take a *long* time. Agents aren't going to drop everything to interview every guy who had access to the flight deck. Rapes, murders, security clearances—they won't just stop to make room for us. And the volume of paperwork we put out will kill a redwood. For you new hires, think about this. Every request for interview on every sailor will have to go out as a separate message, so six months from now, when Norfolk actually gets us a list of flight-deck personnel, we will put out something like five hundred messages for that alone. *Capisce?*"

"One more thing. There's a member of the team some of you have seen around, some not—LT Craik. He's Navy intel. He's on the distribution list. For those of you who don't know it, the officer who was killed and whose plane was brought up out of the Gulf was his father. And don't try to bullshit him, because he'll chew you up and spit you out faster than you can say 'counterintelligence.' Plus, he's a nice guy. Okay, let's git 'em."

Mike walked out. He had wanted more drama, but he thought he had their interest. Funny job for an agent.

AUGUST 1992.

"Please state your full name and rate for the record." Mike Dukas put a small recorder down on the table. It was more a prop than a tool; it established that there would be a permanent record and it focused the subject on a threatening piece of equipment.

The burly figure across from him appeared tense and defensive, but Dukas knew from experience that most sailors and all too many officers hated NCIS agents the way that citizens of Moscow had hated the old KGB. And for about the same reasons.

"Aviation Bosun's Mate First Class James Lake," the subject said.

"Jim, you work on the flight deck, is that right?"

"Yes, sir."

"And you were on the maintenance crew for AE 509 on board the USS *Franklin D. Roosevelt* on July 23, 1990, correct?"

"Yeah, I worked on the skipper's plane."

Mike smiled. An easy one—already giving full answers. "How did you feel about Skipper Craik, Jim?"

"He was fair. He gave me thirty suspended for, um, that thing in Palma. And he told Chief not to take me off his plane. I made first 'cause of Skipper, I think."

"First what, Jim?" Dukas smiled, glanced at the tape recorder, as if the need for precision were not his fault but the machine's.

"First *Class,* sir. I made First Class Petty Officer 'cause of the Skipper, is what I'm saying."

Mike studied him. This guy fit on their revenge list: he had come up twice in front of Mick Craik for a captain's mast, that feared lowest level of discipline; to an analyst, that made him a troublemaker. To Dukas, this cussed human element was what justified the existence of agents like him: on paper, ABH1 Lake was a hard case, an open sore in the squadron, a man with a grudge. Here in this room, however, speaking reluctantly to a man he disliked, he showed that, despite discipline, despite the captain's masts, he felt that CDR Craik had saved his career. This shouldn't eliminate him from the suspect pool, but, in Mike Dukas's real world, it would. End of story.

He had a long list of questions that the team had cooked up, questions about people on the flight deck that evening—who had done what, who had coded AE 509 for IFF, who else was there, was there anything funny?

Jim Lake didn't know. "I can't really remember, sir! It's been a while, and I was dead tired. Don't remember much when I'm tired. Sir, can I ask *you* a question?"

"Ask away, sailor."

"You ever been on a flight deck during cyclic ops?"

Dukas grinned. "No, I haven't. Why don't you tell me how it was, that night?"

"Sir, I just don't *remember!* See, I know how every night went, and I can tell you, but not any one night. You ask me, who was near Skipper's plane. How do I know? How does anybody know? We all wear jerseys, color-coded— I'm a green shirt. But then we wear float-coats—big vests, that inflate, you know?, if you go over the side—and hearing protection, like earmuffs, you know? And goggles, against the fumes and the flares. It's like looking at a crowd on a ski slope, okay? And it's louder than shit—" He looked at the tape recorder. "Louder than anything, until the launch and recovery is over. And when it's dark, it's *black*. Guys walk up, do one thing to your plane, check one thing that got them out of their rack 'cause they forgot it or whatever, they do one thing and they're gone! Sir. Some stay— fuels guys, they cluster round till they're done. We call them grapes—purple shirts. Ordies, they're around a bit, sometimes talk to us lower life-forms. They wear red shirts. But, sir, my own brother wouldn't know me on that deck, not when dark is falling and the launch starts. IFF codes—sometimes they punch them in just before launch. There's guys here, there, running around, get out of my way, noise, we're all doing our own job, you got to believe other guys are doing theirs—man, I can't help you! What I see, every launch, is my job, which I can barely get done in the time I got."

Dukas put his hand on the tape recorder, ready to turn it off. "What's an ordie?"

"Ordnance. You know, ammo and bombs and all that."

"Thanks a lot. You've been a help, really."

And he had. One name could be moved to the *Unlikely* list.

SEPTEMBER 1992.

Bonner heard from a shipmate about the interviews. No secret was made of them. The word was that NCIS agents were crawling all over the crew of the *Roosevelt*. One guy said they were after the three nutcases who had been running dope out of propulsion. But that was bullshit; Bonner knew from the questions he heard about that they were after the IFF on that strike leader's aircraft.

At first, it scared him. Then, when they didn't come after him right away, some of the fear went away. His name started with B; they should have got to him early, first part of the alphabet, wasn't that the way it would go? Or maybe they had some other system. Maybe by rank? No, the Navy didn't work that way. B Priority. "Prioritize," that was the bullshit they talked. So he was low priority—didn't it figure?

He met Donnie in Williamsburg and they looked at the sights and talked about it. Donnie was more worried about his bitch of a wife, pregnant and boozing, anyway. Bonner told him to ditch her, but knew he wouldn't, shouldn't—it was his kid she was carrying, after all.

"Let her have the baby, then throw her out," Bonner said. "She's no good. She's trash."

Donnie looked very young. But stubborn. Wanting not to be a failure at marriage.

Let the fucking NCIS do their interviews, Bonner told himself. They were fishing; let them fish. He practiced what he had been taught about beating the polygraph.

On September 29, Michael Bobby Craik was born, weighing eight pounds, one ounce. Mother, baby, and father were doing well. The investigation faded in comparison with the birth.

OCTOBER 1992.

It just never seemed to end. As urgently as they requested data, data only trickled in. Still, the trickle filled safe after safe, and Mike began to dread the transfer of even one of his original team, who now knew the case so well that they could do the numbers in their heads. They could name names from the flight-deck crew from memory, see at a glance whether an interview was productive or not. Barb, a loaner from Mid-East Area (forties, sturdy, shy), proved a prize—she started a side investigation on foreign intel services; it should have been done years before, and she created a product that served the investigation for its duration—and also justified the money they were spending. It was Barb who noted that the Iranian MO had changed since the Craik incident.

"It's like Sidney Riley?" she said to Dukas at her first

briefing. She had the irritating habit of making everything a question, doubly irritating for a man so often expected to provide answers; it had taken him two or three meetings to realize it was the habitual voice of the smart woman who had been taught not to assert herself. *Hello? It's raining out? The sky is falling? Life goes on?*

After noting his blank response to the Sidney Riley remark, she went on even more tentatively. "Sidney Riley was the original James Bond? A spy for the British Empire? The point is, he was an ethnic Russian, and he went back in the twenties and—disappeared?"

Dukas hesitated. He'd try it himself, he decided. "Disappeared?"

"History says he was killed, but CI analysts note that after he disappeared, the Cheka—the commie intel service?—*(Oh, shit)*—stopped being such bush-league thugs and began to show some promise?"

"You're saying that this Riley defected and changed the Cheka MO."

Barb pulled out some message traffic. "Here are some cases that suggest that the Iranians suddenly got a little more professional? Case in point. They find a Brit sailor on Cyprus with a local girl? Instead of blackmail, their old style, they put a woman alongside the girl and win her over, then move her back to Islam, then run her against her boyfriend. Nice, huh? Also, even, this death in Mombasa? The Iranian the Agency snatched from us? Who committed suicide? That's different, a different feel, like it's a long-term mole kind of thing, not their usual. You follow me?"

"The mullahs move into the twentieth century. Next they'll be building biplanes."

"Laugh if you want—I'll put money down that the People's Islamic Republic bought themselves a KGB spook."

And no question mark! She must really believe it!

Alan fastened on her theory immediately, saw the implications, even knew who Sidney Riley had been. "She means," he said, eyes narrowed, "that a Moscow case officer defected to Iran, and it isn't necessarily a coincidence that it happened *then*, or that some funny missile stuff *and* a piece of espionage happened about the same time. Like—like what?—like the Russian set it up? Like he was trying to get the Iranians' attention? No, he would have had their attention—like he, mmm, started in his new job with a bang?"

"You're guessing."

"No kidding. If this was the Pentagon, we'd call it 'brainstorming.' But think about it, Mike—sure, it might be coincidence, but suppose, just suppose, it isn't—the guy, the spy, the *who* on the *Roosevelt* is an Iranian agent run by a Russian who's moved over: meaning that our man used to be a Russian agent. Meaning that maybe we can find him by finding out what the Russians—the Soviets, they were then—got that a Navy guy could have provided. Well?"

Dukas sighed. "Now all we need is a Soviet spook who's moved to Tehran." He patted Alan's upper arm. "Thanks for making my life more difficult. How's Rose?"

They looked at each other. *He knows I like his wife,* Mike thought. *And he knows I'd never do anything about it.* Alan began to show him pictures of the baby.

OCTOBER 27, 1992. 1520 ZULU. TEHRAN, IRAN.

Yuri Efremov sat at the head of a long table. Men, half of them in uniform, sat down the long sides. The table was heavy, polished, ornate, a faintly overdone version of a European table of perhaps the 1950s. The Iranian flag, three glorious antique tapestries, and a colored photograph of Mecca hung on the walls. Nobody looked at anything but Efremov, however—and not with sympathy, either.

"I have no 'personal agenda,'" he said. His voice was hard. He looked into their eyes. Nobody flinched. Most of them had come to hate him, some to fear him; at best, the minority saw benefit in him.

Next to him, a civilian in a badly made gray suit translated. At the far end of the long table, another civilian in another gray suit checked the translation and nodded.

"We do not expect an Islamic fidelity from you," a general said. He glanced at the translator, who repeated the words in Russian in a loud voice; the other translator nodded. "But we expect the truth. Lies are seeds cast upon stones."

"If you say I am lying, you are a liar yourself."

The others looked from one man to the other without expression.

"The Committee of National Security have no confidence in your project," the general said. The translator shouted it out.

"The Committee of National Security are a bunch of nervous old women." The translator shouted this, too, but in an apologetic tone. Nobody batted an eye. "They have dismissed the Minister of Culture because he said women have a place in government. They are unhappy with me because I do not kiss their feet. We are discussing trivialities."

"These are not trivialities!" The general was on his feet. He was bellowing. "You have removed the iron from our intelligence service and substituted lead! You have turned the rock of Islamic rigor to water!"

"That would be a miracle, General—surely worthy of notice in a religious state." Efremov smiled. The translator blushed. The general pushed his lower lip out and folded his arms. Efremov stood, as well. "I have no personal agenda! I do have a responsibility to an important agent who depends upon my personal help, and I must be free to deal with him!"

"What happened with one of your 'personal agents' in Mombasa? The Americans killed him! A disaster!"

"The Americans did not kill him; he killed himself. He was unstable but brilliant; I have told you and told you—"

"You have told us that you made him your pet and placed him, outside the usual networks, for your personal gain!"

"More lies! I bound him to me, yes, because he was a

pathetic wreck of a man, but with a mind, with training—! I made him an agent with a special loyalty!"

"To *you!*"

"All loyalty is personal, my general—all! If you don't think so, ask those boys whom you had to rope together to make them run at the Iraqi positions around Basra!"

"Lies! Lies!" The general was the color of mahogany. He turned to his neighbors. Several of them were on their feet, too, shouting, "Lies!" The others at the table sat like stones.

"Traitor to Islam!" the general shouted, pulling a Czech 9-millimeter from a belt holster and pointing it at Efremov.

Efremov did not so much as acknowledge that the pistol existed. "I did not think Islamic nations indulged in drama," he said. The translator hid his eyes, in part so as to make himself as small as possible when the shooting started. "If you shoot me, you shoot two years of modernization. Good! Splendid! Do it! Return to the dark ages. You do not deserve me."

At this, a cleric at the far end of the table stood up. Everybody looked at him. He was in his fifties, serious, conservatively dressed in religious garb, bearded. He said one word: "Enough."

Everybody but Efremov and the cleric sat down.

"Your request to leave the country is denied," the cleric said. "Your reorganization is to go forward, but the practice of inspiring personal loyalty among intelligence agents is to end. Allegiance must be to Islam."

Efremov's voice was slightly shaded, just tinged with a respect he had shown nobody else. "One of my agents from my life in Moscow is afraid he will be discovered."

"Precautionary measures are in place, surely."

"They date from the old days. I need to look out new routes, sites, escapes for him—outside Iran."

"That is impossible."

Efremov sat down.

DECEMBER 1992.

There were no big breaks. Dukas estimated that the case had used up thirty thousand man-hours. They were concentrating just then on which crew members had been on the flight deck at night—the night watch. O'Neill, hearing Dukas and Alan talking about it, said, "Ah! Like the Rembrandt painting." They looked blank. "*The Night Watch?*" O'Neill said.

It was news to them, but they liked naming the operation after a painting they had never heard of.

So it became NIGHT WATCH.

That was on the sixth. On the ninth, eighteen hundred Marines went ashore at Mogadishu, Somalia, preceded by a team of Navy Seals and several dozen media people, who met them on the beach. The First Marine Expeditionary Force was mobilized out of Camp Pendleton, California. At Fort Drum, New York, the first of ten thousand soldiers began to prepare.

On the twentieth, Rose came home early and played with the baby. She wandered through the house with Michael in her arms, stopping by windows to stare out at a cold rain as if there was something there to see. She had been back at work for a month, the strange, almost shocking pleasure of those six weeks with her child now a dream. Still, here she was. She fed him, then took him into the bedroom while she changed. She slipped into jeans and a T-shirt Alan had given her, "SuperMom" blazoned in graffiti lettering. She cried a little.

When Alan came home, he knew quite soon that something was up. He had bought an artificial Christmas tree to put up on Christmas Eve; he made jokes about sticking fake branches into holes in the fake trunk, assembling a tree. "Just like God. Only man can make a tree." They had wanted to cut their own, make a day of it, but neither of them had a day, or not a day together, anyway.

"Alan," she said.

He looked up too quickly, like a frightened man. But she was only a young mother in a T-shirt and jeans, standing there with her baby on her hip.

"Yeah, babe?"

She swallowed. Tears stood in her eyes. She had to clear her throat to speak. "What would you think if I went to sea?"

"I'd think you were a sailor. Not funny. What's up?"

She started to cry and he held her and the baby, her forehead on his chest, the baby holding his arm as if it were a whole person. "You're going to hate me," she moaned.

"No—no—tell me, babe, what is it?"

She backed a step. "Mason's taking command of a squadron, he wants me to go with him as ops officer." She cried harder and her voice rose to a wail. "It's fast-track career stuff!" She was blubbering. "I p-promised next time was yours! It w-would be r-rotten! Oh, Alan!"

She stood there, clutching their baby, unattractive as a wailing infant herself, her nose running.

She had just made lieutenant commander. It was a great step. Yes, the fast track.

"Leave here?" he said.

"M-Mayport." *Florida.*

He started to lose it. "But Jesus Christ, you've got a baby! You've got *me!* You said—" And he heard himself, sounding like an infant himself. "Oh, shit," he said, and his voice broke.

All three of them got on the sofa, Alan and Rose half twined together and the baby on top and kind of in between, and they petted and smooched and said a lot without speaking. Then she raised her head and turned her shining, huge eyes on him. "Well?" she said.

"Your goddam career," he said.

She nodded. She breathed in and then out, the air shaky and ragged. "I want to. But I hate to."

"When?"

"Probably June. That's six months we'd still have!"

"What did you mean, 'go to sea'?"

"We'd deploy three months after. The Red Sea."

"Oh, Christ, babe, that's Somalia!"

"It's only humanitarian stuff, Alan—"

"Bull*shit!* Somalia's going to blow! You think Bush doesn't know that, for Christ's sake? He's leaving office, what the hell does he care—send Craik's wife, fuck-all, they can't say it happened on my watch; let the next guy do it!"

"It can't be that—"

"It goddam well can! It's going to get worse and worse; we're going to get in deeper and deeper. You'll wind up flying some fucking special-forces bullshit to someplace you never heard of so they can get shot up by people you don't even know exist!"

She snuffled. She laughed. "Well, at least you care." She cried.

They held each other, then changed the baby, then sat at the kitchen table, holding hands. "Let's get drunk," he said.

"Not very drunk. I've got an inspection in the morning."

He poured wine, a gift from Dukas. "Mike's in love with you," he said.

"I know." She more or less chuckled. "It comes out as food. It always will. We talk recipes." She shook her head. "The best time I ever had was those weeks after Mikey was born. I could stay home, I could cook, I could drink wine." She leaned back and looked at him and shook her head because she couldn't quite talk; and when she could, she said, "I love you so much."

"Yeah, Likewise. That's why I have to let you go, isn't it?"

22

Alan and Rose made the most of the last months before she left for Florida. They were more careful of each other, more aware; both became a little more ruthless with work time to make sure they got home, touched, talked. Michael went everywhere with one or the other of them; even the dog—Rose's dog, soon to be Alan's—got special attention and began to look fat. The group that met for the Saturday socializing (called among themselves the Skeet Club, then the Skeet and Dago Red Society, finally the Clay Pigeon, Merlot and Chattering Class Reunion) became protective of them, a shield from bad things unspecified. Mike hovered around Rose, called her long-distance to chat about food; O'Neill assured them that Somalia would settle down before Rose got there; Peretz and Bea smiled and fussed and said how fast time passed during separations.

The investigation put out tentacles across the country. Information had now been gathered by special agents in cities as far apart as Seattle, San Diego, and Orlando, but few field offices had enough of the big picture on the case to follow the investigation closely. As the tempo of the investigation had increased, Dukas had begged and borrowed a few agents who became his own, to send out for reinterviews or to attend to details of the required police work and police knowledge. Most of the team, whether analyst or agent, could now recite Mick Craik's biography like a mantra; recall every disciplinary action he had initiated since 1975, and against whom the action had been conducted; lay out in detail the scheme of the flight deck of a carrier during the launch of an airstrike. All of them knew that Dukas had hoped to get the list down to a few names in the first year, now approaching its end.

The whole team wrote and supercopied and consulted when Norfolk finally gave them a flight-deck roster, a refined and double-checked list of every man in the ship's company who had been assigned to the flight deck, as told off to an NCIS agent by the air boss at the time of the raid. A now-retired commander went through every rate that had served on the flight deck—fuels, ordnancemen, medical, squadron maintenance, plane captains, aircrew. He looked off into the distance while he tried to think of all the rates that served on the flight deck.

Interviews knocked off more—after eight months, fifty more. Three hundred and thirty-one to go, they told each other.

Carla, the money specialist, had some good days and some bad days. Money trails were tedious, but she liked finance, and money never bored her. She had to stay within the laws to track income and outflow—no taps, no IRS leaks, no bank favors. When she got a lead from one interview that a sailor had acted "rich," she would get Mike to authorize a Lexis/Nexis search and a credit reference. Each one cost twenty-five dollars, however—peanuts to the government of the richest country in the world, you'd have thought. Early on, however, she had tried for credit records on the whole crew, but the total of more than two hundred thousand dollars had shocked the bean-counters, and, more to the point, the Inspector General had reminded her that "probable cause" still had some meaning in a government of laws. Limited checks were legal; five thousand might be construed as intrusive.

When, however, she got to one enlisted man who seemed to be minting money, she asked for legal means to make deeper checks. He had been in Craik's squadron. Two interviews mentioned his Rolex and his BMW. He had had flight-deck access. The credit check showed that he had money, investments, and more rolling in. Interviews revealed a pattern of buying big-ticket items with cash. He was not living on a sailor's pay.

Mike read her report and thought they'd got lucky; this was the guy; indeed, he was so hopeful that he didn't mention it to Alan, a kind of charm against failure. Then another interview on the west coast over that weekend suggested that the subject had had a dressing-down from Mick Craik in 1990 over spare parts gone missing, and everything fit—location, revenge, money.

Carla and Mike held a private meeting in his office, and each came away saying secretly, *This is the one.*

Dukas did the interview and arrest himself. He pulled up in front of Chief Petty Officer Jackson Olean's house, knocked on his door and showed his badge, and sat down in a small, overfurnished living room, ready to confront a spy. And Chief Olean folded as soon as the interview started. He cried. He admitted guilt. He begged for a break. Dukas read him his rights and just kept himself from taking his fists to the big, soft man.

Olean was a child pornographer.

You aim at a clay pigeon, you hit a vulture.

Back to square one.

MAY 1993.

The meeting at the Langley headquarters started forty-five minutes late and had far too many attendees, a common Agency trick to create an excuse for providing no really useful data. If people from Secret Service and Navy and DEA came, no one could expect the Agency to reveal really important data, or so their logic went. The Agency had always felt a moral superiority to the lower classes who peopled the other branches of the government. Knowledge was not only power; it was a sacred trust to be kept from the unwashed. This, however, did not seem to be a normal meeting.

The subject was continuing investigations that seemed to cross bureaucratic lines. The purpose was interagency communication.

Dukas explained in detail what NIGHT WATCH was doing and what the focus was. Some people took notes. Then FBI briefed several counterintelligence investigations that might be related. There were no obvious ties, although a steady, low-level leakage in SHAPE, Brussels, and in the Pentagon seemed the most Navy-related and was more or less right in chronology. When Sally Baranowski got up to brief, she was both the most informal and the most sophisticated speaker, using few slides and no notes but ending with a list of twenty-five code names on a briefing graphic, each with a set of dates and place-names. She was the Agency winder-upper, and she rounded off her presentation with a tone and a smile that seemed to say that the meeting was as good as over, and weren't they all good people for having been so sharing!

"What are those names?" a Marine officer asked, bobbing his head toward the screen.

"Places that the hostile officers noted on this slide have conducted a known or strongly suspected operational act," she answered.

An analyst from Secret Service asked quietly, "What do you mean by an operational act? I mean," he said, as somebody rolled his eyes, "this spy stuff isn't my field. Sorry if it's a dumb question, people."

"Not at all!" Sally managed to imply that it was actually a very good question. "An operational act is a meeting with an agent or an attempt to signal to or communicate with an agent. Well—" She stumbled for the first time in her presentation. "There are actually quite a few types of operational act, but that's what we mean on this slide."

Alan was sitting with Dukas in the second row. Rose was leaving in two weeks; somehow, he managed to have that on his mind and yet to concentrate fully on Sally and her graphic. "Can you tell us more about TORGAU 1416?" he said. TORGAU 1416 was a code name on the graphic for one pattern of operational acts. He was looking at an intriguing coincidence of places and dates.

She smiled at him. "One of the best, considering we have no idea who he—or is it she?—is. Or rather, we have some idea who he/she is, but I'd have to get permission to discuss him in more detail."

She paused for a moment, but Alan had not broken eye contact. She tried a counterattack. "Why?"

"You show that TORGAU 1416 was in Naples at the same time as NIGHT WATCH, the operator Mike Dukas just briefed everybody on. I think maybe Navy has the need to know more about him. Or her."

Alan sank back and listened to the mutters of people who had better things to do. Sally looked to Mike for sympathy. Mike stared at her, swigged from a Coke, and said, "What can you tell us?"

"Nothing."

"That's bullshit, Sally. We're working an important CI investigation, we say you've got something that looks pertinent, you go, 'Nothing.' This is what we mean by interagency cooperation, right? We cooperate, the Agency inters it. Thanks a bunch."

"Mike, we informed everybody of this case at a Jitter meeting months and months ago." She smiled, the nicest, sweetest, most cooperative woman in the world, at the very least. "I'm sure it's in your files, Mike."

"Yeah, yeah, yeah. Come on, Sally! We got a need to know. Do I have to go up to my boss's boss so we can have a really good stink, or do you wanta get your boss to make nice now?"

Sally Baranowski kept on smiling, but she knew she'd

lost one, because Shreed owed Alan and Mike over the Mombasa business, an ethical debt that would have been meaningless had not the administration and the Agency directorship changed, so that everybody was watching his backside. Better to cave on the easy ones.

Before he left that day, Alan knew that TORGAU 1416 was a former Soviet case officer with a thick dossier at the Agency and, at one time, a stable of NATO spies. Now, Dukas wanted to know TORGAU 1416's tradecraft, to know anything and everything from that dossier, but experience told him to be patient and play the game. Alan fumed. Dukas was afraid that Alan would grab the dossier and leave with it. He spoke softly; he urged; he calmed. "You're torqued because of Rose. Don't take it out on Sally Baranowski. She's one of the best friends we got at the Agency."

"They've been holding out on us."

"We play our games, they play their games. Look at the good side: we learned really useful stuff."

In fact, Mike had learned three really useful things.

TORGAU 1416 was Russian.

TORGAU 1416 had fled Russia for Iran.

And the third thing was so precious that he knew that in time he would use it to pry the whole dossier from the Agency. It went far beyond NIGHT WATCH. It was so wonderful that it would allow Mike to start ten, maybe twenty, new side investigations, computer searches, new interviews and interview questions.

It was a name.

Efremov.

That another part of his own government had had the information for more than two years was simply the sort of thing he had learned to live with.

JUNE 1993.

Mike and Alan faced a room stuffed with Mike's Kids. Twenty analysts and the three special agents assigned as Night Watch had intensified sat at three large tables, which filled the briefing room. First Dukas, then Alan spoke to the small crowd. They described their impressions of CIA cooperation and offers of cooperation from FBI, Secret Service, and other agencies. The offers were victories for the team and for Melissa's careful program of bridge building. Until now, Night Watch had been conducted within the Navy; all witnesses, all evidence, even all sites had been subject to Navy discipline and investigated by Navy investigators. Information on handling of the Night Watch spy, on foreign involvement; Sally's theory as to the involvement of a former KGB agent; all of the small leads had been left as dangling threads until the Navy process could be played out.

Now, as they were ready to move beyond the Navy, a new crisis had arisen.

The in-Navy process, instead of reducing the pool of suspects to a short-list, had obliterated it.

There were no suspects who met all the criteria.

Dukas had set the parameters: the shortlist was to have included only those who were on watch, who had had access to the flight deck in the hours before the raid, who knew how to code an IFF gun, and who had had a pattern of unexplained deposits in the bank, a mediocre or worse military record, and some level of contact with Mick Craik. Dukas's intuition had told him that the spy must have known and disliked Craik to be willing to, in effect, conduct a homicide. It was clear from the way that the older agents on Mike's team dealt with the case that they, too, thought of it as a homicide. Grudge, revenge, personal involvement, had been part of the criteria.

Now Dukas was telling them that somewhere they had all gone wrong, and he was reviewing and backtracking and trying to coax them into identifying the self-inflicted wound.

"So this unknown," Mike was saying, "moved out onto the flight deck with ease; a nobody who probably moved straight to his victim's plane, coded it, and left the deck. Maybe he went around and coded other planes after changing the codes. Maybe he went to another job. Jimbo hit pay dirt when he got the maintenance chief in the chopper squadron to admit that a coding gun had gone missing. We'll never know for sure if that gun was used by NIGHT WATCH, but you can bet that if it took us a month to get one chief to admit to a missing gun, then there might be others. Let's say that maybe, probably, NIGHT WATCH tossed the gun over the side as soon as he loaded the codes into the victim's plane. If we believe he did that, then we have to believe that he wasn't in the IFF business, right? He was somebody who had access to the flight deck but didn't usually have a coding gun on him and thus wanted to be rid of the evidence. I know that you can argue this the other way, but stay with me. We have interviews suggesting that virtually every man on that flight deck was near Craik's plane at some point. Our flaw isn't here; we've done this part and done it good."

"Hey, Mike?" Alan said, leaning against the whiteboard behind Mike's podium, looking severe and thoughtful and in fact tormented by problems surrounding infant day care. "When was the aircraft's last sortie?"

An analyst in the second table answered for his boss. "He went on a check ride and scored a trap at 1320L." He looked at his notes. "And his IFF was up and up at that time." The Navy terminology came easily to the analyst's tongue after a year.

"Are you *sure* that was the same plane?" Alan looked intently at the picture on the briefing-room wall, where a haze-gray A-6 had CRAIK stenciled in red below the pilot's side of the canopy. "What was the malfunction that caused the check ride?"

The analyst looked through some notes. "Complaint was concerning some sloppy handling in the trim. CDR Craik downed the aircraft for poor handling after receiving a no-grade for a night trap eighteen hours earlier."

Alan could see his father reporting a faulty plane for a no-grade—read "poor"—landing. On the other hand, he had been a crack pilot and had conducted a check ride, usually the sign of real concern.

"Do you have the pink sheet?"

"Got a Xerox."

Alan's throat tightened slightly at the familiar handwriting on the form. He noted where his father had signed for the plane for the check ride. He flipped through the other sheets in the stack. Then he looked back at the analyst. "Where's the sheet from the combat flight?"

"The original loss investigation took it and appears to have lost it. There are several missing from the raid, but it doesn't look suspicious; I got a guy in Legal to admit that he'd seen it and probably shredded it. Shit happens."

Alan studied a mental image of his father's plane starting its last dive, an image that he had seen so often now that he could recall it by closing his eyes. He focused on a detail that had never interested him until now, the tail number.

"What if I told you that this X by his signature means that he downed this bird for sloppy handling *again*—after the check ride? I believe he flew his mission with AE 504. This sheet is for 509."

"That can't be true!" The analyst was threatened; he glanced at Dukas, then back at Alan. "We've been watching for movement around this plane all this time. I mean, all of the interviews— No, somebody would have told us if we had the wrong plane." He looked around the tables. "Everybody said this was the plane. All you guys. This can't be the wrong plane!"

"Got a photo of the wreckage?" Dukas said. Now he was being the good manager, patient, calming. Inside, he was boiling.

Melissa handed him a photograph. Alan bent over a small sheet with prints from his own FLIR footage. Both showed the same image: AE 504 on the tail, hard to read but there. Both cockpits, however, showed that the strike leader's name had been painted in so that the plane would be fully dressed for the mission. The analysts had not looked beyond the name—they were not military people; to them, names had identity, not numbers. Had an aviator—or Alan—had the pink sheet from the wrecked plane, he would have known in an instant. *How many months, how many interviews, how many reports and tapes and files have these fuckheads wasted?*

The analyst was red-faced, panicked. His hands moved too quickly and his mouth did not seem under control. "We have to look at the times." He raked through the stack of Xeroxed pink sheets, each of which held the complete data on one sortie of one aircraft with one crew. Now he separated out all of the sheets on 504 and thanked his luck that he had copied the maintenance log for the whole squadron, not merely the plane that he thought interested him. He looked up, not a happy man.

"Got it! AE 504 last flew three days before." Crestfallen, he threw his hands up and sat back. "That means that anybody, night watch or day watch, could have coded her in the hangar bay." *Anybody.* Back to more than five thousand suspects.

"But nobody *could* know that CDR Craik would take 504 on the strike." Mike was grim. "Hey, listen up, everybody!" His raised voice brought silence. "If Craik downed 509 and decided to take 504, then he told somebody with enough time that his name got painted on 504, right?"

Alan looked up. His voice was cold. "Night Watch must have had to do it twice."

"No shit." Mike looked down. "He walks up, codes the victim, saunters off, maybe even tosses a gun overboard. Then Craik downs the plane and ups 504 with hours to go." He blew out his breath, muttered, *Jesus,* turned an angry face on them. "Bob, by tomorrow, I want 504's spot on the deck, and Plat camera footage of movement around that plane. Let's hop." He looked at the analyst who had blown the plane ID, at the rest of them. They were very quiet. It was their first really, bad mistake. Perhaps they should have been forgiven a first mistake, but Dukas let the silence grow and grow and then said, "This is shit, folks. This is unacceptable. Jesus Christ, how could you?

"Carla, get Norfolk onto finding the seaman who repainted 504 with CDR Craik's name. I want him interviewed or reinterviewed ASAP. Run his name the moment you get it. Find out who he told about the plane switch. Jimbo, find out who never got off the boat in Naples and use that as an elimination criterion. All right, now you people hope and pray we recover from this, or the shit is going to hit the fan, is that clear? Don't mistake me, people— I'm a nice Greek guy for as long as you do your jobs well, but if you fuck up, we're *finished*. Okay? Everybody got it?

"Okay. Back to our other problem. I'll cut some of the crap I was going to go through; take the review as read. What's new is that because of the meeting at the Pentagon, we're pretty sure what we have is a hostile intel officer, ex-Moscow, now probably Iran, running NATO probes, of which our man was probably one. So, I'm going to back down from my thing about revenge. *Not* revenge. *I* was wrong. Business, not revenge. This is humiliation day, folks—eat-crow day." He looked at Alan as if to say, *And in front of the man to whom it matters most, too!* "So, somebody—yeah, Monica, good—get me a new suspect list based on Jimbo's new eliminations but remove the whole revenge criterion from the model. To recap: our suspect list will include only people who fit the following new criteria:

—on board the *Roosevelt* the night of the strike
—knew that Cralk was to be the strike lead
—knew that the strike lead would fly AE 504, *not* 509
—went ashore in Naples
—had access to the flight deck on a routine basis
—had access to an IFF coding gun
—had money deposited in his accounts besides his pay.

"That's seven criteria. I call six out of seven the short-list. Anybody with less than three out of seven is not interesting to us. Make a list for me to brief the admiral with for Monday. That's Monday, as in four days from now, as in you *will* work this weekend. Then we'll start interviewing again. Go to work."

Two weeks later, Dukas was whipped. No leads had gone anywhere. Dead. Dead ends.

The painter who had stenciled his squadron CO's name on a spare plane was dead at twenty-one in a car wreck, the victim of a drunk driver.

Nobody, not NCIS or the Agency or FBI or Italian counterintelligence, had ever noted a KGB spook cruising around Naples.

Twenty-five names had scored six hits out of his seven criteria. All had been interviewed or were dead or were currently at sea. There was no shortlist.

Only now did Dukas's ignorance of the daily business of naval aviation frustrate him. He had had to admit that neither his team nor their experts *really* knew if they had a list of every man who had been on that flight deck.

The only break had come from the Plat camera. It had caught AE 504 three times as it was moved about the flight deck by a young plane captain. Aircraft are not usually moved so often before a flight, but, clearly, special pains were taken with CDR Craik's aircraft. Several shots showed enough of one crewman that they could find his photo in the ship's cruise book. Roger had been the one to see the left shoulder and glowing helmet top of a man near the IFF device. What Roger noted was that the man was a "white shirt," one who wore the flight-deck jersey worn by many smaller rates but also favored by officers who had business there. No face, no identifying marks.

It turned out that even the squadron admin clerks—even intelligence officers like Alan—all wore or owned white flight-deck jerseys. Dukas thought of that sailor, Lake, and what he had said. "My own brother wouldn't know me." So, NIGHT WATCH might be an officer, might be—who?

Dukas wrote the team a memo: *Add new criterion—a white shirt. Start over.*

Alan looked at a wall he had covered with photos and tried to remember what it had been like at the squadron. One picture, with two laughing enlisted men, tugged at his memory. What had they been laughing at? Something stupid he had done—learning to load FLIR film before he had started to fly. Probably his first time on the flight deck. Two guys from the photo shop, who had helped him load the film because he had been named the squadron photo officer back then and had had no training, and they had thought that was very like the Navy and very funny.

Photo officer.

Photo shop.

Photographer's mates. PH's. In white jerseys.

On the flight deck.

Did the investigative team have the photo mates on their flight-deck list? He couldn't remember. He didn't think so. But, surely—

Alan warmed another baby bottle before he called Dukas at the NIGHT WATCH office.

A week later, the names of the *Roosevelt* photo mates were added to the flight-deck access list. Three weeks after that, PO1 Sheldon Bonner was interviewed. The agent who interviewed him wrote, "Tense, chip on his shoulder, pretty typical rating. Kind of a loser and knows it. Waiting out his twenty years. Follow-up interview recommended— gives nothing unless asked directly, some eye and body language suggests shiftiness. Check financial records. One possible anomaly—he extended his tour on the *Roosevelt*. Odd?"

After the interview, Bonner left a signal for his local contact that he wanted a meeting. He meant that he wanted a meeting with the man he called Carl, but the person who appeared next to him at the dog track was darker skinned, younger, sleek. *Raghead,* Bonner thought. In fact, he was a clerk at the Lebanese embassy in Washington.

"Where's Carl?" Bonner growled.

"I know no Carl."

"Carl, your boss—the guy calls himself Carl."

"There is no Carl."

He irritated Bonner. Nonetheless, Bonner told him about the interview and things he had heard from others of the *Roosevelt*'s ship's company. "They're onto something."

"They used a polygraph?"

"Jesus, no."

"They have nothing. It is routine."

"Routine, how do you know? They're interviewing everybody! They raised the guy's plane, they must know that we—" He wasn't sure how much this unsympathetic stranger knew about the IFF and Carl's plan to down the strike leader. "They know something."

"Well, keep us informed."

"*Me* keep *you* informed? I didn't ask for a meeting to keep you people informed! I need to see Carl, and I want you to set it up!"

"There is no Carl."

"Listen, Mohammed, you tell them I see Carl or I don't see anybody! Get me? I'm not going to lose my ass for you guys. Carl and I have a . . . a relationship; I trust him; he takes care of me. If the Navy tags me, I got a lot I could say. Know what I mean? Now, *get me a meeting with Carl!*"

The sad truth was that the man from the Lebanese embassy had never heard of Carl, not even by his real name of Efremov.

NOVEMBER 1993.

Seventeen U.S. rangers were killed in a botched mission in Somalia. The body of one had been dragged through the streets of Mogadishu. The President had ordered in fifteen thousand more soldiers and had ordered that the U.S. would pull out by the end of the following March.

Rose was still there.

Alan stood in front of a dark room, lit by one slash of bright color where a computer displayed his carefully crafted graphics. His audience was a high-powered one: the Director of NCIS, a deputy for the Director of Naval Intelligence, the Deputy Director for Counterintelligence, their aides. They listened because it was their job to listen. Alan let the images speak for themselves: the tide slide showed his father's plane, dripping seawater, being hauled from the ocean bottom, NIGHT WATCH blazoned over the image. He ran through eighteen graphics, stressing the team's accomplishments and their narrowing of the odds. He touched on the moments of success. He spoke in detail about a slide from Jimbo that outlined some other issues that could have arisen from the same case; he explained the damage that a spy on an aircraft carrier could inflict, especially if he was willing to commit sabotage. He did not mention, even think about, his personal connection. He knew, and they knew.

It's PR, kiddo, Dukas had told him. *It's money and it's personnel, and we need the best talking head we can get, and you're it. Blow 'em away, Al."*

They asked no questions until the end. As he finished his conclusions slide, the Deputy Director's disembodied voice said, "Mike, Alan, give me a rough count. How many names on the shortlist?"

Alan liked to have a reserve slide. It was an old habit. Try to predict the big question. Have a slide ready for it. Look cool. He hit the button on the podium, sipped his Coke, and looked into the dark at the place where the invisible voice had spoken.

"We have eight names, sir. Each fits at least six of our eight criteria for the suspect. One other such man is already dead."

Then Mike spoke from the back, where he had sat, silent, through the brief.

"With what we have now, it's one of these. Four are at sea. The rest will be reinterviewed in the next month and, if we get the okay, polygraphed." He didn't say what they would do then.

Alan departed from his procedure and read off the names.

LTj.g. Harris
LTj.g. Coleward
ISSC Higgins
PO1 Bonner
ABH1 Lourdes
ABH2 Seles
Seaman Wojihowski
Seaman Apprentice Hicks

23

Mike Dukas, sitting in his underwear on Alan's spare bed, held his head. Tomorrow he had promised to take his sister's kid to a Bullets game. He hoped the hangover wasn't too bad. He envied Alan his easy control, his withdrawal from the drinking at midnight. Mike flipped open a fishing magazine and hobbled to the bathroom. *You don't buy beer, you rent it.* He heard his beeper go off in the bedroom. *What now? What now at—Jesus, was it really two a.m.?*

Five minutes later, he had a very sleepy senior agent on the phone.

"Can you drive up to Philly?" the agent said.

"When?" It was Sunday. Sunday morning, he meant.

"This morning. Got a woman on the phone couple hours ago, says her husband is a spy. Not from your boat, Mike, sorry—he ain't your NIGHT WATCH. But I'm a little short on interrogators this weekend, you know—" Dukas saw through that line of bullshit real fast. What he meant was that Mike Dukas was the only unmarried agent/interrogator on the roster.

"What the hell kind of woman says her husband is a spy?"

"One who's smashed out of her gourd, in this case. Pretty soused lady. Still, you know, *in vino veritas.*"

"Jeez, you speak French. You got some balls, you know, asking me to do this at fucking two a.m."

"Yeah, well, you know, Mike—there's other investigations than NIGHT WATCH, right? There might even be other spies out there. Hey?"

"Fuck you. And give me the address. I'll go."

Her husband's name was Donnie Marengo. She had nothing going for her except a pretty face, too much makeup, and a great deal of hate. She was too thin, her eyes too spooky; behind the makeup and the cigarette and the hard Philly accent was a druggie, he was pretty sure. Her accusations ran shallow: her husband was always late coming home; he kept classified material in the house (but she couldn't remember what it was or what he had done with it). He was a lousy father. They had no sex life anymore. (Not the husband's fault, was Dukas's conclusion.) He was too close to his own father, it was sick, like two faggots or something, and the two of them went off places together and left her. When he asked what the two men did, she said something about cars and fishing, and he told himself that they didn't sound so strange as she seemed to think.

Finally, the only thing that interested Dukas was that she thought her husband had a lot of money to throw around, as if he'd hit the lottery or something, because he always paid the bills on time. (A strange complaint from a wife.) She remembered a month when the Navy messed up and the whole command missed their paychecks for a week, and her husband just paid the bills anyway, while everybody else went ballistic. Maybe, she thought, he was into gambling. Or dealing drugs.

"I thought your complaint was about spying, Mrs. Marengo."

"He could be a spy and taking his payoffs in drugs, couldn't he? Whose side are you on? I'm telling you, this is a case of spousal abuse! He's abusing me!" She was like a rubber ball, bouncing around inside a box; nothing connected, except a terrible resentment that bounced from espionage to drugs to the father to their kid to abuse—anything.

"How long you been married?"

"Too long." She laughed. Not a good laugh. An infant, he thought, a pretty, nasty infant. And she needs her pacifier, he thought, seeing her nervous fingers grasping her own arms. They had been married a little over two years, she, told him. Long enough to have a child, then—what the hell *was* love, anyway?

Her husband was a data processor. He had promised her to get out and go to work for the company that serviced his Navy job, a high-tech firm that helped make the military applications of the Global Positioning System.

"You can imagine what the enemy would make of that!" she said. "High-tech, everything like that, you know?" She mumbled something about missiles and blowing up Washington.

"So, you said he promised you he'd get out and go to work for these people—to make more money?"

"You bet more money, that's what he promised, he'd make more money."

"But you say he's got plenty of money, that's what makes you suspicious."

"That and other stuff!"

Bang, bang, bounce, bounce—no logic, all hatred. "So," Mike said, "now he *isn't* getting out of the Navy?"

"He promised me! Now his fucking father goes, stay in, do your twenty, *shit!* Just like that, he changed! Isn't that suspicious?"

Round and round. After an hour of it, he believed he'd heard everything she had to say. He gave her his card.

Driving away, Mike looked out his car window, picked up the cell phone, and started the machinery to put Donnie Marengo in an interview room at the Philadelphia Navy

Yard. It just might be another one like the child pornographer; you never knew. *Shoot at a pigeon, hit a vulture.*

He was an hour early in the interview room next day, and he took meticulous care setting the furniture. He'd get this over with, bang-bang-bang, and be back in D.C. in time to do half a day's work. He chatted up two female agents. What really concerned both of them was that they hadn't been asked to do the Marengo interview.

Donnie Marengo surprised him. Dukas had expected the look of failure and found something of the opposite—not a disappointed man to go with that wife, but a tall, very young, good-looking beanpole of a kid. Donnie Marengo was practically a recruiting poster for the new Navy, intelligence in his eyes, sincerity in his handshake. He seemed wary but eager to please. Dukas remembered her complaints about this kid's relationship with his father and found himself thinking the father had done a damned good job of raising his son.

Dukas brought Marengo a Coke from the office refrigerator, then took him to the interview room and explained his rights, which the young man waived, "at least until I understand what's going on." Mike was disarmed. He showed his badge and credentials, demonstrated the recorder, and explained that the small recording device had no legal standing but was there to help him write his report. He explained that the room had a sealed official recorder.

Then he dropped the bomb. "Your wife says you're a spy."

"She probably also said that I'm gay," the thin young man said, without a trace of emotion. "If you talked to her, you know she'll say anything or do anything. Because she hates my guts, man." He had a smooth, educated voice—something he'd learned?

"Why's that?"

Marengo hesitated. "She's a drunk. She's been crazy around our little girl, and I got afraid she'd get violent with her, and I threw her out." He looked toward the dirty window. "I just want her out of my life. You know? I just want to start over."

"Have you ever removed classified documents from the work environment?" Dukas kept his tone neutral. He couldn't help but notice, much as he liked this kid, that he had evaded his first direct question.

"Yes." Again, the boy sounded neutral. "When I was studying for the First Class test, I took stuff home. I knew it was against the rules. I won't try to bullshit you about knowing that other people do the same all the time. I'm not like that. I don't do things just because guys around me do."

Mike made a note. Interesting. Maybe a reference to the wife, who probably did exactly what the people around her did. And yet, that emotionless tone held a hint of arrogance: maybe *I don't do things other guys do because I'm better than they are?* Mike wrote "better than others" on his pad and looked up, frowning.

"Donnie, I'm not investigating people who try to study for a classified test at home. You and I both know that the Russians probably get the 'one and chief's' study book before the Navy does. I mean, have you ever taken *real* classified material home? Let's say, stuff having to do with military GPS?"

For the first time, Donnie Marengo fidgeted. Finally, he looked Mike in the eye. "Yeah." He looked away. "I don't have much of an excuse. I needed to read code at home, where I could keep an eye on Ruthie. My little girl."

Mike looked at him and changed tack. This wasn't a spy, he was pretty sure, just a young man pretty near the edge. But that note of arrogance went oddly with near despair.

"When did you last travel abroad?" Dukas pretended to take notes.

"Last summer, before Sheila lost it. We went to Toronto for a week. I was on leave and my security manager was notified." This was rattled off in the manner of the first few answers.

"Ever have contact with a member of another intelligence service, Donnie?" Mike smiled at him.

"Never, sir."

Well, that was pretty direct. Good reaction.

"Ever show anything you brought home from work to a third party? To your wife or a friend? Your father?" Mike looked from the corner of his eye. Of course Marengo reacted to the word *wife*, but *father* seemed to hit, too. Showing off for the old man? What?

"Actually, I tried pretty hard to make sure Sheila never saw it, sir." He took a big swallow of the soft drink. "I can't trust her. Not since she changed."

Time for a less direct approach, thought Mike. "When did she change?"

"We tried to meet some new people. She got in with this music crowd—like people who thought they were rockers? Bad news, man. All the things they were gonna do, just one break, think of the bucks, man! And about as talented as that chair over there. They had crack at parties, they walked around half naked. It was too weird. I told Sheila I could lose my clearance. She goes, 'Oh, these are my friends, oh, hey—' She told me she needed friends. They gave her self-esteem. You like that, self-esteem? From these airhead dropouts? Then one night she came home, I mean, high as a kite, her eyes kind of *wild*, man, and she, she, um, had been with a guy, or smelled like it, you know? I yelled some, but *I didn't hit her.* If she says I hit her, she lied. I never hit her. Christ, she hit me enough." The smoothness and the neutrality were gone now. Dukas thought he was now sitting with the real Donnie Marengo, a somewhat confused young man who had lost control of his educated accent and his wife. He still didn't seem a spy, however. In fact, he was likable.

"Shit happens," Mike said. He felt like a celibate priest doing marriage counseling. "What *did* you do?"

"I yelled at her. Yeah, I was 'abusive'—her word, right? Women, man, I tell you, they sit by the goddam TV all day and that shit just pours into them—'Oh, my self-esteem, oh, abusive, oh, I need a support group!' I told her to cut it with the parties, come to the club with me, stuff like that. I told her I knew she'd been with another man. She laughed at me. She left. I followed her and kept her under surveillance all night. Christ, I wish I'd lost her. *She turned a trick.* My wife, man! She turned a trick in Philly, my wife, she's out there like a hooker and she could give me AIDS! Two days later I caught her shaking Ruthie. She said Ruthie had broken a glass, she probably broke it herself, then she was off on some bullshit about losing her chance to be a model because I'd knocked her up. Jesus. I tried to get her to a shrink. I tried to maintain some sort of coverage on her—" He had his hands clasped between his thighs; his shoulders were hunched—a man in pain. "You can bet there was no more sex. Turning tricks!"

Dukas had heard a lot of Navy broken-marriage tales. He thought of the woman he had seen. Marengo was wrong about one thing, however. Sheila was not on crack; she was on smack. He knew the look.

"Donnie."

"Yes, sir?"

"Donnie, the allegation your wife made about you spying is pretty serious. I have to investigate it. Get a lawyer from Navy legal. I'll probably need to do a formal interview. That's like a deposition, written questions. Understand?"

"Yes, sir."

"Good. You got a close friend?"

"My dad, sir."

"Get him to help with your wife. Talk to him about it. You're tearing yourself apart." Mike felt like a fool, but at the moment he was the voice of authority.

"He's at sea just now."

"What about your mom?"

"Not appropriate." Flat, deadpan. The armor was back on; the shields were up. Don't go near Mom. Smackhead wife? Not her problem. Or so Dukas read the boy's picture of his mother.

Dukas extended a gold-embossed business card. "Give this to your division officer and ask him to call me tomorrow. Okay?"

"Yes, sir." Donnie Marengo stood up. Dukas had intended a few more questions, but the kid's life was a little too raw. In a couple of days he would reinterview with a lawyer and close this thing out. And then he caught himself, thinking *Why do I want to do the reinterview? This is the Philly office's business; I'm just a weekend loaner here.* And he was honest enough to see that he had meant to block the female agents from the interview because they might listen to the wife differently: he had already decided in the young man's favor. He had disliked Sheila Marengo—worse, he had despised her. Like the child pornographer. Letting feelings get in the way of reason. "What I mean is, somebody will do a reinterview. Another agent."

They shook hands. Marengo's face took on a strange, eager look; halfway to the door he turned and looked back over his shoulder. His lips parted as if he wanted to say something, but all that emerged was a rather high-pitched "Bye."

Dukas played back the recording, wanting to smoke, not able to because of a local rule. *I followed her and kept her under surveillance all night. I tried to maintain some sort of coverage on her.*

Surveillance. Maintain coverage. Odd terms for a data processor.

Too much TV?

Dukas played the tape again in his rental car leaving Philadelphia. In the dead spot between Wilmington and Baltimore where only country-and-western stations seem to exist, he killed the radio and listened to the tape for a third time.

Dukas frowned. What had Donnie Marengo been planning to say at the end, that he had changed to that limp "Bye"? Dukas had an unfamiliar feeling of failure. That kid, like many suspects and witnesses, had had something more to say. *I've been on Night Watch too long. I got put off by the wife. Well, it's Philly's ball game now.*

1530 ZULU. TEHRAN.

Efremov had everything for which he had left Moscow—a beautiful house, gardens, limousine, driver, mistress, food—except the one thing he had thought he already possessed: control. Control in a religious state, he found, was not exercised in the same ways as in a secular one, nor was it bought or bribed or stolen in the same ways.

The man standing in front of him was obviously a cleric; anybody in Tehran would have recognized him. His power did not concern itself with the things Efremov had wanted: his clothes were simple; he smelled of sweat; he rarely used money. But, it was clear, he had control of Efremov's life.

"I am sorry, my friend. Your request was denied by the Committee."

Efremov, who had been ruthless in eliminating those agents who would not defect from Moscow with him, was nonetheless loyal to those who were loyal to him. "We must bring my American agent out if he is desperate," he said.

The cleric nodded.

"The old escapes will not work—they all ended in Moscow. He has a certain mark he is to leave; I will give you the locations. If one of your agents sees the mark, then he must be brought out—"

"Through Sudan." When he saw Efremov scowling, the cleric said, "It will not do to bring him directly to Tehran from Europe. The Americans watch those flights, the more so if he is running. Sudan—then it is easy."

Efremov scowled even more deeply. He did not know Sudan. Everything would have to be left to strangers.

Later, in his garden, Efremov looked at the day's white card. He had written, "Meeting, Naples, with B." Now, he scratched the entry out and, after a moment, set fire to the card.

DECEMBER 4, 1993. NORFOLK.

The work week was routine, NIGHT WATCH now mere background. Alan was up at five: change Michael, bundle him into whatever gear the weather demanded, walk the dog, Michael in a backpack; feed the dog; change Michael; feed Michael; talk to Michael and the dog, often simultaneously, although he tended to talk baby-talk to the dog and adult-talk to the baby. Mondays, Wednesdays, and Fridays at noon he ran four miles with the rest of his unit; Tuesdays and Thursdays, he met with Marine Gunnery Sergeant Adolph Miner at the gym, where Miner taught him street-fighting and he taught Miner wrestling, and both men came away wiser but bruised.

Then came a weekend in December that he thought would be like all the others, and instead the world heaved.

Dukas came a little late that Saturday; O'Neill and Peretz were already there. It was raining. They were drinking beer and staring at the TV. Dukas said, "I thought I was gonna have something for you today, no kidding. It looked *so good.* A gift. I told you, sometimes lightning strikes, and I thought this was the lightning. Then, *pffft.*" He opened a beer can. "A call-in last weekend. A woman. Boozed. 'My husband's in the U.S. Navy and he's a commie spy.'" He drank. "Her very words. I heard the tape. God, people sound terrible when they don't hear themselves!"

"And you thought it was our guy."

"I did, I did!"

Peretz laughed.

"What's so funny?"

"I don't know many optimists."

"I drove up Sunday morning, *with* a hangover, and I interviewed the wife, who is (a) cute, (b) vindictive, and (c) on smack. Off the walls, folks. But, she says the husband is a spy, and, yes, I'm an optimist. Monday, I interviewed him—hoping against hope, but convinced the kid is blameless because the wife is a bitch. Some cop, huh?"

"I thought you thought he was our guy."

"Nah, by then I knew he wasn't. Never on the *Roosevelt.*" He opened another beer with a snap and a *pfffft.* "Donald T. Marengo. Petty Officer Third Class, Naval Satellite Communications Research Center, Philly. Perfect, right? You imagine a spy in N-SCORC?"

Alan had stopped watching the TV and was looking at his hands.

Dukas sighed. "Hope is a mean bitch, man."

They were all silent. O'Neill glanced at Alan, then at Peretz, and the two gave each other a little look. *Too bad.* Dukas turned his head and opened his mouth to say something to Peretz about baseball.

"Marengo," Alan said. "Where do I know that name from? Hmp. Right on the tip of my tongue—maybe my old squadron? Marengo. More recent than that, like it's real recent—maybe a rating at the intel center when we were checking the new shortlist for the briefing? God, it's right there!" He sounded unconcerned, as if he was talking about the rain. They all looked at him. His eyes narrowed. "It's on the tip of my tongue, but I can't—Marengo. I know I've seen it." He stared into space. "It's in one of the NIGHT WATCH files."

"You sure?" Dukas turned off the TV.

"It's not one of the names, but it's somewhere close. As you said, not somebody who'd been on the *Roosevelt.* But in one of the files. I can see it—*Marengo.*"

The four men looked at each other. Then O'Neill reared himself up. "We didn't have anything better to do, anyway, right, chaps?"

They rushed to their cars, telling the women they would be right back, only a couple of hours, only a matter of going to Alan's office, and they drove through the rain the route he drove every day, twice a day, the traffic less now, showing badges and credentials at the gate, Alan signing them into his building, his office, dealing with the duty officer and the watch, and they dispersed over several offices and began to pull up files on networked computers. Minutes, then a quarter of an hour, then—

"Bonner."

They gathered in Alan's office.

"Bonner, Sheldon. PO1. Photographic Specialist. Ship's company. Divorced. Ex-wife, *Carol Bonner Marengo.* Next of kin, Donald Marengo, Philadelphia!"

Dukas was shaken. "How did I miss him?"

"You can't memorize thousands of names, Mike! This is one of the photo mates, the last group we picked up with flight-deck access. I paid extra attention to them because I was mad you guys had missed them; you were up to your ass managing the operation." He stared at the name, trying to give it human form: *The spy who killed my father?*

"Where's the 'Marengo' come in?" O'Neill said.

"Bonner's ex must have remarried."

Peretz was frowning over his shoulder at the screen. "But it was the next of kin's, this kid's, wife who phoned the FBI about *him.* Bonner was never mentioned."

Dukas rubbed his head. "Marengo's got to be Bonner's kid; he wouldn't name his ex-wife's kid his next of kin. The name—what the hell, one or the other changed his name. Jesus Christ, how did I *miss* that? Unless it was legal, a long time ago—with a child, you know, that wouldn't show up in the normal service record. Whatcha got on this Bonner about marriages? Scroll it— Usually, it's page three—there. Divorced. Okay—wife, Carol. Divorced a long time ago. Children. Three—gotcha! *Donald T.* Look at that—birth date is just about right. My God! and he told me his father is at sea, and I never followed up!"

"Why would you?" Peretz said. "There was no visible connection."

Dukas glanced at the others clustered around the computer. "But shit—if Marengo's wife called about *him*— Jesus. Things she told me made no sense, I blew them away—she said the kid always had money, she didn't know where it came from. It's coming from the father! There's two of them!"

"Hold him down, chaps, he's going into orbit!" O'Neill drawled.

Dukas was annoyed. "Goddammit, this is important!" O'Neill understood, but grinned anyway. "And both the wife and the kid, Marengo, kept using the word 'change'—she said he'd changed; he said she'd changed about a year ago. I'll bet you anything you want to put up that that's when the kid started!"

"Started what?"

Dukas was hating himself. He'd missed everything at both interviews. "Started working for his father," he said slowly, working it out as he spoke. "One of the analysts, Barb, she said the Iranian MO had changed since Mick Craik went in; now we're pretty sure that's when Efremov came on board. He's running the father; now, new rules, he gets the father to bring the son in. It feels right. It feels right!" He shrugged, a kind of apology. "I'm going to my office."

"Holy Christ, that's in D.C.!"

"Yeah, yeah—" He looked to Peretz, the oldest of the four, for understanding. "I won't sleep till it's a wrap," he said.

"Kind of ruins dinner."

"Oh. Well, they'll understand. Won't they?"

Peretz nodded. "Let's pick up the women and I'll go with you. Al, you and O'Neill stay here and the computer whiz can make a secure patch. I'll explain to Bea. And, uh, Pam?"

O'Neill sighed. Pam was his new girl.

"You guys don't have to," Alan said.

"We know that."

By ten o'clock, they had connected Sheldon Bonner and his son and traced the son's change of name, and they had called up and printed their records; they had, as well as their personnel files, the son's file from the credit union, complete security-clearance histories, motor-vehicle records, passport applications, and assorted other files that told them everything—and nothing.

Dukas e-mailed them a last message: *I think we got our man. We got no case. Good night.*

24

George Shreed had eaten in the director's dining room, enjoying the director's special menu, served on the director's special gold-rimmed plates by the director's special waiter, who was paid more of the taxpayer's money to hand food around than many upper-level civil servants. Shreed did not begrudge the director his perks, nor the waiter his salary; nor did he aspire to be the director; he did, however, deplore the time spent being polite.

Still, the food was good.

He hauled his shattered body to the elevator and so to his own floor, where he crawled slowly along, *like a rejected planetary explorer crossing the Sea of Lamentations,* as he described his own progress on the metal canes. People stood back, a mixture of courtesy and distaste that he noted with a grim smile. *Everybody loves a cripple,* he thought for the thousandth time, *just look at them cringe.*

"I'm feeling generous," he said to Sally Baranowski in his office. "Expansive. Caring." He grinned.

"You sick?"

"No, no. We had a man of God at lunch. No kidding,

an actual ordained something-or-other. Southern, but they still count. It makes you think, Sally—a prayer inside the headquarters of the Great Satan."

"Would you believe I don't believe you?"

"Mmm." He sniffed. "Actually—" He pushed some papers around. "It's time I made it up with that little shit Craik. He's been on my mind."

"Guilt?"

"Maybe. Would I know guilt if it knocked me down? I dunno. There's some pressure to make nice to the other services. We're on that swing of the pendulum; next year, who knows? His admiral sent me a rocket last year about— well, you read it. I hate snotty sarcasm. Anyway, that's set the tone since then; it's time we made up. I have that as official policy."

She smiled as if she understood. "Did this come about over lunch?"

"No, actually; lunch was all about family values and putting Jesus back into government. I wanted to jump up— as if I could jump up!—and remind people about the Constitution. Some of them're still in shock about Bush losing; the neanderthals brought in this hick preacher who's got his own PAC and wants to— Where was I? Oh, Craik. Well, we're building bridges this year, so I want to make some sort of gesture, and he's the best-known problem on this floor. Did I tell you I saw 'contemptible' in a cartoon in the men's room?"

"You told me."

"The kid is famous. One word, and he's a folk hero. Or villain. Maybe there's no difference. Anyway, we need to reach out and touch the little bastard. Got any ideas?"

"They're still looking for his dad's leaker, or whatever it was."

"That's going nowhere. They made a shortlist, then nothing. Why, you got something?" Before she could speak, he said quietly, "I wouldn't mind the Navy turning up a spy in their own service, Sally. You know what the word is around here." Neither of them spoke. There was shocked gossip that the Agency had another mole. "Take some of the media heat off us," he murmured.

Sally Baranowski rubbed her forehead. She looked tired—not surprising; her child was ill. "Darya's been very chatty on my e-mail. I think she's got something and wants to share it with us, but she needs an excuse. Darya—Moscow—Efremov?" She offered these like clues in a game. Efremov and his disappearance had been eclipsed by other matters like the Gulf War, in which the Agency had not had its finest hour. Shreed, however, remembered Efremov and Ouspenskaya and the whole thing perfectly well; he waved her clues away.

"What's up?"

"Only a hunch, but after we turned Efremov's computer stuff back to her last year, she said something about 'augmenting it.' It'd take a hell of a lot of augmenting; it was bits and pieces, just mostly dreck the geeks pulled out of his hard drive, but—*but*—she was trying to tell me, body language, hints, they might get more. I think they've got institutional memory somewhere; that says to me an old op or somebody, maybe a colleague of Efremov's, who could vet the stuff and 'augment' it. So, now she's signaling. I might offer her something and see what she says."

"What's that got to do with Craik?"

"Efremov. Remember—the American agent, possible mil, Naples, Iran? We could share whatever we get, even pull Alan in directly. Bring him over here, maybe park him with the analysts for a couple of weeks—share-and-care time? Make nice to the Navy?"

"What have we got to trade to Moscow?"

"How about those four Spetsnaz guys in Canada?"

"Well—I was sort of saving them for a rainy day."

"Maybe it's raining."

He rubbed his nose, pushed out his lips, closed the fingers of his left hand down hard against the palm and jiggled that hand. He made a little sound with his tongue. "Well." He leaned back. "Okay. Signal Darya. If she's welcoming, say we'd like to turn these guys over for, you know, appropriate gestures on their part. Then if she has something about Efremov—"

He swung his chair around and looked at·a big map on the far wall. There was nothing there at all relevant to what he was saying, but it seemed to represent some metaphor, at least in his own unconscious. He put his hands behind his head.

"Set up a meeting for Paris. Tell the Canadians to handle their end any way they like—you know what I mean, *ask* them, *ask* them; Christ, they're sensitive—tell them we thank them for their generosity in sharing information gained from these four criminals, blah-blah, we now have no objection to extradition, blah-blah—and set up Darya's handover of whatever she's got. Hard copy—you know, something tangible, so Craik can see it and see how nice we are. *In English.* Hmm? Invite him along. Paris in the spring, right? Do it through that frigging prig of an admiral, so they know this is a gesture, me to the little shit direct—they'll know what we mean. I couldn't make it clearer if I cleaned his shoes with my tongue."

Sally looked wan. "You could just say you're sorry."

"Never. Never!"

DECEMBER 8, 1993. 1920 ZULU. PHILADELPHIA.

Mike Dukas had borrowed an office that was so like half the other offices he had borrowed that he had a momentary lapse into complete disorientation. He knew that the man a few feet from him was the lawyer; he knew that the kid across the desk was Donnie Marengo, but everything else was blank. He looked at his notes and breathed deeply and then thought, *If it's Marengo it must be Philadelphia,* and it all came into focus—if he raised the blinds, he would see a bleak landscape that would not include Independence Hall but would be Philly; somewhere nearby was his rental car.

"Right," he said. Marengo jumped. Mike Dukas smiled. "Don't be scared, Donnie. I'm not gonna come over the desk at you." Dukas chuckled. The lawyer scowled. The kid winced. Dukas pretended to tick something off his notes. "Okay. Donnie—you don't mind if I call you Donnie this time?—Donnie, you know why I'm here."

The boy scowled. "You're here to screw me, man,"

"Hey, Donnie, come on—!"

"Come on, what? What're you gonna tell me, you're here to help me? Last time you said you were here because she'd called you. Okay. She wants to screw me, man—okay! She's an unfit mother; I'll say that in a court of law! I threw her out, right; I kept Ruthie, *yes,* and she's not gonna get her because she's a sicko bad mother!"

Dukas didn't really care about Marengo's wife at all. She was simply a useful diversion, although he felt sorry for the kid, because it was true that the wife was sick or crazy or just bad; the Philly police had had her in for prostitution, drug possession. She was going to do time, if she ever came to trial. This was a nice kid who had been tied in knots by a bitch, but that wasn't Dukas's concern anymore.

"Have you ever heard of Commander Michael Craik, U.S. Navy?" he said.

The switch worked; Marengo was confused. But his reaction seemed okay. He asked for the name again; said no; looked suspicious.

"Never heard your father mention him?"

"No, sir."

"Your father didn't tell you about Commander Craik's plane going in while he was on a tour with the *Roosevelt?*"

"No, sir. What's this about?"

"Commander Craik was lead aircraft in a mission, and he took a direct hit and splashed. It hit the people on the *Roosevelt* pretty hard. I thought your dad might have mentioned it. Your dad *was* on the *Roosevelt?*"

"Yes, sir. Still is."

"Where at?"

"They're in the Med. Or on the way; he sailed last week."

"Commander Craik's aircraft had been tampered with."

Dukas looked into the honest brown eyes. *What does the kid know?* he wondered. *Could he really not have a clue about his father?* "Somebody on the *Roosevelt*," he said, "tampered with Commander Craik's aircraft and got him killed." He pretended to check his notes. "Commander Craik has a son in the Navy still. Like you and your dad. Pretty tough, to have somebody kill your father." He looked up at the honest brown eyes. "Don't you think?"

"Sir?"

"To have some Iranian spy kill your father."

The boy put things together very quickly. He leaned forward and put a hand on the desk and almost shouted, "I've never even been on the *Roosevelt!* What the hell are you trying to get at here?"

Dukas caused his mouth to smile. "I know *you've* never been on the *Roosevelt,* son. I know *you* haven't." He smiled some more. He, too, leaned forward. He glanced at the lawyer. "Know what a polygraph test is, son?"

DECEMBER 8, 1993. 2030 ZULU. NORFOLK.

Reicher leaned in Alan's door and said, "Hey, American flyboy, you want to go to Paris, France?"

"Very funny. Ha."

"I'm not kidding. The admiral's office just called. Shreed's deputy asked that you personally join them for a trip to Paris to pick up some quote-unquote significant material. Interested?"

Alan refused to be interested. "Significant, how?"

Reicher leaned in the doorway. They knew each other pretty well now, actually liked each other. "NIGHT WATCH."

Alan's eyes narrowed. "It's a con." He meant, *Once bitten, twice shy.*

"The admiral says you're going. It's Shreed's way of apologizing. We're all in cooperation mode this week, so you go and bite your tongue and everybody's happy."

"When?"

"Friday."

"Oh, Jesus, Jack! Rose is supposed to call if she makes port! I've got a child to look after; look at my desk—! We're weeks behind on the Sudan SNIE— Send Wiseman. She doesn't have a kid."

"You're going. You were asked for; the admiral says you're it. If you go, it's apology made and accepted. If we send somebody else, it's a slap in the face."

"Is the admiral going to take care of my kid?"

"That's the breaks, flyboy. You'll find somebody."

"Oh, shit!"

His good uniform was at the cleaner's; somebody was coming on Saturday to give an estimate on painting the trim; the car needed work. The dog would have to go to the kennel. The woman who used to care for Michael had moved away. He didn't believe that Shreed and the Agency were going to give him any "significant data" about his father's case; the significant data were in Philadelphia, a young man named Marengo.

"Life is hard," O'Neill said to him that night over the telephone.

Alan was cooking, with the phone held between his head and his shoulder, while the dog watched, chin on floor, and Michael sang to a bowl of noodle soup. "Why don't you come over and take care of him, you big aristocratic slob?"

"I don't do babies."

"Lucky you."

"It isn't luck, old chap. If you haven't figured out yet how babies get made, I'll be happy to explain it to you."

"Oh, piss off."

He was late for work next day because Michael had to be taken for a routine shot, then all the way back to day care. Among his messages was one from Mike Dukas, which he put off answering until last.

"We need to talk," Dukas said.

"Mike, I'm up to my ass. I've been ordered away on some stupid-ass bureaucratic b.s., and I'm running around like a nutcase trying to settle Michael and the dog. Give it to me on the phone."

"I saw the Marengo kid again."

"Yeah."

"Oh, great, I love enthusiasm! Al, this thing is starting to move!"

"Right, we had the big break, and we got a name, and now we're going to spend five years building a case. I know you're working, Mike, but I'm getting cynical."

"Jeez, thanks."

"Not about you—come on. What'd you get from the kid?"

"Nothing. But that's the point. It was so obviously nothing. Marengo's really been zapped by his wife—a naive kid who discovered he'd married most of the problems to be found in modern America. So all of a sudden his life has turned to shit, and there I am asking him about your father and the *Roosevelt*. Al, look, I may have scared the kid."

"You just said you got nothing."

"Well, yeah, but it was a numb kind of nothing. What I was getting at, I don't think the wife *knew;* I think she *sensed*. And the kid is good; he's believable. *But*—if he's in it, and I scared him, he may do something."

"Is he going to do something before I get back next Tuesday?"

"How do I know?"

"Ask him. Anyway, what can he do?"

"Panic."

"Why the hell should he panic?"

"I sort of threatened a polygraph."

"If he's any good, he'll fake it."

"Well—we'll see. Look, let me know where I can reach you through Tuesday."

"Oh, shit—" Alan leafed through piles of papers to find the schedule that had his Paris hotel on it, some glitzy place the Agency was putting him up to make sure he appreciated their generosity. When he found it and told Mike the name, Dukas whistled.

"Fancy, man!"

"Yeah. Why couldn't they wait six months and make it for Mr. and Mrs. Craik? Paris, alone, my work not getting done—this is a favor?"

"Hey, lighten up. Maybe the kid'll panic. Then we catch him and the old man together, committing treason."

"Thanks, Mike. I'll see you Tuesday."

DECEMBER 9, 1993. 1830 ZULU. PHILADELPHIA.

Donnie Marengo had panicked.

He could have managed one thing—his wife's craziness, the disintegration of that part of his life—but not two things, not *everything*. He believed that the NCIS agent who had interviewed him *knew;* the guy was like some obvious TV cop, slimy and tricky and fake-friendly. He was fishing, but he was fishing because he was sure there were fish to be caught. After he mentioned a polygraph, Donnie knew it was time to tell his father he was in over his head.

That was why Donnie Marengo had gone to the Red Cross and persuaded a very nice but out-of-it guy in his fifties to send a message to PO1 Sheldon Bonner on the *Roosevelt*. He had a copy of the message in his coat now: GRANDAD VERY SICK. DOCTOR SAYS ONLY FEW DAYS. PLEASE ADVISE. The only part of the message that meant anything was the word *grandad,* a signal of things gone wrong. *"Grandad" in the first sentence of anything means trouble,* his father had told him. *Like you say over the phone, I had too much Old Grandad last night. Or you write a letter, "Grandad says hello." Or we meet and I go, "How's Grandad?"* Donnie actually had a grandfather, although he was his mother's father and no relation to Sheldon Bonner. Still, dumbfucks like the Red Cross guy and—he hoped—his division officer didn't check stuff like that.

"Marengo, sir." His division officer was a pale ensign

who looked as if he'd been pushed together from leftover cookie dough. He was NROTC, essentially a college kid in a blue suit. Clueless.

"Yes, Marengo. How's it going?" Ensign Dinkman believed he could be a pal to his men. He gave Donnie a big smile. "What's up?"

"I, uh—family trouble, sir. I thought you might be able to give me some advice."

He had said the magic word. Ensign Dinkman was so eager to give advice that slack muscles quivered all over his body. It took Donnie Marengo about three minutes to cause Ensign Dinkman to advise him that he should take two weeks' compassionate leave to deal with his family troubles.

Donnie hadn't had to produce the Red Cross message; he'd thought he would if he had to, but it was better if he didn't, because the less he said that was specific the freer he would be. As it was, he had signaled the crisis to his father and he had two weeks legal leave (after all, as he told himself, he certainly had real family troubles—didn't he?), and he was absolutely square with the Navy so far.

He had almost decided to tell the NCIS guy, Dukas, what he had done. Then he had thought about his father, and the crazy stuff the NCIS guy had spouted about the *Roosevelt* and somebody's dad being killed by—what, a saboteur? A, what had he said, *Iranian spy,* for Christ's sake? A lot of Mickey Mouse. It was no good making his own peace with the Navy; he had to save his father, too. What his father did was certainly not spying for the *Iranians.* The Israelis. And it wasn't really spying. Was it?

So he had sent the grandad warning to his father, and now he would have to persuade his father that the best thing for both of them was to come clean.

Clean. Yes. He wanted to be clean. He had an image of showering, scrubbing it all away—his wife, the fights, the NCIS guy, everything.

DECEMBER 9, 1993. 1900 ZULU. NORFOLK.

Alan got half the day off and drove north, around Washington and Baltimore, cursing the traffic on 695, and on north into Pennsylvania. Michael, in a child seat, wailed and then threw up.

Rose's parents were waiting at a truck stop. They had all agreed that they would meet "for dinner," a terrible mistake, he saw now. He resented the time spent; Rose's mother resented him and the trip and the inconvenience. She adored her grandchild, but all she could talk about was the traffic and the dangers of the road. Leaving the neighborhood in Utica was a big risk for her.

They ate deep-fried everything in a booth festooned with Christmas tinsel, and Bobby and Alan talked about baseball and fishing. When they had run down and they were waiting for coffee, Rose's mother said, in the determined voice of somebody who has waited all day to speak her piece, "I think the Navy is very unfair."

"Mary—" her husband started.

Her mouth was set. She was short, plump, and supremely angry, difficult for a woman accustomed to being passive. "I said, the Navy is unfair."

"I think that sometimes, too," he said. "It's part of—"

"What right have they got to take a mother away from her baby? Tell me that. Don't try to shut me up, I'm asking an important question! This is that government interference they talk about. You'd think this was damned communism."

"You don't know nothing," her husband said.

"I know a mother's duty to her baby! Sending her off to the Persian Gulf! Where is that? Could somebody tell me, where is that? Who cares? What the hell is the meaning for America of a mother losing her baby to go to some Persian Gulf?" She had addressed this all to Alan, the attack harsh enough to make it clear the questions were not meant to be answered.

"And you, letting her do it. I suppose that's what they told you at Harvard. *Feminism.*"

"Shut up, Mary," Bobby said.

"She wanted to do it," Alan said.

"She doesn't know what she wants! Flying, wearing uniforms, going God knows where—kid stuff! She's grown up, she ought to know better! A woman, she should be at home, taking care of the baby, not leaving it for some man to do!"

"Some man," Bobby said, looking at Alan, "some man—he's Mikey's father, Mary! Put a cork in it, will you?"

"I think it's terrible. I think it's disgusting! You know what I really think it is?" She looked from one to the other. "I think it's ungodly!"

"Shut *up,* Mary." This time he said it so quietly that Alan hardly heard him, but she did, and something about the intonation made her clamp her jaws together. Tears came into her eyes.

"I'm sorry," Alan said. "We're doing the best we can." *Are we? Is this the best?* "It's only a few days."

Michael began to cry.

DECEMBER 10, 1993. 0430 ZULU. NORFOLK.

By eleven-thirty Friday night, Mike Dukas had had enough and was headed home. He would have a Jack Daniel's and water when he was in his own kitchen, he thought; he had had three beers all night long, cruising the singles bars looking for somebody to poke—he put it to himself as crudely as possible, because he hated the situation, hated his need for somebody, hated the stupidity of raw sex—and he had failed, and now he was headed home. No, it was worse than that; he faced the truth—he had deliberately sabotaged two good possibilities, two real come-ons, two women as lonely as he and as desperate for a night in the dark that wasn't a night alone. "Fuck it," he said out loud.

The light on his answering machine was blinking. He

played the tape as he poured himself a whiskey, then leaned in his kitchen doorway, clinking ice in the glass and listening to dead air and dial tones and one computerized pitch for ballbuster auto loans. He started to sip the whiskey, and the voice of Donnie Marengo's wife came on, and he stopped with the glass at his lips.

"Where *are* you?" Her voice was nasal, a constant whine; she was boozed or doped, too. "What's *with* you? H'lo? Where *are* you? Fucking government servant. I need to *talk* to you."

He played it back, then played the rest of the tape. One long silence, with a disgusted breath and a click, was probably her a second time, he thought. He tried her number, got nothing. He called his office, roused the duty officer. Nothing. His office telephone had two calls from her, both as empty as the one here. He called the FBI interconnect and asked them to check for calls from her, although he was pretty sure she would stay away from them; she wanted to hurt Donnie Marengo, and she had long since decided that he could best be hurt through the Navy.

So Dukas sat down to wait. He made himself ration the whiskey. One an hour he could handle, he thought. Every fifteen minutes, he called her number. Then he would try his office phone.

She called back at twenty minutes after two.

"Where the hell have you *been?*" she screamed. He thought she sounded a little less zonked.

"Right here, waiting for you. What can I do?"

"What can you do? What can you *do?*" She laughed. He had been wrong; the laugh was thoroughly drunken. He heard her voice, muffled, as she spoke to somebody else. Was she being coached? What was it? "Listen, you government turd," she said.

"I'm here."

"Oh, 'I'm here.' Oh, smell me! 'I'm here.' I hate your guts, you know that?"

Dukas resisted the temptation to hang up. He was thinking about Donnie Marengo and about having told Alan the boy might panic.

"So," he said, "enough about me. How're you?"

"Oh, you know. You know. I'm doing okay. Why?"

"Just wondering how you were."

"You don't give a flying fuck about me. Get real. Ge-e-e-t real. You think I'm a piece of shit. You think I don't know that?" She started to cry. Dukas sighed and told her, No, he didn't think that; No, he thought she was an unhappy woman; No, she had a hard life. On and on. At last she came to it.

"That shit," she said. "You know what?"

"Tell me."

"He's split. He's cut. You hear me?"

"How do you know that?"

"Because the little shit put my baby with goddam strangers, that's how! He's gone—just gone, for good! My lawyer's gonna ream his ass and get my baby back; that's why I called you. I tried to call his CO, no answer, you think anybody in the goddam government phone system cares a shit about me? To give me that asshole's home phone? So I called you. 'Donald Marengo, USN, has *split*.' AWOL. Ream him."

It took another ten minutes to get the story. The boy had paid another couple to take care of the child—"sold it," according to her, but Dukas doubted that—and she had found it out from another woman by accident. In fact, the couple weren't strangers; they were Marengo's Navy buddy and his wife, with two kids of their own. She screamed that they were unfit; they committed child abuse; they were— When he had had enough, he hung up.

He called the couple. The man was at first truculent, then apologetic when Dukas said he was NCIS, but he was adamant that he did not know where Donnie Marengo had gone.

"Family trouble. He just kept saying 'family trouble.' He had compassionate. Fourteen days. It was all on the up-and-up."

"How do you know?"

"He showed Claire the papers. She made him. She, uh, thought he might be, you know—bugging out? Him and his wife have—"

"I know. So he's not AWOL?"

"No, sir. He's got his leave papers. You can check with his Admin Officer."

"But he didn't say where he was going."

"No, sir."

"When he'd be back?"

"No, sir."

"Did he mention his dad?"

"No, sir."

"He got a passport?"

"I dunno. Probably. He did a sea tour couple years ago. Sure, probably."

Dukas hung up and looked at the time. Past three-fifteen. Nine-fifteen a.m. in Paris. He called Alan's posh hotel, got a lot of smooth French b.s., learned that Monsieur Cra-eek was not in his room. He left a message. *Call Mike D.*

Dukas began to make telephone calls. He switched from whiskey to coffee. He began another round of calls. By six, he knew that the *Roosevelt*'s next liberty port was Naples, which the ship would make on Sunday afternoon. He also knew from an air manifest scan that Marengo, D., had flown to Naples via Rome last evening.

DECEMBER 10, 1993. 1105 ZULU. PARIS.

The International Center for Information Resolution had a suite of offices in a Paris building that had gone up in the Pompidou years, glossy and aggressively French—the sort of building Napoleon would have commissioned if he had been emperor in the 1980s. The Center itself had a library, a sophisticated computer room, four employees, and a luxurious "senior common room," the terminology borrowed from the Brits to please the Russians. Agency funded, it so far existed solely to channel the Soviet Union's records—stolen, borrowed, given—to Washington.

Alan allowed himself to be impressed. Much as he hated to admit it, the trip was proving a pleasure: he had felt himself relaxing on the plane, felt himself turn into warm mush in the huge hotel bathtub. Last night's dinner would have been memorable, even if he hadn't been eating microwaved bat manure for the past seven weeks. The Navy, thought Alan, sends you to the most romantic spots on earth—alone.

"And this is our Russian colleague I've told you about, Darya Ouspenskaya of the SVRR."

Darya made him think at once of everything he had ever heard about "older women"—some hint (or promise?), a kind of femininity now dated in the States, an indefinable combination of makeup, glance, scent, décolletage, that recalled old French films and that might just conceivably be a bit comic. Nonetheless, he liked her at once. They chatted about Paris, which Ouspenskaya clearly loved; she said a few deliberately indiscreet things about Moscow and the SVRR, and he tossed in something about the CIA; she laughed, shook a finger, said she had heard he was "difficult" and had made a famous scene.

"Famous in Moscow?" he said, laughing.

"I assure you!" She leaned close; her scent and her décolletage became more insistent. "'Contemptible!'" She giggled.

He was appalled but went on smiling. Sally Baranowski all but winked at him; she had told Ouspenskaya, he saw, probably as an easily tossed away "confidence" that cost her nothing. Ouspenskaya, then, was a lover of gossip. But no fool, or she wouldn't be where she was. That she had been bought by the CIA was clear enough, but so was it clear that only a carefully demarcated part of her had been bought. Well, that was the way you got an agent, bit by bit.

They moved to a cluster of sofas and armchairs. A woman brought in coffee and small pastries. Ouspenskaya made a face and said something about gaining weight. The two women chatted about the coming evening—perhaps the Comédie? Alan allowed himself to be given advice about sightseeing.

And then Ouspenskaya produced the documents.

Sally made a little speech about the man named Efremov and how he had left Moscow, causing the deaths of thirty people, murdering two agents in Brussels and Amsterdam, and moving on to Naples. When Darya had generously allowed it, the Agency's computer people had taken down Efremov's computer and extracted what they could, among which was a confused, sometimes random, often unreadable set of files that they believed were communication plans.

"You know what a comm plan is, I'm sure, Alan." She smiled at Ouspenskaya. "Alan's work is in another area, Darya. But he has an interest here because of—"

"His father! Oh, I know. So tragic." Ouspenskaya touched his sleeve. "These feelings transcend borders, nationalities. Yes?"

Sally had in fact briefed him the evening before on the comm plans; the pretense that he had never heard the term was part of a little dance with Ouspenskaya. A comm plan, he knew perfectly well, was the complex routine for communicating between agent and handler, with fallbacks, escapes, and signals.

Alan cleared his throat. "So, you had what seemed to be Efremov's directions for, mm, dealing with his agents. Mm?"

"We had *bits*. You know what happens when your computer goes crazy? A screen covered with gibberish? Well, a lot of it looked like that. Then Darya saved our lives."

"Well—" Ouspenskaya smiled. *This is all a game,* Alan thought. The two women might as well have been reading from scripts. He wanted to laugh. Oh, well, the coffee was good, the view was great, and he felt better than he had in weeks.

"Well," Ouspenskaya said, "I did not save lives, not yet,

anyway, but I remembered"—she touched a jeweled fingernail to a curl of hair—"a fellow, a former officer, who had been in what you call 'operations' under Efremov. This man was very old now, but quite alert, one of those terrible old Russians with a face like a nut, eyes like stones! You know the type. We went to him where he had retired, far from Moscow, and we made him quite a good offer, considering what Russian pensions are now, my dears—oh!" She chuckled. "He overcame his—do you say scruples? *scruples*—and worked for, oh, a very long time to make coherence of what Sally has called the 'bits.' " She put her hand on a stack of thin folders in red bindings. "These are the result."

"How exciting," Sally murmured. She glanced at Alan, who, understanding that this was really for his benefit, smiled. He nodded to show that he, too, found it exciting; and indeed, he was getting a little adrenaline rush, a flush of hope, after months of not allowing himself to hope.

Darya passed them each a copy. There was apparently no lack of money in Moscow for printing and binding, anyway. Inside, a page of single-spaced introductory material gave way to about thirty pages of what seemed to be lists, many of them bulleted, with paragraphs of elaboration. Much of the material was in brackets—the product of the former ops officer's memory.

"What we have," Darya said with that careful enunciation that suggests a deliberate false modesty, "are parts of the communications directives for four individuals. We believe that they correspond to the four agents that—*whom*—Efremov controlled distinctly from certain, mm, other—you understand." She smiled, a woman who could not say certain things, as *they* must perfectly well know. They all smiled. "The computer results were—do you say 'spotty'?—but intriguing. They included two code names, for example—a great help to the former officer. One, he recognized from the context, as it were, and in fact had himself dealt with for several years—the fellow who, mmm, met his death in Brussels. The fourth—" She smiled at

Alan. "This will interest you, Alan. The fourth was, he was sure, American."

"He knew him?" Sally murmured.

"No. Definitively not. Efremov's 'personal property,' as he put it. But he knew there was an American. So, my dears, you see, we are able to put two and two together and get five, if not six. I hope our little efforts will prove valuable for you." She smiled at them. She laughed, touched Alan's arm again. "Yes, you may read it now!" She laughed again.

He had not expected much. Therefore, he was not disappointed. More puzzled than anything, he scanned pages, registering mostly their comparative incoherence: there would be a perfectly lucid line, such as, "the third corner east of rue des Morts San Têtes Nues contains the Convent of the Nuns of Charity, a large building of gray stone with ecclesiastical lines, where turn right and—" which might then be followed by "A FG * SSSS3 (of?) the [second?] aisle by the [tomb?] FTZ#####." Whole pages looked like this.

The old man's memory had been very good, however. His bracketed comments did not entirely replace the missing data, but often they explained or at least put it into context: "[Here was a place to leave a signal, the precise mark not now known. Chalk was most often used in this technique.]" He gave the fullest information, of course, for the Brussels agent, for he had dealt with the man himself; as a result, that plan was virtually complete. *Because the guy is dead and nothing can now be compromised?* Alan wondered.

He glanced up at Sally. She was reading slowly, now and then making little sounds to indicate understanding. Was this for Darya's benefit?

He turned pages. A change to another plan was clear; street and village names were clearly English. The data were very sketchy, however; of the four, this one was by far the least informative. *Because this guy is still in place and the Russians are trying to find him?*

Darya excused herself and minced from the room. Alan looked up at Sally and found her eyes on him.

"How good is this stuff?" he said.

"I think some of it's better than other."

"The English agent? Are they holding back?"

"Of course they are! You don't think they want us to have him, do you? I'm sure they tried the signals as soon as their old man made sense of them."

Alan thought it through: if you have an agent's communications plan, you can signal him to meet at a place you already know; if he shows up, you can do as you want—watch him, kill him, co-opt him. If the plan for the American was complete enough, Dukas could put up a false signal, and—they'd have him! His heart began to pound. He turned to the next new plan, and the places were Dutch, German, and a few English; this one was also quite detailed, full—another agent already dead, he knew.

And then the last plan, and pages of gibberish.

And, four pages in, the name "Chiaia." It leaped off the page at him. His thigh muscles tightened. Naples. *The Via Chiaia.* The word was surrounded by gibberish, but a paragraph in clear followed: "signal left in that place, make the telephone call in the calendar order of the separate book (*damn it! what separate book?*) and proceed east along this street to the Galleria, a large space with a roof of glass and ascending balconies to the top. Sit here in the center for at least twenty [minutes reading an English-language journal]. (*Journal? Newspaper?*) At the designated time proceed across the floor [of the Galleria] to the south entrance and cross the street there and find a telephone [where you will be called with instructions]."

He thought of the day they had landed in Naples. He had gone to bed with Kim. Another American from the *Roosevelt* must have gone to the Galleria, waited, crossed the floor to the south entrance, got a telephone call—

"You okay?" Sally said.

He looked at her.

"You look like you saw a ghost."

He stared at her. *Then he went somewhere and met this Efremov and they planned how to kill my father.* He knew that was the way it had been. He had to take a huge breath, suddenly feeling dizzy: he hadn't been breathing. He looked at Sally again. "How operational is this stuff?" he whispered.

Sally shook her head. "No way of knowing. It's been a couple of years."

Alan's eyes darted around the room. "If they're still using it—"

He looked at her, this pretty, intense, worried woman, and saw what she had done for him. This was why Darya knew about "contemptible," why she had displayed such feeling about the death of his father. Sally had made it the price for Darya's continuing participation in the Paris center—give Alan the American agent's comm plan, or else.

"Does Shreed know?" he said.

Her smile was wry.

"You're wonderful," he said.

Darya bustled in with the servant and more coffee and more food, and the atmosphere changed as suddenly as if one theatrical drop had replaced another, zap!, change of scene, new mood. Alan stood and pretended to stretch. His mind was racing. Naples. The man named Bonner. Donnie Marengo. Mike Dukas's call. *The kid may panic.* For something to do, he excused himself and crossed to another area of chairs and sofas and picked up the telephone he had spotted there, called his hotel.

"One message, Monsieur Cra-eek. It says, 'Call Mike D.' I hope that has been taken down correctly. 'Call Mike D.'" The woman sounded apologetic.

He got Mike at home on the second ring. Alan was looking at his watch and calculating the time in D.C., and he heard Dukas's voice and knew he had been asleep, and at once both men were talking and then both stopped and said, astonished, *"What?"*

Mike Dukas said, "I said, the kid's split. He's spooked. What'd you say?"

Alan's legs were trembling. "I said, I have our friend's comm plan."

"*What?*" Dukas began to fire questions, his voice hoarse, coughing, waking up.

Alan cut him off, got full silence, and said, "Where's the kid going?"

"Naples, Italy. So am I. Two hours' sleep, I leave for Dulles in forty-five minutes."

Alan was grinning. "Naples! Well, well." He swallowed the grin. "Where's Bonner?"

"On the *Roosevelt,* headed for Naples. They dock there day after tomorrow."

The grin came back. "Well. Well, well! Mr. Dillon, I think we got ourselves a turkey shoot!"

"We haven't got shit! We got nothing—even the kid's legal, he's got leave! We got no evidence, no observation, no—"

"Tell NCIS Naples what's going down."

"I already did that."

"Tell the NCIS guys on the *Roosevelt* to watch Bonner."

"I already did that. What d'you think, I'm an amateur?" Then Alan could hear that Dukas was grinning, too. "What the hell you mean, you got his comm plan?"

Alan looked across the room at Ouspenskaya, who happened to be looking at him. He winked. "A present from a friend in Moscow. I'll tell you when I see you."

"Where am I going to see you?"

"Naples. Now, listen—tell your guys to stake out the Galleria. That's where the kid will go to make contact. He'll get a signal drop before, but I haven't got that, but he'll come along Via Santa Croce and turn into the Galleria and then he'll sit there. That's where they pick him up. Then he gets a phone call and he'll get instructions for the meet, so they have to be ready to follow. *Capisce?*"

Dukas groaned, but it was the groan of a man who loved his job.

"Listen, Mike, I'll get to Naples as fast as I can, maybe

even before you. I'll be at a place called the Rienzi, ask the taxi driver. I'll have a room for you. *Wait for me.* Got it?"

"How come you're the one giving the orders all of a sudden?"

Alan thought about that, grinned again. "It's my turn." He hugged the red folder to his chest. "Mike—this is it. This is our chance."

"But we haven't got—" Dukas groaned again. "Yeah, maybe it is. But—don't break your heart, kid."

"You just be in Naples," he said, and hung up.

He turned to the room. The two women seemed very far away. Both sat almost primly, as if they had been waiting for him. He crossed to them—miles, it seemed. Sally, he thought, had already guessed. Darya might have been wondering, but then, she might already know.

"Ladies," he said, "I'm afraid I must leave you."

25

In the cramped space allotted the *Roosevelt*'s two NCIS agents, a short man named Alfreds smoked and read, blinking with fatigue and now and then waving his own smoke away with the hand that held the cigarette. He was reviewing message traffic, putting papers into piles that made sense to him and nobody else. When his partner entered, he hardly looked up.

"What a can of worms," the newcomer said. He threw a pad on the desk. Alfreds grunted.

"I didn't get zilch."

Alfreds grunted again. He had been holding the cigarette in his mouth; now, when he tried to take it out, it stuck to his lower lip and he peeled it away as if he were taking skin off.

"So what do I do?"

Alfreds winced. "What are you talking about?"

"The Ruiz kid. PFL 719. Assault?"

"Interview him again."

The partner groaned and poured himself coffee. Alfreds handed him a piece of paper. "What's this?"

"Message from NCIS Washington."

"What, the admiral's dog is missing?"

"Some guy. 'Surveil but do not alert. National security implications.' I pulled him up, Bonner, he's ship company, clean, it's just routine. I gave it a case number." He waved at a dead computer screen.

" 'National security implications.' Swell. What, a terrorist?"

"Probably security violation, like he left classified stuff in his locker. Something. Anyway, check him out, make a schedule for where he's gonna be, watches, the usual. All we're being asked to do is make sure he's here, make sure we can contact him. NCIS Naples will pick him up if he goes ashore."

"Jesus Christ! I got Ruiz; I got the phantom shitter in propulsion; I got nine skinheads maybe conspiring to commit a hate crime, and we barely made it to the Med yet! Give me a break."

Alfreds took out another cigarette. "I did. I took the Jesus freak who says he can hear a fairy giving freebies in the marine head." He snapped a plastic lighter, inhaled. "Can't you just hardly wait until we have women on board, and see what sort of shit we get then?"

DECEMBER 11, 1993. NAPLES.

The Hotel Rienzi had a tattered elegance that had been marginally fresher in Alan's boyhood. It had been an English hotel then, favored by those British travelers who hated Naples on principle and retreated to its tea and chintz and copies of *Queen* as to a little bit of England. These had been the things that had attracted his mother, too, and she had taken him there once for five days when she had left his father—temporarily, that time. Now, it was a bittersweet reminder, a kind of home. He hadn't brought Kim here, of course.

He ate at a familiar backstreet restaurant, thought of Rose (another romantic place, alone). He walked. He tried to think of things to do, but he had done the only thing he had to: he had telephoned Reicher from Paris, told him he was moving to Naples to follow a lead; after a pause, Reicher had said, "Have a good time."

Mike Dukas was exhausted when he arrived late in the evening. "How'd you *find* this place?" he groaned, looking around the Rienzi.

"My checkered youth."

"Pretty checkered. I haven't seen so much flower-printed shit since I visited my aunt at the retirement village. Christ, I'm tired. Anything new?"

Alan told him about the communications plans as they went up in the massive mahogany elevator. Dukas was impressed, at least until he heard that the plans were incomplete.

"How many places?"

"Eleven. I can identify Naples, Rome, Venice, maybe Athens, somewhere in Germany. You may recognize some of the others."

"But you're sure about Naples."

"Absolutely." He told Dukas about the Galleria, the telephone, the eleven o'clock and seven o'clock times. "I've walked over it; it all matches. Tomorrow at eleven, Donnie Marengo should be sitting there. Your people need to stake it out, ditto the landing area from the carrier, then they pick up Bonner and—"

Dukas was making sarcastic, too-vigorous head nods. "Sure they do. *Sure* they do!" He waited until they were in the room, which he looked at quickly with amazement—floral lampshades, flounced bedspreads, duvets, bronze statuary—before he said, "NCIS Naples has eighteen agents. They cover the busiest region in the Med. Italy's a great country, nice people, but they're too chummy with Gadhafi; every one of our guys here has more terrorist leads to chase down than he's got days in the week. They also got the usual caseload of deadbeat dads, petty thieves, busted security—everything a cop in a small American city has, plus terrorists, security risks, gays, you name it. You know how many Navy people are in southern Italy and this part of the Med?" He fell backward on the bed. "I'm wiped, man. But I got a meeting at NCIS in twenty-five minutes to work it out." He rolled on an elbow. "I'll try for a surveillance team at your Galleria with a tap on the pay phone, so we know where the kid is going from there. We'll try to get a double team of followers, two cars and a couple guys at least on foot—the kid may have a car, right?—so we'll ask for ten agents. Probably we won't get them. It's gonna be Sunday, right? Plus at least four, five, will be in Spain or someplace. Malta. I dunno. Oh, man, I'm tired."

"Can you set it up by eleven?"

"*Roosevelt* doesn't anchor until late afternoon. Plenty of time."

"In the comm plan, the first meet time is eleven."

"So what? Marengo goes and waits, his father's still on the *Roosevelt;* he goes to the phone, no call, he goes to his hotel or whatever and comes back in the evening; *then* we get them. Eleven o'clock is a dry run."

"When he should be followed, Mike! You got photos of Bonner?"

"They're supposed to be faxing them today. Anyway, the real work starts once dad hits the beach. Seven tomorrow evening? Good, still daylight. But Jeez, if he doesn't make that meet and it goes over into Monday, even Tuesday! Christ, I'll have a hard time holding all those guys that long. They got jobs to do, Al!"

"We've got to be ready to hit them."

"For what?" Dukas's eyes were red from rubbing. "For what? A kid with leave meets his dad who's on liberty. What do we hit them for?"

"If they follow the comm plan, it's conspiracy."

Dukas shook his head. "No, it isn't. Anyway, your comm plan is pie in the sky until we actually see Marengo in your Galleria. Bonner may have cooked up a completely new plan. I would."

"You're you. Bonner's different."

"How do you know?"

Alan stared at the ladylike wallpaper, not seeing it. "He's a follower. He's afraid. He sticks to things he knows. I see it in his record."

Dukas grunted. "We'll see. Plus we need at least two guys to pick up Bonner when he comes off the boat tomorrow afternoon. The NCIS guys on board'll make him before he leaves the carrier, identify the boat he takes ashore, telephone in so we can find him easily. Then they follow him until he meets his boy. *Then—* If they pass anything, we're made. *Anything.* Pray God they do. So much as a confidential instruction manual, we got them. If not, we'll try to surveil them; if the office here can spring for a focused mike, we'll maybe pick them up saying something incriminating." He pointed at Alan, and suddenly he was not a worn-out, pudgy man but a martinet. "And you stay out of it!"

"I'm in it, Mike."

"You're here for the ride. You let the pros handle it."

Alan met the hard, weary eyes. "I'll let the pros handle it until something goes wrong. I've come a little far to watch this get wrecked by some slob with Christmas leave on his mind. That said, I'm used to flying in the backseat, okay?"

DECEMBER 12, 1993. 0211 ZULU. MEDITERRANEAN SEA.

On the *Roosevelt*'s flight deck, a single helicopter waited for the deck officer's signal to take off. Most of the deck was dark, marker lights and reflectors showing safety lanes and the limits of the deck. Only the chopper pad was lit, waiting for the late COD to Gaeta to leave.

The rotors flup-flupped faster and the engine came to full power. The deck officer gave a signal.

The chopper rose.

A face peered out from the helicopter's rear window.

PO1 Sheldon Bonner was airborne.

DECEMBER 12, 1993. 0835 ZULU. NAPLES.

In the light of early morning, if you have eyes to see it, Naples is a fresh and sparkling place. The sea washes the quays; fishermen wash the stones where they mend nets or unload fish. The bay glitters.

But Bonner did not have eyes to see the life of the place. He hated Naples, hated the thieves and pimps and hookers he thought waited for him in every doorway. And he was afraid.

He had landed at Gaeta near four in the morning, taking the place of another PO1 who was supposed to be bringing in classified photos. The photo officer had okayed the change: Bonner was legal. He had a port-visit card.

Bonner had done what he was supposed to, turned over the photos to the watch officer at Gaeta, then got his ass into town; and then he had had to wait out the hours in places he neither knew nor understood. He knew there were NCIS agents on every carrier; sometime, they might come looking for him, because hadn't they wanted to do another interview in Florida?

And then the message from Donnie. *Grandad very sick.*

His gut heaved. It should be as wrung out as an old mop, he thought, but still it was boiling in there, rumbling, getting ready to spurt out of him, Jesus Christ, the crud was all he needed in this god-awful place. He had gone into the first hotel where he had seen a light, a place full of whores, he thought, a terrible place, not even clean, Jesus. Now he staggered into the tiny head and sat and felt his fear gush, hot, stinking, and he rubbed his eyes and held back a bubble in his throat, knowing there was more, always more, because fear was relentless.

They had got to Donnie somehow. Bonner had had to go to sea knowing that, some goddam NCIS agent jerking his son around, because of that bitch wife, he said. Well, it might be. But not likely. They were onto him, onto Donnie. *Grandad very sick.*

He had lain awake the rest of that truncated night, thinking it all through. Again and again. No matter how he thought it, it always came out wrong. And where was Carl?

Contact Carl. That was all he could think of. Somehow, he had to get to Carl himself. Not the substitute who had showed up, some nebbish, clueless—how could Carl hire such people? He thought of Carl, in Iran or somewhere, maybe out of reach; it was like a knife stab. He *needed* Carl.

Maybe it'll be all right. Maybe Donnie'll be there, he'll remember all the plan, he's smart; he'll go to the Galleria, wait, go to the pbone box, get the call, then we'll meet. Bonner tried to clean himself up, felt dirty all over, stinking, got in the shower. Cold. *Jesus, what a dump. You could get the clap here. AIDS.*

Drying himself, he looked out the window again. The day did not sparkle for him. He was bone-weary and afraid, and he wanted help from his control and he wanted protection for his son, and for the first time, he regretted all of it. Mostly for Donnie's sake.

He had to unlock the hotel's outer door himself to get out. He almost panicked when he saw it—being locked in, it was like prison! How could they lock you in a hotel— suppose there was a fire? What a hellhole.

The streets were quiet, not yet dusty. He walked. A few people out, paying no attention to him. Smells of bitter coffee, bread, fish, He walked and walked. Up the hill, not so far from that road where he had last met Carl, a million years ago. Up there on the Vomero, he found a place that sold him milky coffee and bread and little curls of butter; pretty good. A woman his age who smiled at him as she served him; she spoke a few words of English.

If he could find that place on the road again, he'd have Donnie meet him there. But he wasn't sure where it was. He thought of asking the woman, but then she'd remember him, remember what he'd asked. He could imagine an NCIS agent talking to her, then going to the place. No good.

This place? Not bad—you could see in both directions,

plus an alley across the street you could maybe cut out by. No. No, you needed an escape close by. Jesus, why hadn't he done this years ago? He had meant to; he really had. He'd told himself that using Carl's plan wasn't enough, he should have his own plan, his own escape. But he hadn't. He *depended* on Carl. Wasn't that what he was for? Wasn't that what he made so much money for? Because, of course, Carl must make lots of money.

Bonner's guts heaved and he went to the filthy *gabinetto;* when he came out, the woman smiled at him, pushed something at him. Some little glass of foul shit. "Good," she said. "For the, you know, inside." She had heard him exploding in the head. Jesus. She meant well. She pointed at a bottle: *Fernet-Branca.* He drank it. Bitter! Christ, like the worst thing you ever tasted! But, he thought, something that bad had to be good for you. Then she asked him to pay for the stuff, and he thought it was just more of the old con, and he went away angry.

Down into the city again, avoiding the places he usually went, walking along the seawall but avoiding the docks the Navy used; they might be looking for him. Still, he had his card, good until tonight. But if they picked him up, he thought, he was dead. Until he talked to Donnie, he was dead. Because he was worried sick for the kid's sake, he wouldn't know what to do or say.

Carl would have known. Anger against Carl rose up: *Why the fuck had he got Donnie into this? Why had Carl made him?*

Now they needed help, and where was Carl?

The main thing was for them to get together. Find out why Donnie had sent him the grandad message, then calm each other down. Make up a story, if they needed one. Then contact Carl somehow. But it was hard to think, because he was tormented by questions, seeming to come at him from all over his brain: Was Donnie on the run? What happened when his own liberty expired? How close were the NCIS goons? What had that bitch said? What did she know? Had Donnie screwed up somehow?

Zurich, he thought. If he could get to Zurich, he could get at his money, another passport. Then they could buy their way to Iran.

Or Athens. Athens was the fallback from Naples. It was no good trying to leave a help message in Naples until he knew the place was safe enough to stay in a couple days; he had to feel more secure before he'd do that. Anyway, he hated Naples. Athens was okay. Stuttgart was lots better. Maybe, if he got at his money, he and Donnie would go to Stuttgart, signal Carl, get flown to Iran. If things were bad. If things were really bad.

But maybe they weren't. Maybe it was just that Donnie was new at it and had panicked.

Of course, that was it.

But he was a smart kid, sensible. Had his shit together.

No, it was something serious.

Bonner walked out along the bay toward Mergellina and found a café a little back from the water, about a hundred feet up a kind of alley. A tiny place. You could watch both ways up and down the alley from one of the three tables, and anybody coming up or down would have to be right on top of you before he'd see there was a break in the houses right there next to the café. Bonner walked back there, found a kind of little square, three more alleys going off it. Good. Or not bad, anyway. He walked back to the café, checked it out. Got the name. Figured how to describe it, how to tell Donnie over the telephone. It would work. He felt better. Even his gut felt better. That damned woman's bad-tasting stuff had worked. It would be okay.

It would be a piece of cake.

Unless they followed Donnie. Suppose they followed him? They'd stake out the Galleria, pick him up, they had teams of guys with nothing to do but that, all sorts of electronic shit, detectors and eavesdropping stuff, they could listen to you a hundred yards away. They'd follow Donnie here and arrest them.

For what?

For Donnie being AWOL.

Was he that stupid? Maybe, if he panicked. Jesus, not *knowing* was killing him!

The first meet time was eleven-ten; that was when Donnie was supposed to be at the telephone. He should get to the Galleria about ten forty-five. That was part of Carl's plan, so his people could look Bonner over, check him out for anybody following, stuff like that. Bonner didn't have anybody to do that now, but he saw how wise Carl was. Of course. You checked it out.

He began to walk toward the Galleria. It was a little after nine. He would do two things: check that the phone was there and the number was the same; and go upstairs and look down into the Galleria floor, see what was up. Maybe see Donnie. Then, if anything was wrong—

What?

Warn him. Somehow. The hat. The Orioles hat worn backward as a signal. He had the hat in his tote bag. Christ, that would be iffy.

Bonner walked through the still-clean sunshine without seeing it, past the curving, eroded stones of Renaissance doorways and old grandeur, not seeing them, across the Via Chiaia and along the Via Santa Croce, beginning to fill now with people heading for church, for Sunday-dinner shopping, not seeing them. This was a busy street, a main drag, a thoroughfare of choking traffic and shop after shop after shop; *Donnie will walk along here in an hour.* The thought made him hurt inside.

He walked past the entrance of the Galleria, glancing in, seeing the broad expanse of marble floor, the glass dome four stories above. He had waited here for the call from Carl. Only a few tables out now for the cafés, an old guy walking across in a black coat; a little huddle of men far over. Americans? He had had only a glimpse.

The Galleria took up what would have been most of a city block in the States. It had several entrances. He walked around another side, looked in. There were the same people. Yes, all men. Americans, yes, he thought so. Then he was past. He made another right turn and he was coming up on the south entrance, the street heading down toward it so that there was a flight of stone steps down from the floor level of the Galleria. Making himself walk slowly. There was the telephone. Two guys by the telephone. Behind it, sort of. He passed the entrance, looked in. There was the cluster of men. Four. Americans. One with a beeper on his hip.

Jesus. But Italians were crazy about beepers, cell phones. They called each other up just to use the goddam things. The beeper meant nothing.

The beeper sounded. Bonner made himself slow down. He made himself look away. *Watch the guys by the phone.*

An American voice: "Oh, shit, I gotta call the office. He through with that phone yet?"

Another American voice: "Keep it down, for Christ's sake."

The first voice: "Fuck you, it's Sunday, I'm supposed to be off duty."

Bonner stopped. He turned a little and looked at the two by the telephone.

One of them had the instrument unscrewed and was doing something with a tool.

He was bugging the fucking telephone. In broad daylight!

Bonner was astonished at how calm he made himself appear as he realized that his worst fears had come true.

An hour later, Alan and Mike Dukas were waiting where a side street joined the shopping thoroughfare. The street was busy now, cars and scooters whizzing past, people strolling, smiling, waving. Only a sliver of sunlight made it through the tightly packed buildings, and it glistened as blond hair or white shirts flashed through it. The pace was quick, the air electric, as if everybody in the world would have a good time that day.

Alan thought they stood out as Americans, even American military, maybe even as some kind of cops. He wasn't a cop, but Mike was; Alan felt one by association. "We should have changed," he said. "Into what, Italians?" Dukas growled. He was wearing mirrored sunglasses and a purple warm-up jacket and white cross-trainers, and he did not look inconspicuous to Alan. He was also wearing a headset that connected him with the NCIS team inside the Galleria, but maybe the headset looked like a Walkman.

"What if he sees us?"

"What if he does?"

"He knows you, Mike."

Dukas grunted. He had still not had enough sleep. "Let the Naples guys handle it. They got it scoped."

Alan would believe it when he saw it. He hadn't had enough sleep, either, lying awake, going over and over it, thinking of loopholes, screwups, the scene with Rose's parents at the truck stop eons (what, four days?) before. He willed it away: Rose was flying, his son was in good hands, and this was his only shot.

He didn't like the part where Donnie Marengo was supposed to wait in the Galleria. It didn't feel right. It was okay for Bonner and Efremov, he thought—Efremov had designed it, after all—because Efremov must have had other people and it gave him an opportunity to watch Bonner; but it made no sense for Bonner, alone. *Maybe they won't do it that way,* he thought. But he had thought about a lot of things during the night. Bonner, his father, Rose. And how good life would seem if this thing ever ended.

"There he is," Mike said.

Alan jerked upright; his heartbeat jumped. He stared up the street.

"In the green jacket, the tall kid, no hat. No shades."

"I've got him." Alan had seen a photograph of Marengo; he was not sure he would have recognized him. Now, he thought, the boy looked terribly young and sick with worry or fear. He was coming down the far side of the street toward the Galleria, which was half a block beyond Alan and Mike. He walked steadily and not at all like a tourist, seeming to see nothing, avoiding people by simply swinging his body, never changing his course.

Alan looked at his watch. Ten thirty-six. A little early. If the NCIS guys weren't in place—

When he looked up, something had changed. Faster movement was taking place near Donnie Marengo—somebody moving, Alan thought, toward the boy at an angle as if he or she had sprung from the stone wall. Somebody up there saw it too, felt it as the person shoved past; a head turned; Alan had a quick sense that he was seeing something familiar—*American, out of place here, Orioles, a baseball cap on backward*—and the person, man, it was a man, came up close to Marengo and then turned to the curb and began to run across the street, cars whizzing, a motorcycle roaring up and then trying to turn aside, skidding, the rider starting to spin out—

"It's Bonner!" Alan shouted.

"What the hell—!"

Donnie Marengo—where was Marengo? Alan searched the street. Behind him, Dukas was hissing into the headset, "It's busted, it looks like it's busted!" The motorcyclist had saved himself but had stalled and was heeling over; a few voices were shouting; horns sounded. The Orioles cap had made Alan's side of the street and turned away from him, and he was aware of it out of the corner of his eye and then it was gone. And, almost at the far cross street, Marengo's green jacket was showing its back to him.

"Get the car!" he shouted at Dukas.

"Why?"

"Get the fucking car!" Alan started to run.

"Where? To go where?"

"Stay near a phone!"

He sprinted to the crowd that had formed around the cyclist, searching for Bonner, the baseball cap, some way out of the street that Bonner had used; but every shop had a door he might have gone through, and there was an alley. He cursed, saw the choices like crossed blades, the chance to catch Bonner the broken one because he didn't really know what Bonner looked like and he didn't know where he had gone. He decided to cut his losses and made for the son. He used the crowd as a shield to cross the street through the stopped and now angry cars; making the sidewalk on the far side, he dodged after Marengo's distant spot of brilliant green. He didn't have to sprint then, only trot, saying *scusi, scusi,* the childhood Italian coming back. Marengo never looked behind him. He was good, in a way, because he was obedient: he had got a signal, and he had obeyed. *The hat,* Alan thought, *it must have been the hat, the kid'd know it anywhere.* Naïveté served Marengo pretty well, for he was walking away at a good clip but not running, showing no guilt, no nervousness—a sailor with leave papers in his pocket who'd changed his mind about where he was going.

They went up the Via Santa Croce, Alan a hundred feet behind, Marengo walking quickly; the boy turned down toward the harbor, a damp stone alleyway lined with vegetable and fruit stands, many fewer people; Alan had to draw back, count five, look, and then start down more slowly so he didn't get too close. Now Marengo looked back, only a glance, more likely looking for his father than for pursuit. *Did he make me?* Alan wondered; and, continuing on, he took off his blazer and carried it over his shoulder, then worked the sunglasses out of the pocket and put them on, trying to make himself look different.

Marengo turned right again, crossed a double line of traffic, and headed into the vast piazza above the Palazzo Reale, where two curved arms of stone columns seem to reach to embrace the pigeons and the minivans and the people there.

Alan had to resist hurling himself among the cars—*better to make no waves*—but he was saying obscenity after obscenity inside his head from pure frustration, disappointment, rage. *They had missed him!* Somehow, Bonner had known what was going down and he had warned his son. Now where would they go? Thirteen other cities on the communications plan, and which one would they pick?

He entered the piazza and saw Marengo's green jacket skirting a cluster of men and girls; bright colors fluttered in the breeze that blew from the bay. A glorious day. But not for this.

He had to get in touch with Mike. The Naples NCIS agents had beepers and cell phones; Dukas had taken a headset and a beeper, but they had deliberately not given Alan one. He was to be an observer. Now he was the one following the quarry, and he had no way to communicate. At least Mike would warn the others. And then—? If Mike got their rental car, he would be about three blocks away now, picking it up at the hotel. Then all he had to do was find Alan in a city of two million people.

Marengo left the piazza on the far side and headed into a small street. The green jacket disappeared behind a yellow-brown corner of a building. Alan hurried his pace past the bright skirts and running suits, the laughing young men, a cat washing its underarm, and crossed into shadow on the far side, turned into the small street and—found it empty.

Empty. As if nothing moved there, nothing lived.

Halfway down, a small sign. *Hotel Stella Originale.*

He walked down almost on tiptoe. It was like walking through somebody else's dream.

"Signore?"

The only living thing in the hotel was a middle-aged man with a pocked face, the hooded look of a satisfied hawk.

"C'è un' uomo che è entrado qui, momento fa?" He met the hooded eyes—tough guy, Roman emperor, cynic, poet. *"Un giovane, in verde."* It was like an old film. Alan took out a wallet, removed ten thousand lire, twenty, handed them across the high counter. *"È cosa della mia sorella."* *A matter of my sister.* Well, why not? He would have told any lie just then, to find the boy. The fantasy sister was greeted with the faintest of smiles.

The hooded eyes opened slightly, the brows rose, and the chin went up and to the left half an inch: *upstairs.*

"Telefono?" He handed over another ten thousand. The man took his end of the bill but didn't draw it from Alan's fingers, keeping a link between them like an unsealed bargain; he said in Italian, *No rough stuff.*

"Not here," Alan said in Italian.

A cat walked in from the shaded street and jumped up on the counter and began to wash itself. Not the cat he had seen in the piazza. The man seemed to know it, stroked its head.

There was a telephone in an alcove in a paneled box like something from another century, a kind of sedan chair with a solid door. He found that his hands were shaking when he put the card in; the NCIS office number seemed to ring and ring, and he was cursing inside his head and hating them for the delay, although it was only three rings before a voice said, "NCIS, Moran speaking."

"This is Lieutenant Craik, Case NIGHT WATCH. I've got to get in touch with the visiting agent from the States. Mike Dukas."

"What's this about?"

It's about my life, dumbfuck! but he said what it was about; he said it was an emergency; please, he had to reach Dukas's beeper, do it, now, get on the stick, this is my life! The man on the other end got it the second time around and said he'd see what he could do.

Then he hung up and waited for Dukas to call him. Feeling the time going by like blood dripping from a wrist.

He pushed the paneled door open with his foot and leaned out so he could watch the counter. The cat continued its bath. The man stood behind it with folded arms. Sounds of car horns came in the door. Donnie Marengo came out of the one-lunger elevator and stood by the counter to pay his bill.

Alan balanced the choices—tackle him or follow him—and the telephone rang and he sank back into the sedan chair and pulled the door almost closed and said, "Mike?"

"Where the hell are you?"

"He's ready to split, Mike. He's checking out of his hotel."

"Where?"

"The Piazza Reale. The big one with the arms and the huge empty space? I showed you last night. Oh, shit, Mike, by the Royal Palace—"

"I'll get there. Where?"

"On the west side, there's a little street. Oh, shit. A hotel, the Stella Originale. It's down that street. I'll try to be outside, near the piazza. I'm wearing—"

"You're wasting our time." Dukas hung up.

Alan looked out. Marengo was gone.

"Dove?" he asked the hawk.

The head moved, the chin pointed. *That way. Out.*

"Sparutto!"

But the man was not without sympathy for somebody having a problem with a sister, even an invented one, or perhaps he merely liked melodrama. *"Eh,"* he said. *"C'è un' automobile."*

"Dove?"

A cocked eyebrow, a small gesture of fingers and thumb. Another ten-thousand-lire note passed between them. Then the information: the kid who parked the hotel cars rented five spaces from the police in the No Parking area next to the Palazzo. *Go to the piazza, turn right, down to the—*

Alan was out the door and running, up to the piazza, turn right, down to the broad avenue that ran along the Palazzo Reale—and there was Dukas, driving slowly, looking for him, and there was Donnie Marengo, driving fast in the other direction.

Alan began to sprint.

26

Alan drove. Dukas sat in the passenger seat and chewed a fist and cursed. He tried to raise somebody on the headset and listened and called and finally tore the thing off and threw it on the floor. "Out of range."

"What about the beeper?"

"Oh, for Christ's sake, use your head. We gotta stop at a phone someplace."

"We can't. We'll lose him."

Donnie Marengo was up ahead in the Sunday-afternoon traffic, a green rental Fiat three cars ahead of them. They had lost him in Naples, but an NCIS agent had been waiting on the *autostrada* and had spotted him, and they had picked him up again south of Caserta.

"Are they going to fly somebody ahead?"

"No, they aren't and you know they aren't, and stop asking me! They're sympathetic about the bust at the Galleria; they're not sympathetic about chasing a kid with legal leave papers on a Sunday. Christ, Al, they're doing us a big favor, trying to track the father. Until eight tonight, he's as legal as his kid; when his port card expires, he's AWOL—

big deal, a shore patrol responsibility! NCIS doesn't exist to pull in sailors who overstay their port calls. Where are we?"

"About halfway to Brindisi, unless he turns north at Altamura and heads for Bari."

Dukas groaned. They rode in silence for ten minutes.

"Doesn't this kid ever piss?" Dukas said.

They drove for another ten minutes. A sign said that Serafino was twelve kilometers. The road looked parched, the winter landscape harsher than that around Naples; it was a high plateau, the center of the peninsula, colder and drier.

"I gotta piss," Dukas said. "I can't wait. You got a bottle—anything?"

"Sorry."

Dukas found the plastic bag that the headset had come in. He used that, made a mess, tossed out the window what hadn't landed on the floor or his trousers. He looked disgusted. "We didn't come prepared," he said.

"What would you have brought—Pampers?" He thought of his child.

"I'd have brought a goddam Coke bottle, like you use on a stakeout! I'd have brought a cell phone. I'd have brought a fax machine. I'd have brought lunch, because I'm fucking starving! And what *did* I bring? A STU!" He hugged himself. "I'm also freezing, and my clothes, my razor, and my toothbrush are all in that old ladies' hotel you took me to. Al, this is a lost cause."

Alan had been thinking about that very thing. "You brought the STU?"

"I locked it in the back this morning; I thought we might need it if we made a hit at the Galleria. Ha!"

Between them, they had eleven hundred dollars in U.S. bills (a thousand of it Dukas's), two ATM cards, three credit cards, and a Secure Transmission Unit. "I think we're in good shape," Alan said. "If you want to bag it, I'll let you out in Serafino."

Dukas groaned.

Donnie Marengo turned north and headed for Bari.

Dukas looked at the rental company's map of Italy. "Bari. What the hell's Bari?"

"The major port of entry from Yugoslavia and Albania. Probably also has an airport and a train terminal."

Dukas studied the map. After many minutes, he said, "Venice. He's heading for Venice."

He was heading for Athens.

DECEMBER 12 – 13, 1993. ADRIATIC SEA.

It was the Love Boat from Hell. It had sailed from Bari for Sarande, a port tucked deep into a pocket of the Albanian coast, and Alan and Dukas had waited to buy tickets until they were sure that Donnie Marengo was onboard and had locked himself into his one-person stateroom. By then, all the other staterooms were gone, and Alan and Dukas had had to settle for places on the deck. It was cold, and it was wet: rain had started to fall as they stood on the dock at Bari, watching the oceangoing ferry.

"We're going in that?" Dukas had said. He thought that anything smaller than a carrier was too small to float.

"Where he goes, we go."

Dukas had made a sound like a large dog hearing something suspicious. "I'm gonna hate this," he had said. Still, he had done his best: he had called NCIS, Naples, and persuaded them to have somebody drive the rental car back and return it—the sort of detail that particularly bothered Dukas, to whom expense accounts and vouchers were personal crusades. Alan had telephoned his office from the same pay phone, got the duty officer, and left the message for Reicher that he was still following up a lead. In Bari, Italy.

"He say okay?" Dukas had said. The rain was falling by then; both men hunched under an awning, no rain gear, soaked shoes.

"This ferry goes on to Greece," Alan said. He avoided

the question of whether Reicher had approved of his movements.

"My homeland. I'll have melted by the time we get there."

"What if Marengo gets off somewhere else first?"

Dukas held up a finger. "First stop, Sarande. Fucking Albania, man! You think a KGB officer set up a comm plan to meet an American agent in *Albania?* Give me a break! Stop two, Koloniki, Greece. Maybe. But it's a hundred and thirty-five miles from Athens, according to our map, and no international airport. Not so likely. Stop three, Piraeus, the port for Athens. Yes. Big city nearby, and close to the most porous airport in NATO. More terrorists go through the Athens airport without being stopped than I got hairs on my head."

They had boarded in the rain, in a tight-packed, half-angry, half-jovial crowd that seemed to be mostly some sort of wedding party. Alan thought they must be Italians going to a wedding in Sarande, but they proved to be Albanians returning with the bride and groom from a honeymoon. A group honeymoon. A quite drunken group honeymoon.

Marengo's cabin had a porthole that looked directly over the water, and a varnished wood door that opened on a corridor. "I'll take the door," Alan said. "He knows you, Mike. Go hide."

"I'll go make friends with security. If this tub has security."

In the darkness, they landed at Sarande, and the wedding party got off, gray-faced, unsteady, silent.

Donnie Marengo stayed in his cabin.

"Marengo never eats," Alan said.

"He laid in food at Bari. Also Sarande—he paid one of the stewards to get him stuff ashore. My friend the boat security guy has the steward's attention, meaning the guy will tell us if Marengo so much as breaks wind. The dick wants to arrest him."

"No."

"I know, I know—he's leading us to Bonner. We hope. Anyway, I got in touch with NCIS, Naples. By cable, yet— it's like being on the *Titanic*. They made Bonner in Zurich, only a couple hours behind him. He passed over the border on the train; they got the information out too late to catch him there. He's on the loose in Europe—I don't like it, Al. He could go anywhere. And no," Dukas paused and looked up, slowly, "I don't want to arrest Marengo here. Too public. Italian soil, which could get ugly, legally. But Jesus, Alan, I know this is your crusade, but what if his dad skips without him?"

"He won't."

Dukas looked at him, the look meaning, *Not all dads are like that.* He shrugged, said, "The kid's wife thought they were close, anyhow."

"Something bothering you?" Alan said.

"That comm plan. The one the Russian lady gave you. I don't see an escape plan in it. Even the ones that are mostly gobbledygook, I don't read where he makes a drop and Efremov knows he wants out and they scoop him up."

"Maybe Efremov won't bother to scoop him up. He killed two agents, after all."

"Ye-e-e-e-s, but that was different. You just don't abandon an agent who's on the run. You rescue him; you bring him home. 'Home' in this case being Tehran. That's what worries me—that there's a whole new comm plan we don't know about, and it ends in Iran."

"They followed the old one in Naples."

"Yeah, but that's *Bonner,* not Efremov. Maybe Bonner's using the old plan with his son, but Efremov's given him a new plan for himself. Like Athens. You can fly from Athens to Tehran, Al."

"So, tell NCIS, Athens, to stake out the airport."

Dukas sighed. "Al—NCIS, Athens, is two guys and a toilet. One of them is on loan in Bosnia—I know, because I already been in contact with the other one. The Navy's got very little interest in Athens anymore; it's not a big liberty port; we need the agents elsewhere. So there's one guy, and he's *not* gonna stake out the airport."

Alan, too, looked at the rain. "How about NIGHT WATCH? Can't we get some bodies from there?" he said.

"Who? Barb?" Dukas looked irritated. "A bunch of analysts who've never been on the street?" Dukas looked at his cigarette. "Al, let's make a deal." Dukas crushed the cigarette in a filthy aluminum ashtray. He looked up into Alan's eyes. "If we miss Bonner in Athens, we bag it. Okay?"

Alan thought about it and shook his head. "So long as we're in contact with one of them, I'm staying in. If I have the kid, I'll use him to pry Bonner loose from the Iranians, even if I have to threaten his life to do it."

"Al, we can't do that kind of thing! There are laws!"

"*I* can do that kind of thing. I don't care about laws."

"It's your *career,* for Christ's sake!"

"Okay. It's my career." He put a hand on Dukas's shoulder. "He wasn't your father, Mike. It's as simple as that. If you want to bag it, I'll understand. But I'm in for the whole thing."

Dukas sighed. "Well—I haven't broken any laws yet. I think."

DECEMBER 13, 1993. 1000 ZULU. PIRAEUS, GREECE.

Piraeus was once distinct from Athens, a port crowded, in the fifth century B.C., with wooden ships, and linked to Athens by miles of walls. The walls symbolized Piraeus' importance to the city-state. Now, the walls are gone, and Piraeus and Athens have merged into a megalopolis; yet Piraeus remains a port, and any sailor would recognize it as such—salt air, bars, hookers, the modern equivalents of ship chandlers' tucked away in side streets.

The lone NCIS agent met Dukas at the dock. Dukas had been the first one off, going down the crew's gangway while Alan hovered close to Donnie Marengo. Once, Marengo looked straight at him; Alan had the sunglasses on, but he knew two things at once: that Marengo did not recognize him, and that he very well might the next time. Alan looked down from the rail, spotted the NCIS man with Dukas, and nodded. Minutes later, Dukas and the other agent were off after Marengo, and Alan took the boat dick's advice and found a quayside barbershop where showers cost three American dollars and a shave cost five. An hour later, he emerged from a gaudy discount store with new clothes, looking to himself rather Greek, or at least international. If Donnie Marengo had picked up the blue blazer or the button-down shirt, he would not recognize the man in the baggy nylon warm-ups.

When he got back to the ferry, the boat dick told him that Dukas had called, and Alan was to go to a restaurant in Athens; Marengo had had lunch there, and they might still be there if he hurried. He jumped in a taxi, but when he got to the restaurant, they were already gone. There was an outdoor terrace and weak, late-afternoon sunlight shining on the still-wet streets. Alan was standing there, wondering what came next, when a waiter said in heavily accented English, "Mr. Alan?"

He whirled. The waiter was young, grinning; for some reason, what Alan remembered later was the shoes, which had points like spears.

The waiter held out a cell phone. "From friend Mike." When Alan reached for it, the hand withdrew a little. The grin grew wider. "Ten bucks. He say you give me ten bucks."

Alan had only twenties. The waiter's grin became radiant. "You wait, he say. You wait, he call."

Alan waited. The cell phone beeped.

"Hey, buddy." It was Dukas, without question.

"Where the hell are you?"

"Kritikiou Street, sweetheart, watching Donnie Marengo put masking tape on a telephone pole. No shit, something's going down. Fred—the local NCIS guy—is in a car in case somebody picks Marengo up. You eaten?"

"The hell with eating. I'll eat when—"

"Eat! An operation like this, you may not get a chance for another twenty-four hours! Tell my friend Nickie there to bring you what he brought me; it'll put hair on your chest."

"Mike, how come the cell phones?"

"You got a better idea? Maybe we should rent billboards to communicate? Jesus Christ, I thought I did pretty good! These things are guaranteed for the rest of today; then, I dunno. But the way I figure, we better stay strictly in touch, or we're gonna lose this kid. I think things are moving."

"Mike, where the hell did you get these phones? What's this 'rest of today' stuff?"

"I bought them on the street, what do you think!"

Meaning, they were stolen. "I thought you were worried about laws."

"I'm helping the local economy. You want me to take the time to go to the phone company and become a subscriber? Look, Al, check the comm plan, I'm sure Kritikiou Street is in there, also something about a church. Maybe the church is the meet. If it is, Fred and me are going to hang around and make the bust. I know you want to be in on this thing, but we may need you to surveil Marengo if he takes off someplace else. What we're gonna do is hang with him; if he settles in at the church, so do we. If he takes off, I follow him, you join me—I telephone you first, right?—and we do a team surveil, you and me, while Fred watches the church. Right now, you check the comm plan and see if you can make anything out of the church thing. Is it the meet? Read between the lines, you know. You got the STU?"

"Yeah, and it weighs a ton."

"See if you can raise somebody and get us some help."

"It'll be too late."

"We don't know that. Try!"

Of course it was too late.

• • •

They played cell-phone tag around Athens for three hours, first Mike and Alan, then Fred and Alan following Marengo. The third member always staked out the signal on Kritikiou Street, watching for Bonner—or Efremov. Or somebody. They needed at least ten people, and they didn't have them. For Alan, it was a kind of hellish game, unbearably tense, made worse by his not really understanding surveillance. Yet, oddly, Marengo made himself easy to follow, even spending three-quarters of an hour in a coffee bar, while Alan prayed that it would prove the site of the meet and Bonner would appear.

But he did not.

At six that evening, the trade attaché to the Russian embassy, driving home at his usual hour, saw the marker Marengo had left on Kritikiou Street. It made his scalp prickle. It was mere habit that had made him glance toward the metal post; he and everybody in the business knew that that operation had been wound up two years before. There should never have been that mark on Kritikiou Street now—but there was! He made a U-turn across traffic and went back to the embassy and e-mailed Moscow.

It was not until the next morning that an Iranian with a Jordanian passport saw the mark and signaled it to Tehran. By then, of course, it was much too late.

Fred left them at dinnertime. He had done his best for them, gone the second mile; now he had to go back to his office, handle his calls, make some pretense of fighting the backlog. He was apologetic, sincere, miserable.

That left Alan and Dukas again.

Alan stayed with Marengo. Dukas stayed in Kritikiou Street. At six-twenty, Dukas thought he saw Bonner near the mark, and he followed the man and thought he went into the church. He called Alan from the church steps, fearing loss of his signal when he went inside. "I think he's in there. I think this is the meet."

"I'm still with the kid. We're in Piraeus, just walking around. I think he's looking for something."

"Shit." Dukas's hand was trembling, partly fatigue, partly excitement. "Watch he doesn't make a quick move for a taxi. I'm going into the church."

"What if we lose each other?"

"Then it's every man for himself. Good luck."

"You, too."

Alan put his cell phone in his pocket and watched Marengo study a street sign and then turn left and start walking. They were a couple of blocks from the waterfront—cheap bars, clothing stores, gaudy gift shops. Take your girl a real Greek vase.

At nine minutes to seven, Donnie Marengo sat down at an outdoor table of the Adonai Café. Alan tried to call Dukas and could not reach him.

At seven-ten on the dot, Sheldon Bonner crossed the street and entered the bright flare of the Adonai's lights.

He moved easily, not like a man who was worried about surveillance. He was wearing faded blue jeans and a high-tech fleece jacket and shades, and he looked like a lot of older men along the street. Yet Alan made him at once, because he was watching Donnie Marengo at the moment that the young man saw his father, and he had only to look where Donnie's worried, loving eyes looked.

The man who killed my father. Bonner came casually across the street and up the curb, waiting while a German sailor and a girl went by, and then he moved among the tables toward his son.

Alan had to suppress the hatred. He had to quiet his breathing. *I'll take them both,* he told himself, *the moment he sits down.* He would go forward and hold out his Navy ID and say, "I'm Lieutenant Alan Craik, United States Navy, and you're both under arrest for—" Something. *For killing Mick Craik.* He'd say AWOL; it wouldn't matter. Dukas had warned him to look for a countersurveillance team, people who would be backing Bonner up, but he saw no-body. Dukas was sure they wouldn't meet until Bonner had backup, "tough guys," according to Dukas, "guys with guns, you know—hoods," but Alan had a hunch that Bonner wouldn't have been able to put that together yet. He trusted in the breakdown represented by the archaic comm plan, something gone wrong in Efremov's planning.

And he would take them both. If they resisted, he'd go after Bonner. He'd kill him if he had to. *The man who killed my father.*

Bonner came to his son's table. The boy was standing. The two embraced—

And Alan's cell phone beeped. He grabbed it, terrified that it would warn Bonner.

"Mike," he whispered.

"The church is a bust," Dukas said, "I waited around, I went into—"

"Mike, shut up, he's here, the meet is here—Mike, it's going down—"

Bonner laughed and pushed his son down into his chair and waved at a waiter. He dropped his newspaper on the table. He muttered something and laughed and went inside the bar.

"What the hell, Al— Hey? Al?"

"God damn it! He's gone inside! Bonner's here, he's in-side, the kid is outside—"

"Where, for Christ's sake, *where?*"

"The—oh, shit—Piraeus, the Café Adonai—"

"I'm on my way—"

"Mike, the kid is leaving! Shit—"

"I'm on my way! Taxi—hey—" Dukas began to shout in Greek.

Donnie Marengo had picked up the newspaper and was leaving the lighted restaurant area. At the curb, he, too, began to wave for a taxi. Alan was listening to Dukas, watching Marengo, both trying to get a taxi; it was like a movie with the sound out of synch.

He grabbed a waiter. "Is there a back door? Back door? Door?"

"Bathroom. Inside."

"Not bathroom! Back door! Christ—"

Marengo was moving into the street as a cab slowed.

Alan bolted across the terrace and looked down the side of the bar, where a second door opened on a narrow alley. Bonner, he knew, had already disappeared down that alley and was gone.

"Taxi! Taxi!" He stepped into the street, pulling American twenties from his shirt pocket, waving them. In his left hand, the STU felt like a ship's anchor.

"Mike! Mike, Mike! Mike? Can you hear me? Mike, I've lost you— Hello? Mike—it's-the-air-port! My driver says we're on the highway to the airport. Mike? Hello? Hello-o-o-o." He shook the cell phone. He banged it on his thigh. "Hello, Mike? Mike, I've lost you. If you can hear me, Marengo is headed for the airport. I'll head for the departure area. De-par-ture area, Ath-ens air-port!" He sighed in disgust.

The driver glanced back. "No good, them things. Radio, that's what's good." He laughed. He insisted on telling Alan about his three years in Cleveland. He was tickled by driving somebody who said, "Follow that car."

Were they following that car? It was night now; headlights flared at them; the red tails of cars ahead flickered and glowed and remained anonymous.

Alan thought of being so close to Bonner, then of Bonner's easy moves and confidence. It had been a great act. But it had shown that Bonner was capable of a great act when he had to be. After all, he had gone out on a flight deck with a stolen IFF and committed sabotage.

Alan felt sick.

DECEMBER 13, 1993. 1758 ZULU. MOSCOW

The message from Athens about the sighting of an old Efremov message mark reached an SVRR clerk as she was talking on the telephone to a friend. She had been in the job a long time, knew her business; with the phone propped between her cheek and her shoulder, she typed the sighting into a computer and flagged it for a list called Second Priority Inform. It would be on forty-three people's e-mail in the morning, but nobody would be got out of bed to hear of it tonight. Darya Ouspenskaya's name was on the list.

DECEMBER 13, 1993. 1810 ZULU. ATHENS AIRPORT.

The approach to the airport embarkation entrances was crowded with taxis and private cars and buses. It was the winter holiday season—foreigners arriving, Greeks leaving—and the blare of horns in many keys was like a frog chorus gone mad. Engines raced; drivers shot each other threatening looks and cursed and made gestures; the stink of car exhaust was everywhere.

Alan had lost Donnie Marengo. There had been no question as they had lurched into the lighted airport ramps: Marengo's taxi had disappeared into a line of dozens of other vehicles. All Alan could do was press American money into the driver's fist and jump out into the slow-moving traffic, to dodge from taxi to taxi, staring inside, startling passengers, angering drivers. But Marengo was not in any of them. He was already inside the airport—or not at the airport at all.

In the cavernous building, there was more freedom to move but no less sense of bustle and bottleneck. "White Christmas" was playing, disembodied, alien. Long lines of people and luggage trailed from ticket counters, shuffling forward, people shoving bags with their feet. Marengo was not in sight. Alan guessed that Bonner had given the boy a ticket with explicit instructions in the newspaper he had dropped on the café table, probably for a flight that would board immediately so that any pursuers would be blocked—as Alan was—by the complexity of the terminal. Nonetheless, Marengo would have to go through at least one line, produce a passport and a ticket—unless Bonner had been able to get his son a boarding pass. *Not likely,* Alan thought. Even in porous Athens, he would have needed a passport to get a boarding pass. Bonner probably had had a second passport for himself squirreled away, but Alan tried to reassure himself that he couldn't have had one for his son, as well.

Because if he did, it was all over.

He shouldered his way along the lines. Faces, bodies, all sizes and all colors, none right. Then a console of television screens, arrival and departure times. He checked his watch: almost eight o'clock—1958 local. *So, let's say his father got him a ticket to depart within forty-five minutes, tight but doable, pushing the envelope— Say no later than 2045 local.* He missed Dukas. He missed the man's knowledge and he missed his support. Alone now, he felt as if he were out on a limb and an invisible Bonner was sawing it off.

He scanned the monitor for flights leaving before 2045. There were twenty-three of them. More than half were to cities in Greece and the Balkans; remembering Dukas's rejection of Albania as an Efremov meeting ground, he passed over all these. Ten flights: London, Delhi, Stuttgart, New York, Tel Aviv, Riyadh, Bahrain, Johannesburg, Cairo, Paris.

Good Christ. He could be taking any of them. He looked along the lines of ticket counters. The ten airlines were well separated from each other. He couldn't hope to check each one in the few minutes he believed he had until Donnie Marengo disappeared into the international departure area.

So. A surprising fatalism gripped him. *It will happen, or it won't. I'll guess right, or I won't.* Yet it wasn't entirely guesswork. *You're an intel officer. Be intelligent.* Bon-

ner was trying to get them both to Tehran. He was using
the fragments of an old comm plan that once would have
taken him to Moscow. The old plan would have used London or Paris perfectly well, but for Tehran, those cities
were backtracking; going to them would increase the risk
of being seen. They were U.S. allies, NCIS and FBI outposts. *Bahrain. Riyadh.* Bahrain, maybe. Riyadh, no.
Riyadh was definitely on the outs with Tehran.

New York and Tel Aviv, not a chance.

Five definite noes, one possible no.

Four to go: Delhi, Stuttgart, Johannesburg, Cairo.

Not Stuttgart. U.S. mil, tight security.

Delhi. Sure, why not? And where did that plane stop
along the way? Air India. Probably nonstop, in fact. Delhi?

Cairo. No. Cairo is a U.S. friend, the only Arab state
to recognize Israel, not a likely way station to Iran.

Johannesburg. *When you're in Johannesburg, you're at
the southern tip of Africa.* Nowhere, if you want to get to
Tehran. But wait—South Africa had had to take its friends
where it could get them during the years of sanctions. Did
they have air service to Tehran?

A memory tickled him. *Air South Africa to Jo'burg.* He
hadn't been able to take it because the government required
that U.S. employees and military honor the old sanctions—
no South African airline allowed. And he had been frus-
trated, because Air South Africa had gone to the very places
he had wanted to go. Entebbe, Kigali, Kinshasa.

Entebbe.

As close as you could get to Sudan without a car. Sudan,
which was crawling with Libyan and Iranian spooks. Terrorist training camps.

He began to run. A priority assembled itself in his brain:
Johannesburg, one; Bahrain, two; Delhi, three. Air South
Africa was a hundred feet away, Emirates Air a hundred
in the other direction, Air India at the far end of the line.
Maybe, maybe—

Oh, God, if only he had Dukas now!

An angry-looking woman in some kind of uniform was

standing by the South African Air line. She had been pushing somebody into line; now, she looked at Alan. "Yis?"

"Uh—my friend, I think he's already checked through—Entebbe? Jo'burg?"

"Entebbe, yis, Jo'burg, now boarding. Have you luggage?"

He held up the STU.

"Are you ticketed?"

He shook his head. She looked exasperated. She grabbed his arm and pulled him along the line.

"My friend—I don't want to go without him—tall, thin—"

"American? Yis, I think he is already in the boarding area. His name?"

"Marengo." Unless his father managed to get him another passport.

They were at the ticket counter. The angry woman waved the next customer in line away and said, "If you please!" and almost hurled Alan against the counter. He already had his passport and a credit card out. A blond man began to punch a computer.

"My friend—Don Marengo—has he—?"

The man continued to punch keys, nodding, studying the passport, flipping it shut and pushing it toward him.

"I'll seat you next to your friend, then?"

"Uh—no. No!"

The man stared at him.

"I want to surprise him. When we arrive at, mmm—" Entebbe? Did Marengo have a ticket to Entebbe?

"Jo'burg it is, then, Mr. Craik, one way, hand luggage only. You'll have to run, the boarding area is far down the concourse. Your credit card. Your ticket. Gate number—"

Alan grabbed everything and began to trot. The STU was like a suitcase full of cast iron. What would they do about it at security? he wondered. How did Dukas get it through, as a rule? What did you say, *This is my classified, secret, Secure Transmission Unit?*

He was in line at the security gate when somebody's

beeper went off near him and he jumped. *Nerves shot to hell,* he thought. *I need some sleep.* He had been thinking about what he would do on the aircraft. If both Bonner and Marengo were there, he would inform the flight crew, he thought. Could they get somebody to be waiting for him on the ground? If the plane landed at Nairobi, there might be an FBI office. He'd accept the FBI. Not the Agency, no matter what, no way; he wasn't going to be George Shreed's patsy a second time. But if the first landing was Entebbe, there would be a problem. Uganda had nothing. No NCIS, no FBI. And what was the legal situation, being on an aircraft, not yet through customs—?

The beeper kept sounding. It wasn't a beeper, he realized. Some fool's cell phone. *Answer it, dummy!*

Somebody tapped him on the shoulder. He whirled. A short, stocky black man said in impeccable Oxbridge, "Your cell phone, my friend. You are ringing."

My God, it's my phone!

He pulled it out.

"Al! For Christ's sake, what's going on, you asleep? Listen—Donnie Marengo's on the eight-forty-three to Johannesburg, I just checked it out on a computer. Where are you?"

"Mike—"

"We maybe can get the flight held if you can make it by nine. Where are you?"

"Mike, where the hell are you?"

"I'm on the way to the goddam airport!"

"Mike, I'm in line to go through security for the Jo'burg flight. I'm here. I'm ahead of you. How did you know—?"

"I got your call, babe. No sweat. I been on to airport security, they're Greeks, we got along, they found me Marengo on the computer manifest. Hang in there, Al. What I'm gonna do, I'm gonna call back my pals at security and get them to hold the flight and see if I can make it."

"Mike, Mike—can you get them to make an arrest?" He eyed the black man, who looked rather startled. "If

Bonner and Marengo are both on the plane, we can take them here!"

"Nah, I don't think so. Greece is not big on helping Uncle with this sort of stuff. Nah. All they'd do is, they'd throw all four of us out of the country, let us duke it out someplace else. Nah. We'll have to get them in Jo'burg."

"Mike, they're probably not going to Jo'burg. Bonner bought the kid a ticket to the end of the line, yes, but I'll bet you they'll deplane at Entebbe."

"What the hell is Entebbe?"

"It's the airport for Kampala, for Uganda—jump-off point for Sudan. Sudan, Mike? As in Islamic state, friend of Gadhafi, state-supported terrorism?"

He had reached security. He put the STU on the conveyor.

"I gotta go. Get here if you can!"

"Hey, I'm on my way. Wait up for me, Ma!"

The STU was waiting for him on the other side of the barrier. Nobody questioned it. Athens was porous, all right.

He hurried to the departure gate, showed his passport and boarding pass, and looked around for Marengo. Not there. Already aboard, then.

And Bonner?

A last dribble of passengers checked through as the departure time came, then a couple, then three more. Then it was past the departure time and the attendants were urging him aboard, although at the same time, two uniformed security men were arguing with another attendant and shaking their heads. Another latecomer appeared, then another. They were grateful for the delay.

The minutes ticked by.

The attendants were unhappy.

Then Dukas appeared far down the tunnel-like corridor. He was running. His chunky body seemed caught in space while his short legs flailed to move it, and for seconds he seemed not to make any progress at all—and then he was there, slapping down a passport, gasping, falling through the last gate to a near collapse on Alan's shoulder. He drew a huge breath and looked up into Alan's face. "We've got to stop meeting like this," he said.

Five hours later over Africa, with dinner eaten and the movie watched and turned off, Dukas moved along the half-lighted interior of the aircraft until he came to Donnie Marengo's row. Both Dukas and Alan had been up and down the aircraft by then, looking for Bonner and not finding him. Unless he was wearing some brilliant and incredible disguise, he was not on the flight but was going to meet his son at the destination.

Now, Dukas had waited until the person next to Marengo had gone on stockinged feet to the toilet. Dukas stepped over the sleeper on the aisle and lowered himself into the seat next to the young American. He nudged Marengo awake.

"Hi, Donnie. Remember me?" He held out his badge. "I think you want to talk to me."

DECEMBER 14, 1993. 0515 ZULU. MOSCOW.

Darya Ouspenskaya read the Second Priority message about the sighting in Athens. She knew at once what it meant: an Efremov communications plan had been initiated. She came to a wrong, but inevitable, conclusion—that an old Efremov agent wanted to communicate with his case officer. Only two such agents existed, one British, one American. No fool, Ouspenskaya had put together Alan's departure from Paris and the things Sally Baranowski had told her, and she guessed correctly that a rogue American agent was in trouble.

After a quick meeting with her director, she passed the message to Sally Baranowski in Washington.

27

Kampala is a city of hills in a country of lush green vegetation and red soil. Some of the red is blood, spilled by the bloody Buganda rulers of the old days, by the British, by religious fanatics and slavers, by Idi Amin and rebellion and occupation and war. Yet the people are energetic and tough, capable of bouncing back, capable of rebuilding themselves in this place where rain and rich soil give the bases for human life. The hills of Kampala are seen now as tan and pink rather than green and red, the colors of buildings and roofs, and the greenery lies beyond the city like a memory, like the blood.

Dukas had spent two hours talking to Donnie Marengo, first in the row of seats in the aircraft, then in the empty space by the after galley, and he had finally persuaded Marengo to give himself up.

"See, Donnie, I'm just standing here. I haven't tried to arrest you. All you got to do is say you give yourself up, and it's you doing it. A big step toward making things right. We're just talking. But if you give yourself up, cooperate with us, I'll put it in the record that you did the right thing."

Marengo had been worn out, despite his having had more sleep than either Dukas or Alan. He had felt himself a hunted man; he had been heading toward depression, itself exhausting. "What about my dad?" he had said. Dukas had got far enough in his hours of talk so that they both knew they were really talking about Bonner and sabotage and spying.

"Donnie, you know it's better if we take him in. You really want him to end up in Iran? He'd hate it, and you know it. There's a fundamental dislike there, both ways. You persuade him to turn himself in, I promise you, he'll cut a deal in the States. He's got a lot to trade us. He'll do time, but—" Dukas had explained very carefully that it was Iran, not Israel, that Bonner had been working for. And before that, the old Soviet Union.

Bone-weary, tears in his eyes, Donnie Marengo had said huskily as the sun showed in the African sky, "Okay. I turn myself in." He had closed his eyes, and the tears had squeezed out like juice.

They came in from Entebbe in a taxi, Alan, Dukas, and Donnie Marengo, and Alan went out at once to look for a car and a driver. He found a man he liked, a thin, solemn man named Danio, old for the driving business. He had a beat-up but serviceable Land Cruiser. Alan gave him five American twenties.

Mike had taken Marengo to the hotel to wait for four o'clock. That was when the meet was supposed to happen—four o'clock, the City Market, Donnie Marengo and Sheldon Bonner and—? Bonner had given Donnie the details in the folded newspaper at the café. Was he improvising, or had he made contact with Tehran?

DECEMBER 14, 1993. 1235 ZULU. NORFOLK.

Commander Reicher had settled into his chair with the first cup of coffee of the day and the first piece of paperwork, and then the telephone rang. He groaned. He valued this first quiet half hour of the day, nobody else there now that Craik was gone—the early bird.

"LANTIAC, Commander Reicher speaking."

"Commander Reicher, this is Sally Baranowski at the CIA. I'm trying to locate Lieutenant Alan Craik."

Reicher cocked an eyebrow, both at the question of Craik's whereabouts and at a call direct from CIA. "Lieutenant Craik isn't here, I'm sorry. Can I help you?"

"Well, maybe you can. Three days ago— Look, can we go secure?"

Reicher frowned. "Sure." He engaged his STU, gave her time to do the same. "Hello? You go on your end?"

"Right." Her voice now had the right metallic sound. "Shoot."

"I was part of the team in Paris with Lieutenant Craik. To receive some classified Russian material?"

"Yeah, I know about that."

"He left all of a sudden."

"Yeah."

"Any idea where he is?"

"I have an idea, yeah. I don't want to share it just now."

She digested that for a moment. "Commander, let me be straight with you." *That'll be the day,* he thought, remembering recent contacts with the Agency. "We got a message that a supposedly inactive marker was activated yesterday. In Athens, Greece. This marker was part of, we think, the comm plan that Alan Craik was looking at in Paris. Uh—without going through the whole dog-and-pony show, let me say that it may be part of the comm plan of an American military personnel working for a foreign government."

"Would that by any chance be an American military personnel you knew about for more than a year and didn't tell us?"

"Look, I didn't make that decision! Yes, we had that information for a while; is that relevant? I think there's an issue of importance here."

"Right—when it's us, it's somebody else's decision; when it's you guys, it's an issue of importance."

"I don't want to have a fight about it! Look, time is of the essence here. Is Alan Craik in Greece?"

That was a shrewd guess. In fact, Reicher was looking at a memo from the watch officer, saying that Alan had phoned in from Piraeus.

"I doubt that Craik left the message mark, if that's what you're getting at," he said. Although, privately, Reicher wouldn't have put it past Alan if he thought it would smoke out his man. *My God, could he have done it?*

"Does the name Efremov mean anything to you?"

"Yeah, sure—the ex-KGB who defected to Iran. The guy you didn't share with us."

She ignored the dig. "NSA picked up a transmission this morning out of Athens for Tehran about this same activated message mark. It's got to be Efremov's. But everybody's confused about it, which says to me either Efremov's lost his warrant in intel or he's there in Tehran and can't make contact—I mean, an out-of-date comm plan? It means things are going wrong. It means Alan may be crosswise of a busted operation, probably a busted escape plan. And that's dangerous."

He caught the "Alan," sensed a personal interest—liking? more?—and said, "You have operational experience?"

She hesitated. "I was a station chief in a, mm, certain small country. Yes."

"Why do you think Alan's involved?"

"Because he's obsessed with his father's killer."

"Obsessed" was a little strong, Reicher thought, but she was on the right track. "So?" he said.

"He got a phone call while we were in Paris and he left—with a copy of the comm plan. I've checked and found he flew to Naples, one of the cities in the plan. What's he onto, Commander? Come on, be honest with me—have you guys got somebody on the run out there?"

Reicher thought of Alan and the NCIS agent who was running NIGHT WATCH, what was his name? Dukas. Buddies. And the others who hung around Alan, the big black guy, O'Neill, and the FBI, ex–Navy man, Peretz. Reicher had stayed out of NIGHT WATCH; it was a peripheral responsibility for Alan, a sideshow to his real job. Could they actually have NIGHT WATCH on the run?

"I'll get back to you," he said.

"Quickly," she said.

He thought about that, about doing anything quickly for the Agency, which wouldn't, in his view, give him a pair of dirty sweat socks as a favor. "Okay, quickly." There went his quiet hour.

1300 ZULU. KAMPALA, UGANDA.

The City Market is a maze of narrow aisles under a low roof, with, next to it, a rubble-covered dirt field with more stalls, running down from a shopping street above. It offers scores of vegetable and fruit stalls, as well as sellers of rope and sisal twine, baskets, live and dead chickens, *halal* meat, tourist items, Calvin Klein underwear (only several years out of date), the gaudy lengths of printed cloth called *kitambaa*, used shoes, sandals made from rubber tires, Michael Jackson tapes, baby clothes, and almost anything else that a people recovering from a civil war might want or need, and whatever else the industrialized world can dump on them. At the rear of the building is a doorway that looks out on part of the rubble-covered hill; close to the doorway, sellers specialize in shoes and that essential of Ugandan life, the bicycle.

The meeting was set for four o'clock just inside this doorway.

Or so Donnie Marengo said.

Alan had checked the area, and he knew that to the left of the doorway on the outside, behind the rows of shoes, a wall led to an opening that ran beside a shop and trickled into one of the narrow alleys, a maze into which even a white man could disappear in a black country. To the right from the doorway was only blazing sun, a few poisonously green weeds, and a blank, pocked wall for a hundred feet. Straight ahead was the slope up to the street.

Alan put Danio up there with the aged Toyota Land Cruiser. Donnie Marengo, handcuffed to Dukas, was inside in the shadow. From up there, Dukas could see anybody coming to the doorway well before he got there.

Inside the doorway, in the deep shade, there were stalls against the walls on both sides, and stalls running in rows straight away at right angles, one forming a narrow street from the doorway almost to the front of the building—but up there were two doorways, separated by two meat shops and a fruit booth. Thus, it was impossible to look right through the building or to see anything on either side, except along the immediate back wall.

Alan thought of Dukas's description of a countersurveillance team—"bad guys, hoods"—and wondered if Bonner and his control could have had time to set up an operation.

He hoped not.

He had wanted a gun. Now, standing in the gloom of the market, he saw that a gun would have been a mistake. There were too many people, and the open stalls wouldn't have stopped a thrown rock. You'd aim at a bad guy and kill somebody half a block away.

So it's me and him, he thought. *And them?*

He was carrying an English-language newspaper, as Marengo had said he was supposed to do. He wore sunglasses and a baseball hat and a T-shirt, and from a distance he might look a little like Donnie Marengo. Enough to fool a father? Probably not, but enough, perhaps, to fool a countersurveillance man who had never seen Marengo and who, please God, had not been given a photo of him because there hadn't been time, and who might scout the area and go back to Bonner and say, "He's there."

If there was a countersurveillance man.

Alan watched everybody who came into the center aisle or who moved toward him along the stalls at his right and left. He more or less recognized the people who ran the nearby stalls (but who were not necessarily ruled out as countersurveillance thugs for that reason—after all, if you had time to set up an escape plan, why not plant somebody there?), and he found himself passing over the old and the fat, looking particularly for the long-headed, slender look of the Sudanese. Or would they be Ugandans hired for the purpose? Or resident Arabs? Or didn't they exist?

Alan did not think of any "after today." He was entirely in the present, eyes moving, body ready. It was like the moment before a wrestling match started, waiting for the referee to speak, your hand on the opponent's neck. He had done his thinking of the past and the future, lying on the bed in the hotel room: Rose and the baby; his father; career; Rose, Rose.

Now, he wiped his mind clean.

And then he saw Bonner.

1303 ZULU. NORFOLK.

"Ms. Baranowski? Commander Reicher."

"Thanks for getting back to me. I wasn't sure—"

"We'll sort it out later. Here's the story. You know NIGHT WATCH?"

"I know of it."

He recapped the investigation and what he knew of Alan's movements. "I heard from Craik twice—from Bari, Italy, and from Athens. You were right about Athens, yeah, he was there. So it adds up: Craik and Dukas are after two suspects in the NIGHT WATCH investigation. They seem to be on their own. This is breaking pretty fast, so we think we're behind the curve, and we want to know everything you've got or we think we could lose a hell of a good young officer."

Sally was silent for a long time. Finally, she said, "I wish he trusted us more. I wish we hadn't alienated him. If he'd just let us help him—"

Reicher pulled close the printout that had been made an

hour before from Alan's computer. "Here are my conditions. No recriminations on Alan or Dukas. This remains our operation, Navy to be informed at every turn. You try to screw us, we'll pull out and go it alone. Tell your boss that. Tell him he can scream to the President later, but he's going to have to stand in line because my admiral intends to be there first, screaming about lack of cooperation from your end. Deal?"

"Deal."

"Okay." He turned a page of the printout. "NIGHT WATCH is two people, not one. Names, Bonner, Sheldon, and—"

1304 ZULU. KAMPALA MARKET.

Bonner had materialized in the shadowed space of the aisle that ran away from the doorway. Overhead, a single shaft of sunlight came through a gap in the roof and lit a rectangle far behind him, and a bird flashed through it, brilliant for an instant and gone. Bonner was partly silhouetted, but Alan knew the man at once, something about his bulk and his movements, now very different from the confidence he had shown at the café in Greece.

He seemed to be alone.

"Bonner!"

Bonner had been looking at him, trying to make him out in the shadow. Alan worked his ID holder from his pocket, moving slowly, as if he were dealing with a wild animal.

"Bonner, I have Donnie." He held up his ID. "Craik, Lieutenant, U.S. Navy."

Two men in hats and short-sleeved shirts gaped at him, and a woman paused in the act of whacking a coconut with a machete.

"Bonner, I've got your son. Look out the doorway, up the hill. There's a gray Land Cruiser. He's inside it with my partner. He's turned himself in, Bonner."

Bonner took two steps toward him, near enough now for Alan to hear his breathing, to hear him murmur *Don-*

nie as he looked up the trash-littered hillside. Then he made a small sound, one below language, a sound of helplessness, pain.

"Come with me and we'll take you back, Bonner. We'll testify that you turned yourself in. Bonner—it's over."

He had put his ID in his pocket. Now, Alan reached for Bonner's arm; he took one step, and the two men were close to each other, and for the first time he could touch the man—merely extend his arm another three inches, touch the bare upper arm just above the elbow, close his hand around the muscle. He felt the warmth of Bonner's skin.

Something moved beyond the nearest booth; at the same time, far behind him, Dukas shouted, almost a scream: "Alan, behind you!"

He started to turn, and Bonner was wrenched away from him; he swung his head back, saw two Africans with their arms around Bonner; they had jerked him backward and were now dragging him up the long aisle, and Bonner shouted, "Donnie—Donnie—!" It seemed to Alan that Bonner was struggling, trying to break loose, and something struck Alan with tremendous force in the left side, bending him, breathless, and he turned into the wall, taking another kick on his forearms and forcing himself erect again; and there was a thin black man coming up over the sill of the doorway at him and another just rounding the corner of the booth on his right.

Fight on instinct, Gunny Miner had said in their training sessions. *Don't think about it. Go for the kill.* He met the thin one as he filled the doorway, chopping across his throat and grabbing his hair to slam him into the corner of the booth, then kick him and shove him backward against the second man. Blood spurted; he saw that, a gush down the black face; he went right over it and took the second man in the face, grabbing it as if it were a mask he meant to pull off, and then forcing his fingers in, pushing until the back of the head came up against something hard and the man screamed. Alan sprinted up the long aisle, where Bonner was being hurried out. Bonner had turned the other way now, no longer being dragged but letting himself be led between them. They were his people, Alan saw, or his control's people, the countersurveillance team Dukas had feared; they were doing their job, protecting their agent.

"Bonner!" he bellowed. People were frozen all along the aisle, and even in the side aisles that led off from it, but at the sound of Alan's voice they moved, instinct and the habit of civil war causing them to duck and scramble for cover. Bonner turned his head. Their eyes met, a moment—hurt, hatred, confusion—and Bonner was pulled aside, and he disappeared.

Alan started to run and was hit from the right side. It was a body block, meant to knock him down, not as serious as it should have been, but the Sudanese made the mistake of underestimating him, and perhaps of thinking that he needed only to be knocked off stride to give up. Instead, Alan caught himself on the peeled sisal pole that held up one corner of a booth, swung on it and felt the booth teeter, sending a trayful of small oranges flowing over the floor like billiard balls. He changed the direction of his fall, swung around, and kicked his assailant. The man was quite young, also surprised; he had meant only to cover Bonner's escape, give the mere moment needed of delay, and then he was going to follow. Instead, his testicles seemed to come up into his gut; he bent forward and tried to claw his way out of the place, but a knee crushed his nose and he staggered backward, screaming, and took two wooden cages of chickens with him; one broke, and the birds jumped screeching into the air and flew toward the steel rafters and raced among the oranges. A woman cried out as if it had been she who was struck; she came running, swinging a knife, and Alan turned away from where he had last seen Bonner, back toward the doorway, the hill and the Land Cruiser.

The first man, the skinny one, was on his knees. He had a handgun.

Alan swayed to his own right. The gun roared, rose,

roared again. Birds sprang from their perches in the rafters overhead in a great, shrill babble of cries, and men and women screamed all over the market. The chickens cackled and a rooster crowed. Alan saw the gun come down to aim again; the man shook his head as if to clear it. Blood was streaming from his nose and mouth, and he blinked his eyes as if he was having a hard time seeing. He was about to fire again when the other Sudanese, the one whose face Alan had tried to pull off, grabbed the gunman's hand and twisted. He shouted something in a language Alan didn't know, but clearly it was an order, a negative. At least one of them had the sense not to shoot in there, he thought. Nonetheless, the gun went off again, the shot going up and into the roof. Alan heard a woman start to shout something over and over, incantation or prayer, the voice terrified: hell had come back—war, Amin, guns.

The two wrestled for the gun. Alan vaulted past them. They wanted to get out now, too, he thought; they were supposed to cover Bonner, and that task was over. One of them had meant to kill him as revenge, a personal return for pain; his colleague had ended that. Alan was merely a detail now.

He came through the doorway and into white sunlight, dazzled. Slitting his eyes, he could see movement up at the top. Four figures seemed to be dancing in a circle up there. Dust rose around their feet. The scene cleared a little as his eyes could accept more light, and he saw Dukas swing Donnie Marengo on the handcuffs and slam him into the side of the Land Cruiser. Two Africans were trying to get at the prisoner. Dukas kicked at one, dodged, blocked a blow with his free hand, and took a kick in his belly without going down. Marengo, bleeding, staggered away from the vehicle, pulling at the handcuffs, and Dukas dodged another blow and slammed the boy back against the steel side panel.

Alan started to run. Something in his side hurt like hell. *That first blow—a broken rib?* The hard, dry ground was rough. There were bottles and bits of plastic sack everywhere. His lungs rasped. He could see more now: one of the men had grabbed Dukas and the other was reaching around to the back of his own trousers, his hand under his loose shirt.

Alan snatched a quart beer bottle from the rubble. He came toward the man who had hold of Dukas's free arm and was riding it the way little children ride a leg. The other man held a knife. Alan switched hands so he could swing backhand with his left and swung the bottle all the way across his own body and hit the second man in the eyes and forehead. The man bellowed. Still holding the neck of the bottle and the jagged remains, Alan turned a little to his right and threatened the one who had hold of Dukas's arm. They did a little dance around Dukas, who pushed back against Donnie Marengo, pinning him against the vehicle. Then Dukas shouldered the countersurveillance agent away and swung him toward Alan, and the man let go and ducked the jagged glass and reached toward his midriff, and Alan kicked him.

Dukas, pulled forward by the struggle, tried to wrench himself back toward Marengo but groaned and went down, and he lay there, held half-sitting by the handcuffs, saying, "Sonofabitch! Oh, shit!"

Alan kicked the man again and turned back toward the first one, to find that he was gone, halfway down the hill now, holding his hands over his face, blood running down his forearms and dripping from his elbows. He was screaming.

Somewhere, a police siren was sounding.

Alan pulled Dukas to his feet. The movement made the NCIS man cry out. Alan paid no attention; he shoved Donnie Marengo into the Land Cruiser, bundled Dukas in after him. He pulled himself up into the front seat. *"Twende, twende!"* he shouted at Danio. *"Polisi!"*

"Eh-h-h-h-h-h!" the black man cried, and the sound, which had started as a cry of anxiety, ended as a groan. He gunned the old warhorse, and its engine roared and it leaped forward.

1427 ZULU. NORFOLK.

"*Africa!* What the hell will they do in *Africa?*" Reicher's voice was ragged. He was worried about his officer, and he was worried about the larger issues of the investigation.

Sally Baranowski sounded worried, too. "Alan got on a plane for Johannesburg, South Africa. So did an NCIS agent named Mike Dukas; he's the head of the NIGHT—"

"I know, I know."

"Alan and Mike are off on a wild hare after a guy they believe is a spy and they're nowhere! You can't go running around the world chasing people! FBI does that! We do that! Navy lieutenants don't do that!"

"I think this one does. Why Africa?"

"Oh, shit. Well, your NIGHT WATCH might be trying to make it to Tehran. He can connect in Johannesburg, maybe; he might have an escape route through one of the other waypoints—Entebbe, Kigali, Kinshasa. And then there's Sudan, of course."

"Sudan."

"Southern Sudan is practically a free-fire zone, Christian militias, animist tribesmen with a grudge against the government, the Southern Liberation Army of Sudan— Anyway, it's a mess. But we think Efremov will lift the Bonners out of Johannesburg. Anyway, we're putting our people on every airport where we have a presence."

Reicher frowned. "We're behind the curve. Way behind the curve." His inner self told him that the Agency was betting on Jo'burg because it was the only spot where Alan's and Dukas's aircraft hadn't yet landed.

1505 ZULU. KAMPALA.

Dukas lay on the hotel bed, one leg propped up and a wad of steaming towels under it. Donnie Marengo sat next to him, still connected by the handcuffs. He had Band-Aids on his face.

"It's a muscle spasm," Alan said.

"It's a goddam muscle tear! You ever have one? Jesus, it hurts like hell!" Dukas propped himself on his elbows. "I can't walk, man!"

"You tried to lever that guy off you with one leg, and the muscle tore. I'm sorry, Mike."

"You should be. Jesus." He stared up at Marengo. "No thanks to you, you little shit. I should have killed you."

"I didn't try to get away! They pulled me. It was them."

"Once more you moved away from me, I was going to break your neck. I know how." He lay back and looked at Alan. "Okay, I'll live. That's settled. When do we leave?"

"Danio's getting the car ready. Maybe half an hour."

"What's to get ready? Alan—" He pushed himself up again. "You're not— You're not! You're not going after that sonofabitch again!"

"Yes, I am."

"He's gone! Let him go!" He sat all the way up, groaning when his leg had to be moved. "Goddammit, this is my operation, and I say it's over! I'm taking my suspect home. I'm gonna get on the plane and tomorrow I'll be in D.C. and it's fucking over!"

"There is no plane today. There's one tomorrow afternoon. Change in Amsterdam, eight-hour layover; you'll be in D.C. two days after tomorrow. By then, I'll have Bonner."

"Alan, you can't!"

"Danio's laying in some food, extra gas and water. He agrees they were Sudanese. He and I are going north." He looked at Donnie Marengo. "I'll need him."

"He's my prisoner!" Dukas's voice became threatening. "Alan-n-n-n! Suppose they got a safe house? They'll park him somewhere."

"Maybe. I'll find out."

"This is a huge fucking country. They could go anywhere!"

"There's one road north. There are three border crossovers, but two of them lead into antigovernment areas. There's one Sudanese government army post, about eighty miles from the border. If they're going by way of Sudan, that's where they'll go."

"Al— Jesus, buddy, look, I know how you feel. We've come all this way. I know, I know. But—it's over. Look, there's the embassy. Call them. They've got the resources. Al—"

"No!" Alan's voice was a bellow. "End of discussion."

Dukas sank back on the bed.

Alan took Dukas's wallet from his pocket and took out the American bills and counted them, extracted some, put the rest back.

"I'm going out to buy a gun," he said. " 'Help the local economy,' as you put it in Athens." He started for the door.

"I may not be here when you get back," Dukas said.

Alan hesitated. "Okay. Leave our prisoner, though. Handcuff him to something and put the key on the floor by the door." He waited, thought it through, said more quietly, "Thanks for everything, Mike. You were great."

"You saved my life, you stupid shithead. You think I'm not grateful?"

Alan was gone twenty-five minutes. When he returned, Dukas was still there on the bed, Donnie Marengo limp beside him. Alan took out the huge automatic pistol he had bought on the street and held it up. Dukas stared.

"That's a Mauser broomhandle!" He groaned. "You go out on the street in Africa and you find a Mauser broomhandle! Do you know what those fucking things are worth?"

1655 ZULU. TEHRAN.

From his poolside chair, Efremov heard the car stop at his security gate, start up again, come around the curving drive, stop at the private door. He knew how long it would take the servant to open the door, how long the visitor would take speaking his business, how long it would be before the servant appeared—as he now did—and told him that Mr. Omani wished to see him.

Efremov nodded.

Omani came forward with tiny steps, like a man whose feet had been injured. He was a tense, neat little man, precise in everything, utterly without imagination. He stood before Efremov, whom he feared as he feared the imams, and sweated.

"There is a message from Uganda."

"Yes?"

"They preserved the safety of the father, but they missed the son."

Efremov chuckled, not with any mirth. "I knew they would." He stared at the slightly rippling water of the pool, the thin sliver of a Persian moon reflected in it. "Well, do they say what stupidity they mean to commit next?"

"They are taking the father to safety."

"Which is to say, Khartoum. Do you know where Khartoum is, Omani?"

"Oh, yes."

"Do you know what lies between Khartoum and the Ugandan border, Omani?"

"I—ah—Sir?"

"Nothing!" His mouth jerked. "And the problem is that *nothing* goes on for a thousand miles."

28

They had driven all night through the velvet blackness, the road only a gray-brown wash in the single headlight of the old Toyota. Stars were spread overhead in vast profusion, bright and hard and almost mocking, so different from the warm, soft, dangerous air through which the vehicle moved. After midnight, the car began to overheat. Danio would stop, wait, sit in the dark with the lights off, go on. As the dawn came with its astonishing suddenness, he tapped the temperature gauge and shook his head, and his mouth was bitter.

The road was sand now, "braided," as the locals said— long sections repeated in parallel rows where sand too deep to move in had been avoided by making a temporary path next to it, and then another, and then another. Danio wrestled with the wheel, threw the car into four-wheel-drive; once, in deep sand, the forward movement had torn the steering wheel from his hands and the Toyota had shot up on the verge and come to rest against a wind-toughened little tree. Danio had grinned and shrugged and backed out, shaking his left hand where the wheel had almost broken the thumb.

The sun came up red, then yellow. The sky was yellow, the land below yellow and gray and pale blurs of yellow-green where the wadis ran. They slitted their eyes, which felt now as if sand had blown into them, from the lack of sleep. They went on and on. When they came at last over a rise and looked ahead along another braid, Alan saw a clutter of metal buildings like gray igloos, a couple of trucks, five trees, and he knew they had reached the end of Uganda.

"The border," Danio said. He tapped the temperature gauge and, urging the car forward, groaned as the needle jumped higher, then higher than it had been all night, right up into the red. Alan watched it. The needle went almost to the top, then abruptly fell back into the normal range.

"Aaahhhh!" Danio cried.

"It's okay," Alan said. "It's way down."

Danio groaned. "No good, no good."

They limped up to the border post. Three men in fatigues and khaki T-shirts watched them without expression. Danio pulled the overheated Toyota under a tree and yanked the parking brake. He left the engine running and got out.

"What now?" Dukas said from the back.

"Doesn't look good." Alan got out and stretched. He watched Danio gesturing at the Land Cruiser. One of the men in camo smiled.

"I'll take the dog for a walk," Dukas said, pulling Marengo by the handcuff. He gasped when he put weight on his bad leg and then hobbled off.

Alan watched the little group. Several other men were moving toward them. The camp was chaotic, shapeless, a vehicle down for repair parked next to a generator, a mobile water tank off at an angle, a tarpaulin-covered work area littered with tools and a few weapons. Yet, purpose could be read in much of it, the sort of essential practicality you see around a farm. The group of men followed Danio back to the Land Cruiser and stood looking at it. One leaned through the front window, popped the hood, and they all put their heads under and began to mutter.

"Consultation?" Dukas said when he limped back.

"Mmm." Alan rubbed his unshaven jaw.

"What's the verdict?"

"They're not telling me. Danio looks as if he may burst into tears. The big guy in the boonie hat keeps laughing."

They watched for a while. Alan thought of the minutes ticking away, the car with Bonner and the Sudanese moving along a road like this one. Danio had thought that he and Alan and Dukas might even be ahead, for he had made good time and kept to the road, and he believed that the Sudanese had had to go off into the bush to avoid the roadblocks. It was one thing to come into a military area with a vehicle filled with three white men with American military ID and orders and American dollars, another to come up here with a carload of Sudanese and one white man with nothing but an expired liberty card from Naples, Italy. Danio had talked and cajoled and bought their way through the checkpoints; Dukas's gold badge had been a big help. Would the Sudanese, having thrown their operation together in a few hours, be as well provided?

Now this.

Dukas watched the gathering around the car. "You ever tell your boss where you are?" he said out of nowhere.

"I called from Entebbe." He looked at Dukas, grinned. "At 0300 their time. I didn't want to tempt fate, Mike."

"It might help if somebody knew where we are now."

"Actually, I thought we'd find a radiophone up here." He jerked his head. "They've got an antenna." He wasn't enthusiastic about talking to Reicher.

Danio turned away from the group and came slowly toward Alan. He looked like a man delegated to convey the worst of news. He stood in front of Alan and said, in the tones used by heads of state at funerals, "We think we blow head gasket." He thrust his hands deep into his pockets and dropped his head. He was ashamed because he had failed them.

They all looked under the hood again; somebody turned off the engine, and they talked back and forth in Swahili and at least one language Alan didn't understand, and then the big one in the boonie hat shoved everybody else away, dropped his hat over the radiator cap, and opened it. The entire contents of the cooling system went skyward in one gush. Everybody laughed a lot.

The big man clapped Danio on the shoulder and gave some orders. A tractor appeared and three or four men began to hitch the Toyota to it. The big man clapped Alan on the shoulder. "Okay," he said. "Okay, okay." He held up one finger. "One day. Tomorrow." He laughed.

Danio looked stricken. "They make new head gasket. Very good men. Do everything here."

But it would be too late.

Dukas handcuffed Marengo to the water tank, and they walked to the road past the border post and saw that tire tracks of heavy vehicles went on north. If not the Ugandan military, then somebody else with clout was supplying the Sudanese rebels by way of this road.

"The Sudanese team won't come through here with Bonner," Alan said. "They'll cross over in the bush someplace. These guys"—he jerked his head toward the camp—"are supporting the rebels."

He looked north into Sudan. It looked no different—sand, small rocks, thornbush, the odd acacia giving a scanty shade here and there.

"It's the end of the line, isn't it?" he said.

"You know it."

"You're glad."

"No. I want to catch him. I wanted you to get closure on the thing. But you got no good sense. Yeah, I'm saying it's over. I'm going to get on their radiotelephone and call my office and say we're coming home. As soon as the car runs."

"I thought my luck would hold. I thought—I thought we're the good guys; we can't lose him. I thought—something would be here at the border. But there's just more of the same old same old. Christ, we came so close!"

"It's better we turn back. We got no country clearance. No authorization. No orders. CIA and State could fry us just for being up here. I'm a rules guy, Al—I get nervous when we break the rules this far."

Alan looked at the tire tracks. "Somebody goes up there," he said. Dukas groaned.

Danio joined them, head hanging, and stood just close enough to be noticed, like a scolded child.

Alan looked into Sudan. "I may go in a ways," he said.

"You can't!"

"We've got all day."

"In this sun? There're probably lions out there. Snakes!" Dukas sighed. "Oh, Christ, what a hard-ass you are!" He pointed a stubby finger at Alan. "You haven't really given it up, you sonofabitch! You think you're going to walk in there and find Bonner!" He limped back toward the camp. It is hard for a man with a bad leg to stamp away.

Danio had stood patiently, seemingly waiting to receive a punishment. When Dukas had left, he touched Alan's arm.

"The soldiers here, they are good men. I told them you must go on—it is a revenge thing. It is written on you, plain to see. So they tell me, and I tell you. Just over the border, there is a madwoman, an old, mad white lady. They call her the Vulture. That is all they will say. Say that Sergeant Mwansa sent you." Danio attempted a half smile. "I do my best for you—I am so sorry—" His head hung again.

Alan patted his shoulder. "Does this madwoman have a car?"

Danio pointed at a tire track—deep, crisp. A new tire.

Alan looked back at the camp. The big man in the boonie hat was watching him. Now, he jerked his head toward the border. *Go.* Meaning, *Try it, you'll like it.*

Alan followed the wide wheel tracks into Sudan. A dry wind blew. There had been no long rains that year, and everything looked dusty and unwatered. He felt the heavy Mauser, tucked into his belt in the middle of his back. And yes,

Dukas was right. He believed he would still find Bonner. Or a madwoman. Or something. He believed that he could will it to happen, because he wanted it so much.

After a mile, he swept the yellow horizon, and on a low ridge ahead and to his left he saw an anomalous silhouette. "What the hell is that?" he said to himself. Daring to hope. He walked on. After several minutes, he could see the shape more clearly. An umbrella? Soon he could make out a smaller, clearly man-made shape near it. Another umbrella?

No, a dish—a satellite dish.

He followed the road in a long, braiding curve around the ridge with the umbrella on it. The sand was deep but cool in the morning. Utter silence reigned.

He came around the end of the ridge and trudged along its northern face. Thorny scrub masked it from him, and then the scrub opened and he saw wheel tracks heading toward the ridge, and he left the deep sand of the road and started up the wheel tracks, and he saw that there was a camp ahead of him, with a green wall tent and a green awning jutting way forward from it, and a new Land Rover parked under an acacia.

He walked through the camp. A slim Sudanese watched him, leaning against the Land Rover. Going by the green awning, Alan looked in and found himself thinking with a kind of wonder, *My God, look at all the swell spy stuff!* His unit would have given part of the year's funding for some of it: he recognized a long-distance eavesdropping microphone on a boom, night-vision goggles, three spotting scopes, some big electronic box that he bet was a frequency scanner, a Global Positioning System unit that could be car-mounted and would have done for a tank squadron in Desert Storm. Two videocams. A big video monitor. A laptop with a solar power unit. His immediate conclusion was that it was Sudanese rebel headquarters, and then he realized that of course it couldn't be—the Sudanese rebels couldn't afford stuff like that. More, perhaps, like a mobile television studio.

And now he could see that the umbrella was white and

the satellite dish was gray, and that under the umbrella there was a lounge chair with a woman in it. The woman that Danio had called the Vulture.

She was wearing the pale olive safari clothes that are sold all over that part of Africa; a wide-brimmed hat of the same fabric was slung over the back of her chair. The clothes suggested a costume. He saw that she was talking on a telephone. *A woman who travels with her own satellite phone.* He remembered such people from Kuwait. *Journalist.* He walked toward her, his feet crunching over the little rocks. She was watching him from behind her sunglasses. When he got close enough, he saw that her blond hair was a wig. He thought she looked familiar. He saw that the hand holding the telephone was old, spotted with brown and wrinkled like wet tissue paper. Closer still, and he saw the lines down each side of her mouth.

Memory jabbed. Where had he seen her? *Long ago.*

She turned off the phone and looked at him.

She took off the sunglasses.

She was old now. Under the wig, she was bald. Chemotherapy had done that, not age. He had thought she was dead.

"Adrienne Corvelle. You're Adrienne Corvelle," he said.

She smiled, rather horribly. "A long way for an old fan to come to see me," she said. The voice brought it all back— the slight French accent: *"This is Adrienne Corvelle in Saigon."* Or Katanga. Or the Falklands. The *femme terrible* of the Vietnam War, everywhere on the world's TV screens, outrageous and offensive and daring. Thrown out by the U.S. military and brought back in by the Vietnamese.

She laughed now and lit a cigarette.

She had had lung cancer, he remembered.

"You thought I was dead, like everybody else," she said.

"What are you doing *here?*"

"Waiting for a story." She blew out smoke. "One more story." She sniffed, coughed. "I have an instinct. All my life."

The War Witch, they had called her. Where she went,

wars sprang up, was the gossip; in fact, she had simply managed to be there first, just as they were starting. Beginning in the fifties, she had chronicled the wars that ended the great colonial empires—Southeast Asia, Africa, Indonesia. Soldiers hated her and loved her; you saw her and thought death was coming, and you could say things to her you couldn't say to anybody else, and she had an understanding nobody else had. She had a knack for making people talk, the reason she had been one of the few to interview Pol Pot, the one to get the best interview from Idi Amin.

As if she had guessed his mind, she said, "It's different from the old days. They don't know how anymore. So *timid,* all of them—taking the official handouts like good little children!" She laughed harshly, coughed. "One more—one more, I want to do one more—"

Little of the old, wild handsomeness remained. She looked now like somebody's mother in a nursing home—hence the clothes, he thought, the costume, the denial of the dying body.

"Your satellite phone works?" he said.

"*Bien sûr.* Want to use it? Be my guest."

"How about your car?" He was thinking of all that great stuff, not least the GPU.

"Of course the car works! You think I'm a fool? When they left by the roof from the American embassy in Saigon, where was I? *I* was the one who shot the film of them going! I was the one who reported it live! And I took my own chopper out, my darling. And you think I'd be here without a car that *ran?*" She lit a new cigarette. "I'm ready. I'm ready."

Alan looked down at the Sudanese who leaned against her Land Rover. Her driver. He thought he understood why the people at the border had sent him here. "How come they let you inside Sudan?" he said.

"I contribute to the cause." She laughed, not very pleasantly. "The Sudanese Revolutionary Forces of the South control this part of Sudan."

He looked again at the man by the Land Rover, who

looked young, tough, arrogant. He made a guess. "What rank does he have in the Revolutionary Forces of the South?"

"Very good!" she said. "I am impressed. I think Sele is a lieutenant, and I think he is in communications. The fact is, he wants my equipment and is waiting for me to die. Which is absurd, because he could kill me and nobody would know or care. But—" She gave him her skull-like grin. "I have an aura. Perhaps it frightens him." She blew smoke. "Who are you?"

"I'm the story you've been waiting for," he said. He didn't really want to go after Bonner in a car driven by a rebel officer and belonging to a journalist, but he'd reached the point where he'd take what he could get.

Dukas wouldn't like it one bit.

DECEMBER 15, 1993. 0413 ZULU. NORFOLK.

The telephone rang only once on Reicher's bedside table before he had a hand on it and had ended the ring. His wife stirred but hardly woke, and he said, "It's okay, hon, it's for me," and turned to face the telephone, propped on an elbow.

"Reicher."

"Sir, Duty Officer here. Monson. I got a call from Alan Craik."

"Shoot."

"Call was made in clear at 0406 Zulu and went secure at 0408 Zulu. LT Craik was about to enter the country of Sudan. He has one of the two suspects in custody and NIGHT WATCH head Michael Dukas has made the arrest." Clearly, LTj.g. Monson was reading from dictated text. Reicher smiled: Alan was being careful. "They are proceeding by car to intercept the principal NIGHT WATCH suspect at a point inside Sudan. If the suspect goes beyond 11° 45" north, he will suspend pursuit. This territory is disputed at the present time but is considered mostly—um, can't read my own writing, sorry—oh—mostly *dominated* by Christian and An-i-mist—Animist forces. He will keep you informed by this channel. End of message."

Reicher cleared his throat. "How did he sound, Mons?"

"Hot to trot, sir. You know Craik."

Reicher made a face. Sudan. No country clearance, hostile territory. They better have a plan to bring him out.

He got on the telephone to his admiral, then to Sally Baranowski.

0515 ZULU. RED SEA.

The CO of the chopper squadron had moments of regretting his leap at this command from the fairly cushy confines of an admiral's staff. Great career move, exciting work, important to his fellow sailors and Marines—but. There's just too goddam much of it, he thought. Somalia was the quagmire that congressmen talked about every time the U.S. got involved in something. Well, this one really quags, he thought. This is a quag to get mired about. It already reminded him of Vietnam, so many years ago. His people were flying day and night into Mogadishu, down the coast, into Kismayu, ferrying Marines and rangers, doing gunship duty when close air support was really somebody else's function. And now this.

He read the message again:

"You are directed to generate an operational standby plan ASAP for search and rescue as required of as many as four personnel now on the ground in the nation of Sudan, approximate location south of 11° 45", east of Nile river. This is to be treated as hostile territory. Access COMARX for air-defense capability. Consider all aspects of this operation to be Top Secret and covert. Await definite go-ahead from this source and DO NOT PROCEED WITHOUT AUTHORIZATION. Precise location and time to follow as known. Max 72-hour life; cancel automatically thereafter. Code Name PLAYOFF."

He rubbed the stubble on his short-cropped head and called for a rating. Rescuing spooks with insufficient support. Now it really felt like Nam. "Take this to Lieutenant Commander Siciliano, see she gets it personally and log the time of receipt." He glanced over the map as the man left—Sudan was the other side of Ethiopia; have to overfly, probably at night; need fuel—well, Rose was as good an ops officer as there was; she'd deal with it. He turned to the problem of General Aideed's latest hidey-hole.

Rose studied the priority message and said to herself, because she was tired, *Goddam Agency goons,* although on a better day she would have admitted that they were on the same side. She walked the message down to intel and handed it to her squadron AI, a just-made LTj.g. named Patti Delahanty, who was still wearing lipstick and perfume although they'd been on station for three months.

"Get ready to brief this," Rose said. "Two crews, plus we'll need a ground force, and I'll coordinate with the Marines on that. It's beyond our fuel range, so somebody's gotta provide; go up to the carrier intel officer and get some help and report to me ASAP." Rose thought that the other woman's eyes looked uninterested. Fatigue made her temper flare. "But wipe that goddam lipstick off your mouth and wash that stink off your body so you smell like the rest of us and *get serious!*"

Well, she told herself later, at least nobody else had been there to hear her say it.

1220 ZULU. LANGLEY.

Sally Baranowski steeled herself and walked into George Shreed's office, and she tried to smile at him as she sat down. She had been there since three that morning.

Shreed was reading a newspaper. The *Post.* A slow day, he must be thinking.

"Something's come up," she said. He looked at her past the edge of the newspaper. "I've been here half the night. Alan Craik's in Sudan."

He lowered the newspaper. "Give it to me."

She sketched in the arrangements made with Naval intel: a joint operation, put together in an hour with spit and rubber bands—Navy as Comm channel and rescue standby,

Sally as ops control, NCIS for information and legal support.

"Where do we come in?" Shreed said. She knew this mood—outwardly calm, deep-down dangerous.

"We're going to try to coordinate a rescue if it's needed. I'm Quarterback—lead ops. I want you to authorize a request for Special Forces and Air Force support, George."

"What's in it for us?"

"It's what we do."

He laughed.

"It's what *I* do." She shook her head. "I'm tired, George. I'm too tired to be nice. We do it because it's our job, no glory, no payback—Craik comes out with his prisoner, he and Navy get all the medals."

"We're getting crucified in the goddam newspapers! We need something splashy! Tell them it's our operation or we don't play."

"George, we're past that. I'm past it. Look—I can leave here and make better money on the outside and have a life, as well. Be a mother. A wife. I don't need this, George. Do it my way—please—or I'm through." She shrugged. She hated it that her voice had broken on the last word.

He tapped the newspaper. It rattled under his fingers. He didn't look at her, but his face was heavy, brooding, unhappy. "Okay. Call Jack Dinhausen at the Pentagon, lay on an A Team unit and two Blackhawks plus transport. Navy can't handle this—what've they got out there, ship's Marines? Christ. This kind of operation is for specialists. Get current satellite photo feed direct. You know the drill. Okay, go to it." He picked up the paper. She stood up.

"You're angry," she said.

"No shit."

"I decided to do the right thing, George. If you want me to go, I will."

"Get out."

1240 ZULU. SUDAN.

"Eight hours to come a hundred miles," Alan said. He turned his back on the hot wind. "This is the end of the line, Mike."

"I seem to have heard that one before. Where the hell are we?" Dukas said.

They had left the border post that morning and come north, then turned off the so-called road and crawled across hard-packed rocks and sand, dodging trees, going generally west, then northwest, stopping twice at clusters of huts that were on no map but were nonetheless tiny villages in their own right. The Sudanese named Sele, the driver who was also a soldier, had got out at each one and disappeared, then come back and started the Land Rover and headed off again. Now they were here—wherever here was.

"GPU is still acquiring the satellite," Alan said. "Anyway, where we are is where you see."

Behind them, the remains of a long building seemed to give the place a location, an existence. One story high, the walls only waist height, with poles above them to support the roof, it was now returning to the bush—mud walls, once painted dark red, now rust-colored and cracked, thatch falling in. Adrienne Corvelle came out of the low building and smiled at them. She was worked up by the prospect of action; her eyes looked hot, and Alan wondered if she had taken something.

"This was a school," she said. "Typical interfering missionary stuff. Making Africa safe for consumerism." She laughed.

"Sele took the car," Alan said.

"I told him to. He says your man is coming this way."

He had said that to Alan, too. Twice, as they had wound through endless bush, Sele had nodded southwest and said, *They come that way.* "How does he know?"

"He knows, my dear. They always know. When I was with Castro in the Cordillera, I was amazed at what he knew of what went on in Havana. One day, we were crossing a—"

Mike rolled his eyes. Alan stopped listening. Adrienne Corvelle, who had been a superstar, was a bore. Still a problem, because he had involved her in what was now a covert operation, and perhaps even a threat, but a bore all the same.

Alan looked at the only map he had been able to find, a map of Uganda that included southern Sudan by accident. He thought he knew more or less where they were. But to know that was to know very little. The Nile was over there to the west, of course, but too far away to be visible; towns like Rejaf and Juba were over there somewhere, outposts of the Sudanese Army—"the Arabs," as Sele called them because they were Muslims and he was animist. Far to the east were the northern tip of Lake Turkana and Ethiopia— harsh, rock desert.

"We're not going to walk out of here, that's for sure," he said.

"Thank God we got the Land Rover."

Sele would be back, Adrienne assured them. She started to tell them a story about being marooned in Katanga in sixty-three, and Alan turned to the GPU, and Mike expressed a great need to find a bush, so she went inside and told the story to Donnie Marengo, who was handcuffed to an old iron-legged table. When Dukas came back, Alan said, "Keep her away from that satellite phone."

"Look, buddy, I didn't invite her along."

"Any action, and she'll be reporting us live someplace if we don't keep an eye on her." He looked at his watch. "I ought to check in." He rubbed his beard. "I don't quite know what I'm going to tell them."

An hour later, Sele walked out of the bush. He climbed the mostly bare hill to the mission and squatted in the shade by Alan. "They come," he said.

"When?"

"Soon." He drew with a stick in the sand. "Here—we. There—*barabara*."

"Road."

"Yes." He pointed. A kind of track could be seen curving southwest, most of it made by the Land Rover.

Sele made two marks above the place he had designated as the mission—to the north, he meant. "Arabs."

"What Arabs?"

"Soldiers. Coming down from Rahulle."

"Coming here?"

Sele shrugged. He put the stick in the wavy line that was the road. "Cars coming there. Your man—one *mzungu,* five Arabs." He swept an arm out, ending in a long, straight finger, and where it pointed Alan could see a feather of dust. "Coming here. Meet other Arab soldiers. This place."

So that was where they were—the place where people met in the middle of nowhere.

"Who will get here first?"

Sele stabbed the stick into the road. The cars with Bonner, he meant.

"Okay, we have to make an ambush. You understand, ambush? I have a gun— What?"

Sele pointed down the hill. He made a motion with his entire left hand, long fingers together, as if he were cupping water and bringing it toward him.

Nine men came out of the bush. They were tall, very thin, dressed in ragged shorts and shirts, and not all of them had shoes. However, they all carried AK-47s. Sele pointed at the tallest of them, a man close to seven feet, very black, long-headed.

"Alwa. Others, his *lifida.* Nuer people. My brothers."

The plume of dust came closer.

1329 ZULU. RED SEA.

Rose took a seat at the front of the briefing room and looked over her shoulder at the others. She was there only to listen; this covert op, if it ever went, would need the squadron's senior pilot for overall command. Two flight crews, the Marine officer, his sergeants. Awfully short notice, she thought, but that's the way they were living these days. Anyway, this one was only a contingency; almost certainly, it wouldn't go down.

Patti Delahanty took her place at the makeshift podium. Her lipstick was gone; her hair was pulled back; she looked businesslike. *Good*, Rose thought. Rose had had some sleep. Things looked better.

Then a male voice behind her said, "Hey, Patti, where's the kissy mouth?" Haw, haw, haw.

Rose turned around. LTj.g. Eddie Conner was delighted with himself. When he saw that Rose was looking at him, he mugged—pretended shame, guilt, fear. Conner would be copilot in the lead chopper if this mission actually happened.

"Lieutenant Conner, could I see you for a moment?" she said.

The room became very quiet.

She went out into the passage and held the door for him. When they were out there, she faced him, coming close and keeping her voice low and waiting until another aviator had passed before she spoke. Then she said softly, "You loud-mouthed scumbag, if I *ever* hear you wise off in a briefing again, I will have your ass! Is that clear?"

"Rose, holy shit, I—!"

"Don't you Rose me! One more word and you're off this mission. And if I bounce you from this mission, your aviation career is dead!"

Then she walked back in, again holding the door for him, and she sat down and waited for him to sit down, and she said in a steady voice, "You can start now, Lieutenant Delahanty."

1347 ZULU. SUDAN.

Alan lay on his belly in the wadi, willing the two cars to keep moving. He made himself as small as he could. Adrienne Corvelle lay only a couple of feet behind him, eyes shining, a minicam on her skinny shoulder.

The tall man, Alwa, was so close beside him they almost touched. He wore an ancient khaki bush jacket and cutoff U.S.-issue BDU trousers, and he carried a gleaming AK-47 with a shortened barrel. He seemed unworried by the slow approach of the quarry.

"Why are they going so slow?" Alan asked.

Alwa looked at Alan as if he were a friendly child. "They know this is my country. They fear me. Also, they saloon cars—no good in bush." He smiled. He smiled especially at Adrienne Corvelle. He was enchanted by the idea of being on TV.

Alan kept his head low, half rolled on his side. "All I want is the white man."

Alwa nodded. He watched the two sedans start up out of the depression. They were pale brown with dust, even the headlights and the windshields. One was down on a broken spring in the rear. Both drivers could be seen bent forward, rigid with tension. Alwa appeared unconcerned by their proximity. Instead, he was examining Alan's big Mauser pistol.

"Good gun?" he asked with professional interest.

Adrienne Corvelle leaned over Alan to look at it. "It's a Mauser, darling. They were all over Vietnam. The Chinese made them. When I was up the Ho Chi Minh trail—"

"Old gun," Alan said. He didn't want to talk about guns. He was tense, aware of the nearness of Bonner. The woman journalist bothered him, and he told her to lie down.

Alwa laughed. He took the pistol and held it up. "*Star Wars*," he said. He examined the clip and then handed Alan some nine-millimeter cartridges from his pouch. "Old guns, good guns. New AKs Arabs have not worth taking off the bodies."

The cars were close now. Alan could hear the straining engines, smell the exhaust. *Not like flying*, he thought. *You get close this way. Too close.*

"Once in Cambodia, I was close enough to an armored car to—"

Alwa stood just as the first car began to pass him and shot the driver through the open window at a range of two feet. One of his comrades shot the man on the other seat. The car rolled into a thornbush, all in slow motion, stopped, and the doors burst open and men tumbled out with their hands on their heads. Alan was barely on his feet when he saw Adrienne in the middle of the dirt track, a minicam in place of a head, slowly panning even as the guns roared. Black hands with pistols appeared in the windows of the second car, and the gears ground as the driver tried to reverse; a burst of automatic fire sounded, and the doors opened and men came out bent double, bleeding, and then the driver was kneeling in the road with a rifle at his head.

Alan sprinted to the rear of the first car. Doors open, empty. He ran to the second.

There he was.

One middle-aged white man on the floor of the sedan, his arms over his head. He was unarmed. Alan was barely aware that Corvelle was right behind him, shooting over his shoulder.

Bonner.

Alwa stepped up. "You want him?"

"Yes," Alan said. "Oh, yes."

Alwa looked at him. "He has done you a wrong?"

"He killed my father."

"This is a good day for you, then," Alwa said and slapped Alan's shoulder. He grinned into the minicam. He jerked his head for her to follow him.

Alwa walked to the front of the truck and quite casually shot the man in the road. Before Alan could think to protest, two of the Sudanese who had been at the Kampala Market were also shot, one bullet each in the head. Alan saw a third knifed in the eye and looked back to see Bonner, shaking, looking up at him. The speed of the killings took Alan beyond terror; it was almost fantasy, but the stench of open bowels and the copper smell of blood was very real. The killers and the victims seemed almost impassive. Blood was everywhere; on the cars, in the sand. One of the Nuers, the youngest, made a mark with a finger dipped in blood on the buttstock of his weapon. Corvelle zoomed in to get it.

Alan ignored her. He was looking down at Bonner, Bonner looking up at him. Alan thought that he felt nothing, realized that could not be true; the numbness he felt was from the blood and the killings, not any response to Bonner. Still, he felt no triumph. Not even any sense of its being over. He did it by the book. He held up his Navy ID, there in the dryness of the southern Sudan, and said, "Craik, Lieutenant, United States Navy. PO1 Sheldon Bonner, I arrest you for espionage. Get out."

Bonner climbed out backward, like an animal on all fours. The Nuers laughed.

Alwa came back. "We go back to the mission now."

Alan nodded and motioned at Bonner with the pistol. Bonner swallowed. "I need to go someplace. I messed my pants. I thought they were gonna kill me."

Alan understood why the Nuers had been laughing. "Let's go."

Bonner was looking at the woman with the minicam, and he passed his hand over his hair and turned so the video wouldn't show the stain.

The Nuers began to wire grenades to the engine blocks of the cars.

The colors were changing to rusts and reds as they reached the old building, signaling the coming of dusk. Alwa and his men were cheerful and seemed to be joking. They leaned their AKs against the cracked walls and broke out bits of food. A water bottle was passed around. Corvelle videoed it, kneeling, standing on the waist-high wall, moving in close. Alan made sure that Bonner was handcuffed at one end of the old school and read his rights by Dukas. They put Donnie Marengo at the other end after the father and son had been allowed to embrace and say a few words to each other. With the only handcuffs now on Bonner, Donnie had to be tied.

Alan kept an eye on the satellite phone and Adrienne Corvelle. She was burning to report the ambush, he knew. She would have been in heaven if she could have done it live.

The Vulture.

Maybe she hadn't always been like that. Maybe the cancer had stripped away all the politics and ideas, as it had stripped her flesh and her hair. But the glitter in her eyes was terrible.

Alwa was watching the north with a pair of minibinoculars.

"See them?" Alan said.

Alwa shook his head.

"Soon?"

"Maybe." He put the binoculars in his pocket. "Arabs no good here at night. Fearful. Nuer people kill them with knives at night."

"We should leave. I have my prisoner."

"No good."

"Where's the Land Rover?"

The Vulture smiled. "No Land Rover."

They had been in a Land Rover for eight hours—now it didn't exist?

"We have to get out of here. The Land Rover is our transport."

She thought it was a wonderful joke. She laughed and coughed. "It's gone!" she cried when she could talk again. "Gone *where?*"

"Darling, Sele's taken it away somewhere. Are you stupid? It was his price for bringing us here. Now he's gone."

"I have to get our prisoners back to Uganda!"

She shrugged. She really was mad. "Walk," she said. She wandered down toward the Nuers.

At that point, the grenades on the two shot-up cars blew, and the Nuers cheered and clapped.

He went after her. "Where the hell is Sele?" he shouted. She pointed out into the bush. Far away, dust rose. A car would kick up dust like that. "Why?" he said. He didn't believe in Sele's cupidity. She laughed at him.

He appealed to Alwa. "Sele making a battle," Alwa said. "Arab soldiers come out of barracks to catch you—good, we kill them! Sele going to get more of us."

Alan tried to explain about his responsibility. About Bonner. Alwa was not moved; he said, "You got him. Kill him."

"No! Alwa, we have to go back to Uganda! We can start now; we can walk. I'll pay your people to carry my friend—"

Alwa shook his long, narrow head. He made a gesture with his hand, aristocratic and final. "We stay. To fight. You stay. You fight."

It was getting dark. They couldn't make it alone, he knew. Maybe, if Dukas could walk. "When will Sele be back?" he said.

"Maybe sundown tomorrow. Maybe the morning after." Alwa clapped him on the shoulder and walked away.

Alan looked down the long building at Dukas, who was sitting next to Bonner, resting his bad leg. He looked the other way and saw Donnie Marengo. Outside, a few feet away, Alwa and Adrienne Corvelle were sharing cigarettes, laughing. When you came down to it, there were only Dukas and him, and two prisoners, and the others. And the others didn't care about American law.

He moved toward the satellite phone. He thought she might stop him, but she didn't. When she saw what he was about, she came over, and he thought he might have to show the gun, risk it. But she helped him find the satellite and make the connection.

She *wanted* him to call home. More drama. She wanted a rescue. Action.

He put the call through the STU and got the duty officer and they were efficient and brisk, and he began to read off the coordinates from the GPU, to the hundredth of a second, which was close enough to kill somebody with a handgun. He said they had their man and they were ready to come out. "But we seem to have lost our transport."

"How hot is your situation?"

"Medium cool." He looked over the waist-high wall to the north and saw a gleam like polished copper—the dying sun reflecting off a vehicle window? "Heating up. I think it will be hot in the morning."

Silence at the other end. Then, the voice tighter, "There's a plan to get you out. Twenty-two hours minimum."

"In twenty-two hours we could be about ten hours dead."

"Can you move your location?"

"Negative. I've got a man with a bad leg. I've got two prisoners."

"Hold on." Silence. Alan thought of the satellite-phone signal, of Sudanese surveillance. He glanced where he had seen the reflection, saw nothing now; the sun was down. Maybe it had been an illusion. But he knew, of course, that it wasn't.

"Lieutenant?"

"Yo."

"We have a contingency plan. A much higher risk factor. It will be no-go if the landing zone is hot."

"Understood."

"Well— We'll see what we can do. You're sure you can't hold out for twenty-two hours?"

"I'm not sure of anything. But if you asked me if I thought we'd be here in one piece in twenty-two hours, I'd have to say no."

"We'll try for a pre-sunrise touchdown. Stay in that building. Good luck, Lieutenant."

He felt a surge of rage. They were going to die. *Because of Bonner.*

Alan crossed the long mud floor and stood over Bonner. The man smelled. They all smelled, he thought—sweat, dirt. But Bonner stank.

"You know who I am?" he said.

Bonner's eyes were fixed on the wall. He didn't say anything.

Alan kicked him. "Do you know who I am?" he shouted. He kicked again, savagely, recklessly. Dukas said something, and Alan shouted "Stay out of it!" and he grabbed Bonner's hair and turned the face to him and said, "DO YOU KNOW WHO I AM?"

Bonner licked his lips. "You're his kid."

"Whose kid? Whose kid?"

"The one who died."

Alan squatted in front of him. He held Bonner's jaw in his left hand, the back of the man's head pressed against the wall. "He wasn't *the one who died*. He was *the one you killed!*"

Bonner's eyes were wide. He couldn't speak, because Alan's hand had pushed his lips far back, bared his teeth. Abruptly, Alan put the muzzle of the Mauser against Bonner's forehead. Behind him, Donnie Marengo shouted, "Dad!"

"Jesus, don't," Dukas said, "Alan, man—"

"Why?" Alan pushed the gun hard into the bone of the forehead. *"Why?"*

Tears of pain were running down Bonner's cheeks. Alan saw that the man couldn't speak, and he took his hand away. He took the gun barrel off his forehead. "Tell me. Tell me why, you sonofabitch!"

Bonner tried to say something, had to work his mouth because the skin had been stretched so hard. He said hoarsely, "The money."

Alan looked at Dukas. He looked at Donnie Marengo, then back at Bonner. "Money." He thought of his father's last gesture. His father's voice, his father's hand on his shoulder one day on the ship. "Money! You were on the same side; he never did anything to you; you can't—" He had started to say, *You can't kill a man just for money,* but he knew that Bonner had. It was like hearing an animal say why it had killed. For food.

Bonner looked right at him as if daring him to say something. "And you came all this way to hear that?" Bonner said. He tried to laugh.

"I came all this way to take you back."

"For what?" Bonner threw himself forward. "For what?" he screamed. "For fucking *justice?* Because you and your father are fucking officers and I'm not? Because you got away with it and I didn't? Because you can't stand it that I fucked your fucking Navy for ten years and got away with it?" He spat. He screamed again, "Yes, I did it for the money because that's all people like me get! You're all the same! It's all a crock of shit and we all live in it and you guys get away with it, that's the only difference between us! He died! Good! *Good!* You're such a hot— You think you're— You—" He began to weep.

He squatted again in front of Bonner. He looked into the red eyes. He stared and stared; Bonner looked away, back, away. Alan hoped he would see something. But there was nothing. *For the money.* It would have been better for him if it had been for love of communism, or religion, or even madness.

Instead, banality.

He stood up. "I'm taking you back," he said. "For justice." It wasn't good enough. It wasn't what he meant. Words—justice, honor, loyalty. Bonner had spat out a vicious image: a world of shit, in which they were all trapped. And what Alan had in response was words.

He looked at Bonner, who sneered back. He looked at Donnie Marengo. The boy was biting his lower lip. His face was vacant, eyes a little too wide. Alan realized that it was the first time Donnie had heard his father say what he had done.

Alan looked again at Bonner. "I lost my father. Now you've lost your son."

Bonner leaned as far as the shackle would let him. "Donnie—!"

But the boy wouldn't look at him.

"I did it for you!" Bonner cried. But his son turned away, and Bonner's face went slack, bereft, and he fell back against the mud wall.

"Don't tell yourself that shit happens, Bonner. *You happen. You* did it. To *your* son. You live with it!" He took a step away. "And you better believe you're going to live, because I'm going to take you out of here if I have to carry you!"

1525 ZULU. LANGLEY.

Sally Baranowski braced herself and headed for Shreed's office. He had been curt on the telephone. He looked up when she came in the door; no friendliness showed.

"Well?"

"He's got his man. We have his coordinates."

"Where's our rescue?"

"Special Forces are on the runway in Georgia. Navy have their own operation ready as backup. George, we're going to have to go with the Navy. Special Forces can't be there for twenty hours. That's too late."

"I'm not going to hand this thing to the goddam Navy! They'll either blow it or they'll get lucky, and either way we'll look bad! Tell Special Forces it's a go."

"They can't be there in time! Satellite photography shows vehicles moving south toward his position on two routes. He's going to be overrun before they can get there!"

"He can evade. Hide in the bush. He's such a hotshot, let him—"

"I'm telling the Navy to go for it."

He stared at her. "Sally, you're letting me down. You're letting the Agency down."   •

She shook her head. "George, listen to yourself. Just listen to yourself, will you, please?"

But he didn't. Instead, he was thinking that at least the media were out of it and there'd be no publicity.

1547 ZULU. RED SEA.

The chopper squadron skipper walked the message over to Ops himself. He put it down in front of Rose. "We're go on the Sudan rescue. Urgent priority. Who's commanding?"

She didn't even have to look at the status board. "CDR Jakowitz."

The skipper shook his head. "Jack's down in Mogadishu for hydraulics. Who's the backup?"

She swallowed. She tried to smile. "I guess I am."

29

The flight-deck wind stung with particles of grit carried from somewhere over the horizon to the west. *Where the helos were going,* she thought. Where she was going. It had all happened very fast, so fast—barely twenty hours—that, thankfully, she had not had time to worry. *Grit is not friendly to helos,* she thought with part of her mind now, remembering the attempt to rescue the hostages from Iran back in the seventies. The thought was not fearful, hardly conscious. *We have to do better than that.* Consciously, she was checking out the aircraft and reviewing Delahanty's final brief and thanking her stars that Alan didn't know what she was about to do. *Wanting me to promise to live forever.*

The Marines stood quietly on the deck. They looked nervous but oddly pumped up, more a tough college sports team than a lethal killing machine. There were only sixteen of them, with a young captain and a much older Master Gunnery Sergeant. Rose nodded to the captain when her aircraft check was completed. The flight deck was almost silent: the combat air patrol was launched, and the night's mission package was still forty minutes from go.

Rose thought for a moment about being a woman. She was going to be the senior officer, and *she was a woman*, and everybody had to be thinking about that. If it went well, it would be an achievement, a credit to her and the Navy and to female commanders. If it failed, the failure would be thought the failure of women. The Marines had their own chain of command on the ground, but she was the strike lead and the mission commander, and she would give the no-go if she didn't like the look of the landing zone, the go if she decided they could make it. She would say when to go in and she would say when to come out. And if she said it was no-go, then it was on her head that those four guys on the ground in Sudan, whoever they were, got left there to die.

Rose had been in the Navy what seemed like a long time, but this was the biggest responsibility she had faced. Even a little mission like this usually rated an O5. Only the mess in Somalia could allow a female O4 and a twenty-six-year-old Marine captain to run the show. He looked all right, she thought; wound pretty tight, but so was she. They had been briefed to satiety: Delahanty, shorn of the habit of flirtation, had proved a first-rate AI, one who would get a lot of the credit if they succeeded. (And a lot of the blame if they failed? She thought about *failed*. Failed meant everything from a missed rescue to crashed helos, dead Marines. She sucked in her breath.)

They would be maintaining radio silence all the way in, but the CAG would be up there in a Tomcat, ready to help if help were needed. Sudanese air cover was something of a mystery. Quarterback reported an intercept that indicated Sudan knew the downed team's location, but so far no air scramble had been detected. One defector report said that the entire Sudanese air defense had spare parts for only one aircraft, so there might never be a scramble at all.

Rose would fly in a nearly new SH-60 and then set down in Ethiopia to rendezvous with a British special ops team that would have taken fuel in. Then she and her two choppers and her Marines could go two hours farther to perform the mission. Throughout that time, the Tomcats and the Hornets would be less than an hour away, their time.

The Marines were checking their weapons now. Looking at each other's webbing. All dressed up—and, this time, somewhere to go. Looking vaguely like athletes in some contact sport, in body armor and packs and helmets. The clink and rustle of military gear, surely a sound as old as the Roman legions.

Rose walked up to the gunny. He gave her a smile and barked for silence.

She tried to smile at them. Her jaws felt welded. "You guys look great. Good. Here's the deal, guys: We're going six hundred miles into Sudan under the radar. Every one of you will be airsick. Several times. At the end, we'll have a hot LZ and a firefight, and that's if it's a good day." She and Gunny and the captain had studied the satellite photos of the Sudanese advance on the landing zone, and Gunny had estimated their strength at a couple of companies. "We won't have comms with the guys on the ground till ten miles out, if at all. So please, when we get there, get ready to jump out and kick some ass, 'cause Navy doorgunners don't get a lot of practice and we'll need the help."

The Navy remark got a chuckle. Not much, but some relief of the tension. The hot wind blew over them; grit blew in their eyes.

Rose went on. "The guys on the ground, they're ours and they may have some local help. They won't look very uniformed, so look before you shoot. Sudanese military are uniformed, probably camo and boonie hats and no armor. Just remember, gentlemen, that the Americans out there are pretty much on their own and we are all the hope they have. One chance. When I say *Go*, I mean you're on the ground and running and hosing the area before I finish the word! Got me? Okay. Let's rock."

She wanted to sound more like Patton, but nobody looked disgusted. The captain snapped her a salute and she returned it in the Navy way and pulled her helmet on. *Thank God.* Alan didn't know what she was about to do.

She found herself praying.

DECEMBER 16, 1993. 0120 ZULU. ETHIOPIA.

Fear, boredom, adrenaline; in most bodies they don't mix often, but the SAS team was used to the combination. They sat in deserts pretty regularly, and this sure as hell was a desert. Number Four felt as if he were in the Empty Quarter. The shooter had nothing to track. Only heat.

Five men, well spread out, lie perfectly camouflaged in the arid darkness. They do not move. Careful examination would show two giant camouflage nets covering something, but the team does not encourage any kind of examination at all.

So now I've been to sodding Ethiopia, Four thought. *I always get to see the beauty spots.*

In the distance, a low hum gets louder fast. The shooter tracks two fast movers for a few seconds, then makes a clicking sound. Four knows that these are the birds and they are inbound. He looks at his watch. Nice. This guy is slowing slightly to land on the dot of his time.

The team has the hoses out before the rotor noise begins to die. The American Marines stretch and piss in the sand, and the team wonders why the hell these kids are getting to play in the Olympics while they pump petrol. Still, no biggy. The team have been in the petrol business before.

The birds are gone before the piss in the sand has a chance to evaporate. The team spreads out, leaving the fuel bladders and camouflage netting in the sand. Gone in an hour, with some wind and a little luck.

It's a long walk out.

DECEMBER 16, 1993. 0148 ZULU. SUDAN.

Alan had slept briefly and then lain awake. He was bone-weary, bruised from the fight in the Kampala market, even, he thought, a little in shock from the capture of Bonner. He needed sleep but could not sleep. Thoughts of Rose kept him awake, shot through with fear of the morning. No, not fear: anxiety. Wanting to get on with it, wanting to find how he would face death down here on the ground. And then he would swing back to Rose, to his son, to Rose, who would be asleep now, tired, too, dreaming perhaps of him. *Oh, babe.* He talked to her. *I'm sorry.* Because he would have dropped from her life without a warning or a goodbye. No letter, no phone call. *I'm sorry.*

The ruined school had had no windows, but only open space above the waist-high walls, then a rafter and the sloping roof. It was black inside, but when he turned his head he could see a star. Something stirred, a sound like wings—bird or bat? He listened. Far away, a rising, whooping call. Hyena.

He had been awake for hours. He felt over the dirt floor, wary of scorpions. His fingers found the little flashlight he had placed there, purchased in Athens when he was trying to put some sort of travel kit together. That seemed another life now. Naples and Bari and Athens—easy places, as it turned out, although they had seemed tense and difficult then.

He turned on the flashlight. Donnie Marengo was asleep a few feet away. Two of the Nuers were rolled up with their backs against each other by the wall; one opened his eyes into the light and closed them again.

Alan got up and walked the length of the little building, stepping over sleeping bodies. More Nuer fighters had come in during the night. The air was cold. The hyena whooped again, and far away there was something like a grunt, just possibly a lion or an elephant, probably something less impressive. He stepped over somebody's AK and shone the gloomy little beam on the end wall, where Bonner and Dukas were asleep. Bonner was still handcuffed to the wall. Dukas stirred and opened his eyes.

"It's Alan, Mike."

"Mm."

"Just checking."

"Fucking cold, man."

Dukas was back asleep within a second or two. Perhaps he had never really waked.

Alan stepped to the doorway. He cupped the light in his hand so that only slivers came out between his fingers. Somewhere out there were the Sudanese. Three or four miles. Not so far they mightn't send a patrol close enough to waste a man who carried a bright light, he thought.

He urinated. One of the Nuers was standing only a few feet away; Alan had not seen him and had a moment of near terror, then realized who he was. He was a picket, of course, the reason the Sudanese wouldn't come too close. Alan moved slowly away. Some of the other Nuers were sleeping on the ground, in their center a long mound like a caterpillar with a white head—the woman's sleeping bag and mosquito net. The Nuers had taken to her at once, were protective of her. If they had to choose between the woman and Alan, he thought, they would side with her.

It was cold. He was hungry. Most of the food that Danio had bought in Kampala was useless because they had never had a chance to cook, and here they did not dare have a fire. The woman had gourmet food in tins, but tiny portions, this and that—foie gras, caviar, pesto. She had no appetite and was dying as much from starvation as cancer. She would nibble a bite from one of the cans and hand the rest to somebody. It wasn't much of a diet for men who were going to fight. Now Sele had taken even that away.

Alan went back inside the derelict building and shone the light around again and ended with Bonner. Bonner opened his eyes and looked into the light. Alan looked at him a long time. What had it meant, to tell Bonner that he was taking him back for justice? Was it justice, to be fed well, treated well, alternately prodded and coddled until he told them all his secrets, and then make a deal for twenty years in prison? For they wouldn't kill him; they never did that anymore. He would be too valuable.

Yet Alan knew he had to take the man back. Kill him, yes, if there was no way out of here; yes, he would have to stay close to Bonner in the morning and kill him when it was clear they were not going to get away. That was blood justice. Or vengeance. As if he had to satisfy his father's ghost. But it was a second choice, a distant second choice, because the closest he could get to real justice was taking Bonner back for the Navy to deal with. To make an example of. Once, they would have court-martialed him and then hanged him from the yard of a ship's mast in the presence of as many ships' companies as they could squeeze aboard.

Now, they would trade his life and then years for information.

And as for Alan, they would give him no blood justice. They might very well give him a court-martial, in fact, for crossing a forbidden border, causing an international incident. That or a medal; it would depend on somebody—the President, the Secretary—who would make a judgment based on something far away from justice.

Bonner closed his eyes. Alan turned off the light and went to his place by the satellite phone.

Bonner believed that life was shit. Alan knew he was wrong. It was the only thing about the man that made Alan in the least sorry for him. Otherwise, pulling the trigger would be easy.

He thought of Rose. *Oh, babe—*

DECEMBER 18, 1993. 0200 ZULU. SUDAN–ETHIOPIA BORDER.

Rose knew that she was now flying the edge of fatigue; twice she became aware that she was flying without thinking at all, pushing the chopper over ridges at two hundred feet without any awareness. She was not yet close to falling asleep, but she was eye-weary and leg-weary. The landing in Ethiopia had helped a little; so had the coffee the Marines passed forward.

"Eddie?"

"Ma'am?"

"Ready to take it?"

Eddie Conner flipped his night-vision goggles down on his helmet and nodded, then carefully put both hands on the yoke and felt the control. He took a moment to be satisfied; he was a good pilot, although still afraid of Rose because of the dustup about Delahanty's lipstick.

"Got it."

Rose took her hands off the yoke. "You got it." She took her feet out of the pedals and stretched like a cat. Her right knee was killing her, just as it always did on a long trip. She switched her comm and called the back. She didn't have an enlisted aircrew this trip; they needed his seat for the guys they were rescuing.

Alan'll tell me I was a damned fool to take the risk, but he's going to be jealous if I pull this off, she thought. *Loving, supportive, jealous, angry. Loving.* She pushed the night-vision goggles off her face and rubbed her eyes. She didn't look out the windshield. At this altitude, she'd want to grab the yoke no matter what she saw. She glanced at her watch. Evening in Norfolk. He would be reading, maybe looking up at his swords, thinking of her. Michael asleep in his crib. Peace on earth.

Eddie looked calm and happy at the controls. *Sucks to be a copilot,* she thought. *He'll get his medal, too.* If it worked.

They plowed through the dark. Two furrows of sand and brush swirled in their wake.

Through night-vision goggles the world was a green, artificial place. The ground was featureless now. Behind them, the sky was ready to show light, although ahead the stars were bright.

"Thirty minutes, people." She hoped that some of them had slept. She could use some sleep herself. Eddie had taken the con for an hour and she had fought her impatience to seize it back, to make the mission go faster, to get it done.

Suddenly her radio exploded into static, and she realized that she was listening to the E-2. Hours of comm silence at both ends had let her forget it altogether.

"Noseguard, this is Quarterback, do not answer. LZ is hot and will remain. Noseguard, this is Quarterback, do not answer. LZ is hot and will remain. Proceed to Box Seats repeat Box Seats. It's your call from there. Quarterback out."

She remembered Delahanty's final brief and the enlarged satellite photo. "Box Seats" was a small depression that might cover the helos about one klick south of "End Zone"—what Delahanty said was an old White Fathers mission school where their people were supposed to be waiting. Rose was a little tired of the football lingo; she doubted that it fooled anyone, even in Sudan. The radios were encrypted anyway. Games.

Eddie still looked fine.

She studied a big paper map with her own scrawl on it, and her tactical chart from the computer. Intel had found no large-scale maps of the target area that were newer than World War II; what she'd been given was one of these with a quick update faxed from NASA. She waved the tactical chart at Eddie, reset the intercom so that only he could hear, and said, "You copy that?"

"Yes, ma'am."

"What d'you think?"

"Long way from the target, Rose." He tossed out "Rose" as an experiment: had he been forgiven for the lipstick remark?

"You get a gold star. I think we go in rea-a-al low to Box Seats and then pop to two-fifty, just us. Get a look at first light. Either we put the Marines in with the target tight up to End Zone or we call it a no-go. I don't want to give that Gunny a klick of open ground to have to crawl on."

"Sounds good."

They raced on.

0319 ZULU. SUDAN.

He had been dreaming of Rose. He opened his eyes, the dream still with him, aware that it was nearing daylight and somebody was moving, but thinking of her, a dream of threat, fear—what had she been doing?

But it was all right, awake, because he knew she was far off there to the east, on a carrier that was like a small city.

Then he remembered where he was, and he flashed the light around and down the long open space to where Dukas and Bonner were still lying, and he was aware of three things all at once: the Nuers and their weapons were gone; Adrienne Corvelle was gone; and the satellite phone, which he had left against the wall eight feet away, was not there.

Then the shooting started.

Alwa loped easily up the wadi until his head just cleared the edge. Turning, he could see the top of the mission roof as a mass blocking the stars. The firing started again, closer to the mission now. A Sudanese patrol. He threw himself flat. His *lifida* took cover next to him.

Firefight. Entirely one-sided. Arabs spending ammunition like a man passing water, and with as much effect. The mission's mud walls would stop anything short of an RPG, for a while, if the *wazunga* had the sense to keep their heads down. Mostly, the Arabs were clustered around the remains of the two cars that the white man and the Arabs had come in, the ones Alwa had ambushed yesterday; they were stuck hull-down in a sunken bit of road at the edge of the scrub south of the mission. The Nuers had dragged the bodies into the bush for the hyenas; now, he supposed, an Arab patrol was trying to draw fire from the building to see who was in there.

They appeared to have no thought of him. He smiled. He snapped his long fingers. His brothers came up and lay beside him.

Alwa leaped to his feet and ran toward the deeper blackness of the bush. The entire *lifida* ran with him. At the edge of the brush, they fell as if a string had been pulled, together. Alwa could feel the firing, feel the clump of Arabs twenty yards ahead of him in the brush. The officer must be *there*, he felt; he would be the man in the center of the most activity and the most rifles. That was the Arab way.

Alwa took out one of his precious American grenades. He spat in the dust and used the mud to mark it. He held it up against the sky so the others could see, then rolled on his back and pulled the pin. He pumped his hand in the air three times, then jumped to his feet and threw the grenade hard, overhand, about ten yards; his grunt on hitting the ground might have been satisfaction. The grenade exploded and he sprang to his feet.

Alwa shot all four Arabs, who lay, stunned and wounded by the grenade. Each got one shot from his AK as he ran past, at a range of three feet or less. At the far edge of the scrub, he fell flat again.

The Arabs farther up the hill tried to move back down. The Nuers fired into the blackness of the scrub where the soldiers were trying to take cover, and Alwa, ducking low, moved his people up. When the soldiers were dead and he had got to higher ground, he turned toward the north, seeing only the darkness but knowing that he was facing the enemy that was out there. He had destroyed their patrol, but the patrol was only the beginning.

Alan tried to see into the dark, staring down the hill below the mission. He had been puzzled why the Sudanese had not rushed the building, then had guessed that Alwa had been out there before them precisely because he knew what they would do. Then the Sudanese had started the shooting and revealed themselves. In the mission building, Dukas had pulled Donnie Marengo into a corner and pushed his head down, and Bonner had lain where he was handcuffed, his face in the dirt of the floor. Alan, the flashlight extinguished, had made the circuit of the low wall, trying to see—something, anything: movement, muzzle flashes. Then there had been the blaze and crump of the grenade and the pop-pop-pop of the Nuers' shooting, so much more economical than the "Arabs'" wasteful hosing. Then it was over.

Alwa came into the building, panting and sweating, and he and Alan knelt with their heads almost together. "Soon," Alwa murmured. "They know we are here now. They come soon."

"Let's get out."

"No."

"How soon?"

He could see Alwa's head turn against the lighter darkness of the eastern sky. "When light comes."

Alan heard a distant grinding sound, didn't place it, then knew it was a tracked vehicle. Some Eastern bloc halftrack from the fifties, some rust bucket far beyond its intended life, but coming slowly toward them and probably bringing some sort of gun on its turret. As soon as the gunner could see—

Oh, Rose, oh, babe—I came so close—

He pulled the clip out of the Mauser and pushed down on the cartridge, checking by the feel of the tension that the clip was full. Of course it was full. Why wouldn't it be full? Alwa's long hand came down over his, a signal for quiet. Alwa was silhouetted against the dark sky, head tipped back, head turning and tipping, listening—for what?

Then Alan heard it, too.

Choppers.

"Two minutes."

No fatigue now; only adrenaline and clear, gritty vision.

One minute from go/no-go for her—one minute from command decision, one minute from the time when you send these tough kids to maybe get blown apart or you say the risk is too much and you save them and leave the people down there to die.

Daybreak at End Zone. One hot spot to the west; real hot, on fire or just burned out, probably a grenade. Cooler vehicles a klick to the north; probably where any MAN-PADs would be, with the command vehicle. Trucks moving south toward End Zone. Somebody on the high ground. Ground tactics weren't usually taught to helo pilots, but Rose figured that if the bad guys got a little hill overlooking the mission, the fight was already over. If she put down and they took that hill, it might be all over for her, as well.

Full throttle.

She looked at the monochromatic shadows moving among the trucks, everything without color, the night-vision goggles giving it the color of oxidized copper. Two hundred, maybe more, moving on the target. Calculate distance. Calculate rate of movement. Calculate sixteen Marines, each one as good as ten. Calculate the advantage of body armor, firepower, doorgunners. Calculate lives.

Go/no-go.

She thought it was on the edge of disaster. No way it would be cost-free. Blood, youth. And down there, four unknowns, waiting, about to be overrun. Their blood. Their lives.

She came within an ace of bagging it, and then she thought of what it meant to walk in harm's way, of that willingness to bleed that is part of the contract, and she said:

"Go!"

She hit the comm with the other helo. "Just east of the hill, in the dead ground tight up against End Zone. Follow me in!"

In the back, Gunny looked around. The place stank. The chopper noise blocked thought. Everybody looked pumped and ready. The Navy doorgunner looked ready to fall out. *Go, go—*

"Lock and load!" Shouting it over the noise.

The Marine captain poked his head up front and looked at the landing zone—the LZ. Eddie described it over closed mike, his voice shaking with the chopper.

"The hilltop mission seems still friendly. Three positions north and east hostile. Two vehicles and some armored thing here. A klick away. The LZ is warm but not hot. We'll be hull-down behind the hill if things stay stable."

"Gunny?" Rose's voice sounded tight to him; was she too frightened to take them in? A woman?

"Yes'm?"

"There was a lot of fire down there outbound. Quarterback says there are local friendlies, so take care!"

"Roger, I heard that." Gunny and the captain exchanged nods.

"Thirty seconds!"

Gunny pulled himself into the door. The captain popped up beside him. Great—one good round and the whole chain of command went down. Tradition ruled.

"Ten seconds—!"

Wham into the ground and out rolling moving looking for the hilltop—*Follow Me*—up the hill, captain beside him, be there first, suck air, pump, fall flat.

Black faces. Weapons. *Locals*. Not Sudanese regulars, smiling like Satan.

"Hey, Marines!"

It's good to be loved.

Rose watched them go. She had Eddie do a dustoff back to Box Seats. *Got to save the choppers.* So far they hadn't taken a round. The other chopper followed smartly.

She saw the Marines go up the hill, dark shapes in the goggles. She watched them merge with the stick figures at the top. No shooting. So far like an exercise. Too goddam much to worry about, regardless.

She tried the small rescue gadget that was supposed to give her contact with the people she was picking up.

"Lima Mike, this is Noseguard, over." Zero. How the hell had this guy got through to Quarterback but not to her? "Quarterback, this is Noseguard. Give me special teams in one five."

"Roger."

Two hundred miles away, two F-18 Hornets headed for the tanker.

Alan heard the helos come in, with a lump rising so hard into his throat that he couldn't swallow; he knew his eyes had filled; he blinked, feeling wetness on his cheeks, grateful for the darkness. He sniffed, cleared his throat.

"Let that sonofabitch loose," he said hoarsely, "we're rolling out of here." He knelt with the shielded flashlight in his left hand, shone it on the handcuffs as Dukas fiddled with the key, seeming to take too long, much too long, forever, then opening one and pulling it away from the bar it had been fastened to, pulling Bonner's free hand back and cuffing the wrists together.

"Mine," Alan said. His free hand closed over the cool metal of the handcuffs. "Stand up, Bonner. Mike, you've got Marengo." He doused the light. Should he try to signal the choppers? No, they might shoot. Let them come to him. That had been the last word on the possible rescue—in the building. Stay in the building. He cursed Adrienne Corvelle for having taken the satellite phone, cursed his inability to communicate with the choppers or whoever would be coming up the hill, part of his mind running over a checklist of what had to be done and coming up with—

"The STU." He dragged Bonner almost backward down the dark building. The STU was where he had left it. Would the Sudanese know what it was? Would they care? He hauled it back up the length of the building and tied Donnie Marengo's rope to it and put his hand on its grip and said, "Where you go, that goes."

"Yes, sir."

Bonner leaned across him and started to whisper to his son—*sorry, let me explain, please, not what you think,* and Alan jerked him away and said, "Shut up," and stood listening, hearing the distant half-track, the soft coughing of the helo engines, a bird. *The bird of dawning.* Where did I read that?

The Marine captain came all the way up the hill to the old building, scanning it with NVGs, seeing two of the locals at each end, movement inside. He had left a rifle squad with Gunny on the hill to the east and moved up, keeping the building between his men and the area where the Sudanese were moving down. No firing yet; a lull, because of the choppers, he was sure. Only a couple of companies of low-tech soldiers, moving on foot, not even helmets to protect their heads, and helos come banging in and what do they think? Who is it? How many? What weapons?

Then there was a flurry of automatic fire from the northeast; somebody had made a decision. The captain shook his head. Not enough intel. He led five men straight to the building, ducked, saw four people in a corner, took partial cover behind the wall and aimed his weapon, hearing the corporal spreading the squad behind him.

"Dickerson, U.S. Marines! Identify yourselves!"

"Craik, Lieutenant, U.S. Navy! Dukas, Naval Criminal Investigative Service. Two prisoners—"

The captain scuttled in, waved the corporal and the radioman in.

"I've got a man hurt," the Navy lieutenant said. "He'll have to be carried."

The captain gave orders to the corporal. The radioman was hunched over the radio, a red flashlight in his fingers. "Where's your comm?" the captain said to the Navy officer.

"We had a comm failure." He didn't mention Adrienne Corvelle.

"Shit. You got the helos?" the captain said to the radioman. When he heard a grunt, he said, "Tell them we've scored. Four to be picked up; we're heading down the hill. Then get on to Gunny, tell him the same and prepare to pull back on the choppers. Let's go!"

"You run into our friendlies?" the Navy lieutenant said.

"Yeah, yeah."

"Can you give them cover out of here? They saved our ass."

"We got four seats in the chopper, four, period. No friendlies. Let's go, before those bastards out there get serious." The firing had spread, now was coming from an arc around the north and east. "Let's move, move! Corporal, get the wounded guy down the hill. Okay, let's go, go—!"

Then the world blew up.

Alan felt it more than he heard it, felt himself pushed hard against the low mud wall; he was suddenly deaf, even as the world lit up. Light flashed; something hard struck him in the back, and he lost his grip on Bonner's handcuffs, misted, tried to see, smelled cordite and smoke and dirt. A shot from the half-track, a hit on their first try. Dust and grit sifted down from overhead. He turned back, saw the doorway empty against the last stars, a red flashlight glowing on the floor, rafters fallen, and somebody was moaning. He turned his head the other way. He flexed his hand, feeling for the handcuffs.

Bonner was gone.

Thwack!

Another round hit the hill fifty yards away.

Alan was lying on the mud floor. He pushed himself up and saw a shape move on the top of the wall at the corner of the building, then disappear. Bonner had got himself up there, hands cuffed behind his back, and rolled off. Into the dark, into the firing.

Alan went after him.

•   •   •

Bonner cursed the handcuffs. If he fell in the dark, he would land on his face. He couldn't run. He wanted to run. He wanted to sprint toward his own, toward his friends, toward Carl. He could see the bits of light that were muzzle flashes, hear the rifles and something lower, heavier, a *whum-whum* from the Marines, behind him. He tried to run, and the ground dropped from beneath him, and he plunged down a six-foot scree, steep and painful. He stayed more or less upright, partly on his back, one arm pulled up painfully. Loose rocks and grit gathered in his pant legs as he slid down. The firing behind him rose, then fell off. Another big round exploded, not on the building this time, and he realized what he'd let himself in for, and he cried out.

Donnie. He'd tried to drag him with him. Donnie and the NCIS man had been okay, untouched by the blast; Bonner had butted Dukas, grabbed Donnie and pulled. But the boy had resisted. *Resisted.* Then Dukas had tried to hold him, and Bonner had gone over the wall.

He threw himself down. Where was he? Where was his rescue?

Alan crouched below the wall, trying to see, eyes dazzled from the flash. He had no sound yet, only a buzzing. In the east now, enough steely blue light to silhouette the horizon. He stared north, trying to find Bonner; he could be only seconds ahead. Then he saw movement, black on black, lower than he had expected, and he realized there was a drop-off, then a flat before the bush started; he threw himself over the edge, skidded down, threw himself to the ground. He must be able to hear better, because he was now afraid of the automatic firing crisscrossing above him. He began to look from barely perceived object to object, seeking a doomed man.

· · ·

Bonner tried to get up and move toward what he thought were his own people. His legs were weak. He had been chained in one position. Like a torture, the bastards. *Where was his rescue?* This was supposed to be a lift-out. Carl had always promised him that. Owed him that. That was the contract.

He got up on his knees. He should have been given a signal. Something.

"Carl?"

He stared into the north. Shapes were beginning to form out there, like clouds making animals and faces, only this was the light beginning to come, the gray of predawn, light slowly taking on shape.

"Carl!"

The firing intensified, the muzzle flashes coming closer. He put his face down on the ground. He was sweating, even though it was cold. They were shooting at him! *There was no rescue.* He was in a bad place, and there was nobody, and he was alone.

He prayed to the only god he knew.

"Carl," he whispered. "Carl—please—"

Alan heard him before he saw him. Then the half-track, now a visible dark mass down the slope to his left, fired over their heads; in the flash, Alan saw the white of Bonner's running shoes. He wasn't more than fifty feet away.

"Bonner! They'll kill you!"

Bonner made a sound, a terrible, ugly sound, and he stood, and for an instant he was silhouetted against the pale sky. Then he tried to run. It was not clear which way he was trying to run, only that he leaned forward, put his head down, and tried to move. Alan already had the Mauser out ahead of him. He was rolled a little on his right side, a fine shooting position; the ground gives you steadiness. He saw Bonner move, and something boomed and light flashed, and the front sight came right down in the middle of the rear, and Alan fired, twice, tap-tap, the smoothest shots of his life. Bonner fell, hit in the groin and the left knee.

Alan duckwalked down to him, hearing a Marine heavy weapon behind and above him, hoping it would keep the Sudanese off him. The half-track fired again, and Alan crawled to Bonner, to find him lying on his side, curled into a fetal ball, hands secured behind him. His skin felt cold, his arms wet with sweat. Farther down, he was already wet with blood, and even in the near-dark, the black places where the blood had soaked his khakis were darker than anything else he could see.

Alan lay half on top of him. He felt light-headed and tired. Perhaps it was a trick his body was playing on him. He felt as if he could lie there forever. Bonner would bleed to death; the Sudanese would come.

He dragged Bonner half-upright and staggered erect, his prey on his shoulder, clumsy, heavy. He made himself turn, feeling Bonner's balance shift and almost take him down. The Marine weapons had stopped firing from the mission. Behind him, the Sudanese were coming on. He made himself move, pumping his legs as he hit the steep scree, only two yards high but like a mountain, waiting for a bullet, a grenade.

The mission school was on fire. When had that happened? How long had it been? He twisted away from the end where the fire was, fought his way up over the lip of the drop-off and staggered against the mud wall, then scraped along it to the corner and around to the front.

The Marines were gone. No, there was one down beyond the other end of the building. Alan could hear the half-track again, even hear its turret swinging. The Marine aimed something from his shoulder and fired, a rocket, and the resulting explosion knocked him flat. He got up and started down the hill.

Alan had dumped Bonner and leaned over him, supporting himself on the wall, gasping. He couldn't go on yet. Not a step.

"Donnie?" Bonner said.

Alan sucked in air. "They've gone," he said. The building was empty.

Bonner's eyes flicked right and left, but he didn't move his head. "Am I going to die?" he said.

Gasping, Alan was stunned by the question. Here was a man who thought that life was shit, and now he was afraid of death.

"Don't leave me here," Bonner said. *With them,* he meant. *In this non-place.*

Alan fetched a deep breath, getting ready to lift him again. "I told you, I'm taking you back," he said. He put his hands under Bonner's shoulders. They were both wet with the blood now, sticky with blood. He pulled Bonner's chest against his right shoulder. This is what it had come down to, this dangerous, bloody intimacy. Maybe that's what it had always been, he saw: the two of them. As intimate as father and son.

He moved Bonner's weight still farther back on his shoulder and inched it across his back and tried to stand. His legs were like rubber.

Rose decided to risk the choppers; hers first. She circled south of Box Seats to build speed and hurtled toward the low rise only a few feet off the deck. It was the best flying of her life. Her touch on the yoke was light but sure, and the Seahawk answered nimbly, rising over a small hummock and descending back to within inches of the deck without loss of speed. She aimed for the left end of the friendly hill and popped up. Her doorgunner fired a long, controlled burst with tracer down at the enemy position to the north. He walked the tracers over the position and had the satisfaction of a small secondary explosion. A Marine on the ground fired six rounds from his grenade launcher and then dumped it as excess weight. Two of them were smoke; they fell neatly between the mission and a gully, along which Alwa's silent wolves faded into the murk and were gone. An armored car burned. Rose in her NVGs saw several blurs climb the hill, and for the second time she set down. *What was taking so long down there?*

The mission was on fire, and Alan could hear more armor. The Marine first squad ran for the chopper, while the second, having retired from the mission, covered them from a hilltop. Below him, Marines dropped smoke and ran down the hill, two carrying Dukas. Donnie Marengo moved under his own power, no one appearing to guide him; he simply ran. The second chopper nosed in. Alan halted, readying himself to try to go on. The last man of the second squad was well below him, lost now in smoke and dark. He and Bonner were the last ones on the mission hill.

Rose checked her watch. She heard the thud of a small explosion over the hill and her mouth tightened.

"Chopper Base!" a tinny voice sounded in her phones.

"Roger!"

"Second squad—can you come to us?"

"Hold on—" Eddie had been listening and had the map and a satellite photo out, and he was making a grease-penciled circle on the photo southwest of the mission, about a hundred and fifty yards from their original LZ. A glance told her that they just might have protection from the hilltop there as the Sudanese came up the other side.

"Can do, but we won't be able to sit there more than a couple of minutes! We're going to jump, hold one, and we're out of there! We're losing darkness. Tell him."

She heard shots and another thud in the earphones, and then the Marine comm man said, "We're on our way! Count from now and go!"

She looked at Eddie. He braced and took the yoke in his hands. Rose went to intercom and barked at the doorgunner, "We're going up to one-fifty in forty-five seconds; our second squad will be coming on, so take a good look and then blast beyond them at the top of the hop. Thirty seconds now." She switched to tell the other helo, then turned aside to mutter to Eddie, "You're doing great, Lieutenant!" Then to the other aircraft: "Twenty seconds, hop heading two niner zero. Doorgunner, hose it but watch for our people! Follow us up, Jack—"

Alan had Bonner back on his shoulder. He was covered in Bonner's blood now; it made the carry more difficult. He tried to run toward the sound of the helos. And then he glanced up a knoll east of the mission and saw the thin, olive-green figure with the satellite telephone, standing against the lightening sky. At that distance, in that pale light, he could not see the ravaged face or the lines, but only her defiance and her passion.

0410 ZULU. FAIRFAX, VIRGINIA.

George Shreed's telephone rang and he picked it up. He was still awake, would be awake for hours yet.

"Shreed."

"George, goddammit, I don't know what your part in this is, but you goddam well better have an explanation for what's on CNN!"

Shreed scowled. "I don't know what you're talking about."

"A goddam incursion and rescue is being reported *live!* What the hell, George! Is this one of ours? What's going on?"

He knew the Special Forces team couldn't have got beyond Mannheim, Germany, yet; it made no sense. Fuddled, he said, "Delta Force?"

"The Navy, George! They've sent in the goddam Marines! It's like a goddam PR campaign!"

"I'll get back to you."

He put the telephone down and hobbled to a television and got the channel, and there it was—long, static takes of not very interesting maps and landscapes. The visuals were not live at all. What was live was the voice. *Live?*

"*. . . second helicopter has just disappeared behind a protective ridge. Now, the Marines have laid smoke to my right and up the hill to the abandoned mission where this operation began. There's a Sudanese mortar round! No damage; the fire control is pathetic. Firing continues around the building, where a remnant of the Southern Sudanese Liberation Army appear to be fighting hand to hand—I can't make it out in the smoke—I've lost that for the moment. Now, below me, the Marines and the American officer and his prisoner are running toward the place where the helicopters landed. The Navy–Marine rescue operation has been efficient and quick, and the Sudanese regulars appear to be hanging back along the hilltop beyond the smoke, reluctant to engage these tough, high-tech soldiers who have been battle-hardened in the streets of Mogadishu. And now another armored vehicle has topped the hill! A Sudanese armored vehicle—a squad or more of soldiers sheltering behind it—automatic weapons opening up, firing at—oh!*"

The sound of firing intensified. Shreed heard a distant explosion. There was no voice. Then:

"*This—is—Adrienne—Corvelle—*"

Silence.

0416 ZULU. SUDAN.

"All in?" Rose shouted into her helmet mike. She couldn't see through the hill that sheltered her from the mission, but she could feel the enemy cresting the hill, threatening to fire down on her choppers as the Afghans had against the Russians,

"Wait one." Gunny sounded calm in the back. She leaned forward in her harness to look out through the smoke. She thought the second squad was all aboard.

"I'm out of here in thirty seconds, Gunny." Her hands were ready on the yoke.

"Wait one."

∙   ∙   ∙

A colossal roar of fire rose somewhere behind him, and two shattering jet roars crossed the sky above his head. Alan glanced up and saw Navy F-18s and fell into the scrub at the base of the hill. The chopper was still sixty infinite meters away, and he was out of juice. Behind him, the Sudanese regulars continued to pour fire into the mission. Alan pulled Bonner across his shoulders as if he were going to throw him with a flying mare, then got to his knees, to one foot, and then to both feet, grunting. He started forward.

He could see the chopper clearly now; the Marine gunny was leaning out the door, bellowing at him. Even over the chopper noise, Alan could hear that angry roar. "Move your ass! We're waiting for you, goddammit. Keep going!"

Other Marines yelled, their mouths moving. Forty meters. Thirty meters. The gunny leaped from the chopper, the lance corporal beside him. They grabbed Bonner from Alan under the nose of the chopper, and the release from weight caused Alan to stand up straight and turn his head.

To look straight into the eyes of his wife.

That was the way Rose saw him, coming out of the whirlwind with another man's blood running down him. And a look of shocked wonder on his face as he recognized her.

30

They walked up the long avenue of graves at Arlington, both in winter uniform—dark blue, white hat covers—quiet, somber. He carried their child, who stared around him at the gardens of stone with the same look of wonder that he brought to every new thing.

Alan Craik, Lieutenant, United States Navy, wore the Silver Star, awarded him only an hour before in a private—in fact, secret—ceremony. Rose Siciliano Craik, Lieutenant Commander, United States Navy, wore the ribbon of the Air Medal, awarded two weeks before.

They turned in among the graves and went on, she imperceptibly following his lead, which was purposeful and silent. On he went, turning twice, knowing the way, and coming at last to the small stone that bore his father's name and dates of birth and death.

The sky was gray. The stones, recently wet, seemed luminous, achromatic. The trees, beginning to show leaves, moved faintly in a wind.

He handed the child to her and went and stood alone by the stone. He stood there for two full minutes, looking at it, his head bent so that she could not see his face. Then, quickly, he undid the medal he had just been given, removed his hat, and, bending at the knees, placed the medal on the stone.

He straightened and stood there, hatless.

The child stirred in his mother's arms. He looked at his father, then at her.

"Dada cry," he said.

"Yes." She smiled, tightened her grip on him. "But it's all right. It's all right now."

He stood there a long time. The wind blew, and the silence of Arlington was invaded by the sounds from over the river. Over there is the great city of monuments and public people, the noise of a nation, all the comings and goings, the wrangles and the words, the free acts and the decisions for which the long night watches are kept. And these two people and their child, silent now among the graves, will go there and take up new tasks, for this one is done.